Cassius's Cabin

Suetsmoke Run

Slave Quarters

Slave Graveyard

Overseer's House

rpentry ed

hed

Tool Shed

Tobacco Sheds

Corn Rig

Hay

Large Barn

Small Barn

Stables

R

SWEETSMOKE

SWEETSMOKE

A Novel

DAVID FULLER

New York

Copyright © 2008 David Fuller

ISBN: 978-1-4013-2331-8

Hyperion books are available for special promotions, premiums, or corporate training. For details contact Michael Rentas, Proprietary Markets, Hyperion, 77 West 66th Street, 12th floor, New York, New York 10023, or call 212-456-0133.

FIRST EDITION

10 9 8 7 6 5 4 3 2 1

For you, Liz

SWEETSMOKE

⋘ Chapter One ⋙

July 1, 1862

THE big one closed his hand into a fist and took a step toward the smaller boy. He was tall and narrow, ten years old, and black; his joints bulged in rude knobs, his long bones had grown quickly and suddenly and the meat in between was strung taut like piano wire. A stiff muslin shirt, his only item of clothing, hung to the top of his thighs, barely covering his buttocks and the skin that stretched over his angular pelvic bones. Dust powdered his thin legs and turned his calves pale, and his bare feet left significant shapes in the dirt. The smaller one, the white one, should have been afraid. He wore a gingham shirt with soft trousers held up by suspenders and he had real shoes. But skin showed between shoe and cuff, and the trousers bagged at the knees, shiny there and thin.

Cassius had not noticed the worn material of the boy's trousers until that moment, and wondered if the condition of the white children's clothing was another casualty of the Confederate quartermasters. Then he wondered what the boy's grandmother thought about it.

The white one, grandson of the planter, stood his ground, hands open at his side; in that moment, Cassius remembered himself standing barefoot in the same yard, facing another white boy twenty years before, this one's father. On that day, Cassius had yet to understand that he was another man's property, and now the steam of humiliation flushed through him as if he was standing there again, reliving the past.

Cassius made no move. He had not witnessed the boyhood conflict that had brought on this moment, but he knew how it would end.

Andrew, the tall, black one, should also have known. He had older brothers in the field, and even if by their compassion they hesitated to warn him, he should have known he was alone and surrounded. None of the black children seemed to know, but the white children knew, and one of them ran to the kitchen for Mam Rosie.

Mam Rosie was out in an instant, humping down the steps, wiping her hands down her apron, an old woman lean as a rope twisted tight, coming on fast. Mam Rosie showed no fear, she was high yellow and had privileges, but she was also conscious of the precise limits of her power. She came fast but Cassius knew there was time—the two boys were there in the dirt, the other children were near the wilting camellias by the big house porch steps, and Nanny Catherine watched over her shoulder. No rush at all, thought Cassius, as his eyes drifted toward the work sheds behind the big house. The smokehouse was there, and the sheds for carpentry, blacksmithing, and shoe making. Then the barns and beyond them the shed for curing tobacco—the old woman still running—and Cassius's eyes slid to the low rise beyond which, out of sight, stood the Overseer's house and past that the quarters. Acres of fields rolled out in three directions where maturing tobacco grew tall. The children's gardening chores were done, the butter churn put away, and the air was soft with moisture and sunlight and insects sawing, plenty of time on most days, but not today, as Mam Rosie was quick but not quick enough, and Andrew swung. He opened his hand at the last second and slapped young Charles's ear.

Cassius closed his eyes at the sound. Every child, every adult, every creature in the yard paused, and the future came into Cassius's mind as clearly as he remembered his own past: Tomorrow Andrew would be obliged to work the fields with his brothers and parents.

He would learn about it that night in the quarters, and his heart would be glad because with the news would arrive his first pair of trousers and his first hat and something that passed for shoes. His parents would see his gladness and their eyes would meet in resignation. Their son, their little one, the baby, already going to the fields, two years early. In the morning before sunup, Mr. Nettle would ring the bell rousing Andrew from his place on the pallet between mother and father, torn from sleep with trembling stomach, expected to consume a full meal by candlelight with the sun barely a rumor. He would never again sleep between them. He would eat little and regret it later. Walking in the dark to the fields, his new shoes would pinch and the lower legs of his trousers would cling, wet with dew and cold against his shins. They would assign him a row to pick hornworms off tobacco leaves, the hands working quickly, quickly to save the crop. He was to inspect each leaf top and bottom, plucking hornworms as they grasped with their sturdy legs and strong tiny jaws. The sun would step into the sky and dry his trousers and the heat would gradually increase, unnoticed until he moved, when he would discover his body reluctant, leaden. He would beg for a rest. His mother Savilla would shift in her row to grant him shade from her thick trunk as she continued to pluck hornworms, but then his mother, his *mother*, would guide his fingers back to the work. Eventually she would yield to his complaints and pour hornworms from her sack into his, hastily attacking his section to deceive Mr. Nettle the Overseer. But Big Gus the Driver would know and when he came by she would be forced back to her row. They would not beat him, though, not on his first day. In time, when exhaustion, blisters, soreness, and sweat became routine, he would think back and remember that slap. Andrew would never return to play with the other children.

Mam Rosie cuffed Andrew on *his* ear, a loud and obvious blow that she hoped would satisfy the planter's grandson. Her gnarled fingers squeezed the back of Andrew's smooth dry neck and steered him aside. Mam Rosie pretended Charles was not there, but Cassius saw the boy's reddened ear and knew something would happen. He waited for Charles to order Mam Rosie to bind Andrew's wrists high to the ring on the whipping post, to order her to pull up Andrew's shirt and expose his back. Cassius knew Mam Rosie would do what she was told, whispering to calm Andrew as she secured him to the post while he twisted and bucked in outrage. He waited for Charles to tell Mam Rosie to run fetch the whip. Cassius saw meanness in Charles's face as he controlled his tears, and then Charles's eyes found Cassius's eyes and when Cassius did not look away, Charles saw that Cassius knew, and Charles would have to do something. It was of no consequence that he was ten years old. This was white man's pride.

"Cassius, you git along now and fetch me some water," said Charles.

I don't think I hear you, said Cassius aloud but not loud enough for Charles to hear.

"What's that you say? What's that?" said Charles.

Beautiful day, said Cassius, again too quietly to be heard.

Cassius gripped the heavy hammer in his right hand, nails in his left, and pressed his leg against the fence post where his knee and the top of his foot held the stave in place. A tan and gray feral cat, kitten in her mouth, sauntered into the shade under the big house porch. Sweat coated his skin and fat oily drops clung to his nose, eyebrows, and chin. The air would not cool until long after dark. Mr. Nettle's wife came around the far corner returning from the privy, using her wide skirt to funnel her three small Nettles ahead of her, suddenly alerted by the tension, wondering what she had missed. A bantam rooster lurched with a high step in the yard, one eye warily on the shadow where the cat had disappeared.

"I said git, boy," said Charles.

Cassius probed his own facial expression from within, finding it locked into a blank, uncomprehending stare, reaching back to know it had been just so at the moment Charles had met his eyes. But Cassius still did not look away. His mind remained trapped in the past, barefoot in his own stiff shirt, not yet knowing who he was or what would come of his defiance. Charles's eyes reflected uncertainty; he knew there should be no hesitation. The yard by the big house was unnaturally quiet. Cassius became aware of the song then, the ever-present song that rose out of the fields, brought louder up the hill by a shift in the wind. He did not notice that the smell came as well.

Cassius turned back to the fence stave and expertly angled a nail, bringing the hammer, driving it three-quarters home with one swing.

"I'll tell her, Cassius, I'll tell Grandma Ellen!" Charles said. He spit out Cassius's name and walked to the big house.

Mam Rosie stood with Andrew, looking at Cassius, a warning flashing in her eyes.

On the second floor, Ellen Howard read aloud to her servants a news story from a two-day-old copy of the *Richmond Daily Whig*, reliving General Lee's victory at Gaines' Mill, the third battle fought in as many days. She read dramatically, expecting her servant, Pet, and her daughter's personal servants, Susan and Pearl, to be properly moved. The early months of the war had brought a constant stream of terrible news that had spread a pall over the Confederacy. The newspapers bemoaned the inevitability of the war's rapid conclusion in favor of the Union, and Ellen had been deeply traumatized. The culmination of the bitter news came with the fall of New Orleans in April, and her natural gloom settled into depression. But soon followed the campaign in Virginia, and a series of victories over Union general George McClellan's enormous army brought unexpected joy to the populace. Ellen Howard, however, was slow to trust good news, afraid to emerge from her comfortable cocoon of dread and ennui. Already feared as a thin-skinned and distant mistress, she had grown unpredictable after the news of her oldest son John-Corey Howard's death at Manassas Junction during the first battle of the war. John-Corey had been named for her father, the late Judge Ezra John Corey, a man she had adored. Ellen's bitterness over her son's death grew when informed that the Yankees had ridden out from Washington, D.C. in their buggies with picnic lunches to enjoy the spectacle of their soldiers defeating the Johnny Rebs. She was little cheered to know they had been forced to flee in haste and terror when the South had answered the cocksure Yankees with blood. A number of John-Corey's belongings had arrived with a letter of condolence, his watch but not the winding key, his slouch hat and his precious collection of received letters, many of which were written in her hand.

She was not to view her son's remains. Perhaps because she could not picture him dead, a dreamy part of her was able to imagine the war as unreal, envisioning John-Corey alive on his own plantation outside Lynchburg, or here, in the big house, hiding as he had as a child. As long as she did not see his body, she could pretend that the war did not exist, certain that all this foolishness would soon be revealed as a test of character. On such days the house people would hear her humming, alone in a bedroom, through an open door down a long hallway, and they would look at one another and disguise their anxiety with covert, derisive laughter. Missus actin strange, Missus goin off in her head, Missus havin one'a them days so watch out. Reality would eventually intrude, in the form of the *Daily Whig* with war news, or she would see a soldier on the road or hear the sudden hum-rumble of cannon that sounded close but would actually have come from somewhere far to the north.

But nothing brought on the reality of her son's death as much as the arrival of his people.

Two weeks before, two of John-Corey's negroes had come to Sweetsmoke Plantation in a wagon. John-Corey's other people had been sold, but John-Corey had left instructions that these people were special family and should be kept together. He had neglected to mention his personal body servant in these instructions and so Lewis, who had been by his side when John-Corey died at Manassas and had returned to his plantation to bring to the family the news of his death, had been sold with the others to a cotton and rice plantation in Georgia. John-Corey's last two negroes had spent the winter and spring with John-Corey's widow closing up the big house at Howard Plantation. When Stephanie returned to live with her parents, John-Corey's people had been sent to Sweetsmoke. Two weeks now and Ellen had yet to meet them. Half a dozen times she had called them to the big house, but each time she had been overcome with nervous emotion. John-Corey's special people brought back the pain of his death, so each time she sent them away without seeing them. She even used the excuse she had heard whispered among her people, that the girl was bad luck, a contagion carried from her son's plantation. Ellen knew the girl had been a good house girl, and the man, her father, had carried the keys. Ellen had not had a butler in the house since her second son, Jacob, had taken William, the plantation's butler, to be his personal servant when he had joined Turner Ashby's 7th Virginia Cavalry. Tomorrow, she thought. Tomorrow I'll feel stronger and I'll speak to John-Corey's people. In the meantime, they went to the fields with the others.

Perhaps it was no surprise that Ellen was incapable of meeting her son's people, as her life was now a series of superstitious gestures designed to keep Jacob safe and alive. She had let down her guard for John-Corey. Now she was afraid to alter any of her activities in case doing so should endanger her beloved second son.

In the afternoons she sometimes worked with watercolors, upstairs with the windows open to catch the breeze. Before the war, her paintings had been of flowers and landscapes, but once her oldest son had gone off to fight, she began to create fanciful scenes of the Garden of Eden, incorporating many of the flowers and plants she had painted before, as if her previous body of work was but a premonition. Lately, purple storm clouds crowded the edges of her paintings, and more reds were evident in the trunks of the trees and branches, as if their inner cores were heated, athrob with light. In fact, amid the shortages brought on by war, she was low on blue and green paint and had an abundance of red. Her husband fretted over her work, but the new red pleased her and she reached for it willfully.

Ellen paused in her reading to her people after the pleasure of speaking the words "Gaines' Mill," feeling the syllables in her mouth as her tongue formed the final *l* with a rubbery push off where the top of her mouth met her teeth. The wind changed then and brought the new smell through the open window and she lost the track of the sentence. Her body servant Pet smelled it as well, and unconsciously imitated Missus Ellen's rigid pose. Ellen recognized the smell and envisaged field dirt and sweat, moist body crevices and hidden hair and oil and blood and feces. She waited for the odor to pass. She closed her eyes, her upper lip pronounced, nostrils arched.

"Pet, in my dressing table, bring the bottle."

The bottle from Paris, Missus? said Pet.

Ellen nodded slightly and Pet went to her table. Pet was darker than the others in the big house, thus Pet was anxious about her position, even though she had worked there for four years. When Pet was out of her missus's sight, she opened the drawer and took up the bottle of perfume. But she moved Missus's best petticoat and found the other bottle, the one that held the laudanum, the bottle Missus was using just a little more every day. Pet looked at that bottle long-ingly, then covered it over with the petticoat and with her hip pushed in the drawer. Pet had yet to connect her missus's humming with the laudanum. She returned to Ellen with the Parisian perfume bottle in both hands.

So little left, said Pet.

Ellen took it. She hoarded the precious liquid, chose carefully the occasions to wear it, and even then was miserly when applying the scent as the bottom of the bottle came into sharp focus. She tried not to desire the way she felt when wearing perfume—elegant, cho-sen, French—but this other smell created nothing less than an emergency. She put the smallest possible dab in the hollow of her neck between her clavicles, and when that was insufficient, tipped the bottle to her fingertip and brought it to her philtrum, just a touch of wet applied to her upper lip beneath her nostrils. Her grandson continued to call for her, using that tone, but she did not answer.

C assius was not aware that his hammer drove nails in time with the field song. Even when the wind came around and brought the song, he heard it the way he heard the sun on his shoulders or the sound of his own breathing. They were in the near fields this afternoon, within a mile of the big house.

He heard the song change. He rested a moment and turned his head and listened to the new song that told of death. A surge of ap-prehension drove into his chest. He rested the head of his hammer against the dirt, and the surge pumped in his palms and fingers and made them weak.

He looked down the hill knowing there would be a rider on the road approaching the big house.

Cassius wondered why the rider had stopped in the fields to tell the Overseer. That was how the hands would have learned the news; that was why they changed the song. Big Gus the Driver would have been sure to stand by Mr. Nettle at the moment the Overseer was told. Big Gus, one of the lighter-skinned field hands, worked near Mr. Nettle, and Mr. Nettle let him swing the bullwhip. Big Gus whipped harder than Mr. Nettle, to impress both him and the Master. Cassius pictured the moment, Big Gus bursting with the news, clearing his throat to show off his grand lubricious voice for the women—*I'm comin on to meet you, Lord*—drawing it out so the hands knew he was changing the song. The work would not stop, but the work song would abandon their tongues—*I'm comin on alone*—and spread across the field like a sudden wind spreading a small chop across the glass surface of a lake, and Cassius thought that the tobacco would grow tall humming the song, and those who chewed and snuffed it would taste death—*I'm lookin for to see you, Lord, That me a comin home.*

The rider was close now, pink-necked, flush with news. Cassius knew him, Otis Bornock, a poor white. That explained why he had stopped in the fields, Otis Bornock knew Mr. Nettle. Otis Bornock and other town trash sometimes traded with the blacks. They would trade for things made by the hands late at night, or for things that mysteriously disappeared from the big house. That did not make him a friend. Otis Bornock might benefit from the trading, but he was more likely to turn on a black man than to help himself. Otis Bornock had once sold Cassius a bottle of whiskey so vile and raw, that it had taken Cassius an extra day to finish the bottle. Otis Bornock rode the back roads at night with the other Patrollers, and until three years ago, Mr. Nettle had been their leader.

Cassius watched the man come. Who was dead, and how did this death relate to the plantation? Any death that touched the planter family brought on an anxious time of limbo for the blacks. When a white planter, his wife, or one of their children died, ownership of slaves changed hands. Even the smallest peccadillo in a white man, a gambling debt or an illegitimate child, could propel waves through the slave community. Families might be broken up, wives sold from husbands, children sold from mothers. If they were sold to the cotton states, they would not be heard from again.

The pounding of the hooves slowed, the heat and perspiration of the horse crowded the yard, and Otis Bornock swung out of his sweat-black saddle, the seat of his pants clinging to leather, peeling away. The horse was thinner, surcingle straps hanging long under its belly. Everyone was thinner now. Otis Bornock's pearl-handled Colt Army revolver glinted momentarily in the sun, his sole proud possession that he claimed to have won in a poker game. Others said he found it on a dead man, and whispers that Otis Bornock had encouraged the man's condition before "finding" the gun added to his reputation. Cassius watched him hurry to the porch. Sweat rolled from his stained hat down the ends of his hair and dripped to his collar. Otis Bornock removed his hat at the door and ran his kerchief across his face. Pet came to the door, haughty and superior in the face of white trash, but Ellen came up behind her and greeted him graciously, even as Cassius saw terror in her eyes. Then she allowed him inside, a man like that, Cassius thought, allowed in her home. Cassius saw that she anticipated the worst possible news. Otis Bornock drew a letter from his back pocket and it was wrinkled and moist and Cassius imagined it stank of Otis Bornock's backside. Young Charles followed him in, quiet as a shadow. Charles understood the impact of the visitor, preceded as he was by the song. Cassius knew he would have to be careful about Charles. He had aroused an enemy, and the boy would not forget.

Cassius listened for the owl screech of anguish, but the silence inside stretched and he knew Master Jacob, *Major* Jacob Howard, was still alive. Cassius breathed. The planter's family remained intact.

Cassius straightened his shoulders to relieve the strain on his back, where the scar tissue was like a crust. He picked up a pail with fresh water and moved to the chuffing horse, which dropped its nose and drank loudly. While he knew not to water a sweating horse, this was Bornock's beast and Cassius was carrying out a plan. Cassius looked toward the door to Mam Rosie's kitchen. Once the horse finished, Cassius would walk to the pump by the kitchen to refill. By then, Mam Rosie would know the news.

Ellen came out of the big house onto the porch, the rider standing behind her in the dark of the room. She held the unfolded note in her hand.

"Cassius!" she called.

He set down the pail and stepped away from the horse into her line of view.

Yes, Missus Ellen, said Cassius.

"Mr. Bornock tells me the French gate leans."

That's so, Missus Ellen.

Cassius knew Bornock had said nothing of the kind, nor did he mention that the main gate had been leaning since the day it was built, that it had almost certainly leaned back in France on that vine-yard.

"You go directly and straighten it out."

Yes, ma'am. Right after I finish this fence Master Charles knocked down.

"That will have to wait. You get on down there like I said. And do it right the first time, Cassius, not like your usual."

I will, Missus.

She nodded to the rider, dismissing him. Otis Bornock returned to his horse and remounted. Cassius was not to know the news. Ellen would wait for Master Hoke, her husband, to return from Edensong later that afternoon to tell him. Young Charles stood in the doorway, staring at Cassius. Cassius could not help himself; he looked directly at Charles, and saw malicious satisfaction on the boy's face. The identity of the dead was bad news for Cassius, and everyone knew who it was but him.

Cassius collected his hammer and nails and a coil of rope. He listened to the horse hooves fade down the hill. He did not fetch from his carpentry shed the tools he would require to complete the work. He went directly down the hill to the main gate. One of the house girls, probably Nanny Catherine, was crying in Mam Rosie's kitchen. But he could not go there to discover why. Ellen Howard had made sure that he would not find out.

The main gate was from a vineyard in France, bought off the property by Hoke Howard on a European visit back in the days when money was in season. The field hands often told the story, heard second- or thirdhand, of Master Hoke riding in the French countryside, pulling up when he saw the magnificent gate. Well, Ol' Massa Hoke, he used to gettin what he want and he knows that gate belong not in France but on his plantation in the Commonwealth of Virginie, so he do what any self-respectin massa'd do, he walk on up to that ol' Frenchy's door and offer up a big ol' sack a money like them burlap ones we got in the fields. The hands seemed to think it was so much money—and with every recounting the amount increased—that Mr. Frenchy had been astonished, but when Cassius heard the story, he imagined the Frenchman suppressing a smirk as he allowed himself to be overpaid. Cassius knew that when Hoke was flush, he threw around his money the way he threw around his weight, randomly, in grand pointless gestures. So Hoke had hired people to systematically break down the gate, numbering each piece as a local man made a drawing. The crates were then shipped back to the Commonwealth in one of his merchant ships—before the blockade, when Hoke was still part owner of a fleet—but along the way, the numbered drawing was lost. Here the hands out-embellished one another, describing the Old Master in a comic rage dismissing ships full of careless white men.

The gate was made of cedar, an overblown trellis that straddled the narrow road leading up to the big house, a vain and solitary structure in a vast landscape. While performing his apprenticeship as a carpenter—and it was Hoke who had offered to take him out of the fields so he could learn carpentry—Cassius had helped reconstruct the gate as it emerged from the crates, piecing it together like a puzzle. Hoke had then painted the name of the plantation across the top: Sweetsmoke.

The wind shifted and Cassius heard it move above him, through the highest leaves of the tall oaks where it did him no good, and the immediate air around him went dead and he stood in a hollow of stillness. A sensation of dread came over him, one he had had before: He was living in another man's dream. The dreamer was like the wind rushing through the oak leaves above, indifferent and unaware of his presence. Cassius made no mark on either the man or the dream. The stillness crowded him and Cassius was afraid to move.

He believed he had already lived long enough. He thought he was over the age of thirty—Jacob Howard was thirty, and they had been born around the same time—and Cassius looked that and more. He now studied the land as if he would never see it again, and tried to memorize it as if he might need to describe it one day. Indeed the land was elegant and sculpted and green and fertile, yet he was so unconnected to it that its beauty did not move him. He believed that he made no mark whatsoever on the land. He memorized but did not imagine carrying the memory with him to a better world. He could not imagine any kind of world that would come with death. He simply saw the end of his time, and in the quiet that followed, he found comfort. It would be an end to a life that had given him little pleasure, hope, or ease. He believed that he had turned his heart cold.

A hornworm clung to a long sprig of switch grass and he reached down and plucked it off, its stubborn legs letting go one at a time. The creature fit in his palm. Its head was thick and bulbous with grooves that resembled a series of folds, its flabby legs grabbed at his skin, its jaw chewing on the air. Cassius looked at the small white ovals that ran down its side, outlined in orange with an orange dot in the middle so that they appeared to be a row of miniature painted eyes.

It was early in the season, yet it felt late; the light of the sun seemed darker, older. He wondered if the field song was prescient and the death was his own. That would be a bit of good luck. He set down the hornworm without killing it.

Sounds of the plantation slipped in clear and bright, then were just as quickly muffled, a fragment of work song followed by a ghostly stillness, the drifting laughter of children, blown away by the rush of overhead wind. A deep ache built inside him as he listened to people living, working, and being together. A fierce and terrible melancholy gripped him and he did not understand why the feeling made him desire to live.

Finally, a breath of breeze passed under the brim of his hat and cooled the sweat, and Cassius was released from the moment.

He began to work. He tied a length of rope to the top of the gate and tied the other end around a stone and let it hang to make a plumb line. He secured one end of another piece of rope high on the opposite side, and pulled the far end around the trunk of a tree. With a steady pull, the gate came near to upright and the stone hung closer to the wood. He secured the rope around the trunk and moved to sit in shade. He hooked his hat over his knee to dry. No one wanted or expected this work to be done. Cassius was there to be separated from the big house until Hoke returned. He watched the road. The ruts were deep after the rains in April and early May.

Dust came off the road to the west in the direction of town, and he watched the cloud grow larger. Not Hoke, as he would come from Edensong Plantation in the opposite direction. A neighbor perhaps, or a traveler.

Cassius smiled as he recognized Weyman driving the buckboard of his owner, Thomas Chavis. Cassius remained in the shade, and when Weyman drew near he pulled up the horse.

Woo, Cassius, you hidin out? said Weyman.

Hiding out?

What y'all doin down here, messin with that overgrown door frame? Must be in a heap a' trouble.

No trouble here, said Cassius. He noticed something off in Weyman's manner. Around the eyes, maybe.

Right, 'cause they always send you down here to rest your black backside in the shade.

Can't have the sun looking over my shoulder, said Cassius. Like to make me self-conscious. Could miscalculate and build a gate that leans.

Weyman laughed and Cassius was suddenly curious, never before having heard Weyman force a laugh. Cassius took note of something he might not have noticed otherwise, that he generally was at ease in Weyman's company. Right then Cassius felt like a dog whose fur had been shaved backward with a dull blade.

Coming from town? said Cassius.

Equipment in at the dry goods for Thomas, said Weyman, nodding to items in the back of the buckboard covered by a tarpaulin.

Taking the long way home, said Cassius.

Got a customer over at Edensong.

Cassius nodded and looked in that direction and wondered when Hoke would return. Then Cassius said, abruptly:

Tell me who died.

Weyman looked away and Cassius understood Weyman's unusual manner. Weyman looked back and shrugged.

Wouldn't know, said Weyman.

Cassius nodded and his insides twisted into a knot. Weyman knew and Weyman would not say. This was likely to be bad news indeed for Cassius. From the moment Ellen had shut him out, he had suspected the identity, knowing whose death was most likely to bring him grief, but much as he tried not to be superstitious, he did not want to think of her at that moment, for fear he would make it so.

When you goin make me some more a' them little soldiers? said Weyman.

They take time, said Cassius.

The white children like 'em. Remind 'em of they daddies. I can sell 'em at a good price, people been askin.

See what I can do.

A real good price, Cassius, and you know I always share.

I know you say you do.

Now that's a fact, said Weyman, nodding in appreciation.

One day I'll make you hundreds of soldiers so you can be rich, said Cassius.

Rich. Can't rightly imagine what that be like.

Give it some thought, maybe you'll come up with something, like sitting down regularly to a fancy spread for supper or walking around in decent shoes.

No sir, tell you what I'd do if I ever was rich, I reckon I'd like to own that Colt sidearm of old Otis Bornock.

Maybe a new hat, that one got holes in the holes. You don't look out, pretty soon your hat'll be around your neck.

Got that sweet pearl handle and all, said Weyman, but he pulled his hat off his head and looked at it.

Bornock sooner cut his own throat than give up his gun, said Cassius, shaking his head, amused.

I seen somethin, said Weyman, growing serious.

What'd you see? I know, Bornock coming around to gift you that gun 'cause he's so doggone fond of you, said Cassius, enjoying himself.

No, this serious. Seen your ol' massa consortin with The Angel Gabriel.

Cassius felt a chill run up the backs of his arms.

Maybe you got mixed up, said Cassius, but his smile was gone.

No sir, seen it with my own eyes.

Gabriel Logue, said Cassius, weighing the significance of the name.

Cassius and Weyman looked at each other in silence, roasting under an indifferent sun. Gabriel Logue, nicknamed The Angel, was a smuggler, although he did not trade in human flesh. His goods flowed both north and south, across a porous border. The Confederate Army would be particularly satisfied to have Gabriel Logue in their custody. If Hoke was doing business with Logue, then he was again suffering financial difficulties, and that was not good.

Your old master still lets you ride around in that thing, said Cassius finally, changing the subject with a smile.

Oh yeah, Thomas trust me, he even trust me out here on the road with y'all wastrels and vagabonds, said Weyman.

Now that's the second time you call your old master by his Christian name. Pretty soon he let you lay down with that pretty woman of his.

Weyman laughed naturally this time. He and one other slave, an older man named Bunty, were owned by Thomas Chavis, and they worked his small family farm side by side with Thomas and his wife Martha. The white family sat with their slaves at the supper table and ate the same food at the same time, like equals. For a slave, Weyman's life was good.

Pretty woman? Why, one time, that speckled old hen lean over to make a reflection in a pond and damned if that pond didn't pucker up and soak into the ground.

I heard that, said Cassius laughing. He had never met Thomas Chavis's wife, but Weyman always had a good story about her.

A skunk took one look at her and his stink peeled off his tail end and ran for cover.

Makes a man wonder how old Thomas got her belly rounded, said Cassius.

Some time after dark, I s'pect.

Cassius saw the first indication of a dust cloud to the east, from the direction of Edensong Plantation. He moved casually to the rear of Weyman's buckboard, testing the ropes that held the tarpaulin in place, forcing Weyman to turn his back on the cloud.

But you doin all right yourself, carpenter, said Weyman. Long as your old "secesh" master be loanin you out to other planters. Just keep hidin your half pay from them field negroes and you can buy your freedom by 'n' by.

A free man, Cassius said thoughtfully. Tell me something, Weyman, what does a free man do? Where does a free man go? I better know so I can make plans.

A serious look crossed Weyman's eyes as he said: Free man go wherever he want, Cassius. Free man free to go hungry with no roof over his head, free man free to get picked up by the paddyrollers without a note from the Old Master to keep him safe. Free man free to be whipped like a common slave, since he look no different to the white man.

Well, Weyman, I guess you best stick with your Thomas.

And his handsome nestin wife, said Weyman.

The dust cloud was a certainty now. Cassius watched it peripherally.

Got your story set for Saturday night?

Workin on it, said Weyman, puffing his chest like an old peacock. He had won the storytelling competition three years running. Sunday's Big-To-Do was to be hosted this year at Edensong, Francis Jarvis's plantation, and the hands of the neighboring plantations waited on that day with great anticipation.

You want to practice your story, go right ahead, said Cassius. The dust cloud was larger. Cassius observed it without turning his head.

Well, now, I was just thinkin 'bout that time Old John went on up to Heaven and met Saint Peter at the gate. Old John, he look inside the gate and saw this mansion look just like his old plantation, and he say to Saint Peter, Saint Peter? Why you done built a copy of my Massa's plantation up here in Heaven? And Saint Peter say, Well now, why don't we go on over there and have a little look, and Saint Peter leads John over to the plantation, and it's all big like his plantation but it's different, too, fancy-like, made with jewels and gold and silver, and John is surprised and all wonderin and he says, Why, Saint Peter, this here plantation is even nicer than my massa's plantation, but who that workin over there on the roses, he look just like my old massa hisself, and Saint Peter says, Shhh, that be God, he just *thinkin* he your old massa—

Weyman laughed at his own story, and in the middle of his laugh he looked around and saw the dust cloud and stopped laughing.

That your Hoke?

Cassius smiled and said, That's him.

Weyman snapped the reins and tsked at the horse, turning him around to head back toward town and the Chavis farm, setting off at a trot to build some distance between himself and the oncoming dust.

Guess I'll meet that customer some other time, said Weyman over his shoulder, and he smiled at Cassius, knowing Cassius had gotten some of his own back, after Weyman had held off from telling him who had died.

Some minutes passed before Hoke Howard came up in his carriage. Sam made the wide turn into the road to the big house, wheels coming up over the ruts. Hoke pulled Sam to a stop and looked at Cassius without a word.

At one time, up until five years before, Cassius had been Hoke's favorite. During the subsequent years, Cassius struggled to disguise his hostility toward the man. He would see Hoke most days, but for the times when he was loaned out, specifically the six months he spent building the addition to The Swan of Alicante, Lamar Robertson's plantation. Not once in that time apart was his anger diminished.

Hoke made a clicking sound out of the side of his mouth and Sam lurched forward, carrying them under the arch of the gate.

Cassius sat back in the shade and watched Hoke get smaller. The sun was two hands up from the horizon. An early mosquito tested his ear. They would call for him when they were ready. Cassius knew he was facing a late supper.

C assius was called to the big house after the bell rang for the field hands, and he heard them dragging back to the quarters in the twilight. The sun was gone, the black trees framed a pale blue sky, and the big house grew larger with each step. The indoor lamp flames fluttered and flitted across the warp of the large blown-glass windows. Crickets chirked, a mourning dove warned a mockingbird of excessive celebration, and under it all he felt more than heard the munching hornworm jaws out in the fields.

Something pulled his attention to his left near the kitchen. He saw a figure in the dark and recognized Tempie Easter. Curious that she was hanging around the big house, as she had no legitimate business there. Tempie had come from another plantation, the only slave who insisted on a last name. She had arrived alone, an unattached high yellow, and for a time, the single stallions circled her. They moved on when it became apparent that her mind was otherwise occupied. She had brought with her nice clothes and campaigned to join the big house staff. Cassius thought she might have been what she claimed, a big house negro, as she carried herself in that superior way, with her aristocratic chest and small upturned breasts, her high hips and swaybacked walk. Cassius saw a second head peer around the corner and met Pet's eyes. So it was business. Pet had allowed some trinket to slip into her apron, something Tempie might offer to a customer. Pet backed up and he knew she would run to the side and come through the house to answer the front door as if she had been indoors all this time.

Cassius stepped onto the porch where only hours before Otis Bornock had stood, and Pet opened the door.

Two winters had passed since Cassius had been inside the big house. The subtle smell of fish embraced him, a smell he associated with wealth and power; despite the deprivations of war, they still had whale oil for the lamps. The big house was alive, children upstairs emitting occasional shrieks of delight or misery, their footfalls thunderous. The main foyer opened to a majestic greeting room that extended all the way to the back of the house, where a grand fireplace dominated and the walls were covered with paintings. In the far corner, a door led out to the rear gardens. In the wall to his right was the door to Hoke's study. To his left, the staircase ran halfway up, to a landing at the back wall, turned, and finished its climb to the second floor. On the far side of the stairs, a wide breezeway opened into the dining area and other rooms. The ceilings were high, the rooms large, the floorboards scrubbed clean, the rugs elegant, the windows huge. The volume of light was staggering, coming from a multitude of candles and whale oil lanterns that filled this room and leaked from other rooms, around corners, down the stairs.

Anything left in Mam Rosie's kitchen? said Cassius. Or did all them starving planter children eat up the leftovers?

Pet shook her head at him, mouth set, eyes grim.

Cassius understood. It was going to be bad for him. But bad news was a constant, bad news was forever and bad news would keep because right then he was more interested in his belly.

Pet scrutinized the grime that clung to Cassius from the day's work. She shook her head and rushed out of sight, returning with a damp cloth. She did what she could to clean his face and arms and hands, saying nothing. She left him alone with a warning look.

Cassius heard Hoke Howard's voice from his study.

"I'll not repeat the error of bringing you gifts in the future, if this is how they are to be received."

"This locket appears to be gold. How can we afford it, Mr. Howard?"

"Perhaps it is extravagant, but we can still afford special things."

"That is a crooked path to an answer, husband."

"I had a bit of luck gambling."

"You know very well my opinion of gambling," she said.

"I never bet more than I can afford to lose," said Hoke pompously.

Cassius moved to change the angle of his view of the inside of the study through the slightly open door. He could make out Ellen with her back to the door, but her full skirt blocked Hoke at his desk.

"And you were not gambling," said Ellen decisively.

"Was I not?"

"You have taken advantage of that tax business up North."

"You refer to the Morrill Tariff Act."

"Just so, you and your specificity, the Morrill Tariff Act then."

"There are certain benefits to—"

"You met with that man Logue."

"Now, Ellie."

"Gabriel Logue is a—he is a—"

"Logue is a businessman, no more, no less, just as I am a businessman, and I will tend to my business." His voice was loud and she was silent and Cassius backed up so that he would not be observed. Weyman had told him the truth. "If the North sees fit to tax tobacco, then I am but a damned fool if I do not take advantage. People desire my product and dislike being taxed. Logue offers me an excellent price, but lest you think me greedy, I have held back a portion of last year's crop to satisfy Mr. Davis's government so that we do not incite suspicion. And it is damned lucky I was able to make Logue's deal. You see the condition of the crop. If we do not terminate this affliction, we will need Logue just to see us through the winter!"

"I do not approve of you dealing with men like Gabriel Logue," said Ellen quietly.

"We are at war, and this is man's business."

"War and man's business," she said derogatorily.

Cassius heard Hoke's chair scrape against the floor as he pushed himself back.

"I have summoned Nettle and we will attend to it. It is his fault we are in this mess, I let him convince me to use the south fields for the third straight year and the soil is played out. This winter we will clear cut the parcel I took from Buffalo Channing's grandson. I cheated him out of *that* one, at least."

"Is the Produce Loan from the government inadequate?"

"Will you leave man's work to men, Mrs. Howard!?"

Cassius listened to the ensuing silence. If the Howards sold property to pay debts, life would change irrevocably. His carpentry skills could transfer to a new master, but would a new master allow Cassius to rent himself out? Would a new master allow him to retain his saved money? Cassius might even be sold to a cotton state. At that moment, life seemed not unreasonable in Sweetsmoke.

"Was there word from Jacob?" said Ellen.

"Nothing today, my dear, but do not fret, your son has never been a regular correspondent. Remember that in March we received a collection of his letters in a bundle."

"Does he not understand what it does to me?"

"You must consider that, with Sarah . . ." His voice trailed off.

"Yes, he married a ninny, which does not excuse him from communicating with his mother."

"Hush now, lest she hear through the floorboards."

Cassius glanced up at the ceiling. Pretty Sarah Greenleaf had been a sickly thing well before Jacob had taken her as his wife. She brought him one son, Charles, and in the ensuing ten years had yet to recover from childbirth. Not long after Jacob announced he would be joining Ashby's cavalry, Sarah was rushed to her bed with an undisclosed illness. Her husband, expected to remain behind to nurse her to health, had instead ridden away sooner than originally planned. Her illness persisted and she remained in her bed to this day.

Pet crossed to the Old Master's study and pushed open the door, entering as if she was but a gust of wind. Cassius now saw Ellen and

Hoke standing in opposition, but then Pet closed the door behind her and he heard the latch click.

The knot in his belly tensed. A slave never closed a door. It was difficult to hear through a closed door.

A moment later, Pet opened the door, Ellen emerged and marched past Cassius without making eye contact. Pet nodded that he should enter the study. Cassius did not move. Pet followed her Missus Ellen to the stairs, and spoke rapidly.

I don't know if this be the time, Missus Ellen, said Pet, but I was thinkin that if Missus Sarah was goin get herself a personal servant, ain't no one better than Tempie.

"Do not say 'ain't,' Pet."

Sorry, Missus.

"Tempie, now who is this Tempie?" said Ellen.

Why surely, Missus Ellen, you know her, Tempie Easter, she the one wear them nice clothes and such?

"I will have to consider that, Pet. I have yet to meet with John-Corey's people, and they were in his house."

Oh but Missus Ellen, Miss Genevieve got herself a personal servant and Miss Anne do, too—but Tempie, she been here a while and she know everythin 'bout the place.

From the stairs, Pet caught Cassius's eye and made a more urgent nod toward Hoke's study.

Still Cassius did not move.

"Cassius? Come on in here now," said Hoke.

Cassius entered the study. Hoke sat behind his desk, writing. Cassius noted that his pen hand moved with more deliberation than usual.

Cassius knew that Hoke was not the tower of strength he had once been. In the past, his wife would not have dared challenge him. Hoke nevertheless maintained the image of authority in front of his servants. The calculated time spent writing was meant to intimidate Cassius. But now that Cassius was here, he found himself in no hurry to learn the bad news. He took this time to observe his old master. Age and gravity crept in relentlessly, tugging at his neglected edges. Loose skin draped off his jawbone, gray tufts spiked from the tops of his ears and inner caverns, his eyebrows curled into his eyes, and the backs of his hands wore a pattern of liver spots. At fifty-four, Hoke Howard may have had power, but Cassius took no small satisfaction in his own relative youth, his physical strength and the tautness of his skin. Time had squeezed and bruised and softened Hoke as if he were an overripe pear.

Cassius examined the room. Once it had been a sitting room, but Hoke had chosen to make it his office and the room had been transformed accordingly. Cassius had, in fact, done the work. He remembered back, seven or eight years, to the months he had spent in this room. He had built the wall of shelves. He had erected the wainscoting and created the decorative interior casing for the windows. He had built all of the furniture, particularly the great desk, as well as the chair in which Hoke now sat. The old man had a fondness for wooden boxes of different sizes in which he stored personal items. A low rectangular box held paper alongside a taller, more narrow box with writing instruments. On the shelves were boxes appropriate for chewing tobacco, snuff, and his decorative pipes which Cassius had never seen Hoke smoke. There were boxes for medicines and candies, and some that were either empty or held items about which Cassius did not know. Cassius had made many of the boxes, some simple, others elaborate, but the most ornate boxes had been purchased during Hoke's travels. His eyes moved around the room. Even the picture frames were his work.

Behind Hoke was the oil portrait of his wife, Ellen Corey Howard, in younger days. The painter had captured an expression in her eyes Cassius did not recognize, and it made the portrait appear false to him. Cassius had also not remembered her ever being so pretty. He did not consider that the artist had shrewdly idealized her; only that the artist may have been mediocre or worse, blind. On the opposite wall, so placed for Hoke's pleasure, was the portrait of his sons John-Corey and Jacob. John-Corey was thirteen in the portrait, Jacob ten. The portrait of his daughters was in another area of the house.

"Well, Cassius," said Hoke, looking up. "Did you finish work on the gate?"

No sir.

"No," said Hoke thoughtfully. The issue of the gate seemed to hold little meaning to him, and Cassius was surprised at how quickly he abandoned it. Hoke Howard rubbed the root of his nose between his eyebrows with his left thumb and forefinger. Cassius had seen him perform this gesture many times, and remembered the same gesture made by his son.

"I do not know how things will turn out, I simply do not." Hoke looked not at Cassius but at the space beside him, as if he spoke to someone else. "What will be my legacy, with my son gone to war and showing no inclination to take his natural place at Sweetsmoke? The government raids our essentials to supply the troops, they appropriate the crop before it can reach market and achieve its legitimate price, and yet, and yet, when I consider all things, we are well supplied in comparison to our neighbors. And I'm still in fine health, so there is time for Jacob to come around, still time, still time. It does not help that my children and their families are drawn to Sweetsmoke as if to a center of gravity, yet we nevertheless, with careful management, produce enough to care for them all, Genevieve, Anne and her family, Nettle and his flock of children, good God, John-Corey's people, of course, our people. The burden is great, Cassius, great, but manageable, and yet, so many to care for, so many. My God, on a daily basis, I know only exhaustion, it resides in every fiber of my being, the responsibility, and I worry about my health, Cassius. The responsibility is crushing."

Cassius was alarmed to hear him speak this way. The man had opened up a private part of himself to his slave. Cassius thought back, wondering if Hoke had ever revealed himself to Cassius before, and realized he certainly had not in the last five years.

Hoke looked directly at him without seeming to see him. His eyes were unfocused, as if searching for something within his own mind. "Yond Cassius has a lean and hungry look." His words were sad, spoken as if the words were unrelated to his true meaning, spoken as if he was unaware of an audience.

Cassius was further convinced that everything was different.

Yond Cassius? said Cassius.

"Eh? Oh. I must have been thinking aloud."

You said Yond Cassius.

Hoke lightened for a moment, as if taking advantage of a momentary reprieve. "I named you, Cassius. You were quite the lean sprig when you were born. I thought you might grow to be a runt."

I think I heard you say that once before.

"Did I? Yes, of course. Yond Cassius. From *Julius Caesar*. It's a play by Shakespeare," said Hoke condescendingly. "Julius Caesar was a great general, although when the play begins, he is emperor of Rome. 'A lean and hungry look' came immediately to mind when I saw you and I always trust my first instincts, as I have so often been proven correct. A man named William Shakespeare wrote the play, but you would not have heard of him."

In fact, Cassius had heard of Shakespeare. But he said, No sir.

"Well, have no fear, Cassius is an honorable man," said Hoke and laughed to himself.

Cassius took a step toward the shelves as if looking for the book. Hoke watched him indulgently.

"Would you like to see the book that gave you your name?"

I think I would, Master Hoke.

Hoke moved to his bookshelf, his step assured, abounding with pride. For an instant Cassius saw the young Hoke, with power invincible. But perhaps he had never truly possessed that power, perhaps the young Cassius had imposed it upon him. Hoke reached without hesitation toward the shelf that held the Shakespeare volumes, but then his hand hesitated as he did not immediately see *Julius Caesar*. Cassius had already located it, but said nothing.

"Now where is that?" said Hoke.

Hoke found the book and with his finger atop the spine, drew it from its slot. He cradled it in his hands, then turned its cover to Cassius. *The Tragedy of Julius Caesar*.

"Although I cannot imagine what good it does you," said Hoke. He did not bother to mention that Cassius could not read.

Cassius had been fully aware of the change since the death song in the field, but what pursued him into this room was something quite remarkable. Hoke was not only speaking as if he regarded Cassius with respect, he was revealing personal limitations through candor. Recognizing this sliver of an opening, and knowing it would soon come to an end once Cassius learned the identity of the dead, Cassius decided to press his advantage.

Curious about my name, said Cassius. How it looks written in a book.

"Well," said Hoke. He opened the book and flipped through a

series of pages until he found the name, put his finger under it, and turned the book to him. "See? That word there. That is your name. C-A-S-S-I-U-S."

Hoke glanced away, holding the book carelessly, unaware that the leaves flipped until a different page was revealed, and Cassius read a passage to himself:

> *Cowards die many times before their deaths;*
> *The valiant never taste of death but once.*
> *Of all the wonders that I yet have heard,*
> *It seems to me most strange that men should fear,*
> *Seeing that death, a necessary end,*
> *Will come when it will come.*

Hoke snapped the book shut and returned it to the vertical space it had vacated. "Trust me, were you able to read, you would greatly admire Mr. Shakespeare."

Cassius memorized its place on the shelf. Then he asked the terrible question: Will you keep us together? With things as they are, will you keep us or will you sell us?

If Hoke thought Cassius overpressed his advantage, he did not show it. "I will do everything in my power to keep our family together, Cassius. You are my family, you are aware of that, are you not?"

Cassius held his tongue a moment too long before he said: Yes.

Cassius knew he dared press no further. Hoke returned to his desk and sat in the chair. He set his elbows down and folded his fingers together.

"You were born here, Cassius. This is your home. You grew up with my son. I daresay you and Jacob were friends. He grew tall and handsome, did he not? He did not take you as a personal servant when he joined Ashby. William was an odd choice, I think. But no matter, perhaps he was protecting you, yes, I suspect that was it."

The news is very bad, thought Cassius. The man delays.

"Do you attend church, Cassius?"

Cassius shook his head no.

"No, I suppose not. Church is for women. And slaves. Not for men." Cassius realized Hoke had just differentiated him from the rest of his chattel.

"They have been dancing around you and have only made it worse," said Hoke bitterly. "Everyone knows how she took care of you."

So. Here it was.

Hoke stood. He walked out from behind the desk and onto the long rug, hands behind his back. "Unnecessary intrigue, a lot of damned nonsense. Are you a danger to run, Cassius?"

No sir.

"No, of course not." Then, musing, "Although would you tell me if you were?" Cassius was unsure if Hoke spoke to him or to some unseen person in the room. "You already enjoy a freedom most of our family can only dream about. How I wish I had your freedom." Hoke looked directly at Cassius.

Cassius wished he had never entered this room. He wished to further delay the news. He disliked being treated as if he were more than a slave when he knew so absolutely that he was not. When Hoke treated him as a human being, Cassius was unpleasantly reminded of the past, when he had been Hoke's favorite. Cassius wanted nothing more than to continue hating.

"I will just come out and say it, Cassius, as I know you will handle it, and I trust you will not lose sight of yourself or what you have here." Hoke hesitated, and Cassius saw a tremor in his hand. Apparently the news had been a blow to Hoke as well. "She is dead, Cassius, that is all there is to it, Emoline Justice is dead, and that is that."

The room blurred before his eyes and for a moment Cassius did not know where he was. Time stretched and at any other moment, he would have recognized his silence as dangerous, but at this moment time had little meaning as his head filled with voices from the past. It was what he had both dreaded and expected, but to have it verified took something out of him. His body grew unexpectedly heavy and he feared the floorboards might bow and splinter beneath the sudden weight of his legs and feet. He no longer saw Hoke's study, as in his mind he was looking at the snow piled up outside, against the window, and in that moment he felt her hands on his back, gently applying salve. But before the sorrow could expand and well up and smother him, he remembered where he was and he compressed his emotion and forced it deep down into the darkest pocket of his mind so that he would be incapable of revealing his feelings.

He worked to make his voice sound normal: When?

"Last night. Monday, yesterday."

How?

"Someone . . . Well, from the little I know, someone struck her. Struck her violently at the back of the head, they said."

Who did it to her?

"I do not know that, Cassius. No one knows that."

Someone knows, thought Cassius. The one who did it to her knows. But he did not speak these thoughts aloud. Perhaps she had spoken her mind once too often, and that had led to her death.

"She was . . . she was a damned annoying woman, a prickly, frustrating woman, oh how she could make my life miserable," said Hoke, and Cassius's shoulders straightened to hear her spoken of in such a way, but then he recognized the shiver in Hoke's voice and saw that Hoke had turned toward the window, perhaps to allow himself the indulgence of speaking openly of his grief, for he could do no such thing in front of his wife. Perhaps he could do no such thing in front of anyone else. "She tutored me as a boy, she was of course older, and such a bright and lively creature for a negro. My mother saw it first, saw that certain something in her, and Mother went against everyone and taught her to read. She learned well, so well that Mother had Emoline teach me. You would think she would have been grateful to be treated with such regard, but even then she could be so willful! It shocked me in those days, a slave with such strong opinions, I worried even then that she would go too far. I had . . . I had feelings for her, you may think it impossible, but that is the truth of it. I can still feel her in my arms, so tiny, so tiny."

Cassius did not care to hear about Hoke's affection for Emoline Justice. She was dead, that difficult and extraordinary woman, a free woman, freed by Hoke himself, a woman who still taught when she could, a woman who sewed for the blacks and told fortunes to whites and had already bought her son's freedom and was striving to buy the freedom of her two daughters. Now they would never go free. Cassius knew her son well enough to know he would not work to free his sisters. But Hoke was correct about her certain something, and Cassius remembered the way a room lit up when she entered, even when she was stern and demanding. Or perhaps it was he who lit up to see her. He thought back on her face, and realized that in his memory she never appeared to be afraid.

"I was so young then, and unsure, and you can imagine my amazement, my true amazement when she came to me, it being my first time. It was as if I was being bestowed with a great honor."

Cassius took a step backward. Hoke was lying, he knew that for a fact. Emoline had told him about the times Hoke Howard had come to her bed and how they had made a son against her will. He crushed Hoke's words inside him, Hoke had no right to redefine her memory in that way.

"She did me a great service. She lied to my mother about the identity of the baby's father. Mother was anything but unintelligent, but Emoline created just enough doubt."

Cassius thought with disgust that Hoke still would not mention his own son's name, and his thoughts must have played out on his face because Hoke said, "But I go on too long." Hoke brought a sleeve to his cheek, composing himself. His next words were uttered with renewed strength, charged with his significance.

"Now, Cassius. You tell me how you are with this. I would not like to put you in the tobacco shed again."

Cassius remembered her small home in town with the two rooms. One wall was taken up with a large hearth that housed a living fire and the smell of the room came to him and he nearly lost his balance.

If there is a funeral, I would like to attend, said Cassius.

Hoke considered the request.

"Depending on how you behave the next few days, I shall write you a pass when the time comes."

Cassius nodded. He knew that Hoke would wait until after Emoline was in the ground and then he would tell Cassius it was too late. That did not matter. The living mattered. The dead were the dead. He endured Hoke's examining eyes as to his state of mind. This was his unspoken warning, Hoke would be watching, and then he remembered Ellen and young Charles, and Otis Bornock going first to Mr. Nettle in the fields, and Weyman looking away. He thought of the field hands and their song, and the whispering planter's family. The news had shaken them because of what she had once meant to the plantation, as a former house servant, in her relations with Hoke, and because of what she had once done for Cassius. Now they would all be watching. Cassius scanned the desk for the note delivered by Otis Bornock. He did not see it.

C assius left by the front door, but went around the side to the kitchen. Mam Rosie was outside; she had not gone in to her pallet yet. She looked thinner and more taut than she had in the afternoon with Andrew and Charles, if that was possible.

All I got, said Mam Rosie, is pot likker.

Pot likker, said Cassius.

You heard what I say.

She stepped inside and came back with a deep pan. Cassius took it and touched the pan's side and it was lukewarm. He drank.

That almost remembers being warm, Rose, he said.

He didn't look up as he said it, just lifted the pan back to his lips and drank more. But he felt her eyes on him. No one called her Rose. Only her husband Darby ever called her Rose, and he had been sold more than twenty years ago and never heard from again. She had not even been allowed to say good-bye. Only Cassius had said good-bye.

I s'pose there might be somethin else, said Mam Rosie.

She moved into the kitchen and came back with a small pan of spoon bread.

As Cassius took it, he said: Not like you owe me.

Cassius ate quickly as Mam Rosie watched him.

What you be plannin? said Mam Rosie coldly.

Planning?

I know you, Cassius, don't you even think 'bout sassin your Mam Rosie, you know what I'm talkin 'bout.

You mean with young Master Charles? Guess I'll just have to hope he forgets all about it.

You are a damned sight too smart for your own good, said Mam Rosie.

Cassius looked at her.

And then he spoke: She was a prickly, frustrating old woman

who took care of me once. I am sad to hear that she's dead. But nothing I can do about that now.

Cassius tasted Hoke's words in his own mouth, surprised that they had come out.

She took real good care of you, Cassius, don't you be forgettin that. And she was a good friend to me too, said Mam Rosie.

Cassius would never forget how Emoline Justice had helped him. But he was not interested in saying so to Mam Rosie. He knew that Mam Rosie collected secrets. More than once, people around her found themselves in trouble with the Masters who seemed to know things they should not have known, but Mam Rosie was never in trouble.

This spoon bread is fine, said Cassius. Just the right amount of molasses.

He handed her back the empty pan and sucked crumbs off his fingers. He turned and walked down the dark path to the slave quarters.

-<del> Chapter Two <del>-

WOODEN crosses had been erected haphazardly along the path through the quarters. Tallow-dripping wicks were tied to the arms, spaced evenly and hung long to dry, as if crucified angels had been left to decay, leaving only their shattered skeletal wings. The wicks were now being rolled in partially cooled tallow to add thickness. Savilla had claimed the task of candle-making. She liked her candles thick and no one else had the patience or was willing to devote the time. Unfortunately, the Confederate quartermasters had thinned the herd of livestock, thereby reducing the supply of heavy animal fat, and Savilla had been forced to rein in her enthusiasm. Savilla experimented with the tallow by adding fragrant items to disguise the smell; tonight the lane smelled of animal death and anise. Her sons had been enlisted to help her, but one by one they had slipped away, starting with Joseph, the oldest. Joseph was eighteen, independent and smart, and could appear enthusiastic while doing the least possible amount of work. He had a distinctive tuft of white hair that grew just off-center on his head, which set him apart and gave him a dashing look. He played on his uniqueness and got away with more than his brothers. He was gone before anyone realized it. The next oldest was Sammy and he had stayed longer, but now only young Andrew remained. Andrew maintained a respectful distance so as not to lard his new trousers, his new shoes, or his new hat, all of which he would wear tomorrow for his first day in the fields. And so Savilla worked alone.

Personal chores were performed at night as daytime was for the Master. The hornworm blight had forced them to spend every daylight hour in the fields and they were worn senseless, performing their tasks in a trance.

Heat lingered and cabin doors stood open. The lane was lit by heavy iron frying pans burning grease set on stumps, while a few small fires burned in shallow pits, green logs spraying frequent sparks. Smoke burned eyes and throats, and no one lingered near the flames in the heat.

Cassius approached from the big house, the path barely visible as the moon was setting, a sliver in the sky. He passed Mr. Nettle's home, the Overseer's place, set between the big house and the quarters, visible to neither, so that on this side of the bend he could just make out the glow from the lane above hedges and between trees. Inside, Mr. Nettle's wife shrieked at her children and Cassius knew Mr. Nettle would escape early to patrol the grounds and slave cabins. Cassius rounded the bend and approached yellow firelight and the path went black under his feet. He entered the smoke bloat and identified silhouettes, marking the occasional face lit by low greasy flames. Cassius walked the center of the lane by the gully, named by some previous wit Suetsmoke Run, which was known to swell to a river when it rained and where the women dumped bathwater and other things. His cabin was the last before a cleared area and the woods, and he hoped to pass through unnoticed. To his surprise, they looked at him only to pretend not to see him. He flinched after the third time and examined the ground. To be shunned was worse than to be ignored. Cassius preferred isolation; it served as his cloak and allowed him to pretend to be unaffected by the capricious wisdom of the masters or those in the quarters who schemed for power. But as their eyes brushed off him, Cassius knew that isolation was desirable only when it was by choice. He was surprised to find himself wounded.

He heard their talk in snatches—don' know why Massa ain't clear out a new field this year, I could'a tol' him that one be played out—

—got that thing happenin in my lung, ev'y time I breathe I be suckin through a muddy spiderweb—

—pity 'bout that old woman, used to get potions from her—

The voices dimly competed with the unpleasant chatter in his head. The sharp plunk of a homemade banjo cut into his thoughts, George playing a riff as he spoke: You got to practice, Joseph, I can't be playin so much no more, my fingers givin me fits, and this thing on my shoulder hurts bad.

Joseph replying: When freedom comes, it'll all get better, George, everything better under freedom, and didn't I see you do your shoulder with your own knife?

Don't make it hurt no less. You got to learn to endure pain, boy, and don't give me no sass mouth 'bout no freedom.

Banjo George played a song, and Cassius walked on, listening with his head down so that he did not see Shedd. The Little Angry Man commandeered a wide alley in his walk, expecting all hands to make way. Cassius ran directly into him and the little man stumbled for balance. Shedd found his feet and sprang at Cassius, Shedd's good eye boring in while his other eye wandered off to look at something to the side. Cassius was mesmerized by Shedd's loose eye, as if Shedd's words were aimed not at him but at some unseen other standing near him.

God damn son of a roach! said Little Angry Man, stabbing a thumb at Cassius's face. Starin at your toes like they stuck with diamonds. I been walkin here since before you shit solid, you yellowjack big house whoremonger. Maybe if I seen *you* out bustin your teats squeezin worms off smokeweed, then maybe you see *me* back off!

An ember of fury flamed inside Cassius. He had kept Emoline Justice packed down tight in his chest, but now things churned inside and he was dangerously close to liberating his grief at this pointless little man. At that moment, he disliked Shedd unspeakably, Shedd who held no more claim to injustice than anyone else in the quarters, yet he and his wandering eye wore temper like a skin. Cassius knew he would have a pass from the quarters if he chose this moment to punish Shedd. But Emoline's memory brushed against him and allowed him a breath, and after that breath, another. Emoline had taught him to look for another way to get back his own. Cassius stared at Shedd as all eyes watched.

Cassius's voice was low and without emotion: Go away, little man.

Little Angry Man's mouth twisted into a snarl but no sound emerged. He could live with angry, but *little* man? Shedd framed a response but saw he stood alone. A second tirade would be unwise. He spat in the dirt, held his quivering leg still for an age, and was away. Cassius watched his clumsy-quick shamble, long leg swinging wide as if trying to dislodge a stone. Cassius had been told that Shedd's leg had been crushed on Durning's Hill ten years before when the mule Milady lost her footing in the muck and rolled back on him, but he thought there might be more to the story.

The tension broke and ended his invisibility. They looked at him, they nodded as they returned to their business, they smiled about a thing to be quickly forgotten, nothing important, just Little Angry Man.

He did not like Shedd, but Shedd had done him a service and brought him back to life in the quarters. Now Cassius could become invisible again.

He saw Tempie Easter wearing a clean dress, presenting a fresh facade for an ordinary night of chores. He found her airs tolerable, and appreciated that she paid him little attention. There was something to be said for frank self-possession. He wondered what trinket, if any, she had gotten from Pet, and wondered further if she would slip away tonight, avoid patrollers and meet up with a buyer. It was not impossible that her customer was himself a patroller.

Cassius's cabin was large and more solidly constructed than the others. Cassius could have lived in the carpentry shed near the big house, but chose to live here. He had built this cabin especially for his family. He and Marriah had lived there during her pregnancy. She had never returned after the boy was born, and close to four weeks had passed before Cassius was back. He did not doubt that the cabin might be better suited to a family, but the others had been too spooked to inhabit a place thought to be haunted. If it was, then he was the shade. He had built hidden places in the walls that would be near to impossible to discover, and while most stood empty, one held a book, a dangerous possession if it were to be found, along with a toy soldier he had carved for his son.

He ducked under a wing of candle wicks and arrived at his door. He heard Big Gus's voice and stepped to the outside corner of the cabin to look out on the cleared area near the tall trees. Two women hovered around Big Gus, while a third stayed a few steps outside their circle. Gus was preening, making a pretense of conjuring up a poem right there on the spot to impress them. Cassius had witnessed this act before.

Big Gus employed his pulpit voice: When I 'member your smile, I come back after 'while, so 'gainst the till I lean, 'cause all about you I dream.

Cassius stifled a laugh. Big Gus was forever and always a wretched poet, but was he truly so deaf to his own lack of rhythm? When no uncomfortable laughter followed, Cassius wondered if poor poetry, rendered with artificial ardor, might be catnip to women.

Why, that beautiful, Big Gus, said the deeply stupid Fawn. Fawn embodied the black woman's curse—she was pretty. Hoke had named her as well, her newborn face reminding him of a young deer. As she developed, her body grew curvaceous to exaggeration so that men could not look at her without envisioning fornication. By age thirteen, Fawn's presence was required at the big house when Ellen was away, and sometimes at the smokehouse when she was not.

The second girl with Big Gus was light-skinned, freckled Polly, she of the flat round face that pinched her small features in toward her nose. But she was as clever as she was plain. Cassius wondered why she attended to Big Gus but then knew it was *because* of her cleverness. She played pilot fish to the pretty one, safe in the knowledge that Gus would never amuse himself with someone so homely, allowing her to collect whatever scraps might fall.

You like that? said Big Gus, referring to his poem. He did not look at Fawn. He looked at Quashee, the new girl. He raised his voice a notch and said: Mr. Nettle has expressed appreciation for my poetry, other patrollers, too. One said I ought present 'em to Old Master Hoke hisself.

Quashee had come with her father Beauregard from Master John-Corey's plantation, and the two former house servants had been put to work in the fields. In the wake of Big Gus's plea for flattery,

Cassius considered her for the first time. Quashee was unusual in the quarters where adult field hands were strong and large. Her shoulders were narrow, her breasts small, her hips and legs lean. Cassius admired her face, although he might have taken little notice had Big Gus not blazed the trail. Her eyes were wide-set, an almond shape that swept up and away from her nose. Her forehead was high, smooth, and her upper lip was particularly defined and appealing. In the right company she would be high yellow, lighter than most field hands, light enough to be welcome in the big house. And unless Cassius was mistaken, Quashee was edging away from Gus, a smile on her face that did not encourage him and may well have been indulgent. With that pleasant realization, Cassius came by a measure of respect for her.

Might surprise you to know how many whites be appreciatin my poetry. But I want to know 'bout you, how you like it? said Big Gus.

Oh I liked it, Gus, I did, said Fawn.

No, I mean you, new girl, said Big Gus and Quashee's head dipped in a manner that resembled a nod.

To go against Big Gus was dangerous, almost as dangerous as it was to get close to him. Big Gus was the Driver, and as such, his favorites reaped benefits. Those who crossed him found themselves trapped in unpleasant working conditions while being eyed suspiciously by the Overseer, as Big Gus regularly whispered in Mr. Nettle's ear. Wise to stay on Big Gus's good side, but even that could be treacherous. Once Gus tired of someone, then they too would be eyed suspiciously.

Thought you ought to know, Quashee, your time in the fields can go easier, said Big Gus.

It's not so bad, said Quashee softly.

I got me a fine relationship with the white folk here, he said.

I imagine you do, said Quashee.

And I don't take serious all that talk 'bout bad luck, said Big Gus.

Cassius saw Quashee's head flinch sideways at the words "bad luck."

Big Gus moved to her, taking her hands in his, turning them over to expose her palms. Neither Fawn nor Polly moved, watching the moment play out.

These hands, said Big Gus, ain't used to field work. These be inside hands. See how they split and blister. I can help these pretty little hands return to the big house where they belong.

They just gettin used to new ways, said Quashee. Always that way in the beginning.

Big Gus smiled at her, holding her hands for a beat too long, and Cassius shared his confusion. Was she playing the fool, or did she truly not understand what was being offered? If she did understand, was she being coy or was she not interested? Big Gus could offer good things to a pliant female, and he enjoyed it when women competed to satisfy him. What would cause this new girl to hesitate?

Cassius saw Big Gus for what he was, a fickle boy in a man's body empowered by white people who enjoyed his groveling flattery. If Quashee saw through Big Gus, then she was wise indeed. Maybe even wise enough to play the fool.

Quashee saw Cassius and a brief smile crossed her face. Cassius could not pretend he had not seen it, so he nodded. Big Gus saw her smile and turned his head, thus trapping Cassius.

Hello Gus, said Cassius.

What you lookin at? said Big Gus.

Cassius did not care to start things with Big Gus. Did the new girl imagine that Cassius might protect her? Or was she simply redirecting Gus's attention away from her? Wise, perhaps, but Cassius wanted no part of it. If Gus had a fresh female target, so be it. Cassius's life was altogether simpler when he avoided friction with him.

I was just thinking about your poem, said Cassius easily.

You were thinkin 'bout my poem? said Big Gus.

Heard it when I got to my door. You got that voice, Gus. Might sound good if you sing it.

You sayin I should sing it? said Big Gus. Big Gus was altogether baffled by Cassius's meaning.

Some poems sound better sung, said Cassius.

What that mean? What you sayin, Cassius?

Cassius was clever enough to trust silence, which put Big Gus in deeper torment. On one hand, it resembled flattery, but Gus knew Cassius and, what was worse, suspected Cassius of mocking him.

You think you're better 'n me, Cassius?

Gus, I only know I could never make up such a poem. But that's all I got to say 'cause I am dog tired, so I'll only say one last thing which is good night.

Cassius walked back to his cabin door. He wondered why he had done it, making himself a target so the new girl Quashee could get away.

Big Gus looked back and found only Fawn and Polly. He looked over their heads as they attempted to engage him.

That was nice of him, said Fawn.

Maybe it was, said Big Gus.

But go on with your poem, said Fawn. I'd be lovin to hear it again.

Don't remember it no more, said Big Gus as he saw Mr. Nettle coming down the lane, performing his evening check early. Big Gus rushed now, to walk with Mr. Nettle, who smiled when he saw Gus coming.

Cassius opened his door and saw Savilla's husband Abram sitting inside waiting on the small stool by the cold hearth. Cassius had not kept a fire in the hearth since the rains in March and April. Abram was admiring the carved toy soldiers Cassius had been whittling for Weyman. He set them down in military formation.

Little bit like you go out your way to get his goat, said Abram.

Little bit like he goes out of his way to be a horse's ass, said Cassius. No one can say I wasn't pleasant as a man can be.

You get to eat? said Abram.

Cassius nodded. Got something from Mam Rosie.

Because Savilla saw you were goin be late so she made extra in case you was hungry. You could'a had my portion. Can't eat nothin with my tooth.

Savilla's a fine woman, Abram. You tell her I thank her, but that I'm all right tonight. Time you got that tooth pulled.

Then Cassius caught himself. He had been about to tell Abram to visit Emoline in town, she had poultices that could lessen the pain of an extraction.

Tooth ain't nothin, said Abram. Ain't nobody right. You hear 'bout Banjo George? Got the bilious fever.

Banjo enjoys complaining so much he makes his own pain, said Cassius.

Ain't nobody right.

Abram stood up. He looked at the tobacco leaves hanging off the rafters drying near the ceiling.

Some of them gettin the mold, you best dry heat 'em.

Cassius nodded.

Been out to the traps?

Not in a few days.

Abram nodded. Abram was glad to have his wife cook for Cassius, as Cassius was a lucky trapper and he brought to her whatever he caught, to share with her family.

All right tonight, said Abram with a thoughtful frown, as if memorizing Cassius's exact words so he could repeat them to his wife. Cassius could see that Abram had something else on his mind, and he did not care to hear it.

I'm just going to get some sleep, said Cassius, hoping to ward it off.

I'se heartily sorry, Cassius. If it be all right to say so.

Not necessary to say—

Had a real good likin of that woman and she did not deserve to go in such a way.

That's kind of you—

She always decent to me and mine, and I think that be all I got to say 'bout it.

Cassius had known that Abram could not be stopped from saying what he had come to say. Once Abram set on a path, he had to offer his condolences about Emoline Justice or eventually burst.

Well, said Cassius. Maybe she's the lucky one. You remember to tell Savilla I thank her.

All right tonight, said Abram. Cassius caught a whiff of Abram's breath and knew that his tooth had to go.

Abram was a decent man and in the raw caverns of Cassius's mind, Abram's concern and empathy were a balm. But it was a relief when he was gone.

Cassius lay on his pallet and listened as the quarter settled. Children's voices drifted off as bathing ended and bedtime stories concluded. Low conversations among men replaced them, as well as the activities of women, finishing candles, washing clothes, or mending their only frocks or their husband's one pair of trousers.

Insects and crickets voiced their songs as the air cooled. His mind drifted and touched briefly on Mam Rosie. She had raised him, but Hoke had named him. Which act was more important to his personality? he wondered. Hoke Howard was not his father; his mother had been pregnant when Hoke bought her, although he had not bought Cassius's father. He had sold her four years after Cassius was born, and Cassius wondered if an incident had precipitated her sale. He thought not; Hoke's fortunes had always been up and down, and the turnover in slaves and horseflesh was considerable, new favorites purchased when he was enthusiastically flush, sold off when things went sour. Cassius considered Hoke Howard's name. If Cassius was named on a flight of whimsy, Hoke was named with grave consideration. The third Hoke Howard bore a name of substance with extensive roots. His great-grandfather Horace had built Sweetsmoke; his grandfather, the first Hoke, had made it a monstrous success; his father, the second Hoke, had further expanded it; and he now commanded it. If Cassius was a name from a book, Hoke was a name with great expectations. What would it be like to bear such a name? Cassius thought of the responsibility he had witnessed that afternoon, and for a fleeting moment imagined Hoke Howard as trapped in his destiny as Cassius was in his.

Jenny came to his cabin door. She opened it without knocking, but tonight lingered in the doorway; normally she would have closed the door behind her and begun to undress.

You want me with you tonight, Cassius? said Jenny.

He looked at her silhouette, her arm stretched out with her hand on the door. Behind her, the grease fires were out, and a log shifted and sprayed embers in what remained of a fire by the gully. An instant of flame hugged the log, then dropped back into the glowing red ashes.

Not tonight, said Cassius.

Her silhouette nodded and backed out. He regretted turning her away, but did not know how to be anything but alone this night. Jenny would have been smart enough to provide nothing more than warmth and an easy presence, but he could not have that now.

Back when it happened, Cassius had assumed that the love component of his life was over for good. His wife and son were gone. In the aftermath of that, with a raging and tormented mind, he saw women shy from him the way wild deer shy from a company of soldiers. More than a year passed before Jenny happened by the carpentry shed with something to be repaired. A few days later she visited again. In time, her excuses became careless. He had thought Jenny offered charity for old times' sake. Years before he had courted her, but it was a poor match and she had ended it and he had borne that hurt for some time. Now she came at night so the others would not know.

Cassius and Jenny did not meet often. They rarely had occasion to speak; he a carpenter, she a field hand; and she only came when he nodded to her at some point during the day, granting her permission. She would not always come at his nod, but when she did, she would come furtively and lie beside him where he pretended not to be waiting. He craved the physical element of their liaison, but youthful passion was gone. She had once abandoned him—her punishment was to be ravished, but not loved. Yet she was willing, while others acted as if he were in smallpox quarantine. He better trusted the judgment of the wary women; they saw him as he saw himself, a raging, bitter, coldhearted man. Jenny tried to be near him, the way small children and animals tried to be near him, and this to him was inexplicable.

On his worst days, small children, barely old enough to speak, would hover as if sensing his need. He imagined himself unapproachable, and yet they came, sometimes to sit by him, sometimes to take his hand. And he would grow calm. Domestic animals, independent cats in particular, would approach. Blinded within black storms, he would be jolted by a nudge against his shin, the shock of a cold nose, the amazing strength of a tiny body running its length against him, a layer of fur coating the sweat of his leg or neck or cheek.

It was strange to think of these things, at a time when he was ready to release the demons of his memory.

Cassius dreamed of running. His muscles knotted and anxiety passed through his legs as he slept fitfully on his pallet with his back on fire.

He woke suddenly. He tried to shake off the dream, but it encircled him. On that day, he had been unaware of his back bleeding,
but he had felt a deep cold and searing heat all at once. Marriah was
dead. The boy who had yet to be named was gone. Cassius ran.

The patrollers chased him on their horses with their dogs. When
his mind was right, he knew ways to fool the dogs and evade the patrollers, but that took planning and this was not planned, he had to
outrun them with the only tools he possessed: Stamina fueled by hatred and horror, the stamina to run forever and never stop, not to eat,
not to sleep, just to run until he had outrun all of it.

He ran through the fields, past crops and hedgerows, he ran
across dusty roads and into woods, he ran through brambles and
brush, he ran along the creek, he ran without thinking.

The dogs were close, then far, then close again. He did not care.
He anticipated the moment the dogs would catch him and tear him
apart, a chance to feel again—would they go for his back, would the
blood drive them mad, would it happen quickly or would he have
time to savor his own death?

He ran to the edge of town. A flash through his brain warned
that if he were to run through the streets, he would surely be caught.
He ran through the streets.

They came on, dogs, and horses carrying men, and he ran between houses and past the dry goods store and a boardinghouse and
a tavern, and then his legs were strange, as if no longer joined to his
hips, running full-out in his mind while his legs lagged, as if dragging a dead steer, as if he had plugged into dense muck, thick legs
sucking to pull free, the bottom of his feet shooting roots that dug
in and grabbed. Each step tore his feet out of the ground while the
world rushed and swirled around him.

The first dog was too fast, barking maniacally, dancing around
him. Then came the pack, a thunderous wave of sharp barking and
hot breath chased by whistles, horsemen ordering dogs back, horses
blundering in, dust clouding and choking.

A woman's voice poked a pinhole of light into the scrabble of his
mind, and he pictured the sound coming between himself and the
dogs horses men. Her voice was a safe sound, a barrier, authority
without fear. He quivered with exhaustion as he willed himself to
remain standing. Never before had his body quit on him, never, he

could press it to impossible limits and yet here in the direst of moments, it trembled.

Her voice was close, the patroller's voices responded from far off. In a moment or an hour, the horse hooves backed away and she was in front of him, her arms under his armpits, and they moved, a miracle, but it was her legs doing the work, his own being dead.

He did not know that Emoline Justice had saved him from being hobbled. He did not know that she had confronted the patroller who had unsheathed his blade, readying it for Cassius's Achilles tendon. He did not know that they were soon joined by Hoke on horseback. He did not know that she told them she would take Cassius into her home and that when he was recovered he would return to Sweetsmoke and his duties.

He did not know that Hoke nodded in agreement at the same moment that the others scoffed at her in that high-handed arrogance of the desperate poor who crave a lower creature to abuse.

Hoke turned them back and created a simmering resentment. Hoke informed them that Cassius was a valuable possession and he did not care to throw away property. Neither county nor Commonwealth would reimburse him for the loss of a carpenter, and he suggested that any patroller on their eight-dollar-a-week salary who damaged his slave could repay Hoke for Cassius's fair value. But Cassius knew Hoke Howard. Hoke was an emotional man who trusted his first instincts. In a moment of high dudgeon, Hoke had been known to sacrifice his own best interests for that heady savor of power and revenge. As he healed, Cassius revisited Hoke's choice. That same man three days before had flayed him with a bullwhip, carving stripe after stripe into his back. Planters reckoned that each stripe lowered the price of a slave by five dollars, but at that moment, Hoke was interested only in punishment. Cassius did not consider that something decent might be coiled inside the planter. Emoline alone had seen that.

The first two days spent in Emoline's home, Cassius did not know where he was. His mind was convulsive with fulminating rage, ashriek with images of Marriah and her baby, images that burned inside until he was empty of everything, and yet the fire still would not quit.

Pain gripped and ripped him, pain more intense than his shredded back. His helplessness was his horror, as he could not save the ones he loved. He could do precisely nothing. She was gone, the baby was out there somewhere, and there was no way to find him. By now, the boy was three days away and might well have been sold more than once. How could he force Hoke to name the slave trader and his destination? And were he to escape Sweetsmoke, he had never traveled more than thirty miles from the plantation. He did not know what existed out there. He could not read, and to him, a map was nothing more than a jumble of shapes and lines. He had done every possible thing in his power and it was not enough, it would never be enough. He had bargained, offered himself as proxy to accept the punishment intended for his wife, he had fought, he had run, and still he had ended up here. He had not even been able to defend himself. He was alive and not crippled only because an old freed woman had come to his defense. The wail that rose from his pith blinded him, engorging and splitting open the whole of his skin: Who will love him, who will love the little boy?

Emoline Justice nursed him from the outside. She showed him a different side of her aggressive, opinionated nature. She worked her magic with salves, using extracts from leaves and bark and seemingly every other potion in her possession to soothe and heal him until his back responded. He wondered later if she had borrowed the intensity of her uncompromising persona and transposed it into healing, and he thought some of that persona had inadvertently rubbed in and taken root under his skin.

Emoline had grown up at Sweetsmoke, a house servant and nanny to the children of Hoke Howard's parents. Hoke's mother, Grace, had been particular about the language spoken by her servants, and Emoline was her star pupil. Emoline then served as tutor to the children, one of whom was Hoke, a mere five years younger. After Emoline and Hoke's son was born, she "married" a man in the quarters who gave her two daughters. Marriages among slaves were not considered legal or binding in the eyes of the law, but Emoline treated her marriage as sacrosanct. Hoke's resultant jealousy caught him by surprise. Then Hoke's father died with Hoke still in his young twenties, and shortly thereafter his bereaved mother followed, leaving him the callow master of Sweetsmoke. He attempted to rise to the challenge of his father's expectations, and in a moment of magnanimous sentimentality he would come to regret, Hoke allowed Emoline to buy her freedom. She chose the last name Justice for herself and shared it with her son, Richard, whom she was able to buy a number of years later, when Hoke floundered in one of his depressed financial periods. The man in the quarters she had married now married another, a marriage Hoke had encouraged if not arranged. Emoline, however, remained true to her vows. She called herself a schoolteacher, even as she made more on the side as a conjurer, and it was conjurer money that bought freedom for her son.

Throughout the first week of Cassius's healing, she read aloud. After a number of days he became aware that he was listening, and her words added up to a story. She read about a man named Ulysses, a warrior struggling to return home. As Cassius's interest grew, his rage became intermittent and she began to turn the open book and show him the words. Initially he saw small black shapes arranged in rows on white paper, and as they meant nothing to him, they were little more than magical markings. Yet they somehow conjured up fantastic imagery. In the years that followed, Cassius remembered few specifics from the book, only that it was another salve to his pain. He did remember that Ulysses had been away from home a long time, that when he returned he found more troubles, and Ulysses defeated those troubles in a great paroxysm of violence.

Sometime during the second week, he asked Emoline why, with her knowledge and gifts, she told the fortunes of whites but never of blacks.

She acted as if the fact that he had even asked such a question was a wonderful sign, because any interest in a topic outside his anger meant he was improved. Her explanation was delivered in her familiar, self-assured voice: She told only white fortunes because the future must not be predicted nor anticipated. She would not bring false hope to her people. Their lives were hopeless enough without packing them with lies. She was more than happy to take money to manufacture white fortunes, sewn out of whole cloth and presented in a pretty package, and wouldn't you know, the odder her predictions, the more her clients desired them.

Emoline left her home on occasion to visit these clients and she carried her tools with her, as she would not have others in her home while Cassius was healing. Cassius knew that Hoke sometimes visited her for conjuring, and wondered if during those weeks she ever ventured to Sweetsmoke.

By the second week, Cassius discovered he had less pain. He sat up. Emoline taught him the alphabet. He learned quickly, filling his aching, empty, hungry brain. By the end of the week, he recognized words. By the third week, he read sentences.

Somewhere in the second week, Cassius noticed a distraction in Emoline's eyes and he wondered about it until Hoke sent the first messenger. At the knock on the door, Cassius rose to his feet in defiance, his back bristling. Emoline pushed past him and opened the door herself. The messenger was one of the grooms from Sweetsmoke, saying that Master Hoke was anxious to have his man back. She sent the messenger away without explanation. A few days later, another messenger arrived, this time William, the butler. To him she said simply, "Not yet." But for all her certainty, Cassius continued to identify a nervous energy in her demeanor.

She could heal him physically, but his mental healing followed a separate path. For this she could only offer tools, and she knew her time was limited. She was pleased to see him learn words and sentences, and this new ability, this ability to read, reshaped his mind. For the first time in his life he experienced a nugget of personal power that was not a gift from his master. He did not know what might come of that power, but he knew it was greater than the strength of his arms, the power owned and benefited from by the Master. Reading was his secret power, and through it he recognized the small budding cancer of hope.

By the third week he was moving well, and in between her reading lessons, she put his skills to work. He built for her a false panel between the hearth and the perpendicular streetside wall. She did not say why she desired a hiding place. He assumed it was to protect her money and her free papers.

When the false wall was finished, he knew it was time to return to Sweetsmoke and he was able to pretend to be mentally recovered.

The citizens of the Commonwealth of Virginia marked time from that day, January 16, 1857. But more to the point, slaves living in the Commonwealth marked that day. Many slaves did not know their birthdays, but they remembered the day of the Cold Storm that blanketed the state and brought everything to a halt. It snowed and then it snowed. Snow waves crested under eaves and rolled up against doors, where they froze in place. People did not leave their homes. Cassius could not leave for the plantation, so he stayed another week with Emoline Justice, and his reading improved and his comprehension grew.

He would return to Emoline's home many times in the ensuing years, and she would give him a Bible of his own to read, the book currently hidden in his cabin, and he would return with questions that she attempted to answer. But it was that last week, with snow falling on the roof over their heads, that he felt his confidence grow as he became fluent.

On returning to Sweetsmoke, Cassius walked down the lane of the quarters. Snow melted, a trickle glinting down the Suetsmoke gully under a cover of lacy snowpack. He returned to his cabin on the lane, where it had stood empty for weeks. He stopped in the doorway and took in the large room with the cold hearth barely discolored with soot. He walked around to the back, to what remained of Marriah's garden, blanketed by snow that was unblemished. His shoes crunched through the icy top layer. Black sprigs of a sapling poked through a drift; he had planted it to coincide with the birth of his son. He dug his fingers down in the snow to secure the narrow trunk and wrenched it out of the earth. He threw it aside, where it remained as the snow melted beneath it, until someone sometime later took it away.

The only excuse for a tree or garden was to invest in the future. No future existed. His heart was as cold as his fingers and knuckles had been on that day when he had wrenched out the sapling. He hated Jacob for what he had done, but it was not unusual or unexpected—he hated Hoke more, for protecting his planter son and for the three days in the tobacco shed.

He rose from his pallet fully awake, his legs sore from running in his sleep. He found the cigar that he had hand-rolled earlier in the day, and a Lucifer friction match, and put them both into his pouch and went outside.

The last of the fires sizzled. Wooden crosses surrounded him, dark and erect, fresh bulbous candles dangling off their arms. The smoke had cleared, a few crickets persisted in the night air and the dew cooled his bare feet. Mr. Nettle would have made his final pass down the lane hours ago. Cassius considered going into the woods, but it would be a slow and tedious journey to his traps in the dark. He had decided to go to town on Saturday night. Friday was the Fourth, and there would be celebrations, but Saturday would still see many hands traveling to their abroad husbands or wives. The patrollers would soon tire of checking passes by lantern light for the second straight night, and he could utilize the whole night, as Sunday was free. The Big-To-Do was Sunday at Edensong, the Jarvis plantation, and not even Hoke would dare take that away from his "family," not even for hornworms.

He ran his finger over the piece of string he had tied around the end of the cigar, an inch from the lip end, a personal habit and his alone, then brought the cigar between his teeth and dug for the match. Unable to find it in his pouch, he ducked under the arms of a cross and pushed the other end of the cigar into a banked fire. He stood slowly, drawing in the smoke, thinking that he would have to see if his pouch had developed a hole and if it could be mended. He looked back at the pale dry shapes made by his bare feet in the dew-covered dust where he had walked from his cabin. He smoked awhile standing there, and after many minutes had passed, he saw her in the cleared space beside his cabin. She sat on a log under a tree, and she hadn't moved. His heart raced, thinking her a spirit or an illusion, but when she smiled, he knew she was real and had been staring at him. He walked over to her. As he got closer, she seemed to duck away, and Cassius knew that she had not wanted him to see her. He considered that, and thought that it had to do with her being perceived as a jinx.

Quashee is an unusual name, said Cassius.

Not for an African.

You born in Africa?

No, I was born here.

Your name got a meaning?

What make you say that? she said.

Something I was told, African names got meanings, and you didn't get Quashee from a white master.

No. My father gave it to me. Quashee's a girl born on Sunday.

Ah. So what day were *you* born? said Cassius.

She smiled graciously. And your name? she said.

My name came from Hoke.

So no meaning.

Got a meaning to Hoke. He plucked it from a play. From *Julius Caesar*, by Shakespeare.

Ah. William Shakespeare.

Cassius was surprised. You know Shakespeare? he said.

I heard the name, she said, looking away as if she had revealed too much.

Can you read?

She looked back at him and considered his expression. Then she said: No.

Cassius almost spoke up, but caught himself. She had not asked him if he could read, but if she had, he would also have said no.

Why're you out here? said Cassius.

Why're *you*? she said.

Running from a dream.

My muscles are too tired to run, I lie still and my leg knots up, said Quashee. She reached down and rubbed her calves.

Savilla probably got a balm for that.

Savilla got some witch's brew for most everything, said Quashee.

Guess I forgot, wouldn't be like you to believe in low negro superstition, you being part big house.

You ain't exactly a field hand.

Cassius smiled. No. So why're you sitting here?

Didn't know this was your field.

Most likely that didn't come out right.

It's late. Someone comes out, they like to ask questions, she said. Cassius smiled and looked down. She went on: Over here, I am out of their way.

Cassius nodded, thinking, Out of the path of insatiable young men. Out of the way of gossiping women. Out of the way of people imagining you to be bad luck.

She looked at the cigar in his hand.

Your cigar got a string, said Quashee.

He raised it as if seeing it for the first time. Nodded.

Any reason for that? she said.

He took her in with a full look, then spoke the truth: Did it once years ago, when all I had was an old leaf wouldn't hold together. Some of the others laughed, so instead of explaining I said it made the smoke taste smooth. They believed it, and a few even tried it once or twice, said I was right. I did it for the next one and now it's just habit.

Does it make it taste smooth?

No.

They were quiet for a moment, staring at the dying fires on the lane.

So why're they keeping you down here? You belong up at the house, said Cassius.

They won't see me at the big house.

Who won't?

Missus Ellen. We've been called up, but always get sent back before she sees us. I asked her girl Pet, but she's got nothing to say to me.

Cassius saw Quashee catch herself, letting her literate big house voice slip through. He imagined she was considering revising herself, but she clamped her mouth shut.

I know they could use you, said Cassius, but he remembered how Pet had tried to convince Ellen to use Tempie Easter as a personal servant.

Seems like they already got a full staff.

Sarah should have someone, said Cassius.

Quashee considered that and nodded. She said: I hoped to work for Master Jacob's wife, but she's always in her bed. Not much for a personal servant to do but bring food and empty the slops.

Pet and the others do for Sarah but they don't like it. Ellen is spiting her daughter-in-law.

Then I would surely love to be part of that, said Quashee with a low laugh.

Cassius was aware of an undercurrent of tension.

You think they'll sell you, said Cassius, making a statement.

No good at field work, said Quashee. And now I'm bad luck.

Stupid talk. Something bad's always happening in the quarters. Makes no sense to make it about you.

Seems to be about my master John-Corey.

So I hear. John-Corey dies in the war and starts a run of bad luck, then you come with your father and bring it along.

They say we brought the hornworms.

Hornworms started up before you came. Just another excuse to blame someone else for their troubles.

Sounds 'bout right, said Quashee.

Cassius thought for a moment before he said: I can talk to someone up there.

From what I hear, you ain't got a whole lot of influence.

That from Big Gus?

From all of them. They wonder how you stay so independent. Big Gus would like to have you in the fields.

Big Gus may get his wish, but that would be his bad luck.

She smiled at that.

Cassius was tired of talking. He wanted to be alone, out here where he hoped to avoid thinking. He said nothing more. Quashee may have sensed his desire because only a few minutes passed before she stood and walked back up the lane to the cabin she shared with her father.

Cassius touched the warm dry spot on the log where she had been sitting, then sat on it. He had forgotten to smoke his cigar and it was out. He was unwilling to walk back to the embers to relight it.

He sat until the sky turned pale and Mr. Nettle's bell rang. He heard the field hands rousing from their sleep to face another day battling the blight.

~⊛ Chapter Three ⊛~

CASSIUS opened the door and in the dim light before he found the lantern, he saw how things were. Her belongings had been handled and thrown aside and now lay strewn across the floorboards. He saw herbs and remedies scattered among smashed jugs, bottles, and plates. He wondered if this had happened after the murder or as she fought back, assuming she was able to fight back. He closed the door behind him and struck a match, carrying its timid light until he found the lantern unbroken. The wick accepted the flame.

He sat, and the damaged property made him aware of the violence of her death. The longer he stared, the more he saw the destruction as having a pattern, and he visualized the killer ripping methodically through her belongings. His mind then explored a fresh scenario: Someone not her killer had come hours or days later to paw through her things, perhaps after the sheriff had removed her body. Or perhaps the sheriff and his men had been the vandals. Cassius rejected these narratives and returned to his first instinct.

Upon reflection, he decided she had surprised someone ransacking her home and was killed trying to stop it. She was a conjurer, a hoodoo woman—few whites and fewer blacks would risk the curse of an angry spirit, lingering and furious at its premature death.

The previous night, he had avoided the celebration of the Fourth and gone into the woods to check his traps. He had folded his clothes by the bank of the creek and waded in to a shallow place where the water was quick, lying on his back among the stones and muck to let the chill current rush over him. With his lantern set nearby on the bank, he had watched the pale beam pass through the rivulet, fragmenting and dancing against his skin. His gaze shifted to the water bulging against his fingers just below the surface and curving around his bent knees. He had returned to the quarters with a possum, which he delivered to Savilla.

During the day he had forged a pass for himself, a simple matter despite its inherent danger. Three years before, he had found papers written in Hoke's hand, which he had hidden in the band of his trousers for an entire day. Had these papers been discovered, the punishment would have been swift and severe. In secret he imitated the handwriting until he could reproduce it. But four nights before, when he had been called to Hoke's office, he had seen that his old master's hand had developed a quaver; Cassius's forgery was that of a younger Hoke. He could not imitate his master's shake without a sample, so he was forced to travel with a pass he did not trust. Walking in the dark, he had heard the patrollers singing somewhere ahead. He hid in heavy brush by the roadside and when the singing did not move, he emerged and saw that they were off the road in a clearing. They had liberated their bottles from their haversacks early that evening.

He continued to sit, dazed, in her cabin, slivers of information filtering through to him. The floorboards had absorbed a dark spot, and after staring at it for some time, he understood that he was looking at dried blood. The closest he would ever come to viewing her remains was this stain. Hoke had not bothered to tell him that she was already buried. Cassius remembered that he had also been protected from viewing Marriah's body. His thoughts flowed to her.

He had won Marriah despite being the slow, salacious young bear among swift, adolescent wolves. He had always been slow. He remembered firsthand the trauma of separation when his mother was sold. He was raised by Mam Rosie and for a brief time her husband Darby, as Darby was sold soon after. He grew tall and made to himself a secret promise, that he would be different. He would not love anything. He would make his heart cold. He evaluated the available young females of Sweetsmoke as well as those at other plantations. Opportunities existed to make a match outside the home plantation through the infrequent communal dances, corn shuckings, and the occasional collective rigging of Sunday church. But Cassius decided he was too smart to fall into an abroad marriage; he saw what the lovers were forced to endure—traveling at night, begging Master for a pass, the difficulties inherent in living apart. He limited his courting to the women of Sweetsmoke. His promise to shield his heart made him overcautious, thus the slow bear. Females in their early teens were courted by eager young men, and these couples were kept company by the girls' mammas; if the young men were approved, with permission usually automatic from the big house, they "married." He briefly courted Jenny. He courted Fawn, but men craved her brutishly and his heretofore unacknowledged jealousy flinched. Emotionally stunted Fawn was unable to publicly parade the gown of faithfulness, as she mistook sexual ardor for love. He left her to others, and Cassius entered his young twenties without a steady partner.

Before the war, Hoke Howard's investment in a fleet of ships brought an influx of new wealth to Sweetsmoke, and he celebrated by traveling, purchasing French château gates, expanding his cellars of wine, adding to Ellen's wardrobe, and almost as an afterthought, purchasing the slaves of an acquaintance whose wife and child had died while visiting New England during a yellow fever outbreak. Marriah arrived with five others two years before the Cold Storm. She was older than most available females, almost twenty, but when on that first evening she toted her belongings to her assigned cabin, the wolf pack pricked up. Cassius held back and studied his competition. He learned that she'd had a husband at her old plantation, a forced marriage by the whites who mated couples deliberately and conscientiously, breeding them to add size and strength to their herd. She bore him a son who never took a breath and made that the excuse to push him away. He found another and she was glad. Cassius chanced to be there when Master Jacob first set eyes on her, and he saw the effect Marriah had on him. But Cassius was determined.

When Cassius made his move, he discovered that she had been waiting for him and wondered what had taken him so long. It was the first time Big Gus knew that he was outmaneuvered.

Cassius and Marriah decided to be married. As neither had parents in the quarters, only permission from the big house was required. Genevieve, the unmarried daughter of Hoke and Ellen, took interest in their wedding. Genevieve delighted in matchmaking, but by this time her planter friends no longer agreed to submit to her manipulations. Thus she had turned her sights on the quarters. Genevieve planned a lavish event, the bulk of the celebration being for the planter families, with the marriage ceremony serving as spectacle. Cassius learned of the plan and he and Marriah chose a day and married in secret. On that day they jumped the broom, and pulled on opposite ends of a rope thrown over the roof of the cabin he had built. The rope pull was designed to end in a stalemate so when the bride then moved to the side of the groom and they pulled together, the rope came easily, demonstrating the importance of cooperation. They moved in to the new cabin that afternoon.

Genevieve noticed uncommon bustle in the kitchen on that day and learned from Mam Rosie about the secret wedding. Cheated out of her event, Genevieve summoned Marriah to the big house. When the sun set and Marriah did not return, Cassius was irritated but not overly concerned. He trusted his relationship with Hoke. Cassius was his favorite. Hoke would surely keep his bride from Jacob's bed. Mam Rosie came to the quarters to inform Cassius that one of the planter children suffered with fever and Marriah was to remain at the big house to care for him. Cassius spent his wedding night alone.

Marriah returned the following morning. Only a moment did they share, but she reassured him with her eyes and a touch on his arm. At sunset, he hurried to their cabin, and found her waiting.

She suspected she was pregnant that night.

Marriah evolved into a different person during pregnancy. She went weeks without bathing, the odor of her body changed, small noises caused her to flinch, and he would wake in the night to find only her body's imprint on their pallet with Marriah wandering in the dark. It was as if she hoped to make her baby unwelcome.

The night arrived for the delivery. Marriah asked Cassius to stay away, but when he heard the baby cry, he forced his way past Savilla and Mam Rosie. He lifted the newborn and held it in his arms, umbilical cord still attaching baby to mother, birth blood smeared on his shirt, beholding a child he could not have fathered, a child who could pass for white.

Master Jacob had gotten his way. Cassius's anger was directed neither at the boy nor his wife, and, oddly, he was not angry at Jacob. He felt instead the betrayal of his old master, believing he should have prevented Jacob from indulging his compulsion. Cassius took advantage of a bottle for a day and a night before he accepted what he had known from the beginning, that he would raise the boy as his own.

Ellen traveled to the quarters. She was repulsed by the sight of a white child born to chattel. She returned to the big house and insisted her husband send for the slave trader. Two days after giving birth, a weakened Marriah was directed to join the hands in clearcutting a new field. The winter of 1856 into 1857 was unnaturally cold, and she bundled herself as best she could, returning to the yard by the big house every three hours to breast-feed the infant. Cassius was directed to a job in the second barn. The slave trader arrived in a carriage accompanied by a black woman. The business was transacted in the yard. The slave trader took the still-unnamed boy from Nanny Catherine's arms and placed it in the arms of the black woman, and the three of them rode away. Marriah returned to the yard, breasts engorged. Nanny Catherine said the baby was gone. Marriah did not believe her. She searched until Mam Rosie confirmed the story.

Marriah ran away to catch the slave trader who had her baby. Hoke took a horse and groomsman and set out after her. He returned with the groomsman and a loud conversation was overheard between Hoke and his wife. Hours later, patrollers arrived with Marriah, hands bound, hair in her face, breathing sharply like a wild animal.

Ellen met the patrollers alone, and ordered Otis Bornock, Hans Mueller, and Isaac Lang to secure Marriah's wrists to the high ring on the whipping post and expose her back. Ellen took up the bullwhip and swung it over her head, then snapped it into Marriah's skin with the patrollers looking on. She counted two dozen lashes, set the bullwhip down, and dismissed them. She ordered the yard cleared and strode back inside, leaving Marriah tied there whimpering in the cold, milk leaking down her belly.

At close of day, Cassius approached the yard intending to walk with his wife and son to the quarters. He discovered her alone in the yard, tied to the post with her back in shreds. He cut her down and carried her to the quarters. He learned about the slave trader and left her facedown on their pallet with Savilla attending. At the big house, Hoke would not see him, and he returned to find the pallet empty and Savilla rocking on a stool. Savilla had left her alone in order to fetch herbs from her cabin, and Marriah had run again. Cassius ran after her.

He found her on the road standing on the small bridge, cold and weak and insane, but then the lights of lanterns appeared around the road's elbow, patrollers hunting them, taking them, returning them to Sweetsmoke. Cassius begged to take her punishment for her, but they laughed and said he had punishment of his own coming. Cassius was taken into the shed with tobacco drying overhead and he was shackled to a ring bolt in the wall. He called Marriah's name. Hoke came with the whip which was red wet at its ends. After Hoke laid into him, Cassius was left there.

He had grown up loving the quality of the air of the plantation, seasoned as it was with the sweet, sensual scent of curing tobacco. Cassius had lived his entire life within that luxurious smell, so that it only stepped forward at certain moments, to highlight the freshness of a day, or intensify a moment of human kindness or dignity. Now, chained in the shed, the aroma encircled and forced itself on him. As it mingled with his fury, it became cloying, thick and oily, accented by a creeping suggestion of mold and the acrid bite of tar. By the time he was released, he had learned to despise the smell.

For three days, the hands brought food and salve for his stripes, but despite his questions, no one spoke a word about Marriah.

After Mr. Nettle and Big Gus released him, he emerged from the shed to find Hoke waiting. Hoke said it was over and there was nothing Cassius could do, so he might as well accept it. He told Cassius that he had restrained him for his own good.

He returned to the quarters and found his cabin empty. The women saw him and began to sob.

Where is she!?

She's dead, Cassius.

The sound of Savilla's voice rattled in his mind still. She's dead, Cassius, how precisely it came to him even after the years in between . . .

A sound brought him out of his reverie. The handle turned to Emoline's front door and brought him to his feet.

"I knew someone would come," Emoline's son said, stepping inside. "Eventually." He wore a checked waistcoat over a clean white shirt. He did not wear a hat. Cassius was struck by how much Richard Justice resembled his father.

Cassius watched him prowl the room, stepping over a broken water jug and two smashed plates. He wondered if Richard Justice had been the one to destroy the things in his mother's home, as he would not have feared her curse. Cassius knew that Richard had been hunting for his mother's money.

"Looking for something, Cassius?" he said, indicating the mess.

No.

"This is the first time you've been here since it happened, I wager."

Looks like from when she was murdered.

"Someone searching."

Find anything?

"I don't know, did you?" Richard Justice watched carefully Cassius's response. "No, perhaps not. You were fond of her, as I recall."

Cassius suddenly understood that it was Richard Justice who had torn the room apart. You get what *you* were looking for? he said.

Richard Justice rubbed the root of his nose between his eyebrows with his left thumb and forefinger, just like his father. "And what would that be?"

Cassius smiled, but he felt anger boil up inside him. At that moment, if he were to discover that Richard Justice had killed Emoline, Cassius would kill him and he would get away with it. It was easier to kill a free black. As he was no one's property, you would not be depriving a white man of his future value in the form of hard work. The sheriff would see it as just another dead nigger, which is how he obviously saw Emoline's death.

Who killed your mother, Richard?

"Wasn't me. Was it you? What are you doing here, Cassius?"

You said you knew someone would come.

"And now I find it's you. Did you come out of love, out of respect?"

Why do you think?

"I think you came for her money."

Ah, said Cassius. Her money.

"You were close to her, where is it?"

Don't know.

"Why do I not believe you?"

You think I'd sit here if I knew where it was?

"Do not bandy with me, Cassius, I'm a free man. If I choose, I can have them take you—"

You're free till some white drunk rips up your free papers and sells you for a pint. Don't threaten me, Richard.

Richard Justice raised his hands in a defensive gesture. "Very well, Cassius. Very well. But that money is rightfully mine. And I need it."

Yes, I suppose I know that.

"You know?" Richard Justice appeared suspicious.

Your sisters. You been working to buy their freedom. With Emoline's money, you can free at least one of them.

"That is precisely correct," said Richard Justice.

Cassius considered whether someone else had killed Emoline over money. He did not think it was Richard Justice. Richard Justice liked to gamble. Even a free black was at the mercy of whites when it came to fairness. Richard Justice assumed he was unlucky, but Cassius suspected that his poor luck was aided by the collective design of his gambling rivals.

A face appeared in the window behind Richard Justice. Cassius's eyes met her eyes, but he looked away so that Richard Justice would not know. A moment later the window betrayed nothing.

Cassius wondered if she would wait.

Tell me something. Did you love her? said Cassius.

"She was my mother."

Funny answer. Did she love you?

"She made me what I am."

Yes. Hard and distant, even where it concerned her.

"You neglected selfish. All things that I would need to survive as a black piece of property in this world."

She did you a kindness, then, said Cassius.

"I will be off; I do not like being here."

I will stay.

Richard Justice smiled. "To look around."

Possibly.

"And if you find something?"

You know where I am.

"At the Big-To-Do tomorrow?"

There, too, said Cassius nodding.

"If I hear you've come into an unusual sum of money, we will speak again."

No doubt, said Cassius.

Richard Justice left the door ajar and a brisk hot wind rushed in. Cassius sat a moment, listening to Emoline's son's footsteps move away from the house, then he was up, stepping out and closing the door behind him to eliminate the small patch of light that leaked from the lantern.

Cassius stepped behind a tree and listened. The street swarmed with the song of crickets, flickering lights glowed behind windows, and Cassius leaned to look in every direction. Windows were open in the small homes of the poor whites and he would have to be quiet. He heard laughter from the tavern in the next street. As Cassius was about to move from behind the tree, a thick white woman stepped into the frame of her front door and swung a basin of soapy gray water to douse the roots of a climbing rosebush. She wiped a damp curl off her forehead and returned inside. He stayed behind the tree a moment longer. From his position, he considered the places the woman who had appeared at the window might hide, if she had indeed remained behind.

He stepped around the corner to the window, but found no one lurking under the ledge. Across from the window sat a small house surrounded by low bushes with windows closed and dark. He looked both ways and took a step into the road and something moved behind the bushes. He was quick to round the hedge and grabbed her by the arm.

What're you doing here? said Cassius.

Lookin for Miss Emoline, said the woman. Let go my arm.

Cassius did not let go.

What's your name?

Maryanne. Where Miss Emoline? I ain't seen her in there.

Cassius cocked his head. You telling me you don't know?

What I knows is I'se suppose to meet her. Who're *you*?

She's not here, why you meeting her?

Give her somethin, that your business?

Cassius let go of her arm and said: Better not be seen out here.

Cassius led her across the road to Emoline's door and inside.

Why there no fire in here? said Maryanne. This ain't right, Miss Emoline never be lettin her fire go out.

Miss Emoline is gone.

Where she gone? You mess up her place, oh, honey, she goin be angry with you.

No. She won't.

Maryanne looked at his expression and understood.

I told her it be dangerous, she got herself in trouble and that mean trouble for me.

What kind of trouble?

Oh no, said Maryanne.

Emoline Justice took care of me when I was sick.

You Cassius, then.

After a considered pause, Cassius nodded.

Miss Emoline told me 'bout you. Maryanne nodded now, as if retelling stories inside her head, but inserting the man in front of her into the stories.

So you know you can trust me, said Cassius.

I don't know no such thing, only that *she* trust you.

What kind of trouble was she in?

I'm suppose to give her this. Now you take it.

Maryanne held up a packet. Cassius reached for it, but Maryanne thought twice and pulled it back to watch his eyes. He kept his hand there but did not move it closer. Slowly she moved the packet to his hand.

My massa, said Maryanne, he a cap'n in the Secesh Army, he quartermaster with that General Lee. I travel along, his cook, and

I'se a good one. I gets papers and such from the cap'n when he ain't lookin and bring 'em to her and she give 'em to somebody else who likes to know what General Lee goin do.

Cassius glanced at the false wall he had built for Emoline. Stolen papers from a Confederate captain. Meetings at night, information, secrets.

What's your master's name?

Cap'n Solomon Whitacre, like I say, quartermaster. He got men and they travel 'round gettin food for the army and such. He come through here regular, his wife and children be livin up at that Jarvis place.

Willa Jarvis, said Cassius.

She the one, said Maryanne.

Cassius opened the packet and found a letter from Captain Whitacre to his wife.

This is a letter. How is it he doesn't notice when his letters go missing?

Well, I don't take 'em all. And anyway, he writin all the time, then ask me to mail 'em and the way things is, some get lost.

Cassius scanned the letter and saw that Whitacre was candid with his spouse and had informed her that General Lee was planning to leave Richmond, and General T. Jackson's command was to go north on the Virginia Central Railroad to Gordonsville.

You readin that? said Maryanne.

Cassius refolded the letter, thinking about the meaning of this information. Why did Emoline collect such information? What did she plan to do with it?

I seen it. You read that letter, said Maryanne.

No, I can't read. Tell me about these, said Cassius.

I am done tellin you, and done takin from Cap'n Solomon 'cause he lookin at me like he know somethin.

What did she do with this information? She travel north?

Miss Emoline never leave here. You go on the road on you own, even if you free, bad things happen.

So someone came to meet her.

Don't know for sure. Best not to know nothin. She force me to do it, say I got to if I ever want be free. I knowed all along it never goin happen, and now that she dead, I seen it for sure. Just another fancy dream, gonna be a slave all my life and my children gonna die slaves.

You always come at a certain time?

How I do that? I come when my massa here.

Between you, was there a code?

Code? What that?

Special knock on the door?

Why'nt you just say so?

She showed him the knock that she had learned from Emoline. Rap-rap, pause, rap.

You with your master this last week? said Cassius.

Like I says, we travel together. Came through here for one day early this week, now we back.

Which day?

I don't know what day. Monday, maybe. That right, Monday. Ridin all day Sunday, didn't get no church.

Did you see her, did you see Emoline on that day?

No time for that. Gettin what-all for Cap'n Solomon's supper.

Cassius looked at her with suspicion, but there was little doubt in his mind about Maryanne, she was not Emoline's killer. It was coincidence that she was in town on the same day Emoline was killed.

Cassius asked more questions and got answers he imagined were incomplete. But Maryanne did offer one piece of information: Someone was to meet Emoline here, at her home, after dark on the full moon. The full moon was due on the following Friday.

He watched Maryanne become more anxious as his questions continued. Her eyes rolled toward the windows, her fingers knotted and unknotted, and finally he let her go. She was out the front door and gone like a breath in the fog.

He followed her outside and stood by the tree. He listened to know that Maryanne was away and that Richard Justice had not returned. He went back inside to the false wall and opened it to reveal the secret hiding place.

Emoline's money was there, quite a lot of money, colorful prewar bank notes along with her free papers and copies of both *The Odyssey* and *The Iliad*, her Bible, and a few other books. Underneath the books were a stack of papers wrapped by a ribbon, some of the papers very old. He undid the ribbon and found that these were letters. He looked at the letter on the bottom, the oldest, and he read it. He was still for a long time, and then he sat down to think.

He had recognized the hand immediately, a love letter from his old master before Hoke was anyone's master. One line in particular caught his attention:

> You came to me, and silently, to carry me aloft to heavenly gates of pleasure, O gentle sweetness, O mystery of love, O kindness.

Emoline had lied. This was not the note of a predator. This was the swelling sentiment of a smitten young man enfolded in the throes of love. Hoke had spoken the truth, she had come to him, she had given herself willingly. Emoline had lied.

Cassius considered the meaning of this revelation. It saddened him to come face-to-face with a new and altogether different Emoline now that she was dead. She owed him no explanations, but her lies seemed not casual and careless, but deliberate, and were compounded by lies of omission, as she had not told him about her business with Maryanne. Cassius returned to her hiding place in the false wall.

The bottom of the space was now empty. He felt around and discovered, standing on its end against the side wall, a packet similar to the one from Maryanne. He drew it out. This packet contained not letters and maps, but handwritten notes. Cassius thumbed through them, knowing they were not from Maryanne. Here were transcriptions of official communiqués, inter-army messages, supply requests, supply routes and destinations. Cassius instinctively understood the importance of such seemingly innocuous information; food and ammunition had a destination, and that destination would be General Lee's army. General Lee's enemies would gain a decided advantage with such information in their hands. Emoline had been insane to collect it, the danger was prodigious, and Cassius saw it as yet another example of how her personality blinded her—her arrogant confidence had led her to misguided bravery, which led to her violent death. But who had access to this official intelligence? He reached back into the hiding place, searching with his fingers for anything else, and found in the corner a folded scrap of paper. On it was a small map and he recognized Emoline's hand. It included lines that he imagined were roads, leading to a spot in what he guessed was forest land. Along the top of the paper she had drawn a line of X's. The X's were likely to be railroad tracks. A road crossed the tracks, and she had written something along the road: W York.

He paced the room. To hold something of such importance in his hands thrilled him profoundly and his heart beat high in his chest. But what was to be done with it? Even if Maryanne was correct and Emoline's contact would come for it on the full moon, what did that have to do with him? Was it up to him to hand off this information, so that it could be delivered to someone in the North? The very thought of doing such a thing seemed no more possible than growing wings overnight and flying to the sun. But perhaps he must do just that, for her. He paused in his reckless enthusiasm. And what did he owe her, a woman who had lied to him? He reflected on her lies. To protect her identity as a spy was an impersonal lie, as it protected everyone around her as well, and so he let that be. Her lies about Hoke stung and confused him, but they also explained other things, including why Hoke had been willing to allow her to take Cassius back to her home to heal him. When he thought of this, of what she had done on his behalf, he forgave everything, even her puzzling personal secrets.

He returned to his pacing, and a shard of jug crunched under his shoe. He swept it aside with his foot, his excitement returning. She would not have cared that her things were broken. He now knew her for a different person and her world grew clearer in his mind. She cared for maps and secret information. She cared for the outcome of the war, believing the North needed to win the war if her people were to have any chance to escape slavery. To Cassius, such a possibility seemed remote if not ludicrous. The summer had brought a string of Confederate victories, making the outcome of the war appear to lean heavily to the South, and furthermore, the Yankees did not care a damn for slaves. Yankees would not die for black people. He admired that Emoline had hoped to share her freedom with all her people, but wondered if it had been worth her life. He thought then of how, for a long time, he had been indifferent to death. At least she had risked herself for a purpose.

He thought about Richard Justice. Richard could make life difficult for Cassius. The man was entitled to his mother's money, even if Cassius did not want him to have it. Cassius could have told Richard where to find it, but that would only guarantee its eventual place in the pockets of white gamblers.

Cassius formulated a plan and acted quickly. He counted bank bills and separated out a one quarter share. He returned the bulk of the money to the hiding place. He also returned the packets, believing them safer here than in his cabin at Sweetsmoke. If Emoline's contact knew of the secret place, he might collect the documents without Cassius having to lift a finger. He resealed the hiding place. He found a small tin on the floor and folded the quarter portion of her money inside. He stepped outside by the tree and looked at her garden. He chose an obvious spot where someone had previously been digging, by a green stave that Emoline employed as a separator between herb beds. The herbs unearthed from that spot had been carelessly tossed aside. Cassius dug out the loose soil, then dug deeper into the compacted soil beneath. He placed the tin in the hole, recovered it, and recompacted the dirt. He covered that with looser dirt. He looked around. Down the row, he noticed where an entire patch of herbs had been dug up and were nowhere to be found, as if rather than digging for treasure someone had specifically targeted that remedy. But he gave that scant attention as he thought of one more thing to help his plan and returned to the hiding place, dug out the tin, and carefully separated out a few of the colorful bank notes, choosing only bills on which specific scenes of Southern daily life were etched. This impulsive decision brought a grim smile to his face. These bills he folded and put into his pouch along with three coins.

He walked back to Sweetsmoke, alone on the road, carrying both books of Homer, and was back in his cabin before the dawn of Sunday morning, the morning of the Big-To-Do. Once there, Cassius slept.

~≈ Chapter Four ≋~

CASSIUS opened his eyes to find sun streaming into his cabin through a small high window. He blinked awake and gradually became aware that someone sat across the room on the ledge of the dark and empty hearth. He raised his head.

You missed church, said Andrew.

Andrew rested his chin on his knees, his legs pulled up close and his arms wrapped around his shins.

I try to.

Mamma say you can miss church but not the Big-To-Do.

What time is it?

Afternoon sometime. Some of us already gone over. Mamma said wait on you.

Why didn't you wake me?

Believe I did.

Cassius raised his head higher and saw *The Iliad* on the floor at Andrew's feet. Andrew had dropped it, possibly more than once, which explained the sound of a door slamming in his dream. A folded sheet of paper that had been hidden between the pages had come partway out when Andrew dropped the book. Cassius rose from his pallet and as he took the book off the floor, he pushed the sheet of paper back and put both *The Iliad* and *The Odyssey* out of sight. Leaving out a book was careless, and he could not afford to be careless. He shook off the last layer of sleep and felt the deep exhaustion at his core. He knew that he would drag through the day, and he already anticipated the welcome of his pallet that night.

They walked to Edensong, the Jarvis plantation. Clouds moved in and blocked the sun and a cool wind picked up.

You got new pants, said Cassius.

Andrew nodded.

Cassius did not wish to press Andrew, but he knew that sometimes a young man needed to be prompted so that he understood he was being offered an opportunity to speak frankly.

New hat. New shoes, said Cassius.

Andrew turned his face to Cassius, and for a moment appeared older than his ten years as he searched Cassius's expression for hidden meaning.

I work the fields now, said Andrew.

How's that going?

Andrew shrugged, but a momentary wince around his eyes betrayed him. Cassius suspected Andrew had received a warning from his father Abram to withhold his complaints. It was likely that Andrew's middle brother Sammy tormented him as Sammy himself had been tormented by his older brother Joseph when he had started in the fields.

Was your age when I went to the fields, said Cassius.

I thought you was a carpenter.

Didn't start out that way. Had some trouble with the Young Master.

Oh. Charles? I mean, Master Charles?

No. Different young master.

Andrew nodded and watched the road as he walked. A handful of other travelers were half a mile ahead, dressed up in their finest, but otherwise they had the road to themselves, as the Big-To-Do would already have begun in earnest. The wind came stronger and lifted the hat off Andrew's head, and he reached to catch it, pulling it down snugly.

I remember being a young man, said Cassius.

Andrew said nothing.

Didn't know it at the time, but I had a bad temper, said Cassius.

Andrew cocked his head.

Not always obvious to the one who owns it. You might have a temper and not know, said Cassius.

Andrew shrugged.

What about you? Ever get angry fast, when you don't see it coming?

Don't know.

Happens to me too, said Cassius, nodding.

Andrew looked at him again. With his head angled, the wind snatched his hat and this time Cassius caught it.

You probably want to carry that.

Andrew took it in his hands and said: Yeah.

I remember Old Darby, Mam Rosie's husband, you never met him, was a few years where he looked out for me, and sometimes he'd be watching when I didn't know and he'd see me get all mad and he'd stop me. Ooh, that burned me up, I'd get even madder, man telling you how to be. No, we are not always smart for ourselves.

Cassius saw no reaction from Andrew. He tried again: Darby taught me a little trick. He'd say, When you feel that anger growing and spitting inside, reach down and snatch it, just snatch it right out and take it in your hands and bring it real close, and then when you got a good hold, get it up close in the light, look at the top and bottom and see if it maybe get you in trouble. Sometimes, just thinking about that would be enough and things'd slow down and then you realize the anger be gone.

You sound like my mamma.

Suppose I do. I apologize.

That okay.

For a quarter of a mile they walked in silence. Cassius continued to worry his point in his head.

What I got to say is, you can still be a man. There's other ways to hold on to pride. You don't need to fight and get it all back right then. Sometimes it's better when it comes later, different kind of satisfying. Maybe that way, Master Charles won't see it coming.

Andrew furrowed his brow.

That's a good point, Cassius, said Andrew seriously.

Cassius was unable to stop the laugh that rolled up inside him.

What's funny? said Andrew as his temper raised up its head.

Cassius put his hand on the boy's shoulder. I don't tease you, Andrew, I was surprised to see you look ten years older just now when you spoke.

Andrew raised his hat to cover his head and pulled it down close to his ears, turning back to the road at his feet.

They turned off the main road into the wide entrance of the plantation Edensong, winding through trees and manicured bushes to the big house. The main yard was empty of all but the occasional domestic animal, while the front porch of the big house was thick with planters and their families, the white railing penning them in. Edensong was the home of Judge Francis Arthur Jarvis. "Judge" was an honorary title, honorary and ubiquitous, although when the war became imminent, Cassius had the impression that the number of planters bearing the title "Colonel" increased. Cassius saw that Hoke was there with Ellen and his daughters, Genevieve and Anne; Anne's husband was speaking with one of the Jarvis boys and his wife. Notably absent was Sarah Greenleaf Howard, Jacob's wife, now left alone in the big house at Sweetsmoke, as Missus Ellen would have insisted the house people attend the dance. Lamar Robertson, planter and master of The Swan of Alicante Plantation, was in attendance with his extended family. Cassius recognized Willa Jarvis Whitacre, and predicted that the short man in uniform was the quartermaster, Captain Solomon Whitacre. He noted Whitacre not only because of his servant's connection to Emoline, but because his letters to his wife exhibited a great affection for her, and for that Cassius thought well of him. Cassius was amused to see that the planter children were kept to the porch, underfoot, and not permitted in the yard. The red-faced master of Edensong, Judge Francis Arthur Jarvis, a contemporary of Hoke Howard, struggled to his feet with glass in hand as the two blacks crossed the yard. Lines of sweat coursed down his cheeks and vanished under his collar, soaking the shirt beneath his waistcoat. He dabbed helplessly at his eyebrows with a handkerchief, but his smile appeared genuine.

"Welcome, welcome to Edensong, welcome," Judge Jarvis said pompously. "Mrs. Frances, welcome our late-arriving guests."

Wick-thin Mrs. Frances Jarvis appeared beside her husband as if she had been invisible sideways and had turned to face them like a swinging gate. Frances and Francis Jarvis stood together, a blade of grass and a brick of cheese. She planted a smile on her face and said, "Welcome to Edensong, the others are back there, all the way in back, you cannot miss them. Oh my dear, your glass is empty, may I secure you another, Mr. Francis?"

"Thank you kindly, Mrs. Frances." He handed his half-empty glass to his wife and they both laughed with the other planters at their excellent jest, Mr. Francis and Mrs. Frances, a joke as comfortable and worn as it was anticipated.

"Now don't drink too much," admonished his wife, laughing still.

"These slaves of yours keep coming, Hoke. Are they ignorant of the time?"

Cassius still found it odd to be spoken of as if he were deaf or invisible. It happened often; whites simply said whatever was on their minds in front of their "people," bluntly revealing their thoughts and secrets. He stared at Francis Jarvis with frank curiosity. What would cause a man to reveal himself so nakedly, unless he truly believed he was not judged? Despite the intimate knowledge Cassius carried about the planters and their families, knowing he was taken so lightly made him feel small.

E llen watched Cassius and the boy walk past. She thought again about the death of the free black woman who at one time had lived at Sweetsmoke and had meant something to her husband. She had dreamed about Cassius and Marriah, and when she woke had spent confused moments believing the war had yet to begin. As the years in between filled back in, she had an intense feeling that she was paying for those events with the lives of her sons.

This was a day she always dreaded, a day set aside for the "family," her people. It brought together the families of several plantations, and the gathering was often trying. She would have been in better spirits, as she would normally spend the early morning in mental preparation, but her daughter had chosen that particular time to revive her grievance about sleeping arrangements. Genevieve had whined prodigiously when Sarah and Jacob were given the front bedroom while she was relegated to the rear. Time had not diminished her resentment. This morning Genevieve had harped on the fact that even though Jacob had not returned, Sarah *continued* to enjoy the best bedroom all to *herself*, while from her *back* window Genevieve could see the trees that hid the *privy* and she could *almost* see the quarters. Ellen had made an early visit to her dressing table and had counted out twice the number of drops of laudanum, which brought her calm but did not diminish her hostility. The liquid within the bottle was precipitously low and she would need to speak to the doctor about obtaining more of the tincture. She disliked asking that man for anything, as he always bestowed upon her his most reproving look.

She had spent the early portion of the gathering the way all gatherings were now spent, listening to the men justify the crisis at hand. The war was a necessity, they informed one another as if it were news; the Yankees conspired to terminate their way of life. If given the chance, the bastards—begging your pardon, ladies—would abolish slavery altogether, not just in particular states. And to steal our slaves was no different than stealing our homes and our land, as financially it would be equally disastrous.

Once that conversation was laid to rest, with all in sober agreement—not that it would not reemerge at some future moment in the evening—Ellen simply had to count the hours and pretend to enjoy small talk until it was time to escape.

Ellen looked over to see Hoke approach Solomon Whitacre from behind. Whitacre was a decent enough gentleman, but it had been a surprise to all when he managed to wed the elusive Willa Jarvis, particularly as Ellen still saw him as the cowardly child he had been growing up. Perhaps that was what led him to be among the first to join the army. His effeminate mannerisms had carried into manhood, mannerisms he attempted to disguise with coarse language and bluster. This led to the occasional odd public moment. She had once witnessed him at a social event with his children and wife, as generous a father and husband as you could wish, when suddenly and from nowhere he appeared to notice his surroundings and erupted with an unpleasant epithet, as if to disguise his breeding.

Hoke clapped Whitacre on the back, and Ellen saw him start.

"How do you do it, Whitacre? Why, you spend more time at home than all our soldiers combined."

Whitacre turned to him, manhood under fire.

"A quartermaster, sir, is required to scour the countryside to feed the army, as you well know."

"Certainly, certainly, but must you continually scour *us*?" said Hoke with a hearty laugh. Whitacre did not laugh in kind.

"Beyond that, I have damn well been ordered on a special mission!" said Whitacre.

Willa Jarvis Whitacre's lovely head came around at once.

"I beg your pardon, Mrs. Whitacre," said Hoke. "I may have unintentionally provoked your husband."

"My apologies, my dear," mumbled Whitacre. "Upon my honor, I did not endeavor to be coarse."

Willa turned away.

"A mission, you say?" said Hoke. "Is it usual to entrust a quartermaster with special orders, if you would not find that question to be imprudent?"

"General Lee has plans for me, sir."

"General Lee? I see," said Hoke. Ellen recognized this moment. Hoke was drunk and likely to jab the man's pomposity.

"It is serious business, sir, I am to expose a spy."

"Perhaps you might care to lower your voice, Captain, as that sounds as if it may be privileged information," said Hoke.

Whitacre was surprised by Hoke's measured response and he collected himself, his indignation wilting. "You are very good, sir," said Whitacre quietly, red-faced.

Ellen saw that Hoke was not as drunk as she had supposed.

"I am certain you are the very one for the job, Whitacre, carry on and best of luck to you."

Whitacre saluted then, turned on a heel, and marched into the big house.

Ellen looked at her husband with admiration for his discretion, but luck was not on her side. She saw his eyes fall upon the Jarvises'

youngest daughter, Mary of fourteen years, a girl of seeming inno-
cence and considerable ripeness. Ellen had lately been spared being
witness to his lupine aggression and she was appalled to see him sali-
vate over one so young. She had endured such behavior in the past,
and were it not so painful, she might find amusing the way he always
appeared stunned by the onset of sexual appetite. She watched his
eyes seize adolescent Mary's jaw and glide down her slim neck to
her rubbery collarbones, finally resting on her hidden breast. How
expressive he is, she thought, watching his inner thoughts warp his
face, while he imagines himself impenetrable. He saw women's
beauty as an aggressive personal challenge requiring forceful mascu-
line response. Ellen instinctively drew her own collar to her neck, exposing less so that his implicit rejection of his wife would draw less
blood.

Ellen saw the Judge, his face blotchy and red, move to block
Hoke's view of his daughter. The Judge spluttered, "You, you . . ."
trailing off, unable to find the words, until, at last, he said: "You really must control . . . your *people*, Hoke!"

"I have peculiar control over my people, thank you," said Hoke
idly. "It is, as they say, a peculiar institution."

But the Judge leaned in. "Control," he said. Then he continued
on, and Ellen wondered about his meaning: "Make them fear you;
resort to the whip even in the most insignificant of circumstances
until they understand you cannot be trifled with."

Ellen finally understood. The Judge had recognized Hoke's lust.
Jarvis did not speak of slaves but of his daughter, as she was not to
be trifled with. But once embarked on this parallel path, he poured
all his bile and outrage into it, allowing himself to be carried away.

"I am surprised, sir, that I need to say this to you of all people,"
said the Judge. "Expectations in our negroes are a contagion that can
only lead to insolent behavior and eventually spread across the
county to injure the rest of us."

"Unlike your people, Francis, my people do not require deliberate
excessive correction."

"That last one who walked past?"

"Do you refer to Cassius?"

"He made eye contact with me. And he did not look away!"

"Cassius is a good boy."

"That very fashion of coddling is what leads to rebellion. Have you forgotten Toussaint? No sir, beat them down and you will never hear the least murmur of revolt; if you do not, you will one day wake to find nigras in your bedroom brandishing farm tools!"

"You will cease this sordid talk, Mr. Francis," said Frances Jarvis, coming to her feet. "These are our guests."

The Judge pursed his lips, cowed by her disapproval. After a moment's pause he said with effort, "I will bring my friend Hoke another libation and we will speak of Victor Hugo's new book." The Judge turned, looked at his daughter Mary, and with a forceful nod of the head directed her inside the big house, out of sight.

Ellen saw that Hoke nursed injured feelings, but she glared at him so that when his eyes met hers, he sat upright. He said then, "Yes, Hugo, what did you say it was titled?"

"*Les Miserables*, and I had hoped to dust off my rather dismal French to read it, but with the embargo, well, I know you of all people understand," said the Judge.

"You do realize it has also been published here, in English? *The Miserable Ones*."

"Yes, yes, and I am having someone up North send me a copy, but it is so much better to read it in the original language, do you not agree?"

Ellen listened to her husband lunge and parry with the Judge and she fretted. She may have disliked the time spent with other planter families, but she also feared that the Howards were excluded from the social whirl of the county. She blamed her own personality, feeling that her moody, bitter thoughts leaked and made her transparent to others. But as she listened to her husband she entertained the possibility of another villain.

In a moment of horror, she realized Frances Jarvis had been speaking to her. Ellen turned to her hostess. She knew that Frances would infuse the moment with her code of superiority; she would quash all discord with proper manners.

"I must say, I rarely leave Edensong now," said Frances Jarvis.

"Do you not?" said Ellen.

"I do not and I cannot. It is our people, you understand. They need to be watched all the time, it is worse than ever. I am certain that you experience the same, my dear. The simplest requests, and they refuse to do what is expected of them, always doing things you do not wish for them to do, no matter how expressly you tell them. They are such children, and yet, unlike children, they seem incapable of learning the most rudimentary things. Repetition is not enough, oh no, if I am not present at all times the entire household will go to the Devil."

Ellen watched Frances's words sour her face, and she thought of Frances as a repetitive scold, one whose tyranny had undermined her humanity.

A strange and fleeting image entered Ellen's mind, that of a large cage in a small room. The cage was filled with slaves while their masters were outside the cage squeezed and immobile in the narrow space between cage and walls. This was a queer image indeed as both master and slave were unable to reach the fresh air that beckoned through a wide open door. In that tiny vision she thought she might be experiencing a moment of insight, but it came and went so quickly that she was unable to recall it a moment later. She returned to Frances Jarvis's ramble and was eased back into the comfort of what she had always known, that the negro was inferior and required the guidance and assistance of the white planters. We are, after all, benevolent, she thought, and by our generosity, our people are well served, as they are clothed, fed, housed, taken care of in all the small ways that they cannot do for themselves.

"I do not know why they have so little appreciation for what we do for them," said Frances Jarvis. "We take good care of them, there is no way they could do for themselves."

Little appreciation, thought Ellen. She also had seen the look in Cassius's eye. She knew well that when given a taste of freedom, her people were not grateful. Therein lay the danger of benevolence; a small morsel might bring appreciation, while a grand gesture might bring treachery. She feared them at those moments, imagining that they would indeed resort to offensive methods to obtain their freedom, thereby destroying their own wonderful existence. The Judge had it right. And Cassius was the worst of them all.

"Now," said Frances, smoothing her dress, "perhaps you would care to join us in our cartridge class, Ellen?"

"I beg your pardon, Frances, what is a cartridge class?"

"We gather together a small group of the better ladies and load cartridges for the soldiers. Women all over the Commonwealth are doing it."

Ellen Howard had already forgotten that she had, moments before, been fretful about the Howard family's social position, and she said, "Oh, Frances, I do appreciate the invitation, but I believe I will not be able to attend."

Approaching the small barn, Andrew ran ahead to join his friends. Cassius saw individual exhibitions of vibrant color as everyone was dressed in their finery, and amid the bright oranges and yellows and greens and blues were spectacular splashes of bold red. He took note of his own attire. He had worn drab work clothes without thinking. Cassius had unintentionally estranged himself from the festivities. He wandered down to the orchard, where a storyteller rambled through an overlong tale while standing under a tree dense with tiny clenched green apples. Abram was among the judges, and his eyelids fluttered as his chin drifted to his chest only to jerk back up again. Cassius did not see Weyman, so he ducked behind a line of haystacks that separated the storytellers from the stage. He was surprised to discover Weyman holding a jug.

You already done, Weyman? Sorry I missed it, said Cassius.

No sir, mine just comin up, old windbag James been up there huntin for the end of his tale some ten minutes now, and if he don't finish soon, I'm hittin him in the face with a shovel. Uncle Paul there up next. Uncle Paul, y'all any closer to rememberin how your story starts yet? said Weyman.

Paul nodded, looking green.

Uncle Paul, said Weyman with false seriousness, ain't been real successful keepin down his supper.

Never saw you romance a bottle in advance of your event, Weyman, and you got some hard judges out there, said Cassius.

Y'all know a story tells better when lubricated, said Weyman.

Never saw you lubricate in the past, when you won, thought Cassius to himself.

I'll come back, said Cassius in a manageable lie. He left the orchard and went out to the lane where children shucked corn with their mothers. An impressive rig of green-jacketed ears were piled high against the planks of the small barn, unsheathed one-by-one rapidly and tossed to the summit of a rising stack even as the smallest children plundered the pile from below. The corn was from the previous years' harvest, each cob with teeth missing like an old man's mouth, while the remaining kernels were poorly kept with an intimate knowledge of mold. Cassius filched a husked ear and tasted kernels that ground to mush between his teeth and left a queer aftertaste.

He walked past Tempie Easter and Pet seated high on a horseless buckboard. They preened for a pair of hands Cassius did not recognize, and he assumed they were from the plantation called Little Sapling. Tempie appeared snug and dry in her astonishing red dress, a vibrant revelation among even the grandest of outfits. Pet wore a dress she had borrowed from Tempie, but the red of her dress was a shade deeper and the cut was more ordinary, uncomfortably tight on the plump house girl, with underarm stains that were rimmed by salt down near her waist. The smaller Little Sapling man stood on tiptoes to appear taller. It seemed that he thought Pet bulged in all the right places.

Initially, Cassius thought it a trick of his peripheral vision, but when he looked back he saw the edge of it clearly, a small wooden box that Tempie attempted to hide in the folds of her red dress. He recognized the box, he had seen it recently on Hoke Howard's desk; a box for snuff, predominately green with narrow brown strips inlaid. It had taken him a significant number of hours to carve that inlay. He thought her brazen and foolish to have it out in the open, especially if she planned to trade it for a special treat, and perhaps she recognized her error in judgment as he saw her push the box away, to hide it in the folds of Pet's dress. Cassius met her narrowed eyes. He returned to the path.

Banjo George had found a spot that would both serenade the corn shuckers and carry down the lane. Cassius saw he was lit up and suspected the Edensong men had passed the jug early. Banjo George teased Joseph, holding the banjo just out of his reach.

You gonna play for the folks, Joseph? said George, as the banjo wavered in the air.

Joseph lunged to catch it as it appeared that Banjo George would lose his grip, but his reach fell short when George yanked it back.

Not your fault, boy, you just a young dog sniffin 'round the big dog field, you got to earn the right to play this, said Banjo George.

I know, said Joseph, shaking his head, embarrassed to be there and embarrassed that his teacher was making a fool of himself. Joseph stepped back, looking to escape.

You want to be the Man? Then, earn the right to play. You got to live the pain. You got to suffer, can't just pick it up when you feel like it. Tell you what, we go set this blade in the fire, get it red hot and carve a little decoration in your shoulder, prove you can take it, then you be man enough to play this here banjo.

Cassius stopped close behind Banjo George.

No, I don't think so, sir, said Joseph.

Sure, said Banjo George, goading. Prove to me you strong, show off for the ladies.

Must not be man enough, said Joseph, and Cassius smiled at that answer. You play for us, George.

Not ready to be a man? said Banjo George, louder and with an edge.

Think I'll go check on the dance, said Joseph.

You stay here, said Banjo George sharply.

Cassius stepped in.

You ever see what George here went through to become a man, Joseph? said Cassius.

Reckon not, said Joseph guardedly, thinking two older men now goaded him.

Maybe George'll open his shirt, said Cassius.

His shirt? said Joseph. Banjo George patted his chest.

This man George, he carved so much of his chest, why, if the angels don't weep when he plays, then pain ain't all it's cracked up to be. How 'bout it, George, you ready?

I am ready, sir.

You ready to play like nobody ever played before?

Got me a new song I wrote myself.

A new song, said Cassius in exaggerated awe.

Not just new, this here song inspired by the Lord, said Banjo George, leaning sideways to look around Cassius at Joseph. Lord gifted me when I'se sufferin the great chest tattoo.

Well I'll be switched, George, said Cassius. The Lord.

That so, Cassius, song came with a bolt of thunder from the Lord hisself.

A rumble of lightning, said Cassius happily in the voice of the preacher.

Cassius, on the day I enter heaven, I will sing this song to the Lord.

Cassius's brow furrowed. Didn't you say the Lord gave you this song?

That so.

Well, now you got me wondering. Why give it away? Why didn't the Lord keep his song? If He liked it, you'd think He'd want to hear it regular. I'm thinking the Lord didn't want that song no more.

No, He wanted it—

Maybe the Lord was drunk when he wrote that song.

No sir, Lord warn't drunk when he wrote my song.

Could be the Lord sent it on to you because He woke up and re-membered He'd been a fool with drink the night before, and now He didn't much care to have his song remind Him. Send it down to George, He said, hide this song away from me in the corner of some field.

Banjo George was indignant: He done sent it to inspire me.

I'm just saying, to protect you, George, so you ain't embarrassed flying on up to Heaven with your banjo and He hear you start up and says, Quit that infernal racket, George, I's blind drunk when I wrote that song, and now here you is mockin the Lord.

Banjo George's eyes narrowed. That ain't right, Cassius.

You're right, I know you are, probably not that way at all. Maybe the Lord see you coming and He just real quick send you off to the other place so He don't got to hear it.

Banjo George's mouth opened and closed like a fish on land.

Cassius's eyes found Joseph's and he nodded toward the lane. Joseph was too stunned to laugh. He followed Cassius toward the big barn where the dancing was to take place.

They had rounded the bend when they heard Banjo George's in-strument sing. Joseph finally laughed.

Hoo, you twisted him up good, Cassius. He ain't never gonna play that new song, I tell you that much.

Banjo George ever show you his chest? said Cassius.

Can't say he did. Seem like he always keep it covered.

Looks like a pack of wolves got to him the way he carved and tattooed and scarred himself. You mind that Arkansas toothpick of his and let some other damn fool be his new blank sheet of skin.

Believe I will, said Joseph, and he was grateful. And that there looks suspiciously like Miss Fanny, only this girl is taller and prettier.

Cassius looked where Joseph was looking and saw that little Fanny of Edensong was indeed taller and prettier.

Cassius continued down the lane to the far side of the large barn, close enough to watch the festivities, far enough to be outside of them, and there he found a circle of Sweetsmoke and Edensong men lounging and smoking and he joined them, pulling out a rolled cigar. The men noted the string tied around Cassius's smoke and smiled at one another. Cassius held the far end to the fire and brought it to his lips to suck the cigar alive. He settled back to listen to the discussion.

We been findin hornworms with your name all over 'em, said one of the Sweetsmokes.

Hell, all we done is whisper in they ears that your tobacco be nice 'n' sweet, which it got to be so's to balance out your mean old massa, said one of the Edensongs, and they all laughed.

My massa mean? We done seen yours and he be nastier than a nidderin woodchuck.

Why that warn't no woodchuck, that be your Missus Ellen. My Ol' Massa Francis be the kindliest gentleman in the Commonwealth of Virginie. Got hisself a whole delivery of oranges from that blockade runner, pay top dollar, and give 'em to his slaves, said the Edensong.

No surprise you be confused, seein as how you blind as well as ignorant. He ain't but the second kindliest master. My Massa Hoke one day slaughter up his whole pen a' hogs and give us bacon and ham and pork shoulder and hog jaw and keep none back for hisself, said the Sweetsmoke.

Well hell, that ain't but nothin, my Massa Francis gots a still and he gather up his taters and barley and mash 'em up and makes us some fine Christmas brew and we all happy and not gots to work till Feb'ry. You Suetsmokes back to work by New Year's.

I take offense at you callin it Suetsmoke.

Well, *you* call it that.

All right for us to do.

Then I pass you my jug and apologize.

Cassius smiled as smoke and braggadocio washed over him.

Massa Hoke got hisself a fat new bathtub can fit four hands sittin side by side.

Massa Francis got a whole row of bathtubs, use a different one every night.

Massa Hoke got hisself a new saddle made from the softest pigskin.

Massa Francis got boots made from the skin of lions from Portugal.

Massa Hoke own those lions and Portugal, too.

Massa Francis so rich, he drown his ships come from Portugal after just one trip since he like the smell of when they new.

Massa Hoke, said Cassius elbowing into the conversation, has a desk so large the hands from both plantations can sit around it and still have room for horses and mules.

The Sweetsmokes and the Edensongs looked at him with pure admiration, nodding.

And I built it, said Cassius, blowing out a plume of smoke. On that, he stood up and wandered away. For a moment he heard silence from the men around the fire, and then they started up again. Massa Francis got a chair so big he can sit at Cassius's desk all by hisself and not have room for no one else. Cassius chuckled to himself.

Inside the big barn, men played improvised musical instruments, and a handful of dancers in the middle churned up straw dust. Cassius recognized one of the dancers as Maryanne, Captain Solomon Whitacre's cook, and a queasy feeling came over him. Emoline Justice had been dead less than a week and here he was, bragging and smoking. A shadow crossed his mind; no one would ever know who killed her.

Cassius stared at the interplay of Edensongs and Sweetsmokes, Swan of Alicantes and Little Saplings on the dance floor without seeing them, a swirl of color and motion that hypnotized until a stillness at the center of it all caught his attention, Big Gus motionless on the far side of the barn. Big Gus brought a jug slowly to his lips just as Quashee entered with her father Beauregard. Big Gus lowered the jug and in a step was in front of her, wiping the jug's lip with his sleeve. He offered it and Quashee shook her head. Beauregard allowed himself a polite sip, but Big Gus's eyes claimed Quashee.

Cassius felt his temper breathe, and then Weyman came in and saw him and Cassius was glad to have the distraction of his company so he might push his anger away, as this was not his fight. Weyman leaned hard against the barn wall.

You win again? said Cassius, one eye on Quashee and Big Gus.

Somethin wrong with them judges, said Weyman. Can't tell if they stupid or deaf. I done told that story the best it ever been told but they just look at me like I'se speakin in tongues.

Sorry to hear that, said Cassius.

It's the bad luck, I tell you. It spreadin.

Not you too.

Bad luck all over, like this war. Some say it's good for us, but I say it ain't. They just not tellin folks what it really about. What y'all got with war? More danger, less food, crazier white people, I mean, they a lot more of 'em dyin and that bad for us, see what I'm sayin? I know bad luck when it come.

What's that you're drinking?

Edensong firewater is what it is. Bark juice, busthead, rotgut, pop skull, help yourself.

Maybe later, I had a little something before.

And now your luck done turned worse, 'cause I offered and you said no and now I ain't sharin no more, said Weyman with a smile. After a long tug, he slid down the wall and looked around sadly.

Can't look 'em in the eye, Cassius. Three years I been winnin, and now I'm one sad wicked creature.

Sad wicked Weyman, said Cassius.

Beauregard was speaking earnestly to Big Gus, and Cassius watched Quashee move away. He reminded himself again, it was not his fight. He looked back at Weyman and waited for an opportunity to knock the jug out of reach.

Things bad, Cassius. Dreams keepin me awake.

That's the busthead.

Naw, busthead keep me warm. *Only* thing keepin me warm, women already look at me like I was somethin funny.

Cassius reached for the jug, but Weyman picked it up first.

Gotta have somethin, said Weyman. I am just a poor slave, never be nothin more.

Sure, sure.

Lord write it down in his book, can't argue with the Lord. Ol' Bible say, You a slave, Weyman, you just a slave.

Lord says that in the Bible? Where in the Bible you see that? said Cassius.

Right up there in the beginnin, with Noah and all.

You mean the story of Ham?

Yeah, that the one, Ham, he that son of Noah, saw Noah all naked and got hisself cursed and sent off to be a slave and we been slaves ever since.

Who told you that, the white preacher?

Him and Old Thomas, I don't know, everybody says that.

First of all, Noah cursed Canaan, Ham's son. He never cursed Ham.

It the same shit, still mean the same thing for me!

And why's it matter if he saw old Noah naked? And where in that story, where in the Bible does it say Ham is black?

If he ain't black, why they say he is?

Look, Weyman, I tell you myself, I read that—

Her hand came onto his shoulder, the lightest touch, and Cassius looked, and Quashee's eyes held his eyes for one important moment, and then her hand was gone and she glided away, smiling at someone passing.

Weyman looked at him with drunken, rheumy eyes.

I done talked to someone who read it, said Cassius, letting go of his anger, now imitating Weyman's drunken drawl, and they done told me ain't nothin in the Bible say Ham was black. Don't be listenin to what them preachers and planters tellin you, Weyman, not even your Thomas.

Cassius came out of his crouch and turned casually away, but his secret eyes were alive and feral and they examined the nearby men and women, scanning the faces of anyone who might have been listening. Through the crowd, he saw Jenny. Hurt brimmed up in her eyes and they held each other's gaze. She turned away first and went out the far barn door. Cassius absorbed her pain and had his own moment of loss, and the spot Quashee had touched burned on his shoulder. Cassius knew Jenny would never again return to his cabin.

He took a step to follow Jenny, but Big Gus blocked his path.

Oh Gus, what the hell do you want? said Cassius. His patience was in rags and he was unwilling to pretend otherwise.

Cassius, when you gonna stop botherin that little girl?

Just exactly what little girl am I bothering, Gus?

You already got yourself a girl, what you need two for?

Got a whole collection, now what little girl you mean? said Cassius, thinking, too harsh, too harsh, but he did not care.

Jenny already comin to your cabin, so you stop botherin Quashee or I do somethin about it. She don't like it.

I'll try to remember, said Cassius. It seemed that others knew about Jenny and him.

Cassius began to step around Big Gus, but Big Gus shifted his feet to remain in his path.

Something else? said Cassius, and now he was dangerous.

I'm feelin good right now, said Big Gus.

I am gratified.

Real good.

Real gratified.

And you mock me, Cassius, said Big Gus.

At that moment, Cassius did not remember his words to Andrew, and Old Darby was not there to check him. Every successful To-Do ended in at least one legendary fight, and he was about to make history. Cassius was grateful to Quashee for keeping him from revealing his secret literacy, but her quick thinking had brought him to this. He did not fear Big Gus, but a fight would cause others to take sides and then he and Gus would be defined as enemies, and it would carry on into the weeks and the years. Cassius took the measure of the man. Big Gus was taller, broader, his hands were large and hard, his arm muscles rolled under his skin like iron bars. Cassius expected that he would take a beating, but that was not a sure thing as Big Gus had been drinking and Cassius would be quicker. He devised a strategy, to stay a step outside of Big Gus's reach and let him swing hard and often and eventually wear down. No positive outcome loomed; it would be bad if he won, worse if he lost. If he won, Big Gus would look for a rematch, and the advantage Cassius now held over Big Gus's drunken overconfidence would no longer exist. If he lost, he would take a severe beating and spend his life enduring Big Gus's preening pride.

Would it matter if I say I don't mock you?

No.

Then I won't bother to lie. So explain something. You hear rumors, right?

What rumors?

Rumors that Quashee's bad luck.

Sure, I hear 'em.

Then why do you want her? Don't you think that bad luck'll rub off on you?

Big Gus smiled at him, a leering unpleasant smile.

I see, said Cassius, understanding the unintended double meaning of his own question.

Big Gus turned aside to set down his jug, and Cassius set himself for Big Gus to come up swinging, as was his method. But Big Gus stayed low, and Cassius looked where Gus looked, at Joseph and Fanny dancing in the cloud of straw dust. Cassius saw twirling smiling Fanny, her inviting body imprinting delicious shapes on his eyes, shapes meant for Joseph alone. She reached up and tousled the white tuft on Joseph's head and laughed. He saw Joseph enraptured and reckless, and Cassius thought that all lovers were doomed.

God damn, said Big Gus. I was savin that one.

Big Gus started toward Joseph.

Gus, said Cassius.

Later, said Big Gus.

You don't walk away, said Cassius, wondering why he was doing this. *Gus!*

Big Gus came around snorting.

Fanny's just a girl and that's a good age for Joseph.

You callin me old?

Calling them young.

You lookin at the Driver of Sweetsmoke and I get what I want. Maybe she young, but after tonight she ain't gonna be a girl no more.

I don't think so, Gus.

Big Gus stalked onto the dance area, Cassius moving behind him, but Cassius slowed when he saw Abram across the barn.

Abram caught his eye, then surprised him by turning away and slipping out the door back into the night. Because of that, Cassius missed the moment when Big Gus shoved Joseph. Fanny yelled at Big Gus, but Big Gus pointed his finger at Joseph and Joseph slapped the man's hand aside. Cassius knew Joseph had no chance, young and lean, and round in his cheeks, so Cassius reached for Gus, but three Edensongs stepped in then, men who did not fear the wrath of a driver from a neighbor plantation, followed by Fanny's mother. Cassius chose to let them have him and he walked away with his heart pounding.

Cassius overheard Big Gus say, Mr. Nettle, he trust me, patrollers my friends, you all goin be sold to Sweetsmoke and then you mine, and Cassius overheard Fanny's mother say, You don't git *my* daughter, she ain't betrothin no Sweetsmoke driver, not while I'm her mamma, and he heard Big Gus yell, We in the fields tomorrow, Joseph, so I see you there.

As Cassius left the barn, he saw Fawn weeping openly, having been witness to the whole scene. Irritated by Fawn's tragic tears, he moved away to escape them.

The Big-To-Do went on as night fell over Edensong. Cassius had looked for Jenny but had not seen her since the barn. Perhaps that was just as well, as she might need time to cool down.

So far, nothing had happened that would define the dance as furthering the bad luck. If he was lucky, it would be the first step in changing that tradition. He winced at his own superstition, but knew that when people started to perceive bad luck, any small fool thing reinforced it. The anticipation of bad luck could carry on for months, years. At that moment, as he mused, Richard Justice stepped out of the shadows and took Cassius completely by surprise. Richard Justice had chosen this time and place to guarantee shock and isolation.

"What'd you find, Cassius?"

Nothing, how long you been here? said Cassius.

"What'd you find!?"

What makes you think I found—?

"That smug look on your face, you got something going on, empty your pouch!"

Richard Justice rammed his forearm against Cassius's chest and shoved him against a tree.

Cassius was stronger and taller, but even though he had expected this moment, he had been caught off-guard by Richard Justice's sudden appearance. He did not push back. Richard Justice dug under Cassius's shirt, found the string that held his pouch, pulled it out, and used his free hand to take out the three coins and the folded prewar bank notes.

"Jesus Christ, this is prewar, these are bank notes! No faith paper in sight!"

Cassius had chosen bank notes decorated with colorful depictions of cheerful slaves at work. He did not imagine Richard Justice would notice or care. It was Cassius's own small revenge, and it satisfied him.

"No protest? Aren't you going to tell me you made that money as a carpenter?"

You'd know it was a lie.

"You should have hidden it, Cassius. That wasn't smart, carrying it on you."

Didn't think you'd show tonight.

"Couldn't help yourself, Cassius the clever, flashing prewar bills, showing off to the hands. That's so small of you, they are so easily impressed."

Cassius held his tongue. Richard Justice now thought what he wanted him to think, that Cassius had been foolishly overconfident.

"And the rest?"

Not gonna say, said Cassius.

Richard Justice put his open hand on Cassius's chest and pushed him toward the tree.

All right, all right, back where it was, said Cassius.

"I'll know if you're lying, we can go to your cabin right now."

Cassius slapped Richard Justice's arm away.

So come to my cabin, you won't find nothing. I put it back where she hid it, figured it's good there if you looked before and didn't find it.

"Fair enough," said Richard Justice nodding. Cassius had read him correctly, he was too indolent to bother going further—the money in his hands satisfied his expectation of Cassius's greed, and Cassius knew he had buried enough money to convince Richard Justice he had unearthed her entire fortune.

"So you reburied it. When were you going back?"

Cassius shrugged.

"Don't feel bad, Cassius, it was the smart play, the odds were decent, always a chance I wouldn't come after you."

Richard Justice counted the money again with pleasure. Cassius described where the tin was buried in the garden.

"I looked there."

I dug deeper.

Cassius knew Richard Justice would dig up the money tonight and never return to his mother's home.

"Here, take this for your trouble." Richard Justice put a coin in Cassius's palm.

Cassius again wondered if Richard Justice had murdered Emoline. But he did not believe it. For all his bluster, Richard Justice did not have that requisite inner coldness to crush the head of his own mother. A small voice inside of him spoke, If you don't find her killer, her death goes unpunished. He dismissed the voice.

Which of your sisters will you buy first? said Cassius.

Richard Justice hesitated. "Leave that decision to me."

How would you do it?

"This truly interests you?"

In point of fact, it did. Cassius had no conception of how one would bargain for the life of another human being.

"Dear Lord, Cassius, it's but a simple matter, I messenger a personal note to Mr. Sands, master of Philadelphia Plantation, and his oral reply is returned by my messenger. He would know it was about money and money is what drives such men. He would be obliged to entertain me."

You would go as a visitor?

"I am a free man, Cassius, as such I speak to anyone I choose. Now, if you don't mind."

Richard Justice moved into the darkness, staying clear of the many lanterns that illuminated the dance, buoyant in his step, a whistled tune on his lips.

Cassius returned to the big barn, and was irrationally happy. People drank and danced and ate boiled ears of corn. He had not indulged in more than a few swigs of the dreadful Edensong whiskey, but his head felt agreeably light and disconnected from his body. He warned himself against taking pride in his manipulation of Richard Justice but he could not make the happiness go away. He wandered among the revelers for some time with a smile on his face until someone leaned close to him in order to be heard over the music.

You helped my boy, said Savilla.

Cassius turned and she moved her head closer and said into his ear: I spoke to that Eula.

Eula? said Cassius.

Fanny's mamma, Eula, said you helped my boy. Didn't suppose that from you, Cassius.

Didn't suppose?

Not like you to put yourself out. Want to thank you.

Where's Joseph?

Actin the shamed puppy, probably crawled up inside a jug.

And Fanny?

Got the women all 'round her by the corn rig, keep her there till Big Gus drink himself to sleep.

Savilla left him with a bittersweet taste in his mouth, as her gratitude had been generously salted with the low expectations of his character. The pleasure of manipulating Richard Justice now receded and left him unexpectedly thirsty.

He searched for refreshment, brooding about Savilla's words. Did Savilla think the same about Mam Rosie, that she wouldn't put herself out for others? As a boy, he had tried to emulate his adoptive father Darby. But Darby was gone so soon, and as Cassius grew he was forced to define himself in opposition to the imperious, mercurial, self-centered Rose. Yet it was she he had recognized when Savilla described him.

He found an abandoned jug along the outside barn wall and heard the slosh of liquid within. He carried it up a rise into darkness near a stand of trees. He was glad to be surrounded by the wind which pushed away the noise of merriment. He was finished with this dance, tired of the hands with their opinions and their ominous intonations of dire luck. All that was left was to drink himself stupid and stagger back to his cabin by morning. He sat on a flat divot in the rise but before he could enjoy the contents of his jug, he saw Quashee following in his footsteps. The memory of her touch on his shoulder returned, and a fire grew around his middle as she sat beside him and took the jug.

I didn't know you house folk indulged in the bark juice, said Cassius, friendly.

Oh, I been known to change my breath now and again. 'Course, we used to drink finer fare up at John-Corey's big house, said Quashee.

So, the new girl sips planter juice.

I think maybe I did try it. Once, said Quashee, her smile no more than a twinkle.

She tipped the jug and he saw her try to hide the wince when the harshness gripped her throat, and he laughed. She returned the jug, eyes watering.

Not so smooth as planter juice, said Cassius.

If I'm goin be a hand, I'm goin learn to drink like a hand, said Quashee, voice snagging in her throat.

Showing off, he tipped the jug and drank and it bit back and he knew he had taken too much. He fought to swallow as it burned down his throat into his chest and without warning he hooted. Quashee laughed and rolled onto her side.

Thank you, he said, the words coming in a whisper.

Didn't mean to laugh so hard, she said, still laughing.

Laugh all you want, but I meant for earlier, when you stopped me telling Weyman I could read—hoo mama, that shit burns—'cause if Weyman knows, everybody knows.

You're welcome, she said, wiping a tear of laughter from her cheek.

And when you said about being a field hand—

I'm good with it. See my hand? Look there, see that? No, right *there*, by the blisters. That's a callus.

Does resemble a callus, said Cassius smiling. Might small, but congratulations on your first. Now listen, Quashee, maybe there's a way to get you up to the house.

You goin save everybody tonight?

What, me?

I saw you with Joseph.

Aw, that was, no, forget that, that was nothing.

Taking on Big Gus is a damn fool nothing.

Yeah, said Cassius, you got that right.

Burning's just about gone, pass the jug, said Quashee.

After she had fought down the bad liquor and could speak again, she said: I suppose you know some folks don't like you.

And here I was thinking of running for governor.

Be serious now. Folks who'd like nothing better than to hurt you.

Big Gus, said Cassius nodding.

The hands listen to him.

The hands listen to the Driver.

Just thought if you were warned—

I'll be all right.

You even talk different with them. Not like you talk to me.

Maybe I do, said Cassius, knowing that he sometimes slipped into his field voice when he was with the hands. He did the same with the planters.

I'm glad you don't talk that way to me, said Quashee.

They listened to the music roll in and out with the wind and passed the jug until it was empty. Cassius appreciated her gift for silence. He had noticed it earlier in the week and now saw it was a habit.

I hear you were married, said Quashee.

Doors and windows and shutters slammed shut. Cassius did not move his eyes for fear of seeing himself fly away.

Married, said Quashee. Someone said—

I heard you.

Quashee nodded. A few moments passed before he spoke: I was married.

What was she like? said Quashee.

Not sure I know anymore. Maybe never did.

Know her long?

Marriah. Her name was Marriah. No, she came when Hoke bought the people of another planter.

Nice when it's someone new.

Cassius looked at her, unsure of her meaning.

So you don't know everything about them and they don't know all about you. Not like with someone you grew up with.

He understood the unspoken implication. Humiliations from planters, their families, and every other white man, woman, and child in the county are more easily borne when your new partner hasn't been witness to your history of degradation, thus allowing you to maintain a small measure of dignity.

What do the cackling hens say about my marriage? said Cassius.

Quashee inspected the wild grass at her ankles.

That she had a white child Missus Ellen forced Master Hoke to sell. That Missus Ellen whipped her something fierce, said Quashee.

For once they say the truth.

They say she died but I never did learn why.

Those women can't shut their mouths long enough to chew, said Cassius.

Cassius stared down the hill at the lights along the lane and in the barn, at the drinkers and dancers, at the lovers and the drunken sleepers. He stared at all that intense living that flourished despite oppression, and an image of Marriah's face hovered just outside his vision. He was beginning to forget what she looked like, and the harder he tried to bring back her face, the more it slipped away.

She knew she couldn't run, said Cassius. They'd just keep bringing her back. Pretty soon they'd hobble her. Couldn't be a mother after they took her son. Maybe she also didn't think she could be a wife. She went to the place where the creek runs deep under the little bridge. They were looking on the roads farther out, so she had time.

You don't have to, said Quashee.

Put a large stone inside her dress. Few hours later the planters crossed the little bridge and one of them saw something wave in the water. Buried her before they let me out.

Cassius appreciated more than ever Quashee's ability to be silent. He sat as if alone, hearing nothing. Gradually the sound of the wind returned. He was unsure as to how long they had been sitting in silence; when he looked around, she was in the same position, but the musicians now played a tune he had not heard from the beginning.

They told you a lot, those women, said Cassius.

Don't blame them; I played the spy, asking questions here and there so no one noticed I wanted to know about you.

Cassius started at the word "spy." Intelligence agent, he said without thinking.

When I first came, I thought I recognized you, another bitter, damaged animal, and I know enough to let the damaged ones be.

I am so very happy I helped you out with Big Gus, said Cassius with evident sarcasm. And now you warn me that I bother him like a burr in his trousers.

His trousers, his shoes, maybe a few other places, said Quashee, returning his smile. She passed the jug and said: So after Marriah, Emoline Justice nurses you, and now she's dead and the whole world creeps around you.

God damn cackling hens.

Oh, I pieced some of it together on my own. You been all the talk since she passed.

Emoline brought me out of a dark place. Kept everyone away and just when I had to go back, Cold Storm hit, must've hit you too, snowbound for a week. Extra healing time so my mind could catch up to my body.

Five years ago? I remember that, but we called it Cox's Snow.

What's Cox got to do with it? said Cassius.

Old Dr. Cox from Lynchburg got caught a half mile from his place, frozen in his buggy. Everybody there calls it Cox's Snow.

Sounds funny in my ear, maybe 'cause I didn't know Dr. Cox. More likely call it Emoline's Snow.

Tell me about her.

Well, she was at Sweetsmoke and then Hoke let her be free and after a time she bought her son, and was working to buy her daughters. Taught me to read.

Cassius was tempted to ask Quashee who had taught her to read, but he held his tongue.

They sat awhile surrounded by the wind continually changing its tune, chasing the musical scale through leaves and branches.

Looks like your friend down there, said Quashee.

Cassius saw stumbling Weyman itching for a fight with one of the Swan of Alicantes, who was wisely attempting to walk away from a drunk. Cassius got to his feet.

I'll see he gets home. I enjoyed our talk, Miss Quashee.

I enjoyed it as well, Mr. Cassius.

As Cassius walked down the hill, he sensed Quashee's eyes on his back, which at that moment burned hotter than the Edensong rotgut.

C assius held Weyman's arm around his neck and wrapped his other arm around Weyman's back, walking him out past Edensong's big house to the road. When Weyman drank he rambled on about his early years, growing up in the cotton states. Weyman had been one of the lucky ones. His master had died when Weyman was still a young man and he had been sent north to Virginia as part of the inheritance of his master's son. The son had no use for him and had sold him to Thomas Chavis, and Weyman now lived a very different life. Intermingled with his horror tales of Georgia, he complained about Tempie Easter intruding on his territory.

She sellin more shit to them trash whites and now they don't want what Weyman got to offer, said Weyman. Cassius, y'all got to carve me some more of them little soldiers so I can get my business back.

Sure, sure, said Cassius.

I could shoot that girl Tempie, said Weyman.

Sure, Weyman, you shoot her with your finger, said Cassius.

Y'all think I wouldn't? said Weyman, looking hurt, and then he shut his mouth.

Most of the planters and their children had gone inside, but the two masters, Hoke and Judge Francis, remained on the front porch. They were impressively inebriated.

"You know full well I purchased that land, Francis."

"I would lay odds you cannot produce a document."

"I never bet more than I can afford to lose," said Hoke. "And neither should you."

"Then perhaps you recall that my grandfather, out of the kindness of his heart, permitted Buffalo Channing to clear and plow that land, and Channing's children as well, but never did he grant permission to Channing's grandson to sell it!"

"I purchased that land from its rightful owner and I own it fair and square."

"You waited until he was beyond desperation and pilfered it for a song. You are a land pirate, Hoke Howard!"

"Land pirate!" sputtered Hoke, and his ensuing words emerged coldly: "My dear sir, I know that you will withdraw those injurious words and on your knees beg my pardon!"

The women rushed from the house and surrounded the men, pulling them apart. Cassius walked Weyman out of sight. Cassius might have found the battle between two aging plantation owners comic were it not so fraught with dangerous implications. The planter argument would likely lead to further unpleasantness, and Cassius began to question if there might be some truth at the core of the superstition. Was it possible that the arrival of bad luck was more than coincidence? Francis Jarvis's son-in-law was a Confederate quartermaster, bad luck indeed for the plantation Sweetsmoke.

Cassius scoured the area near the main road and eventually found Bunty, Weyman's fellow slave, who also worked Thomas Chavis's farm. Cassius unloaded Weyman so he could return directly to Sweetsmoke. He would need sleep—tomorrow promised to be a busy day.

⊷ Chapter Five ⊶

CASSIUS stood at the edge of the clearing and drove temporary stakes into the ground. The clearing was on a rise in an
area of deep forest, a tract of land that was being considered to be
clear-cut for the following year's crop.

At dawn on that Monday, the day after the Big-To-Do, Hoke
had accompanied Cassius to the fields. As they walked, Cassius had
listened to Hoke grumbling aloud, "Goddamned Jarvis can't read
French," and "Arrogant prig," and "*I'm* the one introduced Pompous
Pilate to Victor Hugo." Once in the tobacco fields, Hoke informed
Mr. Nettle that Cassius would handpick men to build fences and an
enclosure in a location away from the barns to conceal the livestock.
Cassius had chosen Joseph among the men he knew to be fluent
with hammer and saw. Big Gus protested vehemently, going so far
as to drive his hand into a burlap sack to raise a handful of wriggling
hornworms, as if this constituted proof that Joseph was indispensa-
ble to the counterattack on the blight. He misjudged Hoke's toler-

ance for confrontation and was promptly silenced by Mr. Nettle. Big
Gus closed his fingers into a fist, squeezing hornworms that popped
and oozed in his grip. Hoke looked away, Mr. Nettle glared, and
Cassius concluded that the Driver had severely blundered. As Cassius led the men out of the fields, he saw Big Gus waving his arms in
the air, berating Abram.

It was unnecessary for Hoke Howard to tell Cassius of the need
for haste; Cassius had already anticipated this move and by daybreak
had designed in his head an enclosure that could be built quickly and
strengthened later. Hoke informed him that the livestock would arrive at the clearing by mid-morning. Cassius cordoned off an area
with stakes and rope, and at the arrival of cattle and sheep, he compelled them into that area and continued to build around them. The
hogs would quickly follow, delivered by wagons. The sound of men
and hammers alarmed the beasts and they huddled behind ropes
while Cassius built and re-roped to open new space as individual
sections of fence were completed.

He returned to the quarters at sundown to learn that Hoke's urgency had been astute. Captain Whitacre and his empty wagons had
rolled up in the middle afternoon and requisitioned a patriotic per-
centage of their commodities. Hoke had not been able to hide all his
grain and other dry goods in time, but Whitacre's primary goal—to
reduce Sweetsmoke's supply of fresh meat—had been thwarted, and
he loaded thin, weak, and lame livestock into his wagons as well as
into the Sweetsmoke buckboard, which he also requisitioned. Frus-
trated by their meager gain, Whitacre's men targeted the high-
stepping bantam rooster who frequented the yard outside the big
house. The house servants described the clumsy, off-balance soldiers
in full-bore pursuit of the quick cock, who after being cornered
more than once, feinted and dodged his way to freedom. Children
on the lane mimicked the rooster's moves as their friends imitated
the stumbling soldiers. In the end, Whitacre had moved out with
less than a quarter of his wagons full, wearing the expression of one
who had been obliged to eat an apple acrawl with worms.

The work of the day had been intense and fulfilling, and Cassius
had taken satisfaction in its accomplishment. This rare moment of
personal value led him to seek out Jenny and apologize, as he was
certain, in his charitable humor, that he would surely salvage their

friendship. Cassius found Jenny pulling weeds from between a row of cabbage plants and emerging carrots in the vegetable garden behind the cabin she shared with her sister, her sister's husband, their children, and a blond dog. When she saw him, an expression warped her face that checked his approach. She bent back to the weeds, but a residue of his determination drove him on, even as his prepared apology slipped away. She whirled to face him, eyes blunt with fury.

You make God *angry*! Jenny hissed. That little girl's a jinx, she's bad luck!

He was stunned motionless.

Who do you think you are? said Jenny.

After years of friendship and intimacy, the Jenny before him was a stranger. As difficult as it was to define what they had together, it had brought him comfort, as she had accepted him during his complicated times. An invisible wall was now between them, as if the past had never occurred. The feel of her breasts and belly under his hand, the smoky-sweet smell of her breath, her fingertips drifting along his neck into his hair, all these memories became suspect, unreal. Their past now joined other good times of his life that had been crushed or undermined, as if the real world could accommodate only pain and misery and contempt.

Cassius walked slowly back to his cabin. He stood before the cold hearth and stared at the lightly charred bricks. He attempted to clear his mind, and engaged in the trivial chores of everyday existence. He lit the kerosene lantern from the carpentry shed. He removed his shoes and hung his shirt on a nail hook. He inspected his rations and chose hardtack biscuit and bacon. He ate without tasting, and when he was finished, he tore a segment of tobacco from the oldest drying leaf that hung off the rafters. He rolled the tobacco and without thinking wrapped a small bit of string around its end, then changed his mind and set the fresh cigar aside for another time. Finally, he went for the books he had hidden when Andrew had come to wake him. He brought out *The Iliad*. He opened it and found that the paper that had been revealed when Andrew dropped the book was in fact three sheets folded so they would not be discovered.

He read the list of names on the first page, realizing halfway down that he read only white names. These were clients to whom she gave guidance as conjurer and seer. Beside each name was a series of dates and times, appointments. On the second page was a continuation of white names and among them he found Hoke Howard. The third page was arranged differently with only the names of blacks; beside the names were prescribed herbs. He saw Mam Rosie's name, along with a list of a prodigious number of herbs. This was not surprising, as Rose kept a stock of remedies for the children and others. He noted Pet, Savilla, and Banjo George's names grouped together under Mam Rosie, arranged by location to simplify delivery. He saw Maryanne's name, and he remembered that she had initially come to Emoline as a buyer. Toward the bottom, he saw Weyman's name and almost laughed out loud. He knew that Weyman would never admit to any infirmity, much less one that would require an herbalist, yet here was proof. Cassius ran his finger to her prescribed herbal remedy and saw "jalap." From the hours spent watching Emoline prepare her remedies, he knew jalap bindweed was difficult to grow in Virginia's climate, as it thrived in heat. It was not unusual for her to grow special herbs for clients who required regular dosing. The root of jalap was used for purging, often for children, but had to be disguised with something sweet as its taste was unpleasant. Cassius diagnosed Weyman: His friend was recurrently constipated.

He turned back to the second page, to the name Hoke Howard. The father of Richard Justice might have had cause to visit his former slave. Cassius struggled to imagine them as lovers in the recent past. If that were the case, then it was not impossible that his old master had committed a crime of passion; were Cassius to become the instrument of her justice, Hoke might be his prey. Hoke's last visit had not coincided with her death. He had seen her on the previous day, the 29th of June. It was not impossible that he had discovered she was a spy for the Union. It was not impossible that he had considered it his patriotic duty to end her treason, and it was also not impossible that Hoke had returned unexpectedly on the following day in order to cover his tracks. Cassius allowed pleasant thoughts of revenge to wash over him, but soon brought his mind back to rigor, because this scenario made no sense. Why would a planter bother to cover his tracks? Even if it was discovered he was a murderer, who would hold accountable one of the wealthiest planters in the county for the death of a black woman? Beyond that, Hoke had been deeply moved when he informed Cassius of her death, and that did not suggest a murderer. Cassius knew it was unwise to leap to conclusions, as emotional, half-reasoned explanations rarely resembled truth. Cassius's mind moved to John-Corey Howard's demise at Manassas, the very moment that had supposedly instigated the perception of ill luck that now permeated the plantation. It was not impossible, and perhaps likely, that Hoke Howard was visiting Emoline not for sexual favors but to commune with the spirit of his son, in private consolation.

Cassius recognized that he wanted Hoke to be the murderer. It fit his fantasies and completed the portrait he had painstakingly created of the man. Reality, even sanity, crept back in. Hoke Howard had controlled Emoline's life for years and had granted her freedom. He had visited her, according to the folded sheet of paper, numerous times in the recent past. This last visit was nothing more than coincidence.

He perused the top two sheets of paper and found an appointment scheduled for June 30, the day Emoline died. Sally Ann Crowe was to come in the afternoon. Abigail Dryden was scheduled to meet her the day after she had died, on the first.

All the information swirled and he needed to clear his mind. He knew if he moved on to another subject, the thinking would continue in his subjacent mind, and in time ideas would sort themselves out and be revealed to him.

He sat in his cabin listening to the busy hands doing night chores. He also had chores, but nothing urgent, so he continued to sit. He reached for the rolled cigar, but again stopped himself, not wanting it, just wanting something, and then he realized he still had the book in his hand. He looked at the spine. *The Iliad of Homer.*

Cassius opened the book and flipped through the title page and table of contents to reach Book One. Emoline had called *The Iliad* a book to savor. He now wanted distraction, and the smell of pages and ink brought back the joy of learning to read.

The Iliad. At the top of the page, a paragraph described incidents that he came to understand were to play out in the body of the text in rhyme.

Cassius read the short narrative.

ARGUMENT.

THE CONTENTION OF ACHILLES AND AGAMEMNON.

In the war of Troy, the Greeks having sacked some of the neighbouring towns, and taken from thence two beautiful captives, Chryseis and Briseis, allotted the first to Agamemnon, and the last to Achilles.

The descriptive paragraph went on to explain that an argument erupted between Achilles and Agamemnon over the two captives. As it was Cassius's first exposure to the story, he did not immediately grasp the full meaning of the introduction. He began to read the main body of the story, presented in verse, but the words "beautiful captives" stayed with him, hovering as if on the fringe of the page as he read. The language was difficult, but he persisted and soon discovered the rhythm. Here was a man named Atrides, with kingly pride. He glanced back at the introduction. No one named Atrides was mentioned there. He read deeper into the verse and became convinced that Atrides was Agamemnon.

A simple fact, and yet Cassius found it curious. In this world, men had more than one name. And of a sudden he knew he had heard this before, his mind pulling up Emoline reading aloud *The Odyssey*. No surprise there, he had not been fully conscious then, in a wounded state of body and mind. The god referred to in the opening was first called Smintheus in the verse, then Phoebus, and finally Apollo.

He closed the book on his thumb, brow furrowed. He, Cassius, had only one name. If he had to identify himself away from the plantation, he was obliged to say he was Cassius Howard, which informed any stranger that Cassius was owned by a planter named Howard. Emoline Justice had been Emoline Howard. She needed her manumission papers before she could choose a name for herself. What luxury, to possess extra names. What luxury to know your god through many names. It suggested depth and layers of personality.

Even the god had personality, and never had Cassius imagined a god with moods.

He reopened the book and read on.

The poetic text expanded and elaborated the paragraph of prose that opened the story. A hero named Achilles had taken captive two young women. The father of one of the young women, a priest named Chryses, had come to Agamemnon to beg for his daughter's return. Chryses was a Trojan or at least a Trojan ally, therefore an enemy to Greece. Specific phrases in the text caught Cassius's interest.

For Chryses sought with costly gifts to gain
His captive daughter from the victor's chain.

The victor's chain. Cassius was intimate with the victor's chain. He had been held by that chain for his entire life.

The spoils of cities razed and warriors slain,
We share with justice, as with toil we gain;
But to resume what e'er thy avarice craves
(That trick of tyrants) may be borne by slaves.

Chryses's daughter, Chryseis, was a captive of Agamemnon. Chryses's daughter was now the *slave* of Agamemnon. Cassius read on, feeling a wave of excitement. Soon he uncovered another reference:

Do you, young warriors, hear by age advise.
Atrides, seize not on the beauteous slave;

Cassius again closed the book on his thumb and gazed off in wonder. Agamemnon the king had refused the priest Chryses's plea and sent him away. That was not unexpected. But a great thought had formed in Cassius's mind. If the priest Chryses's daughter was a slave, then was she also black? And if she were black, the priest Chryses might well be black as well. And if Chryses was black, were *all* of the Trojans black?

There was no one he dared ask, for any such question would reveal the fact that he could read and reason. He could not brand himself a dangerous man in such an open way. He would have to reckon this out for himself. He read on with hunger, to discover that the old priest's prayer to Apollo on behalf of his slave daughter brought astounding results.

Thus Chryses pray'd.—the favouring power attends,

Favoring power, that would be Apollo who attends, answering Chryses's prayer—

And from Olympus' lofty tops descends.
Bent was his bow, the Grecian hearts to wound;
Fierce as he moved, his silver shafts resound.
Breathing revenge, a sudden night he spread,
And gloomy darkness roll'd about his head.
The fleet in view, he twang'd his deadly bow,
And hissing fly the feather'd fates below.
On mules and dogs the infection first began;
And last, the vengeful arrows fix'd in man.
For nine long nights, through all the dusky air,
The pyres, thick-flaming, shot a dismal glare.

Cassius was amazed. This was Apollo. A god, breathing revenge. Using his deadly bow to shoot vengeful arrows. Infecting the Greeks. Cassius struggled to wrap his mind around what he had read, fearing that he had somehow misunderstood, or that the words might rearrange themselves on the page and reveal that he had been taken in by a magnificent jest. Apollo, a god, had attacked the Greeks, spreading infection *on behalf of a slave.* For nine days. He attacked dogs and mules and then men. Breathing revenge. For a *slave!*

Cassius sat back and considered this astonishing thing.

It had been clear to him for some time that the God of the Bible was in favor of slavery. The masters spoke of it, and quoted the Bible to prove it. Both white and black preachers preached it, admonishing the hands to abide by the will of the masters so that God would be pleased with them. And what was it in the Bible that exhorted this position? As he understood it, it began with the story of Ham, son of Noah, Ham who was supposed to be father of all blacks, Ham who had committed the crime of seeing his own father naked. Cassius had read and reread that portion of the Bible and had been outraged to discover that the evidence for Ham's blackness was not on the page. It appeared to Cassius that the planters had manufactured this concept for no other reason than to explain Cassius's lack of worth. He did not even try to understand how seeing your father naked could be a crime so heinous as to condemn an entire race of human beings. It would take a white man to understand that.

He had then looked for other Biblical evidence that might offer whites a reason to believe God was on the side of the planters. The most obvious appeared in a passage he had memorized, Ephesians 6:5, *Servants, be obedient to those who are your masters according to the flesh, with fear and trembling, in sincerity of heart, as to Christ.* That passage was read aloud in sermons, word for word. As a boy, Cassius had liked the words, not fully understanding them but warmly believing that he was somehow protected by the words. Even as a man, on the rare occasions when he attended services, Cassius would unconsciously mouth the words along with the preacher. But Cassius no longer needed to accept white man's sermons on faith, because Cassius could read. A further examination of Ephesians suggested a very good reason for the planters to wish to keep blacks from that vile habit. The white preachers may have read Ephesians 6:5 accurately and aloud, but they did not read aloud any later passages from Ephesians, conveniently ignoring Ephesians 6:9, *And to you, masters, do the same things to them, giving up threatening, knowing that your own Master also is in heaven, and there is no partiality with Him.*

Perhaps God's intention was not that blacks were meant to be slaves. And yet, when all was said and done, slaves they were. As they were incessantly informed, God was all-powerful and all-seeing. If God was all-powerful, then it followed that God preferred blacks to be slaves. Cassius drummed his fingers, another thought stealing in. Perhaps the power of God was controlled by the white man, and they had bent God's intentions to accomplish white needs. He let that thought go, not knowing how the idea that God could be manipulated might apply to his oppressed life, as that suggested that if he knew a way to contact God, he (and He) might remedy the situation. Certainly he had heard the argument that slavery was their test on earth, and when life came to an end and they reached that other place, they would be rewarded. But no white man seemed inclined to suggest that he would happily share Heaven with his black slaves. Cassius had often wondered how his life of bondage would work to his ultimate benefit.

The Iliad gave him an alternative. *The Iliad* presented a different god altogether. Apollo could not be ignored, not even by white men. Apollo, with his vengeful bow, actually freed slaves. This brought Cassius a small smile.

He realized with a shock that the feelings he had for the God of the Bible were similar to his feelings for Hoke Howard: dread and relief. Dread because of the absolute power Hoke had over him, relief when any approval or kind gesture allowed him to feel somehow worthy and therefore hopeful. Finally he wondered if the God of the Bible also experienced crushing responsibility.

Cassius stood up and felt a string of spider silk across his forehead. He tried to wipe it away, but after his hand had crossed his brow, he still felt the tiny pull. He wiped again, this time with more determination, and now felt spider silk on his ears and across the backs of his hands. Suddenly he was doing a childish dance, rapidly brushing both hands from his neck to his nose to clean the feeling off his skin. And when the feeling was finally gone, in the ensuing moment of quiet he thought about how Quashee risked her reputation by spying to learn about him, and he thought about Emoline who risked punishment to teach a slave to read. He thought about Apollo bringing plague to free a slave, and he thought about the strange fact that the life of an enslaved black was worth more than the life of a freed black, and he knew as he had known for a number of days now that he would hunt for her killer. It was the danger of recognizing that he had a choice. Friday he would return to town without an official pass to see who might have an appointment to meet Emoline the spy.

-**❧** Chapter Six **❧**-

BY Thursday Cassius worked alone in the clearing, building a
roof over the hog's shed. Groomsmen, brought up from the
barns to tend sheep and cows, idled on the far side of the meadow in
shade as the livestock shifted and grazed in the sun. Cassius had
been sorry to see Joseph return to the fields.

He noticed a crossbar on the fence that hung lower than the others, and he felt with his hand and knew that one of his crew had
driven nails that had missed the vertical stake. The wood was held in
place by one nail. Cassius propped the crossbar with a piece of scrap
wood, dropped to his knees, and rolled himself carefully over onto
his back, gently and slowly sliding over the grass under the bar, nails
in his mouth, hammer in his hand. He babied his back into position
and drove nails in. Points of grass stuck into him through his shirt,
pricked his neck and the back of his head, and the rough underside
of wide grass blades scraped the soft skin behind his ears. He came
carefully out from under the fence to discover someone standing

over him. Cassius rose quickly to his feet, hammer in his fist, without concern for his back which chafed hard against his shirt.

Hoke Howard ran his hand along the wood of the fence.

"Fine work, Cassius."

Thank you, Master Hoke, said Cassius.

"Truly, quite fine," said Hoke. "I have always admired your attention to detail. Even in something as hard-cast and utilitarian as a fence."

It's nearly done, said Cassius.

"Yes yes, there is no rush, Cassius, get it right, that is fine with me, of course, fine with me."

Cassius looked at him warily, letting his grip on the hammer lessen. Concerned that he might drop it, he set it on the fence's crossbar. In the sunlight, he saw that Hoke Howard's left eye was milky with a cataract, that the skin under his eyes was soft and spongy and crisscrossed by telling lines. He considered Hoke's expression and thought he detected sadness, even a longing.

"Quite the spot, is it not? Lovely."

Cassius looked around and nodded.

"I should come here more often. I should visit all my lands. I imagine I might find many such places. Peaceful, yes. Francis Jarvis's son-in-law would have a miserable time finding it, but I would gamble that he does not know to look for it. And I never bet more than I can afford to lose." He paused, taking in the sprawl of his land, his chest full of the pride of ownership. "Peaceful. Perhaps that is what I will do, take a few hours in the mornings away from the shackles of business and wander, appreciate my lands. Perhaps one day you will join me."

Whatever you say, Master Hoke, said Cassius.

Hoke lost his smile and seemed almost disappointed. "We were friends once, were we not, Cassius?"

Yes sir, said Cassius.

"Growing up, you were such a friendly boy. How I did enjoy your company."

The same, sir, said Cassius.

"We all grow up, I suppose."

Cassius heard the wistful note in Hoke's voice and knew, for the second time in little more than a week, that an opening was granted to him.

A question, said Cassius. This is the moment, he thought, take it now. He searched for his best subservient voice, but was unable to conjure it as scrupulously as he would have liked.

"Certainly, anything, my boy," said Hoke.

Your son, Master John-Corey. You miss him?

"I do, I miss my son terribly. God help me, I miss both of my sons, although with any amount of luck, Jacob will return to us," said Hoke. "Would that my legacy will return."

But Master John-Corey, he's your oldest.

"Yes, John-Corey was my oldest."

You taught him your wisdom?

"Well," laughed Hoke, "I did what I could."

But then you trusted him, after?

Hoke gazed off, down the meadow to the darkness of the forest.

"He was such an impulsive child growing up, but I am certain you remember that as well. Such a scamp. Perhaps that is why it took me years to recognize the competent businessman he had become. I gather that means I proved that you can teach an old dog new tricks, did I not? I refer to myself," he said with a smile. "Yes, when all is said and done, I have to conclude that my son grew to be a circumspect and considerate man. I was uncertain about his choice of spouse, but Stephanie was devoted to him, I certainly could never fault her for that. There were times, I must say, when I was concerned that she reflected John-Corey's true feelings about me, but away with that, that is but a fool's errand, to attempt to deduce the motives and secret hearts of our children." He stopped for a moment, as if contemplating the meaning of his words. "I invited her to Sweetsmoke after his death, but she preferred to return to her own parents in Lynchburg."

So Master John-Corey made good choices?

"Yes," he said hesitantly. "Yes. I look back on the things about which we clashed and realize he may well have had prudent reasons for making his decisions. I still may disagree, but in the all, yes, John-Corey made good choices."

Cassius nodded as if something had been made clear to him.

"This line of questioning is curious, Cassius. What brings it on?"

Nothing, Master Hoke; like you said, curious.

"I think not. You have something particular on your mind."

Well, sir, I remember a story about his personal servant coming all the way home after Master John-Corey died in that battle.

"Lewis, yes, returned from Manassas. I believe he was two weeks on the road."

He was a good one, doing that for the family.

"Yes, he was. Pity about him being sold."

And Master John-Corey had that thing in his will, about keeping two other people together.

"Beauregard and Quashee I believe are their names."

You think that was Master John-Corey making good choices?

"I am not certain I follow you."

Well, sir, Master Hoke, if you think Master John-Corey was a smart man, then maybe one of his smart decisions was for his people to come to Sweetsmoke. If Master John-Corey thought they were good at his place, maybe he thought they would be good in his father's place.

"Interesting thought, Cassius, one I had not considered. We do have fine people of our own, of course."

We sure do, Master Hoke, I didn't mean to take nothing from our family. Just thinking aloud, about that Beauregard.

"What about Beauregard?"

Well, sir, Master Hoke, William, he's off with Master Jacob and he was a fine butler, we all know that, but since then it's Pet answering the door.

"Yes, I suppose it would be nice to have a butler again. But my wife is uncomfortable with John-Corey's people."

Guess I understand that all right.

Cassius let that sit for a moment, and then he said:

But one thing.

"Something else?"

Maybe Missus Ellen don't know it'd be an honor to her son's memory to have his people there. I mean, the girl Quashee seems refined, and Missus Sarah needs a servant, near as I can tell.

Hoke considered Cassius with a half smile, and for a moment Cassius thought he had overplayed his hand.

"You speak very well, Cassius, which I take as a compliment to me, as you grew up under my tutelage." He looked away again and said, "Send Beauregard and Quashee up to the house this evening just after sunset. I will see them myself and perhaps I can coax Ellen to take part." Hoke nodded at Cassius, and again Cassius wondered if his smile was patronizing. It mattered little, as Cassius had accomplished his task.

Cassius returned to the quarters early and watched Big Gus lead the hands back down the lane. Big Gus appeared unusually sunny, but Cassius afforded it no significance. He watched for Beauregard and Quashee, and they were with the stragglers, filthy and exhausted. Cassius urged them to find their best clothes so they could be presented at the big house. Quashee came suddenly awake, anxious because her one good dress had been soaking to remove a stain. She could not meet the masters in a wet dress. Others pulled out their best clothing, but every appropriate dress offered was too large.

Cassius overheard whispering women, one of whom suggested that if Quashee went to the big house, the bad luck would follow and the quarters would return to normal.

Cassius saw Joseph bringing up the rear, the last worker out of the fields. Joseph was known to hurry back to his cabin, relishing his evenings and his free time after chores, but tonight he walked with arms crossed, hands tucked beneath his armpits. Cassius understood immediately; Big Gus had fabricated infractions against Joseph and slapped his cane across the young man's outstretched palms. Joseph went directly into Abram and Savilla's cabin and did not return to the lane.

Cassius watched Quashee's anxiety grow with the presentation of each unwearable dress and imagined that she feared offending the planters as she had no time to bathe. Savilla pulled her from cabin to cabin, but no suitable dress was found. Quashee was finally resigned to her work dress and brushed the filth away as best she could. It was then that Tempie Easter approached.

Come with me, girl, said Tempie, leading Quashee to her cabin. Missus likes her house folk to be pretty and presentable.

Cassius was wary of Tempie's offer, but Quashee was frankly delighted. When a person in desperate straits is offered help, he thought, relief can overwhelm good sense. He probed it from every angle, as he did not see how Tempie would benefit from helping Quashee. He could find nothing but charity in her actions, and warily decided that Tempie understood she was not likely to join the big house staff herself and had decided not to spoil another girl's oppor-tunity. Nevertheless, his skepticism persisted and he remained out-side the cabin that Tempie shared with two other unmarried female hands. He heard Quashee's girlish squeals of pleasure from within, a sound so infectious that it brought a smile to his face. Moments later, Quashee emerged adorned in one of Tempie's dresses. Tempie was larger than Quashee, but not as large as most of the women of the quarters, and this dress was suitable. Where it was tight and sug-gestive on Tempie, it had a loose easy quality across Quashee's shoulders and torso, cinched at the waist with a belt where the skirt billowed out and flowed gracefully to the ground. Discreet bows and pockets in the folds completed the look. Cassius's trepidation eased when he saw the relief on Quashee's face.

Oh, Tempie, you are a lifesaver, said Quashee, leaning to hug her.

No reason one of us shouldn't get to the big house, said Tempie.

You look fine, said Cassius.

It's the right thing, said Tempie. You know if you seen Pet that she wears dresses just like this one. Maybe not so pretty.

Cassius noticed that Tempie wore a dress that was strikingly sim-ilar, also cinched at the waist with a billow that dropped gracefully to the ground, also with pockets and bows. If Tempie would wear that dress, then she was not setting up Quashee to look the fool.

Beauregard joined them, erect and elegant in a clean white shirt and dark pants he had brought from Master John-Corey's plantation. The two of them side by side looked out of place in the quarters.

Come, daughter. We should be on our way, said Beauregard. He nodded to Cassius, acknowledging the debt he owed the carpenter for this opportunity. He offered his elbow, she took it and they walked in tandem.

Tempie watched Quashee start up the lane with the back of the dress dragging.

That dress is long in back. I best come along, hold it out the dirt, least till they give you the job, said Tempie, taking a handful of fab-ric and lifting it to clear the ground. Quashee twisted awkwardly to see Tempie walking behind her as if carrying her train.

Oh, Tempie, I can't tell you how much I thank you, said Quashee.

Cassius watched them go, feeling satisfied, but his skeptical mind drove a spike into his pleasure and he decided to follow. He stayed a few steps behind Tempie and Quashee, and again took note of Tempie's dress, a near twin to Quashee's, with cinch, billow, and pockets.

Beauregard, Quashee, Tempie, and Cassius followed the path in the dark, passing the Overseer's place and approaching the big house from the rear, walking more quickly as the lights inside the big house guided them around to the front yard where young Master Charles and other white children were tended by Nanny Catherine. Hoke Howard and his wife, Ellen, sat on the front porch, admiring their grandchildren. Hoke saw the hands and came to his feet, opening his arms to extend a welcome. He smiled in surprise to see Cassius. Cassius nodded, but hung back so that Beauregard and Quashee could properly introduce themselves. Ellen stood but wore an artificial smile. Mam Rosie heard the fuss from her kitchen and came out wiping her hands down her apron. Pet appeared framed in the front door behind them, and when she saw the group, she rushed past and down to Quashee and, with her left hand, turned her around to admire the dress. Then Pet seemed to catch herself and turned and bowed her head to Ellen in apology.

Sorry, Missus, said Pet. It just she lookin so pretty.

Cassius had been watching Ellen for her reaction to John-Corey's people, but Pet's flurry alerted him. Pet had turned Quashee so that she stood sideways from the planters on the porch, with Tempie now behind her. The locations of the lanterns caused a shadow to fall across the backside of Quashee's dress and Cassius could not see Pet's hands. Pet curtsied to her mistress and took a step back to stand beside Tempie. Cassius then saw Pet exchange a glance with Tempie. Cassius alone saw Tempie's quick, impulsive smile, gone before it registered.

A frisson of fear flowed through him as every hair on his arms and the back of his neck set off a shriek of warning. He dug down to engage the lessons of stealth he had mastered so that he could survive as a slave, and he walked carelessly toward the group.

Master Hoke, said Cassius in a strong voice, taking charge before anyone else had an opportunity to speak, I think you know Beauregard here, he was Master John-Corey's butler over in Lynchburg.

Beauregard stood taller and nodded to Cassius in uncertain appreciation. Cassius nodded back.

That is true, Master Hoke, I carried the keys, said Beauregard.

"From everything I have heard, you did a fine job, Beauregard, a fine job," said Hoke.

Cassius moved around Beauregard, behind Quashee. Tempie and Pet were up to something and Cassius needed to buy time so that he might understand what it was.

This here, said Cassius, is our dear Quashee.

"Yes," said Hoke, "you also come with a fine reputation. I am pleased to make your acquaintance."

Cassius glanced down at the back of her dress, now removed from shadow. He saw a flash of shiny green, a small corner not completely hidden in a deep pocket and he understood. From that moment on he knew his timing was everything, he would need to be very good and very quick or all would be lost.

Quashee has been working in the fields, but as you can see, her delicacy is better suited to the big house, said Cassius. He was not fully aware of what he was saying.

He placed his hands on Quashee's shoulder and then let them move down her sides to her skirt, where he appeared to brush dust off the fabric that ballooned out from her waist. In doing this he was able to angle her into shadow. Quashee looked awkwardly over her shoulder at Cassius as if she did not recognize him.

He pressed his leg against her thigh, moving her off-balance, and as she stepped forward gracelessly, he pretended also to stumble and utilized the shadow to slip his hand down into the pocket to secretly grab the small green box. He knew it by touch, the snuff box with the brown inlays that his fingers had formed for Hoke Howard years before. He brought the box up under his shirt as he spoke.

Beg your pardon, miss, clumsy me, said Cassius, then turned back and said rapidly to the planters: Quashee would be a fine personal servant for poor Missus Sarah.

Master Hoke, said Beauregard, breaking in as if he might save Cassius from further humiliation, I hope you will consider us worthy to work in your home, sir.

Cassius nodded, playing the fool, hastily taking steps backward, and others glanced away from his embarrassment. He stepped at an angle and brushed by Tempie Easter. At that moment he understood why Tempie Easter had worn that dress: If Tempie exposed Quashee as a thief, then she might be considered for the position of personal servant to Missus Sarah. Thus dressed for her interview, she could walk directly into the big house and never look back. Cassius slipped the small green snuff box into the side pocket of Tempie's dress and was satisfied she did not feel it.

"I think we may conduct our interview out here as well as anywhere," said Hoke smiling, and he turned to include Ellen. She nodded curtly.

That would be fine, sir, anyplace that the Master deems appropriate, said Beauregard.

"He does speak well, would you not say so, Mrs. Howard?" Hoke said to Ellen, but everyone understood that he was working too hard.

"Yes," Ellen said icily, "our home will be filled once more with the sophisticated tête-à-tête of a butler."

Hoke moved to Ellen's side and spoke with her quietly, leaving everyone standing in the yard at attention.

Cassius shambled over to where young Master Charles watched the proceedings with bored detachment. Cassius's heart pounded loudly in his chest. This was his last trick, and he was counting on Master Charles's dislike of him. Master Charles looked at Cassius as if he was a roach and Cassius sat directly beside the young master, nodding, smiling.

Hoke took a step away from Ellen, who looked off to the side. His smile returned and he addressed his family:

"When you worked for my son, Beauregard, what were your duties?" said Hoke.

Cassius leaned in close to young Master Charles and said: Tempie got herself a plan, but I know the truth.

Charles looked at him, wrinkling his nose.

Beauregard spoke of his duties at Master John-Corey's Lynchburg plantation: I was of course the first one awake, Master Hoke, my position to make sure the house was prepared to welcome Master John-Corey and Missus Stephanie from their uninterrupted sleep, I made sure they never had to give the slightest thought to anything, their bath was—

Tempie Easter suddenly interrupted him: I got somethin to say, Master Hoke, I didn't want to but I got to, this goin on too long. You can't trust 'em, Master Hoke.

"I'm sorry, Tempie, what are you—?" Hoke said.

You can't trust 'em and I got proof, said Tempie.

You see that? said Cassius into Charles's ear. Now it's starting.

I know these two, they are trouble, said Tempie. That girl, she been comin at night, stealin from the big house.

Quashee's eyes opened wide and she looked around her in terror.

I never stole, said Quashee. I never even come near the big house.

Oh yes she do, said Tempie, she come to the big house at night and take things.

Tempie's blaming the new girl, but Quashee ain't got it, said Cassius quietly. Then she's goin come and blame you, Master Charles. But I know it wasn't you.

"What d'you mean you know it warn't me?" said Charles.

You just look in her dress, look right in there, said Tempie. Right in that pocket you find one of your beautiful boxes, Master Hoke.

Quashee looked down at the dress with her arms up in the air, as if she was afraid to discover that Tempie told the truth.

Hoke came down the stairs and put his hand in a pocket of Quashee's dress. When he found nothing, he checked each pocket and then patted around the entire billow of the dress. "What are you on about, Tempie?"

It was there, I swear, she must'a hid it somewhere, said Tempie.

I know it wasn't you, said Cassius. You never took no box. She just muddying the waters so she can get away with it.

"I didn't do it, who said I did?" said Charles.

Nobody said nothing yet, Master Charles, but I heard Miss Tempie say she was planning to point at you. Could be I was mistaken, said Cassius.

Charles stood up and pointed at Tempie. "She's the one, Grandma Ellen, she tryin to get me in trouble. I ain't got no box, Grandma Ellen, not me."

Hoke looked from Charles back to Tempie. He saw the fear in Tempie's eyes, and his demeanor changed. He took a step toward Tempie, who backed up, feeling her own trap close in around her. She patted her dress and felt the box where Cassius had dropped it. Her hands came up directly to her mouth and her eyes closed.

Hoke patted down Tempie's dress and found the small green box.

Tempie opened her eyes and stared directly at Cassius. Her eyes blazed into him with a mixture of hatred and something that resembled admiration for one who had outmaneuvered her. Hoke noticed her eyes and saw the look and turned to see where she aimed her venom. He gave Cassius a full look, sitting alone next to where Charles had been before he exposed the thief.

Cassius was surprised at Hoke's expression, as Hoke's eyes met his own. Out of self-preservation, he had learned to read Hoke's countenance, and he read him now. Hoke knew. Hoke wouldn't know all the details, and he would understand that when it came to his people, with their uncommunicative and sullen self-protective manner, he would never learn the whole story, but Hoke Howard knew enough to understand that while Tempie was surely at fault, she was not the lone culprit.

Cassius saw Hoke make mental plans to punish him.

"Your first order of business as my butler, Beauregard, is to help me take Tempie into the tobacco shed, where she will remain until I decide what to do with a thief."

Yes sir, said Beauregard sadly, as his first order of business was distasteful.

"You come along as well, Cassius."

Quashee turned in a circle in Tempie's dress, uncertain as to what was to happen. Her father had been graced with a big house position, but she did not know if she was to be similarly rewarded or soiled by Tempie's plot.

"You gonna whip her, Gran'daddy?" said young Master Charles, eagerly following the men and Tempie.

"You stay with your Grandma Ellen, Charles," said Hoke.

Ellen came down off the porch and took Quashee's arm. "You come inside with me, Pet will get you started."

Pet stared at Quashee with loathing. Mam Rosie walked over to Pet and took hold of her ear, gripping it hard and twisting it.

Ow! said Pet. Quit that, Mam Rosie! Ow ow *ow*!

Mam Rosie yanked the ear in the direction of the big house and let go, and Pet raced to the steps of the porch and hurried inside ahead of Ellen and Quashee.

Beauregard held Tempie Easter's arm, gently guiding her to the tobacco shed with Hoke and Cassius following. Inside the shed, she was chained with the same bracelets to the same ring bolt in the same position Cassius had known for three days five years before.

You want me to fetch the whip, Master Hoke? said Beauregard very softly.

Cassius imagined Beauregard's mixed feelings. His new job was to anticipate the Master's every whim, and so he would know to offer the bullwhip. But no black man wanted any part in the violent correction of a family member. Nevertheless, Beauregard understood that this woman had tried to destroy his daughter, and would have destroyed him.

"No, Beauregard. She is not worth as much with stripes."

Cassius saw the sag in Hoke's shoulders as he made a decision that concerned his property.

Cassius followed Hoke out of the barn.

"Beauregard, you go on up to the house, have Pet show you the ways. Cassius?"

Cassius stayed behind with Hoke.

"The trader is in town. He is here with a landowner from Louisiana, a cotton and rice man. Even with the embargo, they bring in a crop so they are buying people. I had said we had no one for him." Hoke sighed. "Cotton boys need people, we oblige with our runaways and troublemakers." Hoke looked at Cassius, emphasizing the word "troublemakers." "Tomorrow I will go to town to see this man and take that girl." Old Hoke looked at the green snuff box in his hand. Finally he said, "You will drive me."

Cassius nodded and watched Hoke walk back to the big house. Cassius understood that Hoke had likely not made up his mind whether he was to sell two of his people, or only one.

Cassius held the reins of the carriage, Hoke beside him as Sam pulled them down to the main road. Tempie Easter sat up straight in the black cushioned rear seat of the planter's fancy vehicle, hands shackled in her lap. A gunnysack was wedged under the seat beneath her knees. Cassius did not know who had packed it and stowed it there, but assumed it contained her fancy clothes. He thought the idea that she might be allowed to keep her things was optimistic. Tempie said nothing and made eye contact with no one. Her eyes were dry and her face was calm. Hoke occasionally looked at Cassius pensively, as a teacher might ponder whether a student was absorbing a lesson.

Sam brought them under the château gate, then left onto the main road, drawing the carriage wheels into the ruts. After a few minutes, they rode past a tobacco field and Cassius saw the hands collecting hornworms. One by one they stopped and stood up to watch the carriage carrying Tempie roll by. Cassius saw Big Gus straighten but after a moment, Big Gus saw Joseph come up as well. Cassius watched Big Gus move, raising his cane while still five or six strides away. Cassius wanted to warn Joseph, but he could only watch as Big Gus connected with the back of Joseph's thighs. Joseph went to the ground, out of sight. The hands nearest Joseph looked in his direction, then returned to work. The hands who had not witnessed Big Gus's assault watched the carriage roll out of sight.

In town, Cassius guided Sam to the livery. Hoke got down and walked into the barn while Cassius remained in the seat. He turned fully around to look at Tempie, but she did not look back at him. He had no words for her. She would have put Quashee in just this position, but during the entire ride, his heart had dragged behind them in the dust of the road.

He did not remember a time when the livery had not been there. The front faced south in the full sun, and the whitewash paint cracked and crumbled in scaly patches exposing silver wood beneath. Sunlight leaned in through the open double doors and straw dust glowed against the interior gloom. At the far end, a bright rectangle stood out, the door to the auction tent. Hoke's silhouette momentarily filled the rectangle and was followed by the silhouettes of two men, all of them coming this way. Hoke stopped in the entrance and two white men came out in the sun to take Tempie down. Standing on either side, they compelled her into the livery. Hoke stared at the empty back of the carriage, then looked at Cassius and nodded that he come along. A groomsman took Sam's bridle and led the rig away as Cassius followed Hoke.

Hoke and Cassius entered the gloom of the livery and Cassius smelled dry hay and wet horse, animal feces, leather, and man sweat.

He walked a few steps behind Hoke, who did not look back. Beams sliced through unevenly butted staves and yellow blades of sun cut across them in the dark. They approached the far door where the two men had taken Tempie. Cassius and Hoke stepped through into a tented outdoor space. A small wooden platform dominated, in front of a collection of chairs. A triangle of sun rested on the far side of the white tent and gave the auction area a perversely warm and welcoming light. Outside Cassius heard the shrilling of grasshoppers.

Hoke looked at Cassius and his eyes were burdened with the helplessness of a terrible knowledge. In dismay, Cassius felt Hoke's empathy enfold him and finally understood his punishment. He did not intend to sell Cassius. Cassius was to witness the results of his actions, actions that had brought Tempie to this place, and thus be forced to confront his conscience. The bleached muslin of the tent, warmly lit and close, embraced a history of anguish and grief and apprehension, the last place so many, God, so many people, would ever see their sons and daughters, their mothers and fathers and grandparents, their sisters and brothers and playmates before they were sold, and as the side of the tent bowed and shuddered in a soft breeze, Cassius heard a collective moan.

"This is my man Cassius," Hoke said to a small man. "Cassius, say hello to Lucas Force."

Cassius had heard the name, the traveling slave trader, a name that ran cold through the veins of any black man or woman. Lucas Force was the man who had taken the baby boy five years ago in the cold. He was short with wiry black hair, narrow arms and legs, with tiny feet and hands and a protruding, overindulgent stomach. Cassius had a sudden desire to puncture the man's belly with a sharp object, as if he could expulse beer gas and reduce his middle to normal size. Lucas Force blinked twice as often as other men, thus drawing attention to his thick eyebrows and long black eyelashes. Cassius saw that his hands were pale and delicate and his nails were clean and perfect. Lucas Force's eyes ran up and down Cassius, but as he would not get his hands on him, he looked away.

"Mr. Howard, meet Mr. Plume of Louisiana. Mr. Plume and I have had a successful journey and have already sent two coffles south to his plantation. Cotton and rice is your game, is it not, Mr. Plume?"

Mr. Plume did not bother to rise from the chair on which he was perched. He continued to lean forward on his cane even while sitting, and in Cassius's eyes he appeared to be the most confident man he had ever seen. Soft brown curls rolled out from under his hat, his eyes were sleepy and his expression was preternaturally calm. His chin was smooth as if his beard hairs dared not compel the man to shave. His suit was the subtlest shade of gray, and when he finally chose to stand, Cassius saw that he was not much taller than Lucas Force, while seeming to overwhelm the tent.

"My dear Mr. Howard, how delighted I am to make your acquaintance," said Mr. Plume, and his slight drawl and soft voice seemed to emerge from a core of iron. "When I heard that you had a young woman for sale, I told Mr. Force here that we were obliged to delay our return as I am acquainted with your reputation for knowledge of the flesh. I take it your man Cassius is not to be made available?"

"No," said Hoke.

"Not yet, then," said Mr. Plume, and smiled as his eyes cut into Cassius. Cassius was startled to know that Mr. Plume saw through him, read his mind, and knew more completely what Cassius had done, had thought, and was planning to do than Cassius knew himself. If Mr. Plume was ever to become Cassius's owner, Cassius would never again have the opportunity to consider independent action. He would be driven night and day and if he exhibited reticent behavior, this Mr. Plume would reach down inside Cassius with a sharp-edged spoon and scrape out of him any small dreams of freedom that he might have accrued. He was relieved when Mr. Plume looked away, but felt a raw sensation inside his chest that lingered.

During this time, Tempie Easter had been held by the two large men standing on either side of her. Mr. Plume turned to her, leaning on his cane.

"Remove the shackles, if you would, Mr. Force," said Mr. Plume.

Lucas Force rushed to Hoke, who handed him the keys, and then hurried to Tempie, smoothly unshackling her hands, which she let fall to her sides.

Mr. Plume stepped in front of Tempie. Using the gentlest touch of his cane, he compelled her right hand up in the air, shifting his cane just so in order to adjust Tempie's hands, first exhibiting her palm, then the back of her hand and her nails. He did the same with her left hand. He raised the tip of his cane to touch her cheek and she opened her mouth. He examined her teeth, again giving the slightest pressure to the cane so that she turned to the left, then the right, then tilted her head forward and back so he could see her molars, her tongue, and the roof of her mouth.

He nodded and lowered the cane, took a step back and said, "All right." The two men reached for the shoulders of her dress with fingers the color and thickness of bread dough, but she brought her own hands to the buttons at her throat and undid them one at a time. The two men stepped back and Mr. Plume inclined his head, his sleepy eyes looking that much more lethargic as he watched the slow reveal of her flesh. She finished unbuttoning and with her eyes looking straight ahead she shrugged her shoulders out of the fabric and let the dress fall to the floor, so that she stood naked before him. Cassius knew better than to look away as that would incite Hoke's anger. The two men backed up a step further and Mr. Plume walked around her, carefully inspecting her legs and buttocks, her back and thighs.

"No stripes," he said approvingly. "Very good."

He came back to her front. She continued staring directly ahead. He ran the back of his hand around the underside of her breast and watched her nipple respond. He nodded, wedged his cane under his left armpit, and placed his free right hand between her thighs, guiding his finger up into her vagina. He held it there a moment, then removed his hand and brought his finger to his nose. He stood still for a moment as he smelled her, then turned to Lucas Force.

"Very well, Mr. Force, I will take her." He indicated Tempie's dress that lay on the floor surrounding her feet. "That dress will not do, get rid of it, I believe we have something of sackcloth in the wagon." He addressed her directly for the first time. "You are a Plume now, so remember your name."

As the white men completed their transaction, one of the two large men brought a sackcloth dress for Tempie. Tempie looked at Cassius with flat emotionless eyes, and she held his gaze for a long time. Cassius realized that the sale of Tempie was more real to him than his own life, as he had come to expect misery and degradation and horror. A moment later the man took her arm and forced her out the back of the tent to the wagon.

Cassius followed Hoke through the dark livery to the carriage which waited for them in front. Cassius saw that the gunnysack with Tempie's fancy clothes remained in back. Just before climbing aboard, Hoke turned and Cassius saw his stone-cold face, and Cassius knew that Hoke blamed him for what he had been forced to do to Tempie Easter. As Hoke pulled himself up, Cassius heard the clink of coins in the money purse in Hoke Howard's waistcoat pocket, coins he had not had on the trip into town.

Cassius spoke to no one in the quarters, collecting gear as if he was intent on visiting his traps. He was aware of some sort of uproar, but he paid no attention to it, as he was imprisoned by the uproar in his mind. He took the three loose pages that had been hidden within the leaves of *The Iliad*. He left quickly, avoiding contact with the hands as he assumed the uproar concerned Tempie. In his rush, he left behind the pass he had forged for the occasion. It was the night of the full moon.

He hid his hunting gear in deep woods and changed direction, finding his way through heavy brush, helped by the climbing moon, reaching the main road and walking quickly. He watched the sky as a weather front moved in rapidly, stars consumed by the unnaturally straight line of approaching clouds. When the clouds covered the moon, he lit his lantern and baffled the light down to a narrow shaft, to pick out the road before him. He was just beyond the halfway point, near the little bridge, when the rain came and he pulled his hat down low and continued to trudge as the bottom of the ruts grew slick and muddy.

The rain was his ally, driving idlers indoors, and when he reached Emoline's house he did not think he had been seen. He stopped at the fence that surrounded her yard and looked to see the hole in her garden where he had hidden the money. Richard Justice had not bothered to refill the hole, so it collected rain, but not enough to keep the nearby remedy herbs from being swamped. He noticed the other obvious hole in her garden, where an entire area of herbs had been pulled out. He wondered who else other than Richard Justice had come to scavenge, then remembered that he had seen that hole the night he met Maryanne. Seeing Emoline's garden untended brought a wrench of sadness to his chest, a sentimental wounding so profound that he was taken by surprise. He now projected his own anxieties about abandonment onto the rows of growing herbs. She would not be there to harvest them, she would not grind them in a mortar or mix them in a broth or consume them or share them, they would be gradually overrun with weeds and left to shrivel and fade in the fall. He had spent his life resisting such contemptible sentimentality, but tonight his loss struck primal emotions remembered from childhood and he stood bereft under a pitiless rain knowing that Emoline was gone. She had taken his hand and acted as guide through his grief and she was gone. And then he remembered silent Tempie, and knew it was his part in her fate that had brought him to this moment of pain.

He went indoors tracking mud. He had rushed to town fearing he would arrive too late to meet Emoline's contact and now he was relieved, because he was certain that he had either missed him or that her contact had never intended to be here. Cassius would utilize this time to mourn her and quit this pointless, foolish impulse to expose her killer and exact justice. The broken household items were gone, along with the pots and bottles and remedies; the floor swept, the house tidied. Richard Justice had done more than Cassius had expected. Cassius opened drawers for something dry and found a tablecloth. He used it on the floor, and then on himself. He was soaked and uncomfortable, but the room was warm and close and he did not shiver. After a while, he blew out the lantern and sat quietly in the dark, reflecting.

He considered the events of the past few days. He acknowledged a change in himself: He had experienced fear again, as unwelcome as it was unexpected. After Marriah, fear had abandoned him and he had grown stubborn and bold, at peace with the prospect of his own death. He considered the risks he had run in the five years past and compared them to the last few days. Choosing to hunt for Emoline's killer had given him purpose. He had protected Quashee, Joseph, and Beauregard, but he was uncomfortable in the role of avenging angel, despite his dislike of Big Gus and the tyranny of white planters and patrollers. He drifted off the subject, relieved that Quashee was now in the big house, away from Big Gus. He liked the idea that he would rarely see her. He had helped her, and now that it was done, he could bury his righteous urge, eradicate his fear, and return to the cold heart that provided him comfort.

He heard a noise outside. At first he thought it a trick of the rain, but it came again and he identified it as the sound of heavy fabric being shaken out. Any number of visitors might approach Emoline's empty house; her son, or the sheriff. Cassius kept still in the darkness and watched as the door came open a crack, remaining that way for such a long time that Cassius began to wonder if the door had been that way all along and he simply had not realized it. When it finally swung fully open, a man was revealed. He stepped into the room, reached about the wall and floor until he found Emoline's lantern, and lit it. Cassius knew the man immediately.

"Emoline, where the hell are you?" said the man, holding up the lantern. It was a moment before the man realized he was not alone.

✦ Chapter Seven ✦

GABRIEL Logue was patient. He stood in the doorway, lantern held high, looking directly at Cassius sitting on the stool. His expression did not change and he did not appear to breathe. Cassius would have thought him a statue but for the fact that his eyes occasionally blinked behind his dripping hat. His long tarpaulin coat created a circle of water on the floorboards. Eventually Logue set down the lantern. Cassius stood, keeping his hands visible and open. Logue had not produced a weapon, but he would have one close at hand. Logue was an outsized man, taller and broader than Cassius, appearing more massive in his long coat. Cassius had only once before seen the man, from a distance. Logue stood over six feet tall. His expressive hands were large with a span that brought to Cassius's mind eagle wings. He had a strong nose, a dense mustache, a pronounced chin with a deep cleft that was enough off-center that Cassius intuited it to be a scar. As Logue removed his hat and coat, the lantern below suddenly illuminated one of his eyes, revealing a surprisingly pale blue, and in that moment he appeared unreal. Angel of Death indeed, thought Cassius, and wondered how many men Logue had killed. Then he remembered the man's occupation and thought it odd that he had become a smuggler when he was surely unmistakable in every crowd.

"You here by accident?" said Logue, hanging his coat on a peg, then placing his hat on the same peg. His voice was gravel rolling along milled oak planks.

No accident, said Cassius.

"Looking to get your arse out of the rain, then."

Smart man gets out of the rain.

"Ah, so you think you're smart, but if you think I'm likely to infer dryness and warmth as your primary goal, you got another think coming," said Logue.

Then you're smart, said Cassius.

"*I* was looking to get out of the goddamned miserable rain," said Logue.

Not your primary goal, said Cassius.

Logue smiled coldly. "No," he said, "it was not."

You called her name, said Cassius.

"But I find you. Maybe you got a message for me."

From her?

Logue began to pace. Cassius supposed that Gabriel Logue was wondering if he had walked into a trap. Logue took a long time to respond. "Where is she?"

Dead, said Cassius.

Logue stopped pacing. Cassius admired the man's ability to control his emotions. "Appears to be time for me to be gone from here."

Not before you get what you came for, said Cassius.

Logue glanced toward the false wall by the hearth. Cassius brightened inside. Logue knew about the hidden place.

"All right, smart mouth, what makes you say so?"

Full moon says you show up here.

"Who do you think you are, talking to me like that? Maybe you think I won't take it out of your hide."

You know who I am.

"The hell you say."

Called Cassius. From Sweetsmoke.

"Your name goes unrecognized."

Then she didn't trust you.

"I am away." Cassius watched Logue's winglike hands remove his sodden coat from the hook on the wall. Cassius stayed in the chair.

Now I wonder what I'll do with it.

"Do what you please."

Think Old Captain Whitacre'd want it back?

"Don't know what you're talking about."

But you know where it is. Your eyes said so.

Logue's expression went flat. He replaced his coat on the hook, came around, and sat in Emoline's favorite chair, the same chair she had slept in those three weeks when Cassius was recuperating. The chair expelled a small groan.

"Are you named for Cassius Marcellus Clay?"

I think not.

"The abolitionist from Kentucky."

Don't know him, said Cassius.

"Clay was recently in the newspapers, declined Lincoln's attempt to appoint him ambassador to Spain. I am returned from the North this evening, where I have been for these last three weeks. I take it as a tribute to the ongoing secrecy of our arrangement that I was told nothing of Emoline's death. And you may trust, my friend, that I am kept informed of all things that affect my business. If you know the item, then you know Union men are interested in that niddering Whitacre's correspondence."

Military men? said Cassius.

"Indeed. And as you know about the hidden place behind the panel—"

I built it.

Logue shifted in the chair. Cassius thought that never before in his life had a white man so thoroughly examined his face.

"Where's your partner?"

Partner? said Cassius, puzzled.

"Your compatriot, your second, the gump in hiding with the club or pistol. The one you'll signal once I walk out of here with Whitacre's documents. If you're to extort from me, you'd better have a partner."

Maybe I say he waits outside and protect myself, or maybe I say ain't got one, so you can mistrust the truth.

Logue listened to the answer and a cautious smile infected his face.

"You have the makings of an excellent smuggler, yond Cassius."

Yond Cassius? said Cassius with growing interest.

"Is that not Hoke Howard's affectionate name for you?"

Cassius reconsidered Gabriel Logue. Why had he exposed his lie? Cassius could determine no advantage to it.

Old Master reads Shakespeare, said Cassius.

"How well you mind your tongue, Cassius. Initially I insist I haven't heard of you and then I acknowledge your master's particular words. And you endure my prevarication in silence. You strike me as a man worth knowing. That makes you dangerous." Gabriel Logue spoke with admiration. He shifted himself in the chair, making himself more comfortable, as if he might stay for a while. The chair again complained.

It is said you killed many men, said Cassius.

"Is it indeed?"

Cassius saw that there would be no other response, so he moved on: How goes your business with Hoke Howard?

"Do I conduct business with your good master?"

Hoke Howard needs you, said Cassius.

"He does indeed," said Logue, and his smile threatened to become habit. "The embargo was imposed at the precise wrong moment and his wares were left to rot on the docks, putting him in grave financial peril. Bad for him, good for me, thus he and I are indeed conducting business."

Cassius reflected that sharing information was a game to Logue. And if it was a bartering chip, then Cassius's quid pro quo was about to come due.

"I must say, your conversation is good for clearing a man's head. Frequenting the *bierhaus,* a man tends to imbibe to excess."

The *bierhaus?* In the German part of town?

"Is that so odd? From your reaction I see that my home away from home is likely to continue to fool the Anglo-Saxon planters who would not believe I house with German immigrants. Hans Mueller is in particular need of my talents."

You fear discovery?

"Mostly by my wife, as she would be mortified to learn of my accommodations." He leaned conspiratorially forward. "It does not live up to her standards. No, Mule can't afford to hand me over, I keep him in business, providing certain necessities, readily available in the North, for him to sell. At a profit, I might add. And now it is your turn. Tell me why you're here, so far from your plantation, in the middle of the night."

To meet a man coming for Emoline's intelligence.

"Would you take her place, Cassius?" said Logue as if to a precocious child.

I would know who killed her, said Cassius slowly and deliberately.

"Killed her?" said Logue, standing up. Emoline's chair tipped back but did not go all the way over. "God damn it, you said she was dead, not murdered."

Hit on the back of the head, said Cassius, indicating the stain in the floorboards.

"Who was it?"

Anyone. No one.

"This is damned inconvenient. Who else knows you're here?" He moved to a window and peered out into the rain. Cassius was surprised to see that something frightened Logue.

No one.

"Who saw you come?" He moved to the next window.

No one.

"I was careful, but even I might have missed someone. This is not good, not good at all." He closed the baffles on the lantern and opened the front door. The heavy sound of rain rushed into the room. Logue looked up and down the dark street. He stayed inside the curtain of water and stared for a long time, then returned to the room and closed the door, squelching the sound behind him. "If Whitacre's people knew, I'd be in chains. Unless they want to catch me with the papers." Another test as he searched Cassius's face for any sign that might give him away.

How does Whitacre fit in? said Cassius.

"Whitacre has been charged with capturing the spies known to be operating in this area."

You think she's dead because she was a spy?

"You know another reason?"

Cassius told Gabriel Logue what he knew about Emoline's death. He told him that Emoline's son did not know about the secret hiding place and was only interested in her money. He told him that Captain Whitacre's cook Maryanne had brought a packet.

When Cassius was finished, Logue said, "Well, if we're to be undone, let's at least see what our Emoline has collected."

Logue moved to the false panel beside the hearth. He looked at Cassius over his shoulder. "Tell me, Cassius, did she irritate you as much as she did me?"

Cassius said nothing.

Logue smiled then and said, "I will miss her, too." He opened the panel swiftly, indicating familiarity.

"It appears you did not share her money with her son," said Logue.

And I don't share it with you, said Cassius.

Logue reached in to remove the two packets. He left her money and her letters in place. He brought the lantern to the table and sat. He undid the packet brought by Maryanne. He skimmed the Whitacre letters, then refolded them and resecured the package. He opened the second packet and read that more carefully.

"Do you read, Cassius?"

No.

"No, of course not." Logue paused. "These are intercepted telegraph dispatches. They came from a telegraph operator. They did not come from a cook."

Cassius put his hand on his pouch under his shirt and touched where he knew the scrap of paper rested inside, Emoline's hand-drawn map, W York.

Could this telegraph man have been her murderer? said Cassius.

"It's possible."

Perhaps if the Confederates were closing in and he was nervous and wanted his information back?

"Possible."

And he came back for it?

"All of it possible. But highly unlikely."

Why?

"The telegraph operator's risk comes when making the exchange. Nothing in this packet suggests his identity, so he's safer *not* returning. Beyond that, I imagine there is a middle man."

Cassius said nothing.

"Maybe I should be grateful, this will uncomplicate my life. Without Emoline, I can go about my business without concern for espionage or patriotism. I can be the rascal full-time."

How do you get these north?

Logue considered him for a moment, and when he began to speak, Cassius again saw how openly whites were willing to speak in front of blacks, as if they were speaking to a wall or a chair.

"I suppose you're not likely to afford me competition. Not so difficult as you'd imagine. Unless you're in uniform, there's little difference between the gentleman of the North and the gentleman of the South. When transporting small packages, I simply ride across the border. Man like me doesn't usually get stopped. But I will send something this sensitive hidden in one of my wagons that will join the army train of supplies. Ever see a wagon train? Picture an endless line of wagons stretching for miles, now that is one massive operation, something no one man can oversee alone. Man's got to delegate, and the moment he does, I am in business. They divide their train into little fiefdoms, and in the military, when you see something out of the ordinary, well, that must fall under the authority of Major Body Louse or Colonel Forty-Rod. Pass the buck, Cassius, that's the army way. Quartermaster Whitacre will ironically provide the safe passage of these documents to the North. A greased palm here, a plug of tobacco there, and a handful of extra wagons roll somewhere into the middle of the line. Once at their destination, the wagons split off and after more greased palms, they cross the border. The papers get across, Hoke Howard gets what he wants, I get what I want, Bluebellies get a smoke, Butternuts get coffee, and then the bell rings and they all rush out to eradicate each other. The world is good."

So it's not dangerous? said Cassius.

"Oh it's dangerous."

Cassius nodded. Then he said: Whitacre's father-in-law, Jarvis, dusted up with Hoke. Afterward, Whitacre came to Sweetsmoke—

"Ah, to 'assess' your goods. Jarvis sent his son-in-law to get even with your master."

I knew he was angry, said Cassius.

"Hoke made too much money when he invested in that fleet of

ships, before the embargo kicked his backside. Jarvis cannot forgive him."

Hoke had already moved the livestock, said Cassius.

"Good for him, anticipating Jarvis, you can't say Hoke doesn't have his moments. Wise move, yes sir, that'd put Old Jarvis in a huff. But this is good for me, I will get an excellent price on the tobacco, very favorable terms. I owe you, Cassius."

Pay your bill by leaving Emoline's money behind.

"You imagine you've earned it, then?"

Cassius shrugged.

"Intelligence and greed, you would be useful to a man in my position. Are you certain you won't take her place? Our friends up North will be greatly disappointed when this information dries up. Not that they know how to utilize it. It would amaze you to know of the self-satisfied generals sitting on their prodigious arses who ignore these dispatches. They'd rather get their intelligence from reading the enemy's newspapers."

Can you tell me how to find this telegraph man? said Cassius.

"I cannot. In an arrangement like this, it is best not to know your compatriots. Do you plan to find him?"

If you know nothing of her killer, then he is my only other link. He will have some information.

Logue shook his head as he began to understand Cassius's plan. "And this is information you must have?"

To find her killer, yes.

Cassius indicated the stain on the floor.

Gabriel Logue began to laugh. "You have had occasion to take note of your reflection, in a looking glass or perhaps a puddle?"

Now and again.

"Then perhaps you are aware that your skin is black, that you are only counted as three-fifths of a man, that you are a slave owned and controlled by your master?"

Most days.

"And you would seek poor Emoline's killer?"

It seems that I would.

"In the midst of a furious war, where dead white men are common and the death of a free black woman carries less weight than that of a horsefly, for when the horsefly meets its end it ceases to be an irritant, you imagine that you will find her killer?"

Cassius placed his hands on either side of the edges of Emoline's table.

No one cares who did this to her, said Cassius softly. She nursed me back to health, taught me to be a man when the world treats me like a boy. The one who did it took a life worth something. If he sat where you sit now, I'd take his life in return this very moment.

Cassius realized that for all the quiet in his voice, he gripped the table rigidly and the legs agitated against the floorboards. He let go and his vision cleared and he was looking in Logue's extraordinary blue eyes. Logue was leaning back, an expression of alarm on his face.

Logue said nothing for a moment, then his expression lightened.

"I'd say it's a god damned good thing I ain't the one who killed her. Lord, I'd love to be a fly on your shoulder when you chase down this man. I do believe you would be an investigator of the most peculiar variety!"

Logue laughed, but when Cassius did not, Logue cut it short.

"Do you have any plausible suspects?"

Beyond her spy connections, she also had clients.

He drew the three pages from his pouch, leaving the W York scrap in place.

"Look at you, Cassius, you're like that fellow Dupin in those Edgar Allan Poe stories, no wait, he was based on a real person, Frenchman, that detective of police, what was his name? Eugène something. Eugène Vidocq, that's it. But Monsieur Vidocq had an advantage over you, he began life as a criminal. Show me this list."

She read their fortunes, said Cassius, sharing the list.

Logue shook his head. "You waste your time here, she provided the gullible with a service, when did a conjuring woman envision futures fraught with *misery*? No, these were paying customers, she'd want their return business, her visions would have been hopeful and mysterious. You hold here a list of the only people who might actually mourn her loss."

You make sense, said Cassius, but he knew he would venture to see them, to know for certain.

"Any other suspects? How about the patrollers?"

Patrollers are fond of ropes and trees.

"I suppose you're right, cracking skulls is not their style. Who else?"

Telegraph man. He will have more information. Or he gave her up to the Confederates, said Cassius.

"And you insist on finding him?"

Cassius said nothing.

Logue thought for a moment. "All right, allow me to offer you some small direction. Say you know something I don't, and you got some idea where this telegraph fellow does his business." Logue glanced at the secret hiding place, as if he knew there had been more information therein. "I don't know how a negro could do it, but let's suppose you get to him. He'll be a Union intelligence man hiding out near railroad tracks, as the telegraph lines run alongside. The first question you ask is: Was Emoline revealed as a spy? If so, then her killer was Confederate."

If she was revealed, then the Union telegraph man might be revealed, which would put him in a Confederate prison, said Cassius.

"Then you'll never find him. But they might have left him in place so that Emoline and the rest of the intelligence team could be rounded up without being forewarned. Cassius, this is a massive undertaking."

Maybe the answer comes more quickly than we expect, said Cassius.

"Eh?"

If someone out in the rain awaits you, then you were also betrayed.

"Hah. Yes. Time to find out," said Logue soberly. He stood and put his hat on his head. Cassius saw him shiver as the cold wet band met his forehead. "You are very much like her."

Like Emoline? said Cassius.

"Not so irritating, but she too was strong and determined."

Yes, said Cassius.

"Perhaps, one day, yond Cassius, the peculiar investigator, will do what she did and search for his name."

Cassius took that as a compliment, Logue suggesting Cassius might one day be free to choose his own name. He understood now that Gabriel Logue had known Emoline a long time, longer than he had suspected. It answered a question he had not known to ask. How had they known to trust each other with intelligence material?

Lucky you already got yours, said Cassius.

"My what, my name?"

The Angel Gabriel, said Cassius.

Logue bowed from the neck in acknowledgment, collected water rolled off his hat brim onto the toes of his boots, and he swept his heavy, saturated coat around to cover his shoulders, this time sending a fine circular spray across the floorboards.

Cassius suddenly found himself saying: Gonna find the mongrel son of a sour bitch. Don't care what it takes, I will run him down.

Logue looked at him with wonder and, Cassius thought, awe.

"Perhaps we will meet again," said Logue, and he stepped into the rain and was gone.

Cassius waited, hearing intense rain against the window, listening for a shout, a gunshot, horse hooves. When he heard none of that, Cassius thought The Angel had safely flown away.

Cassius needed to sit, and found Emoline's favorite chair. He had not known that his commitment went so deep. He sat a long time and embraced the emotion with fear and satisfaction.

He did not know how long he sat, but he roused himself, took his lantern, and returned to the muddy road to slog his way back to Sweetsmoke. He estimated that it was after midnight. The journey home would be slow going.

As he walked, his mind brought forth suspects and he tested them for motive and opportunity. He did not care for Richard Justice, but that did not make the man a killer. If Richard had known where to find the money, Cassius might have seen it differently, but that would mean he was counting on finding the money after her death. Her money was well hidden, and Richard would have known how difficult, unlikely even, it would be to find. From Richard's perspective, Emoline might have hidden it in the deep woods. No, for reasons of his greed alone, Cassius did not think Richard Justice had done it. Maryanne had been in town the night of her murder. Cassius dismissed her as a suspect. Logue had rejected the idea that one of her white clients was guilty, and his reasons had been sound. Cassius's thoughts fell to Gabriel Logue. If The Angel saw an old woman as a danger to his freedom, he would not hesitate to kill her. But Cassius had seen the man's face when he had been informed of Emoline's death. As clever as Logue was, that instant of shock was near impossible to conceal. He put Logue to the side, thinking him unlikely. Hoke Howard had been on Emoline's list. Try as he might, Cassius simply could not conjure a motive for his master to have killed her. If her death was connected to her spying, then his best chance for information was the telegraph operator, but to find him, he would need to understand Emoline's map. He began to formulate a plan and realized he would need Hoke's help, albeit indirectly.

The steady rhythm of rain gradually drummed his thoughts away. He was exhausted and as the intensity of the day released, he felt his energy drain. He was cold, he was wet, and he'd had little sleep. His pace had grown slow in the persistent rain, and he estimated he had yet to reach the halfway point home. Reality set in. How could he possibly find her killer? He tried to push that thought aside, renewing his effort, forcing his legs to move faster, but after some two dozen steps his concentration waned and he drifted back to his original trudge. The weight of his sodden shirt and trousers dragged on him. He lifted his feet and his shoes fought back, thick with water as mud sucked them back into the road. His hat brim scraped the back of his neck and drooped so low in front that it blocked part of his vision. He felt as if he was being swallowed whole by despair. He did not know what it would be like to be free. He yearned for that knowledge, and knew it would never come to pass. He was acquainted with free blacks, Emoline and Richard Justice among them, and they could go where they chose, work when they chose, they *knew* they were free. But they still lived in the South, they were compelled to carry their free papers, and if any random white man was to take those papers or destroy them, they could be sold again into this ferocious life.

Freedom. He had grown to despise the word, tantalizing him with flimsy hope, shimmering in the mocking distance. It meant everything to him and brought him irresistible anguish. He would have preferred to know nothing about the state of freedom, to live in ignorance and hopelessness rather than be tempted by something so odiously out of reach. And then a terrible thought crawled through his body: Suppose freedom did come, what then? He considered himself, Cassius Howard, as a man, and in a blaze of clarity realized that he did not believe that he deserved to be free. What had he done in his life that freedom should be awarded to him? He did not envision himself as a kind man or even a decent man, quite the opposite when he listened to the bitter rage that crusaded through his mind. He helped no one and allowed no one to help him, as he would be obligated to no one. But he feared the true reason: He was pridefully incapable of gratitude. Cassius bemoaned his weakness, and the thought of hunting down Emoline's killer now struck him as pathetic. He cast his eyes down and followed the tiny shaft of light from his lantern as it revealed the muck ahead, puddle surfaces frothing with thick-falling raindrops.

He didn't hear them in the relentless drumming of rain. They came up behind him and he was suddenly surrounded by horses, their hooves splashing water up against his calves and thighs, their lanterns angled into his face.

"He the one?"

"I dunno, turn your lantern more."

"It's turned, damnit!"

Three of them. Cassius barely had the energy to look up, but he knew them, patrollers, Otis Bornock, Isaac Lang, and Hans Mueller. Big, ugly, stupid men who had him, they had him and there was no escape. A small voice cut through his resignation: What the hell were these men doing out in this ungodly weather?

"Don't much matter if he is or not, we got him. What you doin out here this time of night, boy?"

Got a pass, said Cassius.

"Oh, you got a pass, well let's see it, boy, we don't got time to waste on you," said Otis Bornock.

"He say he got a pass," said Hans Mueller in his German-accented English. "Give him the minute."

Cassius wearily moved his right hand to his pouch and realized that the three folded sheets were there with Emoline's map and nothing else. He reached for the band of his trousers but found nothing. Now he was awake, realizing he had not remembered to bring the forged pass.

"Give him the pass," said Hans Mueller.

Seems I lost it, said Cassius.

"I told you this boy was askin for it. Been askin for it a long time. You gonna get yours now, you black bastard."

"Aw, hell, we don't got time for this," said Isaac Lang.

"*Das ist richt*," said Hans Mueller. "We need find the other one."

"We always got time to teach our nigras a lesson," said Bornock.

Why you out tonight? said Cassius.

"Runaway," said Lang.

"Shut up, Lang, don't answer him, what're you answerin him for?" said Bornock.

"Friend a' yours," said Lang.

Who? Who's running? said Cassius.

"Y'see, that's what I hate," said Bornock. "This darky always had a sass mouth, never knew his place. This is it, we teach him a lesson right now."

"Joseph," said Mueller. "Joseph run off tonight. Call us outta beds in the rain."

Cassius sagged at the news.

"Jesus Christ, what's the matter with you, Mule, why you tell him that? Now we got to take care of him, teach him his place, and it's your fault," said Bornock.

Cassius knew he was facing a beating. It would be worse in the cold rain.

"You think I'm gettin down, we got a boy to chase, I ain't gettin down; you want to take time to beat his ass, you do it, Bornock," said Lang.

"All right, then just me and Mule. Come on, Mule."

"You spend last three hour accuse me of steal your gun, and now you want my help? Go on yourself, you always say you hotshot, handle anyone," said Mueller.

"Damn," said Bornock. He angled his horse in front of Cassius and pressed him off the road, into a clear area around a hedge. The other two walked their horses down the road to a stand of trees under which they were partly protected from the rain.

Cassius stood his ground in the clearing, in the light from the two lanterns. Bornock sat on his horse, looking at him. Cassius knew he didn't have his full strength, but he gathered what he had.

"I'm beat your ass," said Bornock.

Come on with it, said Cassius.

Bornock came down out of his saddle into the muck and grass. He hooked his lantern over the horn of the saddle. His horse did not move. Bornock was a big man, he outweighed Cassius and was about the same height.

"You git on over here."

Cassius stayed where he was.

"Damn," said Bornock, and he charged, swinging his short whip. Cassius caught his hand and twisted it, and he felt the uncertainty in Bornock's attack. Bornock had expected help from Lang and Mueller, and when it had not come, he expected Cassius to acquiesce. Now he faced an enemy he did not know. Cassius gained strength and power from this knowledge, and he let Bornock's weight work against him, stepping aside so that Bornock slipped and tumbled in the mud. He came up spitting and his fury made him foolish. He found his feet and moved at Cassius again.

Come on then, give me that lesson, said Cassius. Come on!

Bornock came on in the dim light of the lanterns, but Cassius moved at him now, and landed a solid fist in Bornock's belly. He heard an "oof" as Bornock doubled over, dropping to his knees, sending water out in a wave.

"I'll kill you," said Bornock hoarsely. "We gonna string you up so high the birds won't reach your eyes."

Cassius moved in and grabbed Bornock by the hair.

You do that. You call 'em over, 'cause it goin take all three of you, and you tell 'em they gotta help you 'cause you couldn't handle me. You tell 'em that and I'll wait here.

"Damn," said Bornock and he spit something into the mud.

Or you say you did me good, you say Cassius can't stand up. Tell 'em you let me live so Hoke Howard don't come looking for the two thousand dollars it cost to replace a prime hand.

"Uh," said Bornock, squeezing his eyes together at the pain. He got to his feet, holding his stomach. Cassius took his short whip from him and threw it away in the dark. He noticed Bornock did not have his fancy pearl-handled Colt Army revolver, and realized that he had not seen it earlier, before they came into the clearing.

Bornock moved to his horse. Cassius leaned to pick Bornock's hat out of a puddle and spun it to him. Bornock swung himself into the saddle. Cassius watched Bornock ride back to the road, losing him in the rain but for the light splay of his lantern. The three lanterns joined and for a moment Cassius thought his ploy hadn't worked, but then they moved away together. Cassius picked up his lantern and walked back to the road. He followed the group of three lanterns as they moved ahead, growing smaller.

Big Gus, he thought. Big Gus had done exactly what he'd meant to do, he drove Joseph until Joseph could take it no longer, and now Joseph was running. Cassius hoped Joseph was smart and knew how to get north. The rain clouds would hide the star markers in the sky, but they could also help him avoid the patrollers and slave catchers that Hoke would employ. But things would now be more difficult for Cassius, he would have less room to maneuver as everyone would be on edge. Every white man in the area would be alert and the patrols would increase. If it had been dangerous before, now it was worse.

He came to the small bridge and stopped, listening to the swollen creek rush by under his feet. He thought about his escape from Otis Bornock, and he was gratified. Bornock might brag and preen, but Cassius knew the kind of bully Bornock was. Cassius had instilled fear in the man. Bornock would, from that moment on, always be unsure of himself around Cassius, and was unlikely to bother him again. That at least was something.

-*❀ Chapter Eight ❀*-

CASSIUS stepped into Mam Rosie's kitchen and the intense
heat burned his eyes and pressured his forehead, and his brain
pounded as if expanding. Something in the room was unusual, and
he looked to see that her unmade pallet and personal possessions
were out on the brick floor—if she had not found time to tidy her
few belongings, then she had been hard-pressed, cooking constantly
for the hunters of Joseph. Within the demonically heated air dwelled
good smells that were complex, accented by sweet. He looked to the
great hearth; she had built the fire so that it burned at various levels
of intensity across its full width. Up front, the older glowing coals
slow-roasted embedded potatoes; behind that, a hearty flame licked
the side of a hog set on the spit. To the left, heavy cast-iron pots
hung from trivets, and coals rested on the cover of one pot so that the
insides cooked evenly. Hot as it was, the hearth fire alone would not
have made the room unbearable. He looked to the side wall and saw
heat waves from the brick oven in full burn. She had been all night

bringing the oven to temperature in order to bake. The sweetness was the first boil molasses added to cornbread.

All this food would deplete the stores quickly, and he projected a lean winter.

Lot of rumors out there, Rose, said Cassius.

What you doin here, Cassius, why you come in here today? said Mam Rosie. You see what's goin on.

You think I got something on my mind?

Mam Rosie moved at him swiftly, her corded right arm rising to wag a threatening finger. Don't you pretend with me, Cassius, I raised you, I know you, I know how you think! This a dangerous game you playin, you close to findin yourself with a stretched neck.

What you hear?

You expect to come in all easy sweet and I just tell you?

You know me, Rose, you raised me, you know how I think.

Mam Rosie lowered her finger. Her mouth turned down and her head swiveled side to side, wanting to shake him out of her kitchen and out of her thoughts.

Somethin goin on with you and that little girl? said Mam Rosie with venom.

No, there ain't, he said, meeting her venom.

The hell you say.

You ask, I answer.

Pet is like to git you, Cassius, and I can't say's I blame her. What you got against Tempie?

Never gave her much thought. But she hid that box in the dress of "that little girl," so I ask you: What Tempie got against Quashee? You think Quashee should get sold? You think that fair? You think that right?

So now you all powerful with right and wrong?

Rose, said Cassius softly, I did not know what would come to Tempie. I just know she set out to injure someone who did her no harm, someone who belonged out of the fields.

You never thought maybe Tempie belong out of the fields? You not think that?

I think she had her chance and it didn't go her way.

You are the slipperiest, the snakiest, how you get so damn tall anyway? Someone sneaky as you ought be short and oily.

Cassius thought that he got to be slippery and sneaky because of Mam Rosie, but he said: What you know about Joseph, Rose?

And don't be callin me Rose.

Nobody here but us, said Cassius easily. Tell me about Joseph.

Mam Rosie heard it before Cassius knew anything, a subtle change that caused her to cock an ear, then move directly to the kettle on the right, arriving just as froth bubbled over the lip and sizzled against its outer bowl. She took an iron rod with a C-shaped bend at the end and hooked one leg of the trivet that held the kettle, jerking it two inches off the heat, at which the foam fell back and relaxed to an easy roil. She made mental calculations on the rest, added three coals to the top of the covered pot, nodded to herself, and sat on a low chair setting her elbows on her knees, resting her head forward where her palms covered her eyes.

Took off in the rain, she said.

I know that much.

Goin in the rain was smart, no tracks or scent to follow. Paddy-rollers and them dogs havin a bad time 'cause of it. Even got Ol' Mr. Nettle out there, ridin around like some holy prince, and you know Mr. Nettle ain't been on patrol three year now. They got slave chasers and whites comin in from every plantation, don't want no big ideas gettin in the heads of their nigras, got to make a 'xample out of this one or all our nigras goin think they can run, too.

One rumor is he's caught. Another is he's beaten, whipped, even hanged; can't turn around without a rumor that he had everything done to him that white men can think up to make the rest of us crap the hope out of our sorry asses.

Rumors, she said bitterly. Rumors are Master Lincoln goin free us, lot of good that do. Right now I settle for just one of us gettin away.

So he's not caught.

No, she said wearily, not 'less someone right now bringin him in.

Somebody had to help him.

What for, why somebody had to, can't a man just run? said Mam Rosie, her eyes unfocused.

Man can run. Man can hide for a while, but Joseph ain't much of a man, yet, and if they don't have him already, figures somebody helped him. You think he linked up with that Underground Railroad?

Mam Rosie whirled at him, her face animated: Don't talk 'bout that, don't even think 'bout that!

Emoline was alive, she'd've helped him, said Cassius.

Just wipe that Underground Railroad out your brain, you hear me?

Cassius remembered that Darby had often spoken about the Underground Railroad. Mam Rosie blamed his loose talk for getting him sold.

So he didn't come to you, said Cassius.

Come to *me*?!? Ain't no way that boy comin to me 'bout no railroad. He just a boy, I ain't never sent nobody, specially not a boy.

All right, Rose, all right.

She stared at him, a hard, mean look in her eyes.

He was the only one allowed to call me that, she said.

He called you that in affection, said Cassius.

He was a good man.

Took real good care of me, he said.

You sayin I didn't?

You didn't need a little boy to love you, Rose. When they sold Darby, they took all the love you had.

Mam Rosie stood straighter, and he saw her forcing her mouth tight to cut off the tremble of her lower lip, but in that struggle her entire head began to tremble. She turned away suddenly and made a nervous tour of her kitchen, testing the hog's side and peering into the pots with her back to him, using her apron to wipe her brow and then her eyes and cheeks. After a long moment, she came back to where he stood, cocked her head, and shifted it back to look at him.

You eat today? Look like you could use somethin, she said quietly.

What makes you think I didn't eat?

That thin look in your cheeks.

You living in a dream, said Cassius, feeling exposed.

That's right, thin cheeks and your chin gets sharp and bony, so don't show off that surprised look, Cassius, you think I don't know you? I know you.

Cassius tried to think of something to say, but nothing came, so he waited before he said: Could probably have some of that cornbread you got baking.

Won't give you none of that.

He felt his temper shift.

Thought you just offered, said Cassius.

Missus Ellen got to feelin mean since that boy run off, she come in here and spit in the batter, then say I should cook it up and serve it to the hands. Well, I cooked it, but I ain't goin serve it 'less I serve it to them paddyrollers. Maybe I wait a day and serve it back to her.

Cassius turned to go. Mam Rosie came up behind him, quickly packing something in a clean rag, which he imagined was bread and pork cooked the day before.

You watch yourself, Cassius. Pet like to kill you for what you did, and she whisper in Missus Ellen's ear. Pet be scary when she got somethin to be mad about, and she got somethin to be mad about with you.

All right, Rose.

Never did much like that Tempie, but gettin sold, oh Lordy. She a hard one, but the punishment rainin down on her now, wouldn't wish that on a dead dog.

Cassius again felt strange, responsible, a small fist closing on his heart. He did not trust himself to speak, so he left the kitchen and stepped out into the hot humid day and was glad after the hellish heat of the kitchen to have the sun cool against his skin.

White men came and went in a prodigious show of force, the men who had not gone to war, some who had bought their way out or had more than twenty slaves, some older men with families and businesses and small farms, some from other plantations, some from the town or from neighboring towns. Had it been a premeditated display it could not have been more effective as the hands applied themselves to their work while keeping eyes averted. Every one of the hands understood the white mood and therefore the danger. Cassius felt the planter rage, a rage specific and self-righteous, born of their belief that something that had been settled was now unsettled and they were forced to revisit the issue. Lessons would need to be re-taught, harshly this time, so they would not be forgotten, so that it would be settled once and for all, and this, by God, would be the last time. When these men rode off to hunt Joseph, they rode in a fashion determined to impress the blacks, wearing their strength and authority and supremacy on their sleeves. Any minor slip by their people, misinterpreted or even accidental, would bring on instant, short-tempered retribution, overwhelming force in response to indiscretion, an avalanche of righteous indignation far beyond its warrant. And yet, Cassius contemplated their ferocious masks and recognized something behind them, a hint of fear. He respected their numbers and their rifles, backed by their laws and their authority, but he began to understand their power as tenuous. These men believed that if their slaves were to rise up in revolt, the planters could well reap the whirlwind. As Cassius watched them throughout the morning, he saw their authority as theater.

"Cassius! You there, Cassius, come here now, boy!" said Ellen.

She stood tall on the porch of the big house, her arm raised in the same manner as Mam Rosie's nagging finger, but Ellen's finger was crooked downward, beckoning him to the foot of the wooden steps. He walked evenly to the spot, not rushing the way she would have liked, but not ambling defiantly. He expected to see Pet standing a few steps behind her missus, and he was not disappointed. He tried to anticipate Pet's revenge, but it occurred to him that Pet had not had enough time to manufacture a plan, much less time to insinuate her plan into her missus's ear. Cassius did not underestimate Pet, but he also did not overestimate her intelligence, and he thought that, for the moment, he would be safe.

"Cassius, take the carriage to town to the dry goods and fetch supplies. Mr. O'Hannon has our order so you will not require a list. As everyone else is out capturing the runaway, it will have to be you."

Happy to tote for you, Missus, said Cassius.

"I don't know that I would send you under these circumstances if I felt there was another way," said Ellen.

I understand, Missus.

He did not move from the spot.

"Well? Be off with you," she said.

Need a pass from Master Hoke.

"You know perfectly well that Master Hoke is away bringing back that runaway, and, oh, very well, I will write the pass for you myself."

Ellen disappeared inside and Cassius watched Pet through the door. He tried to see inside the house behind her, to know that

Quashee was all right, but as he was standing in bright sunlight, the room behind Pet was too dark to discern anything.

Pet moved away. Idling, Cassius turned to see Mr. Nettle up on his huge roan talking to Big Gus in the road that ran past the yard. Big Gus carried Mr. Nettle's second rifle across his forearms, offering Mr. Nettle the gun. Mr. Nettle would have found him in the fields and sent him running to his home to fetch it. Big Gus looked up at Mr. Nettle in the saddle and on his face was an expression of humility and faith. Mr. Nettle balanced the rifle between groin and pommel and put his hand on Big Gus's shoulder affectionately, and Cassius curdled inside.

C assius drove the carriage to town. He tried to concentrate on what he would say to the women on Emoline's list but his mind refused to focus. His thoughts wandered to Joseph, and then to Pet, as if he had missed a warning. He knew this was a unique opportunity, rarely did he have permission to enter town alone, and for that reason he needed to utilize this time in the carriage to strategize, as a black man contacting white women was a pernicious act. And yet there was Pet in his thoughts as if she constituted a danger more immediate. Had she suggested sending Cassius into town on his own? Was this journey her plan for revenge, and where would he come upon the trap? He was concentrating so intently that he barely noticed crossing over the little bridge. As he approached town, an odd thing occurred to him: He had seen no patrollers on the road. Clearly the hunters had expanded their circle, reckoning that with each passing hour Joseph was farther away. Cassius wondered if Pet was so clever as to consider that fact. He turned it over in every possible direction. By the time Cassius reached the main street, he had carefully dismissed each of his complex theories and come to the simple conclusion that Pet hoped he might see this as an opportunity and run as well. That would resolve her vengeance, as the punishment he deserved would be meted out by the patrollers, planters, and hired slave catchers who already scoured the countryside. He was relieved by this conclusion, and stopped trying to outthink her. But now he had no time to plan his approach to Emoline's clients.

He guided the carriage down the alley alongside the dry goods store and stepped down, walking to the back. He looked for Frederick the stock boy, but Cassius saw no one among the crates and sacks. He idled a minute, then entered the stockroom and made his way to the door to the main store. He leaned in and saw O'Hannon with a customer, and stepped back. He did not want to deal with O'Hannon. Frederick ran a little business on the side, and Cassius sometimes held back from Weyman a few carved wooden soldiers and other pieces to trade directly with Frederick for hard liquor or other items. Frederick treated blacks in a manner as close to honest and straightforward as could be hoped for. Cassius leaned forward again. The customer was a white woman whose name escaped him. She fingered bolts of fine cloth laid out on the long table that served as O'Hannon's main counter. O'Hannon gazed at her hands with blank disinterest. She would buy nothing off this bolt, nor any of the other high-priced bolts he had laid out for her, but he dutifully brought down the special cloth and waited patiently until she finally called for the rough linen or cotton or the indifferently loomed wool that she would purchase. The cabinet behind O'Hannon was as high as his waist, the shelves above held ewers and clay jars and jugs of various shapes and sizes. O'Hannon kept his small scale there, while the larger rusted scale stood on the floor for bulk items. Along the far wall were the big barrels brimming with barley, oats, and cornmeal, small shovel scoops thrust into the grain. Closer was a barrel holding tools with handles splayed out in myriad directions, hoes, axes, hammers. On the floor in front of the cabinet stood copper pails, large crock pots with flat covers, rough unlabeled muslin bags, and the small barrels holding nails.

He had not meant to loiter and was surprised to hear O'Hannon say, "Cassius, I don't have your whole order together just yet." Cassius's acknowledged presence had broken the spell, as O'Hannon walked away from waiting on the woman so that she was able to enjoy the fine fabric without O'Hannon hovering.

I got time, said Cassius.

"Probably be half hour, Frederick's out on delivery. Mrs. Howard will be most happy about the watercolor paints she was waiting on."

Cassius went out the way he had come.

He walked down the back alley behind the businesses where the mud was thicker and the trash stank. He was safer walking here and made his way east. The easternmost area of town housed the poor whites, the greatest concentration of whom were in the southern section, primarily the Anglo-Saxon community; in the northeast were the German immigrants, clustered in a smaller enclave. The small German farms spread out to the north, farming some of the poorest soil in the county. In between the two communities but closer to the Germans were the homes of the few freed blacks, but as the white communities expanded, they began to interlock around the black homes.

The houses were small and gave the impression that they were in need of repair. Cassius attributed that more to hasty design, shoddy raw materials, and apathetic craftsmanship rather than to a lack of upkeep. He located the house for which he searched and, after his confident march, looked at it with uncertainty. Many of the homes were similar. He knew her front door was white and this door was white, but so was the door to the neighbor's dwelling. He hesitated. He now doubted his memory. He chose a circle of shade under an ancient maple and stood against its trunk, hoping for a chance sighting of the house's inhabitant. The street was empty. For the moment, he was aware that he was not surrounded, and he had an odd sensation of freedom. Yet he had little time to spare on personal pleasure as a black man here would soon attract attention. Minutes passed and his uncertainty grew as his need to get off the street increased. Another minute and he decided to be bold. He would approach the house and pay the price if he was wrong. And then he did not move, muscles betraying his mental choice. In a burst of brio, he propelled himself out of the shade to the wooden door painted white. He raised his fist to knock.

She opened the door and he removed his hat and lowered his eyes, relieved. He would need to access his best subservient manner, and he was never certain he could rely on it to appear when beckoned.

"What you want?" she said with displeasure.

Missus Crowe?

"Yeah, I'm Mrs. Crowe."

Sally Ann Crowe?

"I don't think you better be usin that name."

Sorry, ma'am, but I just had to come.

"You had to come? What's that mean?"

It's the message, ma'am.

"Well, why didn't you say so in the first place, give it me."

Well, ma'am, I'se awful sorry, but it ain't that sort of message.

"Do you have a message for me or not?"

Yes ma'am.

"Then give it."

He looked at her—pale bloated face, small bland eyes too far apart, long stringy dishwater blonde hair that clung to her cheek, fleshy nose, weak chin—and he said: This a message from Emoline Justice.

He watched her expression for the flicker of horror that might come from a murderer realizing she had not finished her crime. He saw only confusion and imbecility. The moment passed in a flash, but convinced him that Sally Ann Crowe had not murdered Emoline Justice. Nevertheless, he had to carry out the remainder of his plan so that he raised no suspicions.

"Emoline? But she died a few weeks ago."

Like I say, ma'am, this a different kind of message.

Sally Ann Crowe's expression changed to one of wonder. A great intake of air, and she said, "From beyond the grave!"

That's so, ma'am.

"Go around back," she said and disappeared into the house closing the door in his face. He walked around to the back, where he waited. She came out the rear door and sat to face him, fussing with her hair, as if to fancy up before receiving the message.

"Tell me, tell me about her message," said Sally Ann Crowe, and Cassius thought that if she had been a child, she would have clapped her hands in anticipation.

He could easily have told her something simple and hurried away, but her enthusiasm brought out the sadist in him.

Well, ma'am, it go back alla way to the whole reason you was goin to see Emoline in the first place, said Cassius, needing her to fill in a few blanks if he was to pull this off.

"So it's about Lawrence. He all right? He not killed?"

Ah, there, thought Cassius, something to work with. Sally Ann Crowe had visited Emoline worried about her husband Lawrence.

To be sure. It about Lawrence.

"Yankees git him yet?"

Emoline say Lawrence be all right, said Cassius.

Sally Ann Crowe exhaled. "Emoline must've looked around Heaven for him, and seen that he warn't there," she said quietly. "'Course, never know where he end up."

I do believe that's it exactly, said Cassius. He was flush with power, a white woman hung on his every word.

They give the special ones a high perch up there, and we both know how special Emoline was, said Cassius.

"Oh yes."

How he enjoyed exalting Emoline. Sally Anne Crowe would never argue with a message from beyond. Inside, he was as giddy as a child.

But you know Emoline, she may be gone, but she remembers the good folks she left behind.

"Dear Emoline."

She tell me she want you to know she lookin out for the special ones.

"Lord have mercy, she is a good woman." Sally Ann Crowe smiled a heartbreakingly innocent smile of pleasure. Oh my, he was enjoying this.

She lookin down on what's happenin right now, said Cassius.

"A woman of amazing gifts."

Said she been able to see through the mists and seen your Lawrence.

"She can see him, too?"

Down there on the battlefield, thinkin 'bout you.

"*My* Lawrence?" she said looking mystified and Cassius missed the clue.

Wishin he was back here with you.

"So he could slap me around some more."

Cassius leaned back in surprise, and the giddiness abandoned him in a rush.

"Didn't get enough 'fore he left, so he learned new tricks in the war, come on back and try 'em all on his dutiful wife," she said with revulsion.

Lawrence hit you? said Cassius, suddenly tentative.

"Make sure Emoline warns me when he's comin back. Best thing ever happened when he went off to war, every night I pray some

Union Bluebelly gits him 'fore our boys finish teachin them Yanks a lesson so they can all come on home without him."

Emoline will surely watch for you, said Cassius cautiously.

"Lord knows, somebody needs to."

He was more tentative when he said: I got this other message, you know a lady name of Abigail Dryden?

Abigail Dryden had been the last appointment in Emoline's pages, the one scheduled for the day after she was murdered.

"You think I'd know someone like that?"

Cassius held his tongue in the face of his second misstep.

"I seen that trollop bringin men in the back of her house, the first one not three weeks after her Chester went off in his uniform. Abigail Dryden." Sally Ann Crowe's cheeks had colored. "It worse when those quartermaster boys come through. She just as well leave her back door wide open."

Cassius came to the belated conclusion that he would have made a poor seer. Emoline had obviously collected more and better information before she waded in with advice.

Why you think Abigail goes to see Emoline?

"Women things, of course, potions," said Sally Ann Crowe, then caught herself as if she had revealed too much.

Cassius made an excuse to leave and found his way back through the empty alleys to the dry goods. Logue had been right. He mentally scratched Sally Ann Crowe and Abigail Dryden off his list. He considered Sally Ann Crowe's disapproval of Abigail, and imagined that Sally Ann had her own competing business, paying back her Lawrence by renting out his bed by the hour.

O'Hannon had a new customer, one Cassius did not recognize, but her clothes were fine and her manner rigid, likely a newcomer to Little Sapling or Philadelphia Plantation.

"I am so sorry it has taken so long, Mrs. Worthington, but the quartermaster was in earlier to supplement the assessment he gets from the locals."

Worthington would make her from Little Sapling, the niece come down from Maryland.

"Yes," said the planter woman, "we are fully acquainted with the quartermaster's assessments."

O'Hannon laughed uncomfortably. "Well, apparently there are things that cannot be gotten from a plantation."

"How disturbing," she said with wintry sarcasm.

Frederick came in behind Cassius. "I'll take care of you, Cassius."

Out in back, Cassius and Frederick loaded the carriage with some difficulty, as it was designed to haul not goods but passengers. Frederick informed him that he had a bottle for sale, but Cassius had brought nothing to trade and declined.

Quartermaster comes to dry goods for supplies? With the whole countryside to forage? said Cassius.

"Word is, Whitacre and his men hunt for a spy. Other than that they wouldn't bother, but quartermasters aren't issued ordnance the same as fighting troops so they came for ammunition and rifles. Probably tried to assess them from the plantations unsuccessfully. Now you sure you don't want that bottle?"

So he hasn't found his spy yet?

"Not so's I've heard. Apparently they've gone north looking for someone."

Cassius flicked the reins. Sam lifted his chin and stepped forward and Cassius knew he needed to do nothing more as the horse was familiar with the way home. Whitacre had gone after the telegraph operator. He wondered if Whitacre knew about W York. Cassius felt the pressure mount, he needed to get to the telegraph operator first.

-=※ Chapter Nine ※=-

MAM Rosie ventured out to assist Cassius as he unloaded the carriage, but he waved her off. Pet came out the back door of the big house holding up the bottom corners of her apron transporting a small treasure, walking briskly toward the kitchen with her head down, lost in thought. Halfway there she raised her eyes and stopped as she saw him. He smiled at her. Unable to disguise her dismay, she stumbled to hurry back inside, releasing one corner of her apron, and a dozen small green tomatoes tumbled to the ground. Then it was quiet but for the buzz hum of insects and the fierce caw from a crow. He wandered over and stooped to collect the tomatoes, wiping dirt from their thick skins with his thumb, finding them too immature to be bruised. He left them in a pile by the rear door and wandered back to the carriage. He returned to the unloading, and shortly thereafter Quashee emerged from the rear door, stopped to note the tiny green pile, and crossed through the vegetable garden to the carriage. His deliberate indolence had brought him his reward.

I knew you were back when I saw Pet's face, said Quashee.

She was sorry not to see me in chains.

You mean she wishes you in chains, or she thought it might happen?

Possibly both, said Cassius.

You all right? said Quashee with marked alarm, and her eyes ran up to the second-story window of Ellen's bedroom. The curtains did not move.

Way I see it, she told Ellen to send me hoping I'd follow Joseph into the bushes.

But, you been to dry goods before?

Not usually alone.

And she thought this time was different?

Patrollers all spread out after Joseph. She hoped I'd jump at the chance. Anything about him yet?

Nothing, said Quashee.

Maybe he got away, said Cassius.

Too soon to know. Lot of patrollers. You see Savilla?

Hard for her, she hopes he gets away, but maybe that's bad for Sammy and Andrew. Old Hoke could break up the family from spite. I don't think she sleeps, I hear she fell exhausted yesterday in the fields.

Terrible to have children, said Quashee.

Terrible?

In this life. Terrible to love something, all they do is rip it away, and that's just 'cause they can, said Quashee.

Never heard you talk like that.

Saw it all when Master John-Corey died.

Cassius nodded, but said nothing. She looked off in the direction of the fields and the harsh crow scolded them.

How is it for you inside? said Cassius.

Work's same as Master John-Corey's. Hard to care for invalids, they get mean, but the bad parts are over quick and it's quiet awhile before she yells again. Missus Sarah don't read aloud to her servant, and Pet don't want me near Missus Ellen, thank you for that, so I got a bit of my own time. Pet won't help me none, which when I think of it, is likely a blessing, but Nanny Catherine acts nice and says Missus Sarah happier with someone to boss. Pet can't look at me. I see her eyes red from crying, and can't help but feel sorry for her.

She'd've had you in chains bound for Louisiana.

All right, but I'm still sorry.

Can't say that I'm sorry, said Cassius, although he knew he was.

She's sneaking a look out Missus Ellen's window, carry something inside, said Quashee.

I don't care—

Go on, don't be a fool.

They both carried sacks into the kitchen, and Mam Rosie gave them a significant look, then stepped outside to leave them alone.

I got to get into the big house, said Cassius, stepping close to her and speaking quickly and quietly.

What, being a fool ain't enough, now you got to be a crazy person? said Quashee, and she also spoke quietly, matching his urgency.

Got to get something from Hoke's study.

I'll get it.

No, Pet's watching you just waiting for a mistake, she'll get you linked to a coffle to follow Tempie. We make a signal after dark, you let me know when the planters sleep and it's safe. That leaves you on your pallet so if I'm caught, no one knows about you. The only way I do it, said Cassius.

I don't like it.

Or I come in when I think it's right.

Her expression revealed what she thought of that idea.

What kind of signal? she said.

Where do you sleep in the house?

Attic over Missus Sarah's bedroom, so I can hear her at night if she needs me.

Alone?

One night there was Nanny Catherine, but she usually stays in the young'uns' bedroom. Most sleep on the floor near their masters, Pet like to hold Missus Ellen in her arms if she could, and Miss Genevieve and Missus Anne and all them, their servants sleep in trundle beds pulled out from under their mistress's beds.

Your attic got a window?

Small one, in the gable.

Got room to set a candle there?

Think so.

You light it and I'll know family's down for the night.

How do I know what night?

Cassius looked at the fires in Mam Rosie's hearth as he thought for a moment.

You watch for a signal from me, said Cassius.

Can't see the quarters from the big house.

No, but you can see the carpentry shed.

No window in that one.

Watch the chimney, I saw a stack of elm logs somewhere and even old elm makes good smoke. Make that my signal.

Lit candle if it's safe, said Quashee.

Good. I'll watch tonight.

No. Not tonight. Too many patrollers come in and out at night, and Master Hoke's not even back yet. Not tonight.

Then watch for the smoke tomorrow. After supper. Look for it.

C assius spent the better part of the following day working in and around the carpentry shed. He located an old pile of elm logs near the slave graveyard and rolled them to the shed in a wheelbarrow. He climbed the shed roof as if checking for a leak and looked to see that the view was clear from the attic's gables. He walked around the shed to locate an innocuous place from where he might see Quashee's signal. He found a likely spot. He rolled a wide log and stood it on one flat end, the other end his seat. He was ready for night to fall, with the sun still high in the sky.

In the middle afternoon, a vibration came through the ground, almost unnoticed until the tools in the shed softly chimed as they touched. The vibration grew until he looked up with the air throbbing deep in his ears and in that moment he knew fear. They were coming, all of them together, men and horses, and that meant things had gone bad. Hooves agitated the hill and he knew the dishes would be rattling in the big house and every living soul would be running to the windows and he didn't want them to witness what was about to happen. He moved to the door of the shed and came off the step onto the ground, holding the doorjamb as if the vibration might knock him off his feet, but it wasn't vibration that made him unsteady, it was the awful weakness in his legs. He walked to the front yard and they were coming up the hill, he estimated at least a score. Dust trailed them and the wind came around briefly and blew the dust ahead, burying them in a cloud from which they emerged, bigger, closer, closer. Their expressions were grim not in defeat but with self-satisfied victory. Cassius expected them to stop in the yard before the big house, but they did not turn at the gate, riding instead past to the quarters. He saw one riderless horse and realized that a body was secured across the back of the horse face-down, arms and legs lashed underneath. The trailing cloud of dust rolled silently over him and consumed the big house. When it passed, they were out of sight around the bend, most likely already passing the house of Mr. Nettle.

Cassius ran down the path to the quarters. The pounding of the hooves stopped suddenly and he knew they had reined in and now waited in the lane. He arrived to see Otis Bornock and Hans Mueller cut the body free and pull on its arms to drop it facedown in the dirt. The others sat waiting on their horses as Mr. Nettle's iron bell rang. It was a few minutes before the first hands came in from the fields, and they made a semicircle facing horses and men, staring at the body in the lane. Cassius had hoped for his sake that he was dead, but then Joseph moved and Cassius heard a dry pitiable moan rasp out of his throat and Cassius's heart sank lower, to scratch its own place in the dust. Blood was everywhere on Joseph with none of it on the ground. Trails of dried blood coursed along the outsides of his arms and down the backs of his hands and made a perfect line along each of his fingers to where it collected in small oval bubbles on his nails. Blood was slick on his neck and his hair was matted with syrupy nubbles of coagulate grume. His trousers were soaked a deep luxuriant red, and as Cassius looked at his back, he felt his own quiver with empathy and felt wetness inside his shirt. Joseph's back was slashed and furrowed and swollen and shreds of his shirt had been driven deep into his wounds. And yet, when Cassius looked at the back of Joseph's legs, he knew the worst was to come. They were waiting for the hands to assemble before performing surgery. He saw the dull bowie knife in Otis Bornock's hand, and he was almost glad because Bornock was a dull and impatient butcher and might bungle the job and Joseph might yet lose enough blood to allow him to die.

Fawn began to shriek into her hands as she drew close, dancing from one foot to the other with her eyes set on Joseph's back. Banjo George leaned in, inching forward as he gaped with fascination, absorbing every last mark of Joseph's pain.

Savilla ran up the lane from the fields. One of the hands stepped in her path, but she pushed him aside. She went straight at Fawn and slapped her soundly across the face, and Fawn's eyes went round and she stopped her noise. Abram came behind Savilla but held up a few yards short and Cassius saw that Sammy and Andrew were farther down the lane and would come no closer. Hoke nodded to a rider Cassius did not recognize, and the rider spurred his horse to block Savilla, but she bellowed and with her heavy legs and tree-trunk arms tried to push the horse aside to get to her son. The rider finally quit and she was around him standing over Joseph. She could not safely touch him without causing more pain, so she just stood there, her legs wide as if he had only then emerged bloody from her womb, her arms reaching out in an empty embrace, hands opening and closing in a gesture so helpless that Cassius felt tears burn his eyes. She whimpered for her baby boy and no one moved to her side. Abram stayed back and the others shied away. Big Gus marched up the path, saw Savilla, and walked straight for her. The unattractive Polly reached out, a subtle but knowing hand catching his forearm to hold him back. Big Gus stopped, looked at it, and she took her hand away. He then continued his march to Savilla. He offered his broad chest, steel arms moving to enwrap her. She accepted the welcome gesture, unable to take her eyes off her boy, but then she recognized Gus's smell and her head reared back and her eyes opened wide in feral revulsion. Abram quickly came, surrounding her arms before she could lash out, guiding her to the older women of the quarters who smothered her fury. Abram turned to Big Gus, and Cassius saw what would come and moved to support him, but then Abram's head dropped, mimicking a bow. Big Gus put his hand on Abram's shoulder affectionately and they stood that way, a frozen moment, and Cassius thought he would be physically ill.

Cassius looked up at Hoke and saw that his whip encircled the pommel of his saddle. Blood from the ends had darkened the leather with drops that ran down toward the stirrups, spreading sideways. Splatters of Joseph's blood resembled a pox on the backs of Hoke's hands with more hurled up his sleeve and across the front of his shirt, while a red streak remained on his cheek from where he had tried to wipe his face. In Hoke's eyes Cassius saw no satisfaction, only a deep exhaustion from the grueling search that had lasted many days and nights. Hoke would pay each man for his part, and Cassius wondered if there was coin enough for all or if Hoke would give them paper. That would disappoint them.

"Do it," Hoke said, and his voice was pitched high, thick with phlegm.

Otis Bornock wiped the dull blade against his shirt and dropped to one knee, rolling up Joseph's trouser leg. No one moved to help him, and he looked up and said, "Get down here and hold him!"

Hans Mueller stepped in and Isaac Lang quickly came off his mount. One held Joseph's foot and the other leaned his entire bulk against his legs and buttocks, staying clear of his back. Bornock angled the knife, choosing an awkward angle that would do the most damage, and he commenced to split the skin with great effort too high above the heel, sawing through muscle until he scraped the Achilles tendon. Joseph's head and back reared up and a sound came out of him that chilled Cassius, a sound he would not soon forget. Cassius thought of young, pretty Fanny at Edensong Plantation and knew that as much as she liked that white tuft in Joseph's hair, she would settle for a husband with less damage. Not one of the hands made a sound but Banjo George smiled, and Cassius thought the insects and birds had gone dumb. Bornock looked up when it was done and said, "The other one?"

Cassius almost cried out, ready to intervene, which would have been worse than pointless as it would have brought him into the circle of Hoke's rage, but Hoke said, "No, that will do."

Cassius turned away, but his eye caught the eye of one of the hunters, Thomas Chavis, the owner of Weyman. He saw the disgust and horror in the man's face, and was grateful for that small shred of human conscience. Cassius walked away, and behind him heard Hoke issue orders, "Take him to the tobacco shed and shackle him."

Cassius did not remember anything of the rest of that afternoon. He did not remember hearing the men on their horses come back up to the big house to get paid, did not remember hearing them ride off singly or in small groups, but after a time he knew they were all gone.

Cassius, come, come quick!

Quashee was running toward him.

Something wrong with him, hurry!

Cassius ran, swiftly overtaking her and came around the side of the big house where Beauregard was trying to drag Hoke inside with his arms under Hoke's armpits. The women were bees bursting from the house, Genevieve at the door, Anne in the lane, Ellen at Hoke's side, all buzzing madly, pointlessly.

Set him down, said Cassius to Beauregard firmly.

"Don't put him down, get his feet!" said Ellen, and her corrosive panic sprang at him.

No, Missus, said Cassius quietly, with grave authority.

"Get the doctor," said Ellen. "Someone take the carriage, go to town, get the doctor!"

"I saw the whole thing, he got off his horse, the groom took it, and then he was on the ground," said Genevieve to anyone who would listen.

Cassius knelt over Hoke and looked for signs of a wound, but the only blood on him was Joseph's.

Hoke spoke quietly and Cassius moved in to hear. "Time to meet the angel," he said.

Not yet, said Cassius so that no one else could hear.

"He awaits me."

House servants crowded them as they saw Hoke speak, and Cassius stood and his cold expression forced them back. They would never understand the pride Hoke took in maintaining his power in front of his people, and despite Cassius's anger, he did not want his master to be seen like this.

"Cassius," said Hoke, his voice thin.

You know me?

"Yes, of course," said Hoke, sounding more like himself.

Are you injured? said Cassius.

"That stupid boy, that stupid stupid child," said Hoke, shaking his head mournfully.

Joseph, said Cassius.

"Get him up!" shrieked Ellen.

Just wait! said Cassius severely, and Ellen stepped back, shocked and silenced.

"I am so tired, Cassius, so very tired," said Hoke.

I know, said Cassius gently.

"Poor stupid boy."

Been out after him for days, said Cassius.

"Barely slept, cannot remember what it is to sleep."

You'll sleep soon and you'll be well, said Cassius.

Cassius slid one arm under Hoke's back, the other under his knees and lifted him in his arms. Standing, he saw Pet in the door. He scowled, looked around, saw Quashee and nodded to her.

Make a path, said Cassius.

Quashee moved ahead and he carried Hoke through the door and to the cool inside. She led him to the staircase and he followed her up directly to Hoke's bedroom. He laid Hoke down on the bed and removed his left boot. Ellen breezed in behind him, followed by her daughters with the servants hovering in the hallway, scandalized that Quashee and Cassius should be in the Master's bedchamber.

"I did it, Cassius," said Hoke.

Over now, said Cassius.

"My fault, mea culpa, I did it. You try to be a good master, you do not mean to kill, they are your property," said Hoke.

With any luck, he'll live, said Cassius.

"I love them all, you understand," said Hoke.

You're tired, said Cassius.

"You most of all."

You'll sleep.

"Oh Lord I killed her."

Cassius stopped then, the second boot halfway off, and he moved up near Hoke's face, put his hand on Hoke's forehead and felt fever.

Who did you kill? said Cassius.

"Lord forgive me. We both did, we both killed her."

Emoline?

"Emoline?" said Hoke. "What do you mean Emoline?"

No, thought Cassius, it had not been Hoke. He had known it before, but this made it final. Cassius weighed what Hoke was saying, and suddenly knew Hoke spoke of Tempie Easter. Both Cassius and Hoke had been involved in her sale, and her life expectancy had grown suddenly short. Perhaps Hoke had had news about her from Lucas Force, the slave trader.

Cassius shook his head. He could more easily live with the responsibility as Quashee had been saved from Tempie's fate. But Hoke felt it and it ground him down. Cassius was not inclined to make Hoke's conscience easy.

Cassius got the second boot off and left the rest to the others. Hoke would sleep first and they would clean him later. Cassius turned and his eyes met Ellen's, and the full look she gave was something unknown. Later he would wonder if it was jealousy, but the ambiguity of the look made an impression on him.

Cassius walked by Quashee and said: Tonight.

She appeared startled, but he knew, with the house in an uproar, the time would never be better. He walked down the hallway to the stairs, then through the downstairs and back out into the hot sun. The yard was free of planters and servants, leaving him with the occasional cat and a high-stepping bantam rooster, a strange and astonishing emptiness after so many men, horses, planters, and hands had passed through on this foul and rancid afternoon.

⇜ Chapter Ten ⇝

THE lights in the big house were snuffed, but he remained seated on the log he had positioned for the occasion. He had long since allowed his cigar to go out. It was late enough that the moon had risen. He watched the roof where moonlight etched the triangular shapes of the three gables. He had not bothered to burn elm logs in the carpentry shed hearth. Quashee would light her candle when it was time, there in the window on the far left, two stories above Hoke's den. So intent was he on the triangles under the moon that his eyes played tricks and he watched the shapes change, bloom and contract until they degenerated into dancing dots.

It was some time before a glow lit the inner top rail of the sash, grew brighter as a hesitant flame quavered into the left lower pane, then settled to a steady burn. He abandoned his cold cigar on the stump. He made his way to the back side of the privy, which was built to be hidden from the big house, in a cluster of trees. He again fingered the pouch inside his shirt, as he had obsessively throughout the evening, to know the friction matches he thought he would need remained safely therein. He clung briefly to the rim of the trees, his eyes checking every window until he settled his gaze on the rear door closest to Hoke's den. All remained quiet and peaceful as the candle burned for him in the third-floor window. He had heard Mr. Nettle finish his final rounds hours before, locking barns and sheds to prevent theft by the hands—he left the carpentry shed to Cassius—but the big house doors were generally kept unlocked. Cassius left the shadow of the trees, quick across the open land through the moonlight, skirting the vegetable gardens, rushing to the big house, and reaching the shadow made by the big house in the moonlight, glancing one last time up at the gable. From his extreme low angle he saw the glow in the window abruptly vanish and he thought the candle was extinguished. He paused right there, in shadow but still in the open. A warm breeze passed through the rows of vegetables, shivering the tomato plants while broad flat watermelon leaves scraped dryly together. An emerging cauliflower head nudged his knee. He weighed his options. Had she blown out the flame, or did the angle deceive? He backed up a step into moonlight and was convinced the candle was out. Quashee was clever but also cautious. She may have extinguished the candle because she had seen him cross, making the signal no longer necessary. Or something had happened and she was attempting to warn him. He had to move from this exposed place, but retreat to the privy, or press on? He knew this to be a unique opportunity and he had but a small window to complete his mission; the family would be exhausted by the ordeal of the runaway, followed hard on by the master's illness. Optimism and hunger for information trumped caution and he ventured forward. The door was unlocked.

He stood inside at the back of the great greeting room near the large fireplace and allowed his eyes to adjust. After a few moments he was surprised at how well he could see. Silver light from the plump waning moon angled in through the large windows in front, and he could readily make out the stairs to his right as well as the breezeway that led to the dining area and other rooms. To his left was the closed door to Hoke's study. He moved to the middle of the room but rather than rush to his task, he stopped and was still for a moment. He listened attentively to a particular quiet that he had never before experienced. This was his first visit to the big house in the dead of night when the planter family and their servants slept. He heard the cavernous hush as the outdoor world was kept at bay, banished by strong walls and windows and multiple stories piled above. Within that hush came small irregular creaks as wood cooled and settled, or someone above turned in sleep. He focused on the quiet, a sound that so amazed him, he was in danger of becoming hypnotized. He became aware of his own shallow breathing and then noted in his ears a high-pitched whine. He attributed the whine to the heft of moonlight pressing great silver rectangles against the floor. He took a step toward Hoke's study and a floorboard creaked under his foot. He stopped and listened for warning shouts and running feet, but heard none. Just as he was about to move again, he saw a flash of movement on the ground and felt something tickle his leg and his heart leapt, and he used all his strength to prevent himself from crying out. He looked down to see Charles's favorite black-and-white cat running the side of her head against the back of his calf. He tried to slow the racing of his heart, which was so forceful his chest felt as if it might burst. He knelt and gave her a scratch around the ears as prelude to shoving her away. She returned, bumped again, and commenced to purr. Her purr was unacceptably loud and he walked rapidly and silently, cat trailing, to the study door. He touched the knob, she slithered between his ankles, the door opened a crack and the cat bumped it wide open with her head, bounding inside. He closed the door behind him to seal in her treacherous noise.

Ellen Corey Howard gazed down at him from her portrait on the far wall beside the bookshelf he had built. His heart slowed to a tolerable pitch. He could see equally well in here as another great window invited the moon. He observed the way moonlight bent, coming through the blown glass windows, the whorl pattern creating light and dark spots on the floorboards and rug. Charles's cat sprang into Hoke's chair, rolled herself into a ball, and lifted her hind leg straight up, licking its length with a purr that occasionally slipped into nasal clatter. He slid open the flat wide drawer with Hoke's maps and carried an armload to the window to examine them in the light. He found a recent map of the county and another, older map of the Commonwealth of Virginia, and set those aside. He found maps of the Mediterranean Sea, Southern France, and the ports of England.

Hoke had marked the shipping lanes, following the routes of his fleet. Cassius found maps unrelated to shipping, maps of land-bound European countries and Asian countries, maps that Hoke collected for the sake of collecting. He found maps of coastal Northern states, several maps of the Chesapeake Bay, a map of New Orleans, as well as a number of maps that detailed the Mississippi River. Some maps were works of art and some were indifferent presentations of basic information. He returned all but the first two to the drawer. He rolled up the county map and the Virginia Commonwealth map. He started to the door, but returned to the shelves on a whim, reached for and liberated Hoke's copy of *The Tragedy of Julius Caesar*. Charles's cat sat up, alert, leg still high, looking at the door. Cassius saw moonlight glint off her eyes as she looked at him. She thumped to the floor and Cassius moved to the door, book under his arm, rolled maps in his hand. He opened the door quietly, hoping the cat would leave first, providing an explanation to any curious family member as to the source of any suspicious noise. But Charles's cat was not there. Cassius looked back and did not see her. As this was a poor moment to be polite to a house pet, he slipped back into the great greeting room and heard the soft click of the door behind him. He listened to detect from which direction the danger would come. The ambient sound in the house had changed. Initially he was unable to identify the cause of the change, only that the hush was no longer prevalent. He angled his head and determined the sound came from above. He moved to the shadow of a wooden chiffonier. He narrowed himself within the shadow, as it would have been impossible to reach the door to the outside before being discovered.

Gentle footsteps along the upstairs hallway had arrived at the top of the staircase. It was clear to Cassius that the person stepped quietly in an effort to remain undiscovered. This gave him hope that Quashee would descend the stairs. But he hoped with his emotions; his analytical mind knew it was not Quashee. By revealing herself, she might reveal his presence, and that was a thing she would know not to do. With chilling apprehension he realized it was Pet. She had discovered his plan to steal into the big house and had waited for him. He had underestimated her; she had lurked in the upstairs hallway while he finished acquiring that for which he had come, waiting for him to emerge from Hoke's study with his thieving hands full of evidence, and now she was coming down the stairs anticipating her sweet sweet revenge. How idiotically bold he had been, making the sort of mistake every slave learned to avoid in childhood. Cassius girded himself for exposure.

He saw a bare foot placed on a step, the hem of a floor-length dressing gown stretching to follow, her other foot dropping to the next step. But these were not Pet's feet, her skin was African dark with light-colored soles. The feet on the stairs were as pale as the dressing gown, and step by cautious step she descended until she was at the bottom, a casual hand on the banister. From his shadow, Cassius was wholly amazed, as he did not recognize this woman with her black tangled hair that spilled to her shoulders. He became convinced she was an unearthly spirit. She turned and moonlight reflected from a low angle, illuminating her face, and he recognized Jacob's wife, Sarah, a woman he had not seen in at least a year.

Sarah pressed her feet flat against the floorboards and he heard her toes excitedly drumming against the wood. Her hands reached down in a gesture common to a formal ball and between forefingers and thumbs she lifted her gown so that the hem rose and exposed her legs up to her knees. She curtsied to an invisible partner, leaned her body one direction, then with a wide smile she released in the opposite direction, her feet moving rapidly in an ecstatic, silent waltz. Her handsome partner led her, and she spun and circled the room. Her dressing gown was buttressed by imagined petticoats, and she swept around chairs and on and off rugs, into and out of the moon boxes on the floor, a dance of exultant freedom. She twirled close to him at one point and he heard that she murmured a tune as she whispered the one-two-three, da-dum-dum that propelled her dance, and in her wake he smelled her acrid bed sweat.

Cassius understood at that moment that Sarah had been feigning illness, confining herself to her bed to punish her mother-in-law, Ellen's daughters, and the big house servants. He was grudgingly impressed with her willful manipulative power, to have carried out this charade for almost a year out of sheer spite. He wondered how often she danced alone in the night. Perhaps this was a regular occurrence, her nighttime exercise, a preventive to atrophied muscles and bed sores.

But his wonder gave way to immediate alarm as the dance continued. With each sweep of the room, he was in ever greater danger of being discovered, and this threat was more extreme than if he had been trapped by Pet. He might talk his way out of that trouble, might indict Pet herself, might bribe her or find some other way clear of her accusations. But a black man who watched a white woman dance in her nightdress with her legs exposed was as good as dead. He would be lynched and no one would wait to hear his explanations; the moment he was discovered, they would secure his hands and drag him to the nearest branch to be hoisted high in the air by the neck. So certain was this punishment that he struggled to breathe, feeling the rope closing around his throat. He tried to make himself smaller in the shadow, but he dared not move lest she peripherally perceive the motion.

Sarah circled the room a fourth time, a fifth, and Cassius heard a gentle scratching as Charles's cat tested the door from inside Hoke's study. He tightened further at this wretched timing. The cat then quit scratching and emitted a soft meow. She bumped the door with her head. Silence. Suddenly her scratching took on a frantic aggression. Cassius clenched his hand in a fist, trying to will the cat into silence so that she didn't give him away.

He hoped that Sarah's dance was just loud enough, not to wake the others, but to drown out the cat's exertions with her own. She chose different pathways around the furniture with each rotation, and at any moment she could turn her head and be looking directly at him. He waited for when she would stop and shriek, and he wondered if he should run and risk being recognized. How long would she dance? He hoped she might change her route to waltz through the breezeway to the dining area; if she did that, he would make a break for the rear door.

She stopped abruptly and looked toward the top of the stairs. The cat meowed with greater impatience behind the study door, and Sarah's head twitched in that direction as for the first time she realized the cat was closed in the study and the noise she made was Sarah's enemy. Cassius had been unable to hear anything but the cat and Sarah's dance. Sarah, however, had heard something else. She struggled to control her breath, her eyes open wide. In the skewed rectangle of moonlight with the whiteness of her gown aglow, she let the hem drop. If another person joined her there in the greeting room, the likelihood of Cassius being discovered increased, and he felt the window of opportunity rapidly closing. She did not move and still he heard nothing. The silence rushed in and then a faint voice from above broke into the hush.

Missus Sarah?

She fled to a shadow between the staircase and the breezeway, in position to rush upstairs if the opportunity presented itself. Charles's cat meowed, and Cassius was convinced that Sarah also cursed the animal.

Missus Sarah? That you I hear down there?

Cassius recognized Quashee's whisper. She was risking the displeasure of her mistress in order to help Cassius escape. Cassius saw Quashee's small feet descending the stairs, weightless on her toes. Quashee's nightdress did not fall below her knees and her person was revealed step by step until she reached the bottom. If she knew Sarah was hidden on the far side of the stairs near the dining area, she did not show it, as her head turned directly toward Hoke's study. She came toward Cassius, whispering again, Missus Sarah? As she drew close to him, she raised her hand in a surreptitious gesture that warned him to stay in place. She walked to Hoke's study and opened the door, releasing the cat. The cat scampered out in a maniacal thunder, only to halt midway into the room, embraced by moonlight. Free at last, the cat casually chose a chair and made it her own. Quashee continued all the way inside the study. Cassius admired the wisdom of this move, as Sarah now rushed up the stairs unseen by her servant. Quashee then poked her clever head out of the den with a knowing smile on her face.

I'd just set up the candle when I heard her leave her bed. Tried to get the flame out to warn you, she said quietly.

I saw it but wasn't sure.

I'll tell her I was sleepwalking. She'll believe anything if it'll help keep her secret, said Quashee, looking upstairs.

I didn't want you in danger.

You just get away from here, she said shaking her head, looking at the rolled maps and book in his hands.

But thank you anyway.

Make up your mind.

You're lucky for me.

Quashee smiled with satisfaction.

You are something, said Cassius, and his joy at the narrow escape made him reckless. He stepped close to her and kissed her on the mouth and felt her small sweet body against him. He expected her to push him away, to rush him out the door to safety, but she did not. She returned his kiss. He held her for as long as he thought reasonable, but Quashee then put a warning hand against his chest. He nodded and made his way to the door, then watched her move silently back up the stairs. He carried the book and maps outside into the warm breeze, the memory of her lips transporting him through the moonlight and back to the shed.

He was unable to rest and went to see Joseph. The door to the tobacco shed was unlocked, which was Hoke's way, remorse following his spasms of rage. This allowed the women to come in the night to clean and dress wounds. But Hoke was in no condition to have made that decision. Cassius wondered if Mr. Nettle had left the shed unlocked out of tradition, or if Ellen had given the order. He found Joseph out of his head. A plate of food waited by his side, uneaten except by flies and unidentified things that crawled. He was likely to be shackled there for a period longer than Cassius had endured after his whipping. Healing would be difficult and prolonged. Joseph would never run again, and would struggle to walk. He was unlikely to be the same curious, animated young man, and Cassius mourned the death of his younger self. Joseph was, however, likely to remain at Sweetsmoke, as his value was now decreased after the whipping and hobbling. His worth would be estimated at a half hand, although Shedd, The Little Angry Man, did his share with a worthless hip. Cassius projected Joseph as The Second Angry Man.

Cassius returned to the carpentry shed where he had earlier hidden the maps and the book, and he slept until Mr. Nettle's predawn bell. He visited the quarters as the hands ate to make certain that everyone saw him. He heard the talk then: Joseph had been caught near Springs Junction, which was an Underground Railroad station. Had he made it there, he might have reached Canada. The hands wondered who had helped Joseph, as it became clear that only one or two of them had known about the station until that morning. The hands then went to the fields and Cassius went to the big house yard and was busy until mid-morning.

The big house was obsessed with the bedridden Hoke and once Cassius identified the new patterns of comings and goings, he returned to the shed, trusting that he would be undisturbed. He unrolled Hoke's map of Virginia and removed Emoline's hand-drawn scrap with "W York" written on it. He set her map on the larger map and started by locating the town near Sweetsmoke. From there he slid the scrap of paper along railroad tracks, first left, then right, comparing road shapes, and looked for the words "W York." Initially he was stymied; there appeared to be no north-south road with the name York. He broadened his search and discovered a York Road parallel to the tracks that briefly turned north and crossed, and when he compared other indications on her map, he believed he had found what he was looking for.

He estimated three days as the least time needed to complete the journey, a day and a half in each direction. If he was to do it, he had to leave soon, as Whitacre's men were already somewhere in the northern part of the county, hunting the telegraph man as a spy. The more he thought about it, the more he thought he could be away for a few days without drawing attention. It would take a bit of luck, but the timing in and around the household was good. The planter family was caught up in Hoke's illness. They were likely to be uninterested in the comings and goings of the carpenter. It was not so unusual for him to be absent. He was sometimes loaned out to other plantations, occasionally for days, one time for six months. He did not answer to the Overseer or the Driver, and they often did not see him for days at a time. He had made a conspicuous show of not sleeping in his cabin, so his absence on the lane would raise no questions. Pet worried him, but she was no longer studying him as closely. That did not mean she was off her guard, and if she happened to discover him missing, she would gleefully inform Ellen and destroy him, but he thought that a reasonable risk.

His strongest ally was Hoke's illness. He could explain that Hoke had laid out a mission for him before delirium set in. Hoke would be unable to remember, but it was not out of the realm of possibility. Cassius simply needed to muddy the waters enough for three days.

He had one more thought to help cover his tracks: to find someone to say they had seen Cassius around in case someone became suspicious. He considered those he trusted in the quarters, Abram and Jenny, but things were not good with Jenny. He decided against Abram, who was a good and decent man, but might not be thinking clearly with his son in chains. He considered Savilla, but she was too much the gossip. He decided to speak to Quashee.

He met her in passing and they carried on a brief conversation. He asked her to say, if anyone questioned his absence, that she had seen Cassius going to the livestock clearing with his tools to repair fences. He appreciated that she did not ask about his plans.

He spent the early part of the evening doing what appeared from the outside to be his normal chores; in fact he was collecting supplies for his journey. His initial impulse to go had occurred during his conversation with Logue in Emoline's home, made in emotional haste when the reality of the journey was so distant that it mattered little if it was unrealistic. Tonight, he saw it in a different light. He knew his logical mind might argue against it, might even have a legitimate argument, but when he looked at his life, at what he was and had always been, when he thought of what it would mean to him to give up his quest and return to all that, he knew he would not be able to face himself. Living the predetermined life of a carpenter at a plantation was no longer enough. He had experienced too many small freedoms, he had tasted the knowledge that his search for Emoline's killer had already brought. He was determined to find this telegraph man, he was determined to learn what he could. Cassius drove himself toward his journey in a step-by-step fashion, willing to risk everything, to know. To *know*.

Once finished with his preparations, he sat down to write himself a pass. With that done, he thought again, then wrote two more passes, so that one would rest in his pouch, the second in his hat, and the third in his shoe. Anyone who might destroy the first pass would not imagine he carried others.

It was late when he brought out Hoke's copy of *Julius Caesar*. He was curious to know Hoke's inner mind, what his choice of the name Cassius revealed about Hoke's attitude to his slave. He sat by the lantern and held the book open close to it and began to read from the beginning.

Caesar's reference to "yond Cassius" appeared early in the play, and Cassius was amazed at the emotion it evoked. Looking at the words "a lean and hungry look" on the page, the precise words that Hoke had used to describe him after he was born, he had a profound sensation of ownership. He then took pleasure in Caesar's dialogue, that "he thinks too much, such men are dangerous."

As he continued to read, he found he did not care for Caius Cassius. He had hoped to admire his namesake or at least find some redeeming value in him, but instead he was embarrassed by him, as if he and Shakespeare's Cassius were connected and the other Cassius's personality reflected back on him. Shakespeare's Cassius was intelligent but conniving, an arrogant plotter with a thin skin, an inciter who used others to carry out his desires. Shakespeare's Cassius was unpleasantly envious of Caesar's exalted position. The thought of Hoke naming him after such a man humiliated him. It reflected poorly on the memory of the relationship he and Hoke had enjoyed when he was younger.

He caught himself dozing off and knew he would not finish reading that night, nor would he tote the book to W York. It might be some time before he could finish the play and have a full understanding of Hoke's perspective. He mulled over what he had read, and thought that perhaps he recognized himself in Cassius.

He replaced the book in the hiding place, stepping back to be certain it would draw no attention. Satisfied, he settled onto his pallet.

As he drifted off to sleep, he remembered that Hoke had said Cassius was an honorable man. Perhaps his early inference was wrong and Shakespeare's Cassius would ultimately surprise him. Gabriel Logue had said Cassius might one day be free to search for his name. Perhaps he did not need to search, now that he was familiar with the source of his name. Perhaps Hoke had aimed accurately and Cassius had carried his true name from birth.

He slept briefly, but was awake before the bell, wanting to be away before questions could be asked, planning to travel by day with his passes.

-⸙ Chapter Eleven ⸙-

E LLEN Howard was not amused by the smirk on her grandson's face. Something devious had entered his mind and he was preparing to act on it.

She had tried over the years to like her grandson, but Charles had inherited his personality from his father and grandfather, too much of it unfortunate. He had an annoyingly high opinion of himself, earned not by deeds but by accident of birth, and he was intolerant of those who did not share this glorified perspective. Her husband, Hoke, had passed on that particular character flaw, most flagrantly displayed when he took action in the world of business. Something inside of her was satisfied when she saw Hoke encounter his comeuppance. But he did not fail often; in fact, he exhibited a flair for wealth accumulation. In the early years of their marriage, she had perceived this flair to be happenstance, but over the years he had demonstrated it with too great a frequency to have been mere dumb luck. How full of himself he became when he was flush. Hoke was so imprudent with money that after prolonged bouts of profligacy he would be forced to sell people and animals to make up the shortfall. She found those times painful and humiliating. She was especially moved when it came time to sell the animals. She remembered a particular horse, a glorious bay named Ahab, which Hoke had gifted to Jacob. A few months later, when they were overextended, Hoke had sold the horse without warning, giving Jacob no opportunity to bid Ahab farewell. Jacob had been heartbroken in a way that only a trusting young boy can be when betrayed by a father. It exposed Jacob's stubborn streak, as it was years before he publicly forgave his father. Jacob was too young to understand that his father was deeply mortified by his fiscal weaknesses and had been ashamed to face his son.

And so began Jacob's history of mulish behavior in the face of his father's disapproval, which led to his greatest obdurate blunder, his marriage to Sarah Greenleaf. When Jacob finally took a good look at his permanent wife and understood the enormity of his error, rather than admit his folly, he fled, initially to bury himself in his business and later to bury himself in war. And yet there was precedent for his obstinacy. She remembered how Hoke had insisted on Ellen Corey as his bride, and oh, how Grace Howard had frowned on that! Grace Howard. Ellen's mind ran to her mother-in-law. Lord, what a frightening creature. Ellen was terrified of her, spent the entire first year of marriage skulking around her. Grace Howard was a force of nature, so intelligent, so certain, so inflexible. She had even infused her personal servant, Emoline, with those traits. The two of them, in the same house, surrounding Ellen the young bride. She shivered to think of it. Ellen had not felt safe in the bosom of her husband's family until John-Corey was born. At the instant of motherhood, she fell completely and utterly in love with her son, and no longer recoiled at her mother-in-law's caprice.

Grace had not lived to meet Jacob. Grace had acted as if she would live forever, and what a surprise her death had been, not the least to herself. A woman that powerful and determined, and yet she was unable to go on after the death of her husband. Grace left Hoke behind to take over Sweetsmoke. How young he had been emotionally, a new father still struggling to cope with the death of his own father.

"Grandma Ellen?" said Charles coyly.

"Eat your breakfast, Charles," said Ellen.

Charles had a few unpleasant traits that were all his own, one of which was that he thought he was sly and clever, when he was in fact obvious and transparent.

"Where was the carpenter going in the middle of the night?"

"Please do not share your dreams at the table, as they are unappetizing," said Ellen.

"It warn't no dream, Grandma Ellen."

"And please do not bite into the second muffin before you have finished your first one."

"I was up in the night and saw him."

"Saw whom, Charles?"

"Saw the carpenter," said Charles. "Cassius."

"I do not see how you could have recognized him in the dark."

"It was almost dawn and I was using the chamber pot."

"Do not speak of such things at the table, Charles."

"But I was, and before I got back in bed I looked out the window and saw Cassius sneaking off. He had Daddy's old bag and his hat. Where was he going? Is he a runaway too, like Joseph?"

"Cassius has been with us a long time, Charles," said Ellen, but she was interested in this information.

Ellen Howard disliked Cassius. Hoke had always favored him and she had never understood it. Cassius struck her as unexceptional, no different from the others except that his closeness to her husband gave him permission to parade his bad habits, such as being willing to look a planter in the eye and speak his mind. If he had run, it was almost certainly because of Hoke's illness. Cassius would know that Hoke's protection was now at an end and he would not be indulged as he had been when Hoke was alive. She caught herself. She had thought "when Hoke was alive." A superstitious chill gripped her and she looked to perform some act of contrition, now that she had to protect her husband from her dangerous thoughts the way she protected her son. Hoke was alive still and would remain so, she was convinced of it. What had brought on such an appalling thought? She would punish herself; she would avoid laudanum for a day, no two, and drink her tea without sweet. Was it not difficult enough being forced to learn the everyday workings of the plantation? Now she had to defend against evil thoughts.

Ellen's mind turned to the plantation. She played a complicated game with the other owners. Women were not acceptable masters, so she pretended her decisions were made by her husband, even though everyone knew he was incapacitated. The other planters likewise pretended that Hoke was making decisions as that allowed business to flow smoothly. When they disagreed with one of her decisions, they demanded she inform her husband that his decision was unacceptable. She would then pretend to carry their response to him, and return with a new decision. In one case she simply reiterated her original decision and they accepted it without comment. Beyond that, she manifestly did not enjoy being in charge. So many questions, Missus this and Missus that. She preferred the old days, when she only had to inform her husband of her opinion to have her will thus carried out.

Ellen was now forced to suffer through direct interactions with the personnel. She found Mr. Nettle a bore, consumed with minutiae, and she dreaded his evening report on the state of the plantation. Sometimes she refused to see him. She would need to invent a new system. If there was little to report, he could wait two or three days, perhaps even a week. Today was likely to be particularly difficult. Food stocks were increasingly low, and she had delayed confronting the problem. Hoke had hidden grain and preserves from the quartermaster, but had neglected to share with her their location. She had to pretend to know, however, because if she were to ask her people, they would recognize her ignorance and go dumb, and subsequently raid the stocks for themselves. She could not abide her people taking advantage of her. She thought to include the new butler from John-Corey. Beauregard seemed loyal enough and willing to please, but of course it was early in his stewardship, and he would want to appear capable. That would change in time, it always did. It was decided then: She would speak with him, and be careful not to tip her hand. The butler should know the goings-on of the plantation.

Lord, she thought, where is Pet? I will need my laudanum drops if I am to get through the day.

"So you know where Cassius was going?" said Charles.

"Yes, of course," said his grandmother.

Ellen would have to find out if Cassius was on the property. She did not appreciate the spurious expression of shock on Charles's face.

After breakfast, she spoke with Beauregard, and asked for the *condition* of the hidden food stocks, expecting a full report to be detailed by their location. By mid-morning, Beauregard had reported back with an itemized list that included the locations, and went further to report the condition of the hidden livestock. Ellen's hands were rock steady, as she had increased the number of drops and was feeling quite normal in her altered condition. She had forgotten her superstitious promise until after her indulgence, vowing immediately to curb her use the following two days. She asked Beauregard if he knew Cassius's whereabouts, and was informed that Cassius had been seen going up to the area that held the livestock, probably to work on the hog pen. Ellen was satisfied with his report and relieved to know that Charles was wrong. But she would have Mr. Nettle account for Cassius to confirm that he remained on Sweetsmoke property. She would need to exert control over that one. He had too much independence. She preferred to loan him out to other plantations, as then she would not not have to see him day in and day out. If Hoke were not to recover, perhaps a sale through Lucas Force would be in order; but she would never do it unless Hoke was gone. With his skills, Cassius was likely to fetch a fine price.

-◈ Chapter Twelve ◈-

C ASSIUS walked in bluish gray light, fog clinging to hollows in
the surrounding fields as he traveled the turnpike. The sun was
still hidden behind the low hills. He enjoyed the coolness knowing
the midday heat would test his stamina. He carried Jacob's old
haversack, a boy's bag and hand-me-down given to him ten years
before. Inside was a kerchief that wrapped salt pork and ashcakes,
enough to last him two days, after which he would need to scrounge.
He carried no water, but the map foretold a series of creeks, and
he had no reason not to trust whites when it came to mapmaking.
He stopped under the little bridge and drank, lingering for only a
moment as the swift current rushed by. At the fork, he turned north
away from town and approached the small farm of Thomas Chavis,
where he looked forward to speaking with Weyman.

He saw the Chavis barn shrouded in ground fog so that the upper barn and roof appeared to float. He drew closer and an air current twisted a horizontal sash of fog into a coil as if someone unseen

had run through it. The barn was in questionable condition, in need of paint with the random missing board, but the siding that was in place appeared unwarped and flush. He thought that if Thomas Chavis had a better than average harvest, Cassius might convince Hoke to rent him out to work the property. With each step the farmhouse emerged from behind the barn, small and simple and well kept, and he thought that on Sweetsmoke it would have been mistaken for a shed. He slowed to a deliberate pace, expecting to see them leaving for the field, and when they did not, he hesitated. He began to walk on, but the ominously quiet house made him curious, so he crossed to the far side of the turnpike and sat on a stony spot alongside grass still damp with dew.

After a few minutes, Bunty emerged from the privy, pulling tight a rope belt, and walked unhurriedly toward the farmhouse.

Cassius called out to him. Bunty turned, saw Cassius and nodded, then continued inside. A moment later Weyman came out and waved him over with a full arm movement. Cassius made his way, admiring the worn but well-kept tools lined up alongside the house under the makeshift porch roof: butter churn, washboard and tub, large crock pots, small barrels, and a heavy iron pot that had a hole in its side. Weyman greeted him at the door.

Cassius, what y'all doin out here?

On a task for Old Hoke.

"Come in, Cassius," said Thomas Chavis from inside. "We are slow to the fields today as it is Martha's birthday."

Cassius removed his hat and stepped inside, bowing his head to her.

A good one to you, Missus, said Cassius.

"I thank you, Cassius, have you had your breakfast?" said Martha Chavis.

I'm fine, Missus, thank you.

"Nonsense," she said, and scooped beans and meat from a hog jowl onto a tin plate. Cassius noted that she was in no way the disagreeable creature Weyman often made her out to be, as she smiled at him with her small handsome face, leathered by weather and brutal years, but all in all pleasing to behold. Her pregnancy was evident, and as he glanced around at the one-room farmhouse—an area with a curtain for the married couple, pallets on the floor across the room for the hands—he wondered how they would arrange the sleeping once the baby was born. He sat gratefully and ate, and was surprised at the intensity of his hunger. He looked up midway through the plate, aware that he ate alone for an audience, and remembered that everyone in Thomas Chavis's home sat at the common table and ate at the same time, Thomas at the head, his wife opposite, Bunty and Weyman facing each other on the long ends. The other plates had been cleared and Thomas indulged in what Cassius imagined was his second cup of coffee, which smelled like the coffee in the quarters, made of roasted okra flavored with molasses. While Weyman had often spoken of it, to physically consume a meal in the company of a master and his wife brought the experience home with a considerable jolt. Weyman had a most unusual life for a slave, in that he lived in conditions which were better than for many poor whites in town. Cassius envied him, treated with decency and dignity, and he flashed on Hoke waxing poetic on the idyllic life of the happy-go-lucky slave with no crushing burden of responsibility. Surely this was Weyman's world, and Cassius's envy lasted but a moment longer when he suddenly grasped that he was ensnared in white man's romantic twattle. Weyman was not free, he—was—not—*free*.

Cassius finished the food on his plate, and Thomas stood.

I thank you, Missus, said Cassius.

Bunty and Weyman stood as well, and Cassius understood that Thomas had waited for him before leading his people to the field. Politeness was something Cassius rarely experienced, and it was the second jolt of the morning. He nodded and smiled at Martha Chavis, who took the plate from him as he tried to put it in the bucket to be washed. He followed the men outside, and as Bunty went with Thomas into the field, Weyman walked him to the road.

Just looking for a chance to say hello, said Cassius. Didn't expect a meal.

Yeah, y'all got more'n hello this mornin, said Weyman proudly. That look to be a full belly.

Not so full as your ugly mistress.

She a possum hound, ain't she? said Weyman.

Just the way you described her, with a litter on the way.

Didn't want you feelin too jealous, Cassius, said Weyman grinning.

I see why you're happy, said Cassius.

A look of incomprehension entered Weyman's eyes but was gone that fast.

Nice job y'all did on that Tempie, gettin rid a' her that way, said Weyman. My business done picked up considerable.

Cassius winced and was about to answer, but he stopped himself.

Where you off to, again? said Weyman.

Work for Hoke.

I done heard that. What, some mystery task?

Something he needed done.

Word is he laid up.

Heard you were getting herbs from Emoline, said Cassius, turning the conversation. He knew to protect Weyman from knowing anything about his journey in case things went wrong.

Now where you hear 'bout that? said Weyman, looking shy.

Maybe you got the gout from that fancy cheese and wine you been putting down your throat? said Cassius, meaning to tease Weyman, but Weyman did not laugh.

Naw, somethin else, some herb I done forget the name of. Start with a *M* or somethin.

Yeah, one of them letters of the alphabet, said Cassius, looking at him out of the sides of his eyes.

Yeah, one of them.

Emoline's papers linked Weyman to jalap bindweed. Cassius had not expected Weyman to be embarrassed about it.

Getting it from someone else now? said Cassius.

Weyman looked at him slyly: I got Bornock's shooter.

That pretty pearl-handled revolver? said Cassius.

Colt Army. Doin some business with them paddyrollers and saw the chance, took it right under his nose.

Cassius remembered he had not seen the revolver on Bornock's person that night in the rain.

Guess you can make a nice profit, said Cassius.

Could at that, but now that I got it hid, I kinda like havin it around.

You got those patrollers mad at each other. I heard Bornock accuse Mule of stealing it.

Weyman shook his head with glee: I remember what y'all said at the Big-To-Do.

What was that?

You 'member, when I said I like to shoot that Tempie and you said I could use my finger, but I already had the way and you didn't know it.

No, guess I didn't, said Cassius.

They said their good-byes. As Cassius walked along the turnpike, he saw over his shoulder Weyman joining Thomas Chavis and Bunty in the field.

Cassius walked a ways and then he got lucky. A worn-out buggy pulled by a worn-out but game horse named Carolina drew up alongside him. A worn-out freed black man by the name of Ralph offered him a ride. Ralph was heavy and gray and he did like to talk, but Cassius could not for the life of him remember afterward what they had talked about. They were not bothered to produce passes, as Ralph was a frequent traveler and well known on the road. The whites treated him with jocular humor, all at Ralph's expense, and he laughed effortlessly, although at one moment Cassius thought he sensed something lurking under Ralph's friendly demeanor. Some hours into their journey, Ralph called him by his name, and Cassius was surprised, not having remembered introducing himself, but after he gave it some thought he decided that he must have done it when he first accepted the ride. By midday, sooner than Cassius had estimated by looking at the map, they reached the spot where Cassius was to continue on foot. Ralph steered him left, informing him that York Road would eventually cross railroad tracks, and he'd been over the bridge there hundreds of times. Cassius asked if Ralph had seen soldiers in the area, and for the first time in their short journey Ralph was silent.

He walked York Road for an hour, and one time heard the whistle of a locomotive way off to his right. He knew from memorizing Hoke's map that he was walking parallel to the tracks, and hoped to arrive at his destination by nightfall. He had, of course, left the map behind, hidden in the carpentry shed. The heat made him lightheaded, and he fell into a dreamlike state. He had committed to memory the thin lines from the map and expected the road to turn sharply north. As he continued he was unaware of the gradual shift of the sun's angle as its force concentrated on his left shoulder. His thoughts ran to punishment of Emoline's killer, gratifying himself as he imagined different methods of revenge, some rapid and charitable, others slow and cruel, with each possessing its own allure and charm. In time, his mind moved on to the first two acts of *Julius Caesar*, which was as far as he had read. After his initial irritation, thinking Hoke had named him after an unpleasant fellow, he realized Hoke had had no sense of his slave child's personality when he chose the name. It was but idle whimsy on his master's part, a book he happened to be reading, a passage remembered at a coincidental moment. If Cassius had grown to resemble the man in the play, perhaps Hoke was prescient. Or perhaps Hoke had molded Cassius, inadvertently or otherwise, to resemble this Cassius of Shakespeare. Or perhaps Cassius was reimagining his personality through the prism of Shakespeare's Cassius.

He heard the babble of moving water to his left and scrabbled down an incline to the muddy bank of a creek. He left his haversack on dry ground and, with cupped hands, scooped cool water to his mouth. He removed his hat and submerged it, bringing it back onto his head, letting the cold clear stream cascade down his skin, returning to him the memory of local creeks and reckless boyhood. He rested in shade wondering how far he had yet to travel, when he heard a steady growl much closer than expected. As the sound grew, he detected a regular beat, wheels clacking rhythmically on a track propelled by a chuffing steam engine. He took his haversack and scrambled low along the bank, coming out where the creek spilled into a lean river not sixty feet across. The steel trestle above was immense but with wide spaces between the girders and he feared it would not hold the train. The iron horse came on and charged across, leaving behind a great cloud as though the air bled smoke. Cassius had never in life seen anything move with such speed. He stood in motionless awe. This was an astounding creation, of steel and smoke, of heft and heat. The thing that rolled above him devoured his vision. He marveled at the men who had imagined and built it. Smoke filled the shape defined by the girders and rolled over the sides and down the walls of the ravine to the water. He realized that had he continued on the road a few minutes longer, he would have reached the trestle. He had arrived at his destination with most of the afternoon before him.

The locomotive and its dozen freight cars were long gone before he no longer heard their thunder or breathed their smoke. Cassius listened to the moving river and considered a plan of action. He chose a concealed position high in the ravine from which he could view trestle and York Road. He had a decent view of telegraph poles planted beside the tracks. He continued to wonder about the *W* in W York, and after taking in the land, he decided it was not a proper name but a direction, west of York Road, which put him on the wrong side of the river. He was at a disadvantage as he was not intimate with the terrain, and the man who might have information that could lead to Emoline's killer could be anywhere. He decided to devote the following day to luring him out. He considered returning to the road, to reach the west side by crossing at the trestle, but thought better of it.

He heard horses on the road. From his vantage he momentarily viewed shoulders and heads of men wearing butternut kepis. He counted three, but the sound of the hooves suggested more. They rode ahead but did not cross via trestle. He moved again, staying high on the ravine's bank. From his new angle he made out a modest bridge not a quarter mile beyond the trestle, and saw five riders continue on toward the forested hill. If Whitacre's men were patrolling, it was likely that the telegraph man was still here.

Cassius made his way down the ravine to seek a ford. The river appeared deep and he could not swim. He scouted upstream and saw a place. A tree had fallen across much of the river's width. Boulders narrowed the river on both sides, and the current ran fast through the gap. He judged the distance and thought he could make the jump. He reached the spot where the tree came closest to a boulder on the opposite bank. Up close, the distance appeared more ominous. Slowly, warily, he balanced on the trunk.

As he shifted his weight back to jump, the trunk dipped and water swamped his shoes. He hit the boulder sliding, grabbing an edge. His grasp held and he caught his breath as the pain from his banged knees diminished. Gradually he moved to the next boulder and was across.

He spent the next hour and a half in motion, becoming familiar with the terrain. Under the trestle he looked for evidence of the telegraph man's camp near the stanchions. He approached the cart and pedestrian bridge, a sturdy wooden structure whose planks clattered when a farmer crossed in his cart. The reality of his situation became clear. He had scant knowledge of the terrain and hiding places were countless. The quartermaster had numerous troops and unlimited time to find this elusive man, and to date they had been unsuccessful. His mission more and more resembled a fool's errand.

As he could not return before morning, he chose to make the most of it. He found what he judged a well-concealed position where, through leafy branches, he was afforded a view of trestle, wood bridge, and river. He became still, and gradually the rhythms of wildlife were revealed, as upstream a doe came to the water to drink, and two young foxes tumbled down the far side of the bank in raucous play. Travelers came upon the road at irregular and unpredictable intervals. His belly nudged him, and he reached for his haversack, only to find it gone. He patted himself, then the ground around him. He backtracked, no longer as cautious, returning to the riverbank and the fallen tree. The haversack had snagged on an erect branch off the tree's trunk. He understood how it must have slipped off his shoulder when his concentration centered on his leap. The haversack was dry, but to retrieve it he would need to leap twice more, over and back again, unless he wanted to cross the wood bridge twice. He decided to risk the river.

He walked out to the slippery boulder near the trunk. He managed foot- and handholds and stood shakily. He considered his objective. The trunk across the river appeared more unstable from this side, and he feared the sudden weight from his leap was likely to sink it where the current moved swiftly in the gap.

Cassius swung his arms to build momentum and leapt. The trunk plunged under his sudden weight and he was submerged. The current grabbed and held him under. His eyes bulged—he had exhaled on the leap—panicking now, clinging to the trunk, stretching head and neck for the brightness above that was surely the surface. He was afraid to let go. He kicked his legs. His body twisted first to one side, then the other, then he was upside down. He gasped for air, inhaling water. His left foot hit something and he pushed against it and his head miraculously surfaced, choking, coughing, gasping loudly, never in his life so relieved to breathe. After a minute of clearing his lungs, he comically realized he was standing, water moving rapidly around his chest.

He waded against the current with one arm on the trunk, lifted his haversack off the branch, and waded back. He removed his soaked shoes and emptied the muck and stones out of them. He was no longer hungry.

He sat in a sunny spot and his clothes dried quickly. He revisited the good vantage point but made only a modest effort to conceal himself. The day faded.

The Confederate soldiers did not return. He thought to move closer to the bridge, but his belly spoke to him again. He reached for his haversack and pulled out salted pork. He bit into it and it tasted fine, and he leaned back on an elbow to chew.

He scrambled to his knees when he realized the presence behind him, a man aiming a handgun at his chest. He did not know how the man could have silently come up on him.

Don't shoot, mister, said Cassius.

He discerned a small emaciated man in breeches, knee-high boots, frock coat, and a white shirt with a cravat. His clothes were in absolute tatters and hung loose off his shoulders and waist. The man wore a brimmed hat which had once been fancy. He affected elegance, but had been living in the outdoors too long for this act to be effective.

"What the hell you doing here?"

Just, don't know, seemed like a good spot.

"Hiding out. Who are you?" said the man.

Cassius Howard.

"Runaway?"

No sir, got a pass.

"*Who* gave you a pass, where's it from?"

Sweetsmoke Plantation. Could you turn that away? said Cassius, nodding toward the handgun.

"Sweetsmoke?" said the man, as if it rang a bell.

Handguns sometimes go off when you least expect.

"Then you better hand over that food before it does."

Cassius held out the salt pork. The man came forward, took it, and backed up, then looked at Cassius as if he hadn't imagined anything could be so easy.

"Dear Lord, actual sustenance," said the man, speaking to himself as if Cassius were not there.

The man sat down, his handgun no longer aimed at Cassius, and rushed food into his mouth.

Seem like you ain't had food in a while, maybe you ought slow down, said Cassius.

The man stopped and inspected the pork in his hands. Then he suddenly ate again just as quickly as before.

You a Northerner, said Cassius.

The man looked in Cassius's direction, but not at him, as if he looked at someone sitting beside Cassius. "Northerner," said the man.

Telegrapher, said Cassius.

The man spoke to the food. "There have been raids."

You're the one, said Cassius.

"Runaway," said the man, but again he looked alongside Cassius, not directly at him.

Got a pass, said Cassius.

"What does one say if one has no pass?"

That they got one, said Cassius, admitting the truth.

Again the man looked at his food. "Do not address me in such a manner, or I will eat you more slowly."

Emoline Justice, said Cassius, and studied the man to judge his reaction.

The man stopped eating and even in the grim light of dusk Cassius could see he stared at him. "I know of one named Emoline."

She was my friend.

"'Was.' Sad when a couple has a falling out. Happened to me once."

She's dead.

The man sat in silence and nodded. The man connected in short bursts, then faded, to speak with himself or inanimate objects. He had been starving and alone a long time. The man finished the last bite of salt pork and licked his fingers. Cassius hoped to draw him into a longer conversation.

The man spoke to his dirty fingernails. "I am not much of a hunter. Can't fish to save my life. Eating grubs for weeks. Never thought I'd get to like the taste of insects. Some truly are more palatable than others." He rubbed his greasy fingers on his mustache and then curled his upper lip to smell it. "That will smell good for a week." He looked up suddenly. "How did she die?"

Hit on the back of the head, said Cassius.

"Then we are discovered," said the man absently, rubbing his fingers together. "This will close our operation."

You think you are discovered because of Emoline? said Cassius.

"I am recently discovered by a squirrel. He reads my thoughts therefore I cannot catch him. No matter how hungry I am, his desperation is greater."

No one left to pass on your intelligence.

"Ralph is merely a conduit."

Cassius was interested to know about Ralph. He recognized Emoline's hand, recruiting a simple popular freed man to be an intelligence courier. Could the middle man have effected her violent end? A question for later. Cassius reconsidered the moment Ralph had called him by name, and knew that Ralph had recognized him, most likely from Emoline's description.

The emaciated man lifted the revolver again, turned it, and looked at it, briefly pointing the barrel toward his own ear. He spoke to himself. "If this handgun went off, it would be nothing short of a miracle."

Why is that? said Cassius.

"What? Oh. Not loaded."

How'd you get here? said Cassius.

"How'd you?"

Walked, mostly.

"That is good." The man's mind appeared to wander. Then he spoke as if to a third person. "I work for Mr. E. S. Sanford, formerly of the American Telegraph Company, now of the United States of America. Barnes. Where the devil is Barnes?"

I don't know Barnes, said Cassius.

"Jefferson Barnes? Oh, you should meet him sometime, he's military, came south with me. Didn't wear a uniform, though."

Barnes, you say, said Cassius.

"I knew a man named Barnes. He knows this area, has family down here."

Where is Barnes?

"Over there," said the man, pointing.

Can I talk to him?

"Can if you want."

Take me to him?

The man snickered. "Not likely to talk back, though. He's that way, Barnes."

Why won't he talk back?

"I do believe it would be the bullet," said the man. "Got shot while out hunting for victuals, dragged himself all the way back here but forgot to bring the food. His sacred dust is but a half mile that way. This is his," he said holding up the handgun as if he had just discovered it. Then he whispered: "I accidentally buried the ammunition with him, but I didn't have the stomach to dig him back up."

When was the last time you saw Emoline?

"Emoline? You mean Emoline Justice? I never saw Emoline Justice."

What's that, never?

"Never met her. Heard about her."

Do you know if she was revealed as a spy?

"Did you notice that Ralph likes to talk?"

Sir. Was she revealed as a spy?

"Who?"

Cassius exhaled. This man knew nothing about her murder.

"Ralph brought food, but not since the Johnny Rebs moved in."

You know a man name of Logue? said Cassius.

"I know a man named Georgevitch."

Gabriel Logue? Angel Gabriel?

"The Angel Gabriel came to Daniel. 'And when he came I was afraid and fell on my face.' Is that it? I may have forgotten. Been some time since I saw a Bible."

Never met Emoline and you don't know Logue. You're just a spoke on the wheel.

"Well you goddamned nigger, is that how niggers talk to white folks down here? Spoke on the wheel? I work for the United States Government, I was recognized by President Lincoln himself." He dug into his frock coat and pulled out a worn piece of paper. He held it open for Cassius.

A list of dry goods, said Cassius, reading in the last light of the day.

"Ah. So you can read," said the emaciated man, his animosity vanishing as if he had never been offended, folding the piece of paper and returning it to his coat. "I congratulate you on your skills."

Cassius made a fist and knocked on a piece of wood, rap-rap, pause, rap, imitating the code he had learned from Maryanne. The man appeared puzzled so Cassius repeated it.

"I believe the door is open, sir."

Emoline's code knock, said Cassius.

"How do you do, my name is Morningside."

Mr. Morningside, said Cassius.

"A man was here just a moment ago," he said.

What man?

"Negro. He was clever the way he found me." The man spoke directly to Cassius this time.

You think I found you?

"A very clever method, he taught me something: If you're ever looking for someone that you have no hope of finding, make him come to you."

Make him come to you, repeated Cassius in wonder.

"Sit out in the open, take out your dinner and start eating. He knew it would bring me out."

Because you were starving.

"Smart. He started by lowering my opinion of him as he made himself out to be ridiculous. Fell right in the river so that I would underestimate him. Most amusing. I'm sorry you weren't here to see it."

Amusing and amused, thought Cassius, to be given credit for such cleverness. It pulled him out of the sense of sinking into which he had fallen, which had begun the moment he had started to speak to this man. He would learn little about Emoline's death here, and it was clear that he was not in the company of her killer.

"I don't meet a lot of negroes up north. And down here I've met only Ralph, who is free. What's it like being a slave?"

Cassius was so surprised by the question that he answered truthfully: Don't know.

"That, sir, is an interesting answer. Why is it you don't know?"

Because I don't know what it is *not* to be a slave. I know my life ain't my own. I know my time ain't my own. I know I can't make big decisions for myself, and small decisions get changed when some planter gets tired or moody or just plain stupid. Maybe planters know, since they're free but also chained to slavery. We make them rich but to stay rich, they got to watch us, take care of us and guard us. Their whole lives they're surrounded by the enemy, because we're always looking to be free.

"I'm no abolitionist, after all, those people are godforsaken lunatics, but you sir make a fine case against slavery."

Grateful to hear it.

"You mock me," said the man, with a convoluted smile.

Not without cause.

"I haven't carried on a conversation in a good long while, perhaps one time you'll join me?"

Cassius laughed to himself and shook his head.

"What a foolish man you are," said the man to himself, "you mustn't put pressure on this sad fellow. They have proven that negroes have smaller brains, although I met one in the woods who seemed unusually intelligent for his race."

Thank you, said Cassius not bothering to disguise his sarcasm.

It was dark. Cassius could no longer make out the trestle and bridge.

"I think I will climb my pole." Morningside came to his feet.

Your pole?

"Have you not met my pole? I gather intelligence from it for my government."

You think that wise?

"I have done it many times before."

There are men out here looking for you.

"You have an opinion. I am enchanted. A negro with an opinion. How good of you to share it with me. But do leave this decision to me. The men are gone."

Your friend Barnes, what did he do before you—?

"Have you ever seen a climbing iron?" Suddenly the man was excited.

No.

He scrambled to a place a few yards away; Cassius could barely see that he pulled something from a hiding place in the dark, and came back with it in his hand. There was just enough light for Cassius to make out a pair of metal bars with one end a spike. Morningside attached them to his boots so that the spike was worn like a bayonet, and Cassius saw the cleverness in the design and how it would allow him to climb the pole.

Cassius followed him up the side of the ravine to the cleared space, across which were the tracks and the telegraph poles. Morningside set down his haversack. Cassius remained in the brush as the man set out across the open toward the telegraph wires. Midway across, he pointed to a telegraph pole that Cassius was unable to see, as it was deep in shadow. The next moment the man was in flight, feet off the ground, twisting unnaturally in air, the tatters of his clothing bursting out in every direction, his flight concluding as quickly as it had started as his body flopped suddenly to the ground. The retort of a gunshot was almost instantaneous but still too late for the man to have known what hit him. The open ground came alive with men closing in from three sides, seven of them emerging at once. Cassius held still a moment as they converged on the body.

"Look there! Over there, I see something!" One of the men pointed directly at Cassius.

Cassius grabbed Morningside's haversack and scrambled down the incline just far enough to be out of sight. He knew he could not outrun these men. He tore off his shirt and his trousers, rolling them into a ball with the two haversacks. Naked, he moved back to where they had seen him and he hid the light-colored objects underneath his body as he curled up on fallen leaves around the trunk of a small bush. His skin was his ally, becoming one with the shadow under the bush. Voices came closer, and a horse cantered directly at him. He thought he had made a mistake, wishing he had run, at least then he would have had a fighting chance. Two men crashed into the brush beside him, running in the direction he had originally gone. More horse hooves came on, moving along the edge of the brush.

A voice above him, close, oh so close, said, "Spread out, he can't get far."

The man on horseback stayed right there, almost on top of him, and Cassius made his breathing shallow, as insects crawled on his skin.

The man above him bit into an apple and chewed with an open

mouth. His horse dropped its head and munched on something near Cassius's feet. Cassius had a moment of terror, that the horse would step on him and he would cry out.

Another horseman rode up.

"Haven't found him, sir."

Cassius took this opportunity to glance up, assuming that the man and his commanding officer would be facing each other. The officer's lantern allowed Cassius to see that he was a small man sitting his horse, wearing a tan slouch hat. The officer wore his hat with an unusual affectation: He folded up the front of the hat's brim so that it looked as if the wind held it vertical against the crown.

"Assuming there was another man," said the officer, spitting.

"Sir?"

"Lewis sees things. Ghosts and such. Goddamned rot."

"Captain, Lewis has seen the elephant."

"Yes, I know, and you'll get your own damned chance when Lee hands over to me the command he promised."

Captain. Captain Solomon Whitacre. Cassius moved his head for a better look. Whitacre had a lantern, and he opened it to light the end of his cigar with the burning wick.

Cassius would not have recognized Whitacre from the glimpse he'd had of him the night of the Big-To-Do. Solomon Whitacre was a small man with a full beard but no mustache. By the way he extended his pinkie when lighting his cigar, Cassius thought he had the manners of a gentleman, but he wondered about the man's abuse of the language. Whitacre seemed unnecessarily coarse.

"You see the clothes on that whore's chinch?" Whitacre said, motioning to Morningside's body. "Mr. Fancy Hat in rags. Been out here weeks. If he had a partner, surely one of them would have gone off for food."

"I imagine that's true, Captain."

A second rider joined him. "Nothing, sir. But he's out there somewhere. We may need to wait until morning."

"Morning?" said Whitacre. "God's balls, Lewis, I'm not waitin till mornin. Far as I'm concerned, there warn't no second man. We got our spy, and I am anxious to take my leave of this place. If we stay longer, they'll order us to wait on the harvest. Let some other backwater captain rape the people of their crops, I am dog tired of scrapin this damned county bald. No, we are goin to join the wagons and follow them to Lee. The whisper is, Lee will take the fight to the Yanks. Imagine it, boys, an invasion of the North. If I get that command, I promise you won't miss out. You either, Lewis, don't want to miss the last battle of the war. Once we take the fight to the Yanks on their ground, they'll give it up."

"Yes, sir."

"Lieutenant, assemble the men and convene on the far side of the bridge, we're goin north."

Whitacre turned his horse and rode away. The two others held their ground.

"You really see someone, Lewis?"

"Don't matter now. Reassemble on the other side."

Cassius was left alone. He stayed on the ground, motionless for a while longer, listening to the distant voices, shouts, and horse hooves, and finally to nothing more than the sounds of the night aging around him. He sat up. He was alone. They had taken Morningside's corpse, but he had the man's haversack with his papers. He slapped at the places on his body where he had been bitten, then put on his clothes. He took the papers from Morningside's haversack and hid them in the band of his trousers. Then he stepped onto York Road, to follow it south to return to Sweetsmoke.

≁ Chapter Thirteen ≈

CASSIUS walked until the moon came up, at which time he moved off the road to sleep. He dreamed of Emoline moving through an open field, then suddenly flying with her legs and arms snapping off in every direction. In his dream, he combed the field to find each piece so that he could put her back together. He was awakened by a nudge on his shoulder, and opened his eyes to find Ralph standing over him. He looked around and saw that the place he had chosen in the dark, assuming it would be concealed from the road, was obvious to any passerby. They said nothing to each other and climbed into Ralph's buggy, and Carolina pulled without Ralph doing a thing. Ralph and Cassius exchanged a look. Cassius understood the question in Ralph's eyes and shook his head no.

"Dead?" said Ralph.

Cassius nodded. Ralph looked away.

Remember the last day of June? said Cassius.

"The day she died?" said Ralph.

Remember what you were doing?

"Same as yesterday. Same as tomorrow. Odd job here, odd job there. Want to know if I killed her?"

No, said Cassius. He already knew the answer.

Cassius stared off and then he was asleep and the next thing he knew, they had stopped. He roused to find they were close to the town near Sweetsmoke. He climbed down and thanked Ralph for his help.

At the fork Cassius turned toward town walking away from Sweetsmoke, but he took the small road that ran around the town to reach the northeast section, and on the outskirts approached Hans Mueller's *bierhaus*. As he approached, he saw that Mueller had fashioned a sign, and Cassius took a moment to consider it. "Bierhaus." The letters were ornate, painted in a style of writing with which he was unfamiliar. The capital *B* was identifiable as a *B,* but was preceded by an outstretched bar at the top, a forelock perhaps, and there was a thick decorative bar parallel to the main ascender. The round backs in the *B* were made with straight lines that came to hard corners. This was all in imitation of a broad pen nib. The dot over the *i* was very nearly a diamond shape, again as if made by the slash of the same broad nib.

Mueller had built his *bierhaus* as an extension of his home. Cassius stepped inside, into coolness and the sour urine smell of old beer, with a great deal of uncertainty about the reception he was to encounter. The room was long and narrow, furnished with two long tables side by side, both with equally long benches that in the old country might have encouraged conviviality and conversation.

Cassius's eye was drawn to the intricate woodworking in the furniture, done in a style he found unfamiliar. In particular, he noted a clock on the wall. It was handmade in the form of a house, and on its face was painted a garden scene, chipped and worn, perhaps from travel. Around the entire clock house was elaborately carved latticework. He would have liked to spend more time, as carpenter and woodworker, examining it, but he turned his attention to the room. The sole patrons were two German men, one with a tall elaborate stein. They met his eyes, then turned away. Mueller was at the far end inspecting his glassware and when he saw Cassius, he took a step toward him.

"You cannot be in here."

I look for a man.

"I am a man, so you have found one, now go."

Not you.

"As you see, just these gentlemen and no one else. *Auf Wieder-sehen.*"

Cassius held his ground for a moment, and as he was about to back out the daylight behind him was blocked and the long room grew darker. He turned to see Gabriel Logue filling the doorway.

"It appears to be my old friend Cassius," said Logue.

I'm here to find you, said Cassius.

"Once again you expected me?"

Said so yourself. When in town, you're here.

"Damned imprudent of me. Why'd you think I'd be here on this particular day?"

Hoke said, and I hoped you weren't gone.

"I thought your master was indisposed."

Said he had to meet the angel. I thought he meant death. Then I knew he meant you.

Logue nodded and Cassius detected a thaw. "Well sit down, then."

Cassius hesitated. This was not proper. Even if Logue insisted he was under his protection, this was likely to turn Mueller against him, and Mueller was a patroller.

"Oh, go on, have a sit down, don't worry about Mule, he won't say nothing, will you, Mule? Care for a beer?"

No, said Cassius. That would antagonize the German unnecessarily and he knew he would need his wits later on.

"Fair enough. Just me, Mule. I take any and every opportunity to indulge."

Mueller tapped Logue a beer and brought it, foam still building as he set it down. The head rose dense and creamy and finally boiled over the side, touching the table as a golden puddle. Mueller gave Cassius a wintry look, and Cassius pretended not to notice. It was done now, he had a new adversary with which to deal.

"They call this Teutonic swill a lager. I'm a porter man myself, but I'm damned if I won't develop a taste for it, as my beer here is gratis."

Cassius nodded, but still kept an eye on Mueller walking to the far end of the bar. Mueller's son, perhaps fifteen years old, blond and very pale, came in the far door. Cassius did not remember the boy's name, but he remembered that the boy was brain simple. He offered a large bowl to his father. A moment later, the pleasant smell of fresh baked goods reached Cassius.

"Mule and me, we got an arrangement; I deliver certain items from the North for him and he affords me a home away from home and a ready supply of piss juice." Cassius decided that this was not Logue's first lager that morning, as he was surprisingly talkative. "Mule doesn't get a lot of customers, so he supports himself trading my wares. Anything you need, you'll do better here than the dry goods."

I think you made him my enemy.

"Mule? Nah, he's all right."

Cassius said nothing and Logue looked up to see Mueller approaching a second time, setting down a bowl deliberately in front of Logue. Logue pushed it toward Cassius, and he saw what appeared to be thin sticks of bread. Mueller stared at Cassius with grave malevolence.

"Well. I could be mistaken," said Logue.

Cassius kept his eyes on the objects in the bowl.

"Pretzels, try one. German food. Also got a thing called sauerkraut, damnedest food you ever ate."

Mueller went off to the far end of the room, but Logue waved him all the way out. Mueller looked at him coldly, but he took his son by the arm and they both left. Logue did not care to be overheard. Cassius looked at the two Germans who remained. He met Logue's eyes.

"Forget 'em, those boys don't speak English. By the by, in a minute that clock is going to announce the hour," said Logue.

Cassius looked at the clock and saw a small door come open, built in under the clock's roof but above the clock face. He heard the wooden mechanism whir as a tiny carved bird poked its head out.

In unison and without emotion the two Germans said, "Koo-koo, Koo-koo." The bird pulled back into the clock and the door closed.

"Cuckoo clock," said Logue. "Had a little accident on the way over from the old country. Everything works but the bellows, so the bird doesn't sing."

It's all carved? said Cassius.

"German farmers do 'em in the winter, or so they tell me. What else is there to do when you're snowed in?"

Every moment brought some new thing, and Cassius understood he had entered another world, so near to his home.

"If you're here, you got something for me," said Logue, and Cassius saw him distracted and decided that his early morning drinking, his willingness to talk, and his hearty warmth were disguising something that disturbed his mind.

You got some sort of trouble? said Cassius.

"Me? Hell no. Me?" He sipped his beer. "Naw, nothing important."

Cassius left Morningside's papers in the haversack and waited. Out of nowhere, and to Cassius's surprise, Logue spoke up.

"You know anything about women, Cassius?"

Cassius's head came up straighter.

"I'm damned if I know what to do about this, me, a married man."

Of all things, here's something I didn't reckon, said Cassius, fighting back a smile.

"Just got a letter from my wife, caught up to me, or I suppose I caught up to it since no one knows where I am, and at first I was glad to have it, until I read the damn thing."

How odd, thought Cassius. He is about to tell me about his wife.

Sorry to hear it, said Cassius solicitously. She got someone else?

"Someone? No, hell no! She doesn't want to end the marriage. God knows she couldn't afford it. No, she's offering lessons on manners. In a letter. Napkins and soup spoons and, and etiquette! Haven't seen her in eight months. Etiquette!"

I see, said Cassius.

"No sir, you do not. My wife is from one of those fancy waistcoat families up in Massachusetts. First time I saw her, Jesus wept, what a pretty little thing, like she stepped off a cameo, never imagined anything so dainty could walk and talk. And I fell for her, damn fool, I did, I mean she was a great challenge for a man like me. Acted unimpressed and above me, my own damn fault for taking it like a red flag in front of a bull. What pride won't do to a man."

But then you caught her, said Cassius.

"I chased her, but I did not catch her, no sir." A fine and healthy eructation gathered in Logue's belly, he fought it down, but it finally climbed through his chest and up his neck and escaped loudly. Cassius thought he could detect in the air a mist of lager.

But you said she was your wife, said Cassius.

"I got snared, Cassius. Snared. Walked right into it. A trap is what it was."

Cassius did not understand why Logue was telling him this. Unless it was similar to the way planters spoke indiscreetly in front of their people.

"I had a reputation by then, honed it myself to scare folks, get their respect, but I didn't think it could be used against me."

You named *yourself* The Angel Gabriel? said Cassius.

"Very nearly The Archangel, but then I thought that was a might ostentatious."

Cassius was amused to discover Logue's moniker was self-christened, but not surprised. He was now convinced that Logue had also never killed a man.

"That delicate little thing knew that someone with my reputation would need to claim such a prize, that was her trap, but she understood something else. She understood that I was the prize because I have the gift; I know how to make money off this good land. Her father came from old Europe and the old fool squandered his inheritance in bad deals. Only thing left of the family fortune was their manners. You are looking at the one and only breadwinner of my wife's noble ancestral clan."

That's power, then.

Logue slammed his fist on the table. "Now you'd think so, would you not? But all I get is disapproval. Money buys a seat at the table, and the right to follow their rules. I try, though. I try to use all those good manners. And now, refresher lessons in a letter."

She thought it easier to change you than learn how to make money, said Cassius.

"That precisely." Logue leaned in close and spoke conspiratorially. "You're around them, Cassius, tell me what to do."

Around *them*?

"Planters, rich folk. People with manners and culture, how do you deal with 'em, how do you handle 'em?"

Angel Gabriel, said Cassius, hiding his smile.

"Yes?"

The Angel Gabriel.

Logue sat back and cocked his head. "All right, I see where you're at. I got the reputation, I got the money, why not just let her and her kind have it?"

Why don't you?

"I guess I love her."

Ain't that a funny thing.

"Don't know what to do about it."

Maybe that's all you can do.

"What?"

Love her, said Cassius.

Logue sat up. He nodded and a light came into his eyes. "Show the woman that you love her and then maybe you don't need to change and get all fussy and grow manners. Love makes up for all that. I do believe she will like that. I knew you were the man to talk to. You certain I can't get you that beer?"

No beer.

Cassius reached for Morningside's papers in the haversack. But as he was about to reveal them, he said:

Why did Emoline lie about Hoke?

"Emoline lied about Hoke?"

She said Hoke came to her bed the first time when I learned that in fact she went to him.

Logue smiled. "Emoline was smart. Hoke took special care of her after that, which I think she counted on. Emoline knew, of all things, how to survive."

But why lie to me about it? said Cassius.

"Seems obvious enough to me, Cassius. Vanity. She did what was necessary, but when she got what she needed, she wanted to be seen as above it. She liked how you saw her. It was how she wanted to see herself."

Cassius had not considered that as a possibility, but it made good sense to him and after a moment's thought, he was relieved to have the secret explained.

With a smile, he laid Morningside's papers on the table. Logue looked them over, then looked up at Cassius.

"Where did you get these?"

You know what they are?

"Of course I know what they are, they're from Morningside," said Logue.

Cassius nodded. Logue had pretended that the members of the spy ring were unknown to one another, so everyone was protected, and yet the name Morningside was on the tip of his tongue. Cassius appreciated the man more every time he saw him. Logue looked at the documents closely.

"This tells us Lee's movements. Indirectly, but it gives us everything we want to know, as it says where supplies are being directed. Good information. It would have been a boon for the Union brass . . . three weeks ago. This is old intelligence. When it's past its time, it's useless."

Your man died for it. He was far gone as it was.

"You continue to be the bearer of bad news."

I saw him. Starving and talking crazy.

"Tell me he died of starvation."

No, Whitacre's ambush. Shot dead.

"Did you lead Whitacre to him?"

Whitacre was there before me.

"Then I have less time than I thought. I will endeavor to skedaddle, although I can't leave until tomorrow the earliest. I reckon that allows you to feel somewhat more contented."

Why contented?

"With your murderer revealed."

Not Morningside, said Cassius, genuinely mystified.

"Of course not. Solomon Whitacre killed Emoline."

Whitacre?

"He's on to us, removing us one by one. I won't underestimate him again. He'll come next for me."

Cassius felt a chill crawl under the crust of his back. It all came clear to him. He thought back and in his mind the pieces fit together. Whitacre. Of course. It made perfect sense. Maryanne had said that she and Whitacre were in town the week, no, the very day Emoline was murdered. He had only considered Maryanne as a possible culprit. Strange that Whitacre had not entered his consciousness. But there it was. Whitacre had been ordered to expose the spy ring.

While Cassius did not experience emotional satisfaction in the knowledge of Whitacre's culpability, rationally he knew it was right. It seemed that Whitacre had not bothered to give the order, but had carried out her death himself. It fell in with what Cassius knew of Whitacre's nature, a man of bluster committing a cowardly act, attacking a female spy from behind. Cassius pictured him bragging to his men that he alone had destroyed the key to the spy ring. Cassius looked at his hands with grief. He had been close to Emoline's killer and had not realized it.

Whitacre said he's returning to Lee. He won't come for you, said Cassius.

"He said that?"

To his men.

"He caught you?"

No. I overheard. Said Lee's taking the fight north, an invasion.

Logue's expression changed and he sat forward. "That is good information. He said those words?"

Close to them.

"I thank you for that, Cassius. That is news I can carry."

I heard a man speak once of the rascal's uncomplicated life.

"I did say that, did I not? Can't seem to help myself."

Cassius's gloom consumed him. His sense of hope slipped away.

If Whitacre's her killer, then I've lost him, said Cassius.

"You, Cassius? No, I think you will find a way. In time, Whitacre will return to his wife and family. You will have your chance then."

Not before year's end, at Yule celebration, and he anticipates a command so probably not even then. How would I get to him otherwise, he is an army captain, always surrounded by his men. And what am I? Just another man's property.

"Maybe someone else will carry out your revenge for you. Some Yank with a musket."

I made her a promise and failed.

"You carried it a good long way, Cassius, longer than any reasonable man could expect."

Cassius snorted at the idea that he might be perceived as a reasonable man.

I got to ask you a favor, said Cassius.

"Ah, Cassius, I'd take you along but now I got to travel in a different manner. Under other circumstances you could be my body servant, but not this time."

No, something else.

Logue smiled. "A favor from a smuggler? A favor from a dangerous man? A favor from the Angel of Death?"

Yes.

"I am all ears."

Emoline's money. Take it and buy her daughters.

"And I had such high hopes for you."

Give them their free papers. What hopes?

"I imagined you would keep that money, and here you prove me wrong. All along you wanted those girls to have their manumission papers. You're not dishonest enough to be a smuggler, Cassius. We will have to work on that."

Will you do it?

"You would be wise not to trust me."

Will you do it?

Logue was motionless as he thought. Then he nodded his head once. "I will find a way."

Then I will trust you up to that moment and distrust you after.

A sparkle passed through Logue's eyes.

"I will miss you, Cassius."

You don't ask the amount.

"No need. I had a look," he said with a gleam. "There may be enough if I do it right."

Thank you, said Cassius, and his sincerity was evident.

Cassius walked back from town, leaving the road well before Sweetsmoke so that he could approach undetected through forest. He had not realized that he had been away from the odor of the tobacco until he returned. It coated the back of his tongue and brought back the hard memories, but he forced it all aside. He went to his cabin, the quarters empty but for dogs and chickens, as the hands were in the field and the small children were up in the big house yard with Nanny Catherine. He ate from his rations and washed, then walked the lane to the carpentry shed.

With everything he had faced on his journey, he knew that he now faced the greatest danger. If he had not been missed, then he would go on with his daily life. If anyone knew he had been gone, there was little he could do. He would face dire consequences and perhaps the loss of his life. Confronting this stark possibility, he wondered why he had not done the same as Joseph. Once at the railroad trestle, he was well on his way out of the county. He had been unprepared to travel farther, but others had escaped knowing less.

He desperately wanted freedom and yet he had come back. What happened to his obligation to Emoline if he was unable to finish her justice? Accept defeat and run. And yet he had come back.

He gathered tools and went to the yard so that he might be seen.

The bantam rooster saw him first and lifted up on his toes, then ran fussing in the other direction. Cassius entered the yard and set down his tools by the wooden fence that he had repaired weeks before. Charles came out the front door and down the steps and he saw Cassius and stopped cold. Cassius stood tall and gave him a full look. Charles did not react at first, but Cassius saw the telltale surprise in his eyes, and at that moment he knew.

Charles ran triumphantly back into the big house, yelling that the runaway slave Cassius had been returned.

Cassius did not move from the spot. After a moment Ellen emerged gripping the bullwhip, spindle fingers white with tension. He saw the blaze of righteousness in her eyes, and the whip slowly unfurled from the handle in her hand, stretching down to her feet, and continuing its slow roll down the wood stairs, shaped by each individual step, until it laid its abradant head upon the dirt to wait, a swollen snake with a twitch. Charles leaned to see around her skirts.

Her voice came out strained, spit chasing the words. "Cassius, you vile, you *treacherous* fiend! You ungrateful *whelp*! Go to the post directly and remove your shirt, *someone secure him*, two days missing, *two days!*"

Cassius faced her with manifest calm, but he could scarcely hear her words for the roaring in his ears. Ellen had tied Marriah to the post and whipped her savagely and left her bleeding in the cold. But when Cassius did not move, Ellen hesitated, and in that moment Cassius understood that Hoke still lived. She was a powerful adversary and she held every card but one: He was still, in her eyes, Hoke's particular property. He had known the risks when he left the plantation, had known that this moment might come, but now that it had, it was worse than he'd anticipated. His life dangled by a thread. His reply needed caution and patience, and even then he saw little hope to elude her fury.

Quashee came from deep within the house, framed by the front door, and he saw terror course through her like a disease in the blood and his hope was further undermined. Up to that moment he had thought he could take his whipping, but right behind Quashee stood Pet with her delighted vengeful eyes. Peripherally he saw Mam Rosie come from her kitchen, and he turned his head to see her stop suddenly as if she had lunged against the limit of an invisible rope. He recognized her inner struggle, stay or go, bear witness or shrink from the abject humiliation of another human being. She stayed, as he knew she would. Cassius also knew that from now on his audience would only grow.

"Get to the post and strip, or by God I will lash you where you stand!" said Ellen.

It's true, Missus Ellen, I was gone, said Cassius and he was surprised to hear strength in his voice.

His comparative calm fanned the flames of her outrage. "How well I know *that*! Nettle inspected your cabin and the shed, you slept in neither! We sent a man to the clearing, you ran from Sweetsmoke, you cannot escape this!" She came down the steps, whip throbbing, optimistic snake. "Charles saw you creep away in the night."

Master Hoke didn't want you to know where, said Cassius.

She slapped him ferociously and the sting bit into his cheek like white-hot needles. "With my husband upstairs, I *command* this plantation, and I *will know* what he knows!"

Quashee wavered in the door. Mam Rosie covered her mouth with both hands. Nanny Catherine arrived with Mrs. Nettle and the children, and then Genevieve and Anne came and he was surrounded. Every one of them wore an expression of glowing anticipation. His degradation would be a circus act performed for women and children. He was convinced that escape was impossible; her indignation had grown so immense that she could not back down. A massive urge welled up inside him, to grab and choke her, to batter her physically if only for the small dignity he would gain by giving willful cause for his humiliation. He repressed the urge, but his temper was alive in his arms, pumping into his palms and fingers.

I'm loyal to Master. And you repay me with stripes, said Cassius softly, but inside his head, where the blood rushed hard, his voice chimed.

"What is *between* you?!? Some satanic connection? What is it about you that entrances my husband? What, tell me *what*!"

The exertion of her words exhausted her. Deep bruises encircled her eyes, and he knew she had not slept. He pictured her sitting beside her husband hour upon hour, praying that he might emerge from his fever, and Cassius knew her fatigue fed the blaze of her outrage.

Master Hoke sent me so you would face no danger, he said. The words came easily and surprised him as he had not anticipated them.

"*Me* face danger?"

I told him you're strong, that you can do what needs to be done, but he would protect you.

The urge to attack her grew and he feared he could not control it. And yet words came easily, as if from another.

"Then you tell me, Cassius, you tell me what needs to be done," said Ellen fiercely, but her grip on the bullwhip eased and the snake exhaled in the dust. "You tell me what my husband would not!"

Pet angled her head, her eyes losing their smile. She too felt the change, and Cassius's overwhelming compulsion to strike out took a small step back.

Master Hoke sent me to see a man.

"How could that be? Who would meet with you?"

The Angel, Missus Ellen.

"Oh Lord," she cried out with full understanding. "Oh my dear sweet Lord."

For Sweetsmoke.

"The smuggler, dear Lord, I thought that was ended."

You thought me a runaway?

"No, I— After Joseph I did not know— And then Charles saw you steal away in the night, so I was certain of it, and Mam Rosie confirmed it, saying you had told her. But here you are, so how could you be running? Everything around me is intolerable and bewildering, everything."

Master Hoke can't meet with Gabriel Logue. It falls to you.

"You tell me it falls to me? You tell me my business? You? One of my people?"

She spoke as if the decision had been made without her consent and she was forced to accept it.

Mr. Davis's government would trade worthless paper for your crop. Gabriel Logue will make a fair arrangement.

"I cannot. No. It is impossible; I cannot speak to that odious man."

I got no authority and Master Hoke not able.

"Mr. Davis's government," she said shaking her head. "You sound exactly like Mr. Howard."

Ellen Howard was disgusted that she was obligated to take action, and further disgusted that one of her slaves compelled her to that action. She did, however, understand that Cassius was correct. With Hoke indisposed, she needed to rise to every call of the Master's responsibilities, including distasteful decisions necessary to maintain Sweetsmoke's survival. She considered whipping Cassius anyway, if not for the bold expression on his face, then for the fact that he perpetually took liberties. He needed to be reminded that if an idea was to enter the mind of a slave, the threat of punishment would be its eternal partner. But while she had the strength to plan his punishment, she had not the will to follow through. She thought to call Mr. Nettle from the fields; he would be glad to exercise the whip. But that thought fled as a familiar twinge grabbed her hip and she slid into the place of discomfort only laudanum could relieve.

Cassius had seen the moment of danger flare back up and then recede, and he knew it was done. He breathed deeply and his breath pressed through him like fingers digging into hidden places he had given up for dead. He looked past her at Charles hanging on to her skirts and then at Pet in the doorway, and as he came back to life he smiled at them both. Charles looked as if he had been properly disemboweled, and Pet slipped away into the cool darkness of the big house. Only Quashee exhibited relief, her mouth open to welcome oxygen, her back leaning hard against the doorjamb. Nanny Catherine scuttled off with her charges like a hen shepherding chicks, Ellen's daughters wafted away, and Cassius turned to Mam Rosie. He was not surprised to find that she was no longer there. She had told Ellen that Cassius had planned to run when Cassius had been careful to tell her nothing.

The gentleman is at the *bierhaus*, Missus. Best you be going this afternoon, as you won't find him tomorrow.

Ellen nodded, her revulsion now complete as she would need to enter the German section of town.

❧ Chapter Fourteen ❦

CASSIUS met her near the stand of trees that shielded the privy from the big house. He waited while she emptied chamber pots and noted the flowers blooming around the structure. She set the pots aside in a clump of tall grass shiny in the sun and they moved back but still out of sight of the big house. Face-to-face with her actual person, he realized that a dream version of her had accompanied him on the road and he knew that he had exaggerated their moment, a single impulsive kiss that she had likely found inconsequential. She glanced nervously in the direction of the big house and he read that as an onerous sign.

Good to see you safe, said Quashee.

How is he? said Cassius.

Doctors came. They bled him, but no change.

He nodded, and thought about what would happen if Hoke were to die.

She reached out and took his hand as if reading his mind: He won't die, Cassius. He's strong.

Her hand was warm and dry and he was reassured, but now he thought of how fragile the connections were when others held the power over their lives.

Sometime you got to tell me about where you went, said Quashee. But I got to get back soon.

I'll tell you everything, said Cassius. He smiled then, remembering something else: You ever imagine your Sarah a dancer?

I wait up every night but she ain't been dancing since. Sorry, Missus *hasn't* been dancing since. What dance was she on about?

It's what they do at white dances, call it the waltz, one two three one two three. Pictured herself decked out in a fancy dress. I got to wondering who was dreaming—the invalid from her bed, or the slave breaking into his master's study?

Is that so, she saw herself in a gown? said Quashee, and her face opened up with the wonder of a child.

He imitated Sarah lifting the fabric of her nightdress: Held it so, looking in the eyes of a partner who was a might taller than her Jacob, and did a curtsy.

That poor, sour old thing. You'd never know, listening to her— Quashee get me water, Quashee I'm too cold, Quashee now it's hot—a gown and handsome partner. Always wondered why she don't want me sleeping in her room. Would've ruined her secret.

The back door of the big house slammed shut and they heard a child scream and laugh, another one chasing, all out of sight.

Got to be careful, said Quashee. Pet watches me. She pretends now, like she's my friend, but sometimes I see her face when she thinks I'm not looking. Got to get back before I'm missed.

When do I see you?

In the afternoon, she said and picked up the empty pots on her way back to the big house.

They were not able to meet that afternoon, nor in the afternoons that followed. With Cassius returned, Quashee was under greater scrutiny. They were limited to brief moments of conversation in passing.

Ellen Howard had gone to see Gabriel Logue on that afternoon, but had not left the plantation since. Nothing about their meeting

had reached Cassius's ears. Beauregard had driven her in the carriage, but he had remained outside and she had revealed to him no
indication of its success or failure. Cassius had been directed to town
the next day to collect the post and newspaper. He had looked for
Logue, but by then The Angel was gone.

Joseph was released from the barn after a week of confinement,
and was carried facedown on a litter to Abram and Savilla's cabin
where his rehabilitation continued. Cassius was sad to see that his
tuft was no longer a unique mark, as the hair on Joseph's head had
gone completely gray. Hoke's condition was unchanged.

Cassius returned to the drudgery of plantation life as July moved
into August. He thought often about Whitacre, but did not know
how to resolve his promise to himself about Emoline. He often
worked close to the big house, to be near Quashee, near Hoke. Cassius was taken for granted. He had not run when given the opportunity, and had so earned Ellen's trust. He was sent with regularity to
the town to conduct basic family business. He drove the carriage, but
as it was not a buckboard, it resisted transporting supplies, showing
wear and distress. Cassius's presence in town became no more unusual than a shadow. He created a routine, stopping initially in front
of the dry goods to review the lists posted of the local dead. As
most of the men were members of the same unit, when they saw
battle, multiple casualties were common. He made a show of pre-
tending he could read, entertaining the townspeople. Thus he was
able to spend time perusing the list. To maintain his secret, he would
eventually ask one of the passing whites to read him the list, keeping
the game alive by saying he had something in his eye or could not
make out the handwriting. The white would chortle agreeably, a
willing partner in Cassius's charade of intelligence, and while the
white read aloud, Cassius pretended to listen. Upon his return, the
Howard family would rush to meet him and he would inform them
of Jacob's absence on the list. Once they knew Jacob was safe for another day, they would ask for news of others, always double-
checking his memory.

"Are you sure William Anderson was on the list?"

Oh yes, ma'am, Mr. Morse told it to me particularly.

The women would mourn the names and make plans to visit
widows or mothers. But the overall mood was good, as their Jacob

was alive, the war continued to go well for Lee and the Army of Northern Virginia, and they anticipated an overall Confederate victory within weeks.

He did not seek out Mam Rosie. She would come to him, in time.

He finished reading *The Tragedy of Julius Caesar* and was disappointed. He read to discover in what way Shakespeare's Cassius was an honorable man, only to find that those exact words were never uttered. Mark Antony, or Antonius, spoke of Brutus as an honorable man. He said, "So are they all, all honorable men," a reference meant to include Caius Cassius. Brutus was "honorable" many times over, while the honor of his ally Cassius was but inferred. Cassius understood that Mark Antony did not mean what he said. Mark Antony's speech roused the Roman masses and by its conclusion, "honorable" had come to mean "traitorous."

Within the shadows and hollows of a hot and unusually dry August, Cassius reviewed Hoke's meaning when he had said Cassius was an honorable man. Had he meant to be injurious? Was he enjoying a laugh at Cassius's ignorance? Cassius decided that the irony worked against Hoke. When Hoke had not prevented his son Jacob from taking Marriah to bed, Hoke had been an "honorable" man, while Cassius—to use Mark Antony's sarcastic words— would choose to wrong the dead and wrong himself rather than wrong such an honorable man. When his temper retreated in fatigue, he wondered if perhaps Hoke had known all along that he had wronged Cassius, and had intentionally pointed the irony back at himself.

Cassius grew increasingly unhappy with his name and began to weigh alternatives. But each new moniker he tried on fit him no better than a costume; he tugged and stretched them until abandoning each one in turn.

Cassius made weary plans to return the book to Hoke's library.

Work in the fields took on a normal, seasonal urgency. The blight was long defeated, the occasional plucked hornworm now an anomaly. The summer aged. The hands primed and topped the tobacco plants, removing leaves close to the ground, as well as flowers, seeds, and compact leaves from the head of the plant. Harvest was weeks away, its timing to be decided by Mr. Nettle, and he was meticulous in his inspections, shuffling from row to row, touching each plant, contemplating the sun, anticipating precipitation, rolling handfuls of soil in his palms, calculating, calculating. The hands did the same, arguing among themselves about the optimum moment. The sun hung lower in the sky and the days were shorter, with daylight pinched from both ends. Ellen surprised her people with unwelcome visits to the fields, more visits than her husband had been known to make. Her ignorant fingers grasped leaves that seemed to waver and withdraw from her touch. Savilla recognized her urgent desire for a triumphant harvest, and she followed Ellen discreetly, superstitiously touching the same leaves as if to calm them.

One afternoon in town, Cassius met Weyman loading supplies onto Thomas Chavis's buckboard. Weyman paused and allowed himself to be entertained by watching Cassius rearrange sacks of grain to fit in the carriage.

I see y'all Sweetsmokes take your dry goods real serious, said Weyman.

How's that? said Cassius.

To me, that's just a sack of barley.

It's barley, so?

I'm just sayin, barley is barley, and if you don't look out, you goin spoil it.

It's not spoiled, Weyman. It's fresh.

Lugging it around in the fancy-nancy carriage, I bet y'all sing it to sleep with a lullaby.

Cassius caught up to Weyman's joke and joined in: Dry goods getting pretty dear around here, Weyman. You don't treat 'em right, they likely to run off to war.

Cassius wanted to stay and banter with Weyman, but he had a week-old copy of the *Whig* as well as a letter from Jacob to his mother, and he was anxious to read them.

Once outside of town he eased off on the reins and Sam slowed to an amble. Jacob rarely sealed the envelopes that carried his letters and this one was no exception. Cassius opened it. It was cautious and newsy and told him nothing except that at the time it was written, Jacob did not know of his father's illness. Reading between the lines, Cassius understood that Jacob was changed by the war, but that Jacob knew his mother well enough to pacify her with platitudes. Ellen however would not be fooled. He unfolded the *Richmond Daily Whig*. A battle had taken place at Cedar Mountain and General Thomas Jackson, referred to by his nickname "Stonewall," had driven Union general Nathaniel Banks from the field. Cassius refolded the newspaper, and snapped the reins to lift Sam out of his lethargy. He would learn later that Ellen read the newspaper aloud to her unconscious husband, but he did not hear if she had done the same with Jacob's letter.

Throughout this time, Quashee continued to be watched closely by Pet and even Sundays when the hands were free, Quashee's presence was always urgently needed at the big house.

Cassius tested boundaries. Some nights he slept in the quarters, others in the carpentry shed. He noticed no increased suspicion, from either Mr. Nettle or Big Gus. He gradually recognized his opportunity, and began to contemplate a plan to shadow Lee's army in search of Solomon Whitacre. With the decision still unresolved in his mind, he began to mend his clothing and hoard food. He built a new pair of shoes and did not skimp. He carefully measured his foot so that there was room for his large toe to spread when he walked; he used the best leather he could find, leather reserved for the planter family's shoes; he rejected exposed stitching to make the more durable pegged soles, but once that was done, he decided to disguise his handiwork by adding exposed stitching, thereby making the shoes appear of lower quality. Once finished, he scuffed and dripped paint and glue on them.

On a night when he planned to sleep in the quarters, he saw Jenny hovering near his cabin. Her intention to speak to him became obvious when she did not rush away. She waited for an opening. He surmised that she had come to offer a truce. He stepped out his door and sat on the extended step that served as a small deck. He nodded to her and took up his whittling knife and set to carving. She stayed a few steps off in the lane.

I have missed my friend, said Cassius without looking up.

I was missin you, too, said Jenny.

Everybody been busy.

She took a step toward him.

I brought some things from my garden, said Jenny, opening her apron and revealing carrots, radishes, and okra.

Glad to have them, I thank you. Sit?

So I guess you heard, then, said Jenny without moving closer.

Not sure, said Cassius.

'Bout Big Gus?

Not a word.

She came over and sat, setting out the radishes and carrots in a line.

Mind you, it a secret from Abram.

All right, said Cassius, not certain he wanted to know something that was to be kept from a friend.

Abram been tellin things to Big Gus, confidin, you know.

Abram and Big Gus?

Told Big Gus things 'bout you and that little girl.

Cassius nodded as his mind raced, fitting pieces together. Jenny was speaking to him, for which he was grateful. She continued to hold a grudge against Quashee, but that did not surprise. Abram had betrayed him to an enemy. He set that aside to be considered later and said nothing.

He's just doin what he can to protect his boy, said Jenny.

Before or after Joseph ran?

Both ways, before and after. Even after Joseph got stripes. Big Gus sayin to him that it could still go worse for him.

Cassius set his mouth in a line.

So Savilla keep her plan secret from a husband who can't keep a secret from the Driver, said Jenny.

Poor Abram.

Maybe, maybe not. One day we's all out there mindin our business and Big Gus he come over to Savilla's row and want to see where she at with her primin and all, so she show him her bag and it only 'bout half-full. Now Big Gus lookin for anythin to keep that family down, so he nod and smile pretendin that everythin okay and such, but he go right to Mr. Nettle and say, Oh Mr. Nettle that wicked Savilla not doin her work!

Why that son of a—

No wait, said Jenny. Big Gus come back with Mr. Nettle and they walk on up to Savilla and Mr. Nettle he say, Open your bag, Savilla, and Savilla she open her bag and lo and behold, it full of tobacco leaves. Mr. Nettle look in and then he look at Big Gus and he say,

Now Gus, don't let me find out you got it in for this family. He got a inkling Big Gus drove poor Joseph to run.

How about that Savilla, said Cassius with admiration.

Ain't the half of it. So Big Gus go 'way mad, and he thinkin 'bout what he can do to get even. He don't like it much when Mr. Nettle not trustin him.

No, I reckon not.

So we all know Polly been sidlin up to Big Gus 'cause she like the special treatment.

Polly's no fool, said Cassius.

And everybody know Fawn can't keep her mouth shut to save her life.

Fawn can't keep her mouth shut to save her breath, said Cassius.

So next day come and some of the older ones go over and be primin and toppin near Fawn, and they talk all in a hush so Fawn can't help but listen. And one of 'em say Andrew done it, he run off, like his brother, and Fawn, she hear that and she likely to burst. She go right to her friend Polly and tell her Andrew done run away, and Polly don't even pretend to hide it, she call Big Gus over wavin her arms and tellin him directly. Big Gus get that wide smile he get when he plannin to give it to someone? And he go right to Mr. Nettle and say, Mr. Nettle, sorry to say, but we got ourselves another runaway, and this time it be Andrew.

But Andrew's ten, said Cassius looking around for any sign of Andrew in the lane.

Just wait now, so Mr. Nettle he march right over to where Abram and Savilla workin and he say, Your boy Andrew done run this morning?

Big Gus is with him?

Right by his side, and Andrew, who been hidin from Big Gus all mornin pop up his head and say, I am right here, Mr. Nettle.

He's a good boy.

And Mr. Nettle, he turn on Big Gus and say I done warned you, Gus. I trust you to be fair with all our people and you done undermined my trust.

He said undermined?

He say undermined, and I like to think he whip Big Gus right there, but he done give him a sack and send him off down a row away from everybody and told him to start toppin and primin.

So wait a minute, where's Gus now?

Hidin out in his cabin. You shoulda seen Abram, he was swearin and cussin out his Savilla, sayin he had Big Gus calmed down and now she got him all riled up again, but I think Big Gus not be comin back to Driver no time soon.

So Big Gus finally got his, said Cassius with satisfaction.

Sure seem like it, said Jenny and they laughed together.

And Savilla, how 'bout that, said Cassius.

She a strong one when it come to her boys.

Good to have someone looking out for you, said Cassius.

Jenny looked at him pointedly and said: Real good to have someone look out for you.

Yes it is, said Cassius, continuing to chuckle as he played it out in his mind, picturing their expressions and body language.

Take me with you, Cassius, said Jenny suddenly.

How's that? Cassius stopped laughing.

You heard, take me with you, I can't stand much more, I got to go with you.

What makes you think I'm going?

Please, Cassius.

Cassius looked at her but now said nothing.

She stood up abruptly. Please, she said. Think about it.

She walked quickly away leaving radishes and carrots and okra in a line on his step. If Jenny knew he was planning to run, then everyone knew, and he had thought he was undecided. He had also thought he was inscrutable, only to find that he was no less transparent than Fawn. He watched Jenny go along the gully and out of sight up near her cabin.

The next day Mam Rosie came to see him. She came in the afternoon with the sun high, and he thought of Jenny and wondered if Mam Rosie also knew. She had removed her apron, and wore her good dress, and she found him outside the barn repairing a wagon wheel.

Cassius was impressed that she was not apologetic.

I ain't had no chance to see you since you come back, said Mam Rosie.

You been busy.

Busy? Always busy, what you mean busy?

Hoke ill, people coming and going, doctors and visitors, said Cassius.

Mouths to feed, that so.

Well, it's a fine surprise to see you.

Mam Rosie winced, but he kept the smile firmly planted on his face.

Cassius, you know's well as I it ain't no fine surprise, said Mam Rosie, thus marking the deliberate course change in their conversation.

Cassius looked at her and allowed his easy smile to fade. He knew she knew that he would not make it easy, but he would also not make it impossible.

I didn't mean it the way it come out, said Mam Rosie. I didn't mean it the way it happened.

Never thought you did.

Didn't do it to hurt you.

All right.

I thought you was gone, clean away. I thought you was smart to do it, too. The way you think about everything all the way to the end. The way you plan things out.

You flattering me, Rose?

No, Cassius. Just me and you.

All right, Rose. Tell me how you thought.

Master Hoke sick, said Mam Rosie. He not there to lead them paddyrollers after you, and you know them paddyrollers, if he ain't there, they don't care the same way. And the way they just got paid paper money for Joseph, too, how much they get worked up for another runner after that? They go hard in the bush for Joseph, and now they got another one? No, sir, they never find a smart one like you. I was glad for you. I knowed you was away for good.

So you saw an opportunity, said Cassius.

Now what you got to say that for?

I know you, Rose. Don't you think I don't.

Mam Rosie remembered how she had used those very words on him, and her face twisted in recognition and pain.

I deserve that, I do. But Missus Ellen, she promise me some old clothes, fine linen, hard worn, but nice, you know how that be. I do be likin that soft cloth. But after she say that, it never come so I figure she done forgot, or maybe she promise in her happy time with that secret bottle. I knowed you was safe, so I figure ain't no harm to give her somethin, so maybe after she trust me a little and I can ask her again for them things she already promise.

She give them to you?

Give what? said Mam Rosie.

After you told her I said I was running, she give you the linen?

No. She done forgot.

You never got them.

No.

Never.

Mam Rosie understood his meaning as he reemphasized her betrayal of him for soft linen.

Who you think you are? said Mam Rosie.

She turned and walked away, back to her kitchen, and he went back to repairing the wheel.

❧ Chapter Fifteen ❧

QUASHEE found a piece of time to slip away and met him outside the carpentry shed. She was different, girlish, and he did not immediately appreciate that she was flirting. Finally she took his hand and led him into the shed. Her eyes did not wander but remained fixed on his. Her clothes carried the aroma of fish from the whale oil lamps in the big house, and Cassius was again pleasantly reminded of power and privilege. He felt himself aroused, in proximity to a strong, exciting woman who desired him; better still, a woman who had chosen him, someone who smelled good in an influential and elegant way, and he welcomed the moment, turning his head slightly and closing his eyes to breathe her in. She was very close, and his memory brought back the night in the big house so completely that he felt the sensation of her warm mouth against his and then something turned in his mind and he forced himself to step back and he moved away from her across the shed.

You all right? said Quashee and he saw the awkward tilt of her shoulders and the confused hurt in her eyes.

I am. No. Guess I'm not, said Cassius.

I thought maybe this time was good for us, said Quashee, and he had never before heard insecurity in her voice.

It would be. Should be, even might be.

Her eyes opened wider as she contemplated the enormity of her error, believing she had completely misread him.

Oh, said Quashee. I'm sorry, I thought something else.

You didn't think wrong.

No, I did and I'm sorry, said Quashee and she backed up toward the door.

You're not wrong, Quashee. But something changed.

You don't got to explain, I best be getting back.

No, not yet. Hear me.

She stopped at the door, and her girlishness was gone and he was sorry. Her shoulders tried to close around her heart and her eyes were large and moist in her face. He saw that she was alone, and it broke his heart.

I—I got to go again, said Cassius.

You only just come back.

Something to finish.

I will miss you, said Quashee, and she was another inch closer to the door. She opened it a crack. He saw that she wanted to be away to keep private any display of emotion.

You don't understand, said Cassius.

I do, said Quashee.

You don't. Listen now.

She turned her face away, and a slant of brightness from the open door swelled in her liquid eyes.

I see you, said Cassius. I see you in the yard or by a window or coming down the lane and my poor heart flies. I think on you when I'm alone just working and I smile inside. You come to my dreams and I wake up at peace. I want to know what it is to touch your hair, to know if your back is smooth or striped, to know how you sound when you breathe while you sleep. I want to know that everything'll be all right. And when I think that, I get afraid, and remember how it was when I was cold because I didn't want and didn't offer. That was a good time—they couldn't hurt me and I couldn't hurt because no one got close.

Only Emoline, said Quashee softly.

Only close enough to mend so I could stand again.

I think she did more.

I wasn't afraid then. If they hurt me I could take it. If they killed me, then the thing that I am stops and I could take that too. I didn't care, and now that's changed and that says I can hurt you, and I can't take that. I don't know how to say you should give up love, but if you don't, then they got every power over you, every one. If you don't love, then there's one thing they can't destroy.

That's a compliment, only it means you won't be with me, said Quashee.

I could be, I could put a whole life of you in my last days here, but where are you after? A man on the road, and you not knowing where or if he's coming back. I got to go. If I'm a gambling man, I don't bet on my chances. I am tired of the hurt and I don't want to cause more.

So I did this.

How you mean?

You opened to me, and it made you afraid.

No, that's not right.

But think, Cassius, if you don't let it happen, that fear and pain all be for nothin. 'Cause that's all you got, fear and pain, so you got none of the good that goes with it. It's the good lets us stand the pain.

Cassius closed his eyes and exhaled.

Never thought I was unlucky, said Quashee.

No no no no, said Cassius.

But I look around and there's Pet close by every day.

It's not better in the big house than the fields?

When you outside Missus Ellen only hear what someone say about you in her ear, she can't see you every day—

And see you're good.

Okay, but then every day she also reminded about you.

Cassius opened his palms in a gesture of helplessness.

Master John-Corey was a straight-up man, said Quashee. Different from his father. Simple.

I know, I remember, said Cassius.

Old Hoke, he's like other planters, grand and poetic and naming plantations Swan of Alicante and Edensong and Horn of Plenty and Sweetsmoke, while John-Corey Howard just made his Howard. Howard Plantation.

John-Corey's great-grandfather made his Sweetsmoke.

I'm saying John-Corey was not complicated. Straight-up. And I fit in. I knew what was expected. I was proud of what I did. Life was slow, but it was safe. I had a man at John-Corey's.

I didn't know.

I know you didn't. We didn't jump the broom or nothing, but we had each other for a time and it was something for me. He was in the big house, too, and he was straight-up. Straight up and good to me. It was nice to have someone. When John-Corey got killed, he got sold with all the rest, all of them but my father and me. I cried, but it was over quick. That was a surprise 'cause I found out I didn't love him. He was a good man, and I miss him, but I didn't love him. I had kept back some part of me when I was with him. After that I was at Howard Plantation for months closing it, and I got easy with the idea I would never love. And then I got unlucky to meet you, and more unlucky when you said no.

Quashee pushed the door of the shed wide, and the sudden sunny green of the outdoors shocked his eyes.

My back, she said, is smooth.

She ran out the door, and he followed to see her go from the sun into the shadow of the trees on the way back to the big house.

S he hadn't been gone more than an hour when he heard her call: He's worse, Cassius, come quick!

He dropped his tools and saw her running to him, slowing as he started in her direction: He's worse. Come now.

He ran with her to the big house, and followed her in and up the stairs. She stopped at the door to Hoke's bedroom and Cassius passed her and removed his hat. Hoke's eyes were open, but he saw nothing. He spoke but in words that Cassius did not recognize. Hoke raised a trembling hand and then down it fluttered and he was quiet, but his open eyes looked wildly around, as if he could not understand the things he was seeing, and those things frightened him unimaginably.

Cassius stared at the man on the bed, knowing how different things would be when he died. Then he realized that Ellen was speaking loudly in his ear.

"Go, Cassius, go now, fetch the doctor, do not simply stand there gaping," she said.

Cassius returned in the carriage with the doctor following in his own buggy. Cassius trailed the man up the stairs, but the doctor closed the door to shut him out. Cassius went to sit near the front porch, and within the hour the doctor emerged alone, snugging his hat on his head and going for his buggy; things were not good. Cassius heard no crying within, so the old man wasn't dead. Genevieve came to the yard and walked the long way around to the kitchen, as if she could no longer remember what she had set out to do a moment before. He watched the comings and goings inside the house, and through the window he saw Ellen Howard descend the stairs and cross the large greeting room to Hoke's study.

He stood and dusted off his trousers but did not bother to put his hat on his head. He stepped up to the front porch. He caught a glance of the bantam rooster and he made an abrupt move toward the little cock and said: Go on now. The rooster ran in a circle then went around the corner out of sight. Cassius felt sour in the pit of his stomach. He entered the big house without knocking, crossing the large greeting room to Hoke's study. He stopped there, and saw Pet's shock at his brazen entrance. He handed her his hat. She looked at it with stunned disapproval, set it down on a sideboard, and scurried away. He knocked on the study door.

"Yes yes, come in," said Ellen.

Cassius did so.

Ellen Howard commanded Hoke's desk in a way different than her husband. Hoke embraced the wood; he touched it and gathered strength from its warmth and grain. Ellen acted as if she could rise above it. Cassius sensed that her power was precarious.

"Cassius," said Ellen, and her tone of voice betrayed her lack of tolerance.

Missus Ellen, if time is short, then make the best of it.

"You continue to take many liberties."

If so, it's for family and Sweetsmoke, said Cassius.

"I forbid you to use that tone with me, Cassius."

You think Master Hoke won't live long.

Ellen glared at him, and for a moment he thought he had gambled too recklessly, but then she looked away and he knew he had won.

"The doctor is not optimistic."

Cassius remembered the lessons he had learned from Emoline, and he conjured up a story on the spot: You been having dreams.

"How did you know?"

Dreams about your family.

Her carriage went rigid.

Good news comes about the war and you believe you got to pay for it somehow.

"Oh God," said Ellen, and her arms crossed in front of her, hands to her shoulders as if he had torn off her dress.

Cassius intended to prey on her fears. He only wished he could unsettle her more.

I had a look at your dreams, said Cassius quietly.

She kept her arms crossed and her head drew back in surprise.

You're not careful, Missus Ellen. Letting down your guard. You were protecting Master Jacob, but now your energy goes to Sweetsmoke. The line to him is weaker.

"Do not speak to me in that way, Cassius," said Ellen, in a whisper close to a hiss.

I can help you.

"How can you help me?"

You best remake the connection to your son in a hurry. You can't lose both.

"Aah!" she cried out, loudly, her deepest fear rended from her insides and laid out fresh and wretched.

Bring him home, said Cassius.

"How can I? How? How is that possible?"

Someone's got to tell him his father's dying.

Ellen's mouth made a flat line.

Someone's got to bring him back.

"Who can go, who can do that?"

I can.

"*You?* How would you do that?"

First find the army, then find your son. Bring him home, but then it falls to you, you make him stay.

Ellen's eyes went wild much as Hoke's had done earlier, but in her madness she saw possibilities. Cassius glanced at the portrait behind Hoke's desk, and in that moment, he recognized what the painter had captured.

You got to have Jacob back, said Cassius simply.

They worked out the details. The carriage had to remain at the plantation. Cassius would find whatever transportation availed itself. She wrote out a pass and an accompanying letter explaining who he was, and that he was on his way to see his master who was with the Army of Northern Virginia. Her letter was concise, and he was impressed by it.

She said that at dawn, someone would take him in the carriage to the outskirts of the town and then he would be on his own.

He took the letter and the pass and walked to the door of the study and opened it. He saw Quashee on the other side, halfway down the stairs, supporting herself with her hand on the banister, staring at him. From behind him, he heard Ellen say, "You will do this, Cassius? You will bring him back? You won't just go off, you will fulfill your duty to us?"

He looked back at her, and Ellen was standing in almost exactly the same pose as Quashee, supporting herself with her hand on the bookshelf.

Cassius looked again to Quashee and said: I'll come back, if I am able. I will make you that promise.

He went to his cabin in the quarters to collect his things. From the secret hiding place he removed the stash of money he had earned from being loaned out as a carpenter, leaving the soldier he had carved for his son. There was more money than he had remembered. He thought back on the six months spent doing finish work on the addition to Swan of Alicante's big house, and realized Hoke had not taken his half. He folded the bills and slid them into the small panel he had sewn into the inside of his trousers leg, up near the left knee. He put one stitch in the top of the panel so that the money could not accidentally fall out.

His decision hardened in his mind. He would accept nothing less than the death of Solomon Whitacre. His death for hers. It no longer mattered what happened to him afterward. He was absolute in his final promise to himself, that he would kill Emoline's murderer. No matter the cost.

He filled Jacob's old haversack with salted beef and pork and ashcakes. He inspected his hat, and was sorry he hadn't taken the time to repair it. It would have to do. He would go out later, when the sun went down, to his traps. He would give any trapped animal to Savilla, and then he would shut them down for good. He would not allow an animal to starve to death inside an abandoned trap.

He heard a light knock on his cabin door. He opened it to find Shedd, The Little Angry Man.

Let me in, said Shedd.

Cassius backed up and The Little Angry Man dragged his bad leg into the cabin.

Shut that door, said Shedd. Cassius did so.

What brings you—?

Shut up. I know you're gonna run, said Shedd.

Not going to run, said Cassius.

You are. I seen it. New shoes, mendin trousers, everybody seen it.

Cassius wasn't surprised. Jenny had known, so others knew as well. Shedd's wandering eye darted around his cabin, and he saw that Shedd was having difficulty remaining still. Shedd's leg hurt him and he got jumpy and fidgety if he didn't keep it moving.

Not going to run.

Shedd gave Cassius a violent look.

Don't need to, said Cassius.

What's that mean?

Got a pass from Old Missus. She's sending me.

Hah!

Think I'm lying?

You listen up 'cause you can't make it with that.

Not taking you with me.

You think I go with *you*?

Cassius was caught off-guard: Then why're you here?

I'm the one sent Joseph to the Underground Railroad.

You sent him?

'S right.

He got caught.

Not my doin.

How do I know, how do I know you didn't set him up?

Cassius took a menacing step toward Little Angry Man, but Little Angry Man did not go off.

He almost got there, said Shedd. I talked to him after, in the barn. Joseph did it hisself, even said so. Tried to stand up to a paddy-roller when he was almost safe; I warned him, you can't run on hate, you got to run smart. He got hisself caught. You ask him, he'll say. But that don't matter to you, you won't do stupid like Joseph.

Cassius backed up across the room, sat and looked hard at Shedd. Shedd began to twitch, needing to change the position of his leg. He finally turned it inward, clamping his hip at a taut angle, forcing thigh muscles to grip so his leg would stay there, then looked back at Cassius with an unforced grimace.

You don't got to trust me, Cassius, don't know why you would, except you smart enough to know when somethin's right. So listen close, you son of a pox whore's bastard, this what you look for. The song ain't lyin, "Follow the Drinkin Gourd." Star up there called the North Star.

You think I don't know this? said Cassius, impatiently. I know north from south, even at night.

I know you know, but I'm sayin it anyways, you follow it, 'cause that where it leads. Travel at night, that give you the best chance.

I told you, I got a pass.

Hah, big head big shot got hisself a pass, only you take one step outta this county and that pass only good to wipe your ass. No one outside knows a white Howard from a white magnolia.

Cassius knew it was true. Shedd was offering authentic advice.

Why you helping me?

Just shut your hole and listen, swole-headed prick. Go at night and duck them paddyrollers, they get nastier the closer you get to the North. Plenty of work up there, grabbin runaway niggers. Folks always greedier when they got more. You get yourself to a town call Shamburg, they got a safe house, part of the Underground Railroad.

Cassius paid strict attention.

You wait till night, look for a light on a hill. They leave a lantern up when it safe, not the house on the top, but about halfway. You go to the front door. But don't be a mule's ass, keep your eyes open, 'cause shit changes. And don't look down, look up and watch, you see a white man catch your eye and make a sign with his hand, like touch his chin or his nose, he offerin you a safe house. You follow him, understand?

I understand.

Be careful, Cassius. Don't talk 'bout what you doin. Don't tell no-body at Suetsmoke when you're goin.

I know that, but why say so?

They try 'n' queer it for you. They resent you.

Not all of them.

You Hoke's boy, always been. You got more leeway, you don't get punished the way others get 'cause your master favors you. But you ain't safe. Big Gus aimed for you, and you damn lucky he missed. And if Hoke dies, there be more comin after you. Who knows, maybe I be one.

Shedd headed for the door, his wandering eye taking one last look around.

White man make a sign, said Shedd, you follow.

Chapter Sixteen

THE afternoon of the first of September promised heavy rains.

Mr. Nettle drove him in the carriage. Cassius sensed his seething resentment at being assigned this chore. The ride unfolded in silence, giving Cassius time to consider Ellen Howard's surprising choice of a reinsman, wondering about her motive. Had she taken into account the coming harvest and the demotion of the Driver? If so, then she was taking Cassius's journey seriously, delegating a white man to convey him. As they rode past the fields, the hands watched them ride off the rim of the property.

Mr. Nettle dropped him at the fork and stared at him coldly.

"Reckon the next time I set eyes on you, you'll be in chains."

Mr. Nettle swung the carriage around to sprint back to Sweetsmoke. Cassius began his walk north. He passed the Chavis farm and saw Weyman far off in the field, but this time he did not stop.

Cassius was obliged only once to show his pass on the road, and he offered the one signed by Ellen Howard. The man reluctantly accepted it as real, and Cassius had the impression that he could not read.

By midday he had arrived at his first destination. Ralph had described the location of his isolated one-room shack, and Cassius had no difficulty locating it.

Ralph gave him food and, despite Cassius's objections, insisted he sleep there that night, as he anticipated a full day's ride. They would leave in the morning. Although impatient to begin, when the thunderstorms arrived, Cassius was glad they were not on the road.

Cassius told Ralph as little as possible, but he did say that he wanted to get to Lee's army. Cassius asked about Shamburg and the Underground Railroad. Ralph told him that he was not likely to see that town as he was to travel in a different direction altogether if he was to find Lee.

Ralph's roof leaked under the aggressive storm until the interior smelled of wet lamb's wool and something musky. The raucous thunder habitually stomped at the very moment Cassius was nodding off, so he slept poorly and woke ahead of the sun. Ralph, however, was not a man to be rushed. He had waited most of his life to be free, and reveled in the languid pace of his current existence. He woke late and ate slowly. He owed speed to no one, and made no apologies for his torpor.

They set out under a strong sun, Cassius staring at Carolina's backside as she pulled them. They avoided the large milky brown puddles, staying to the center of the road as trees dripped on both sides. The road gradually dried, but the journey was not unpleasant as the coating of rain kept dust to a minimum. By nine o'clock Ralph informed Cassius they had left the county. Cassius considered the journey ahead. He had memorized the maps, but lines and shapes and names could not prepare him for reality. From here on, the world would be unfamiliar. He could not control the large things, so he concentrated on the small. He would not use Ellen's pass again, trusting Shedd's wisdom, and hoped the forged passes would suffice. He had filled them out with planter names that he hoped would be common throughout Virginia, names like Johnson and Smith, fudging the signatures so that they would be tricky to read. He thought to affect a stutter if questioned, in hopes that any slave catcher or patroller would suggest a local name out of impatience. He did not need to implement his plan on this day, however. They passed farms, travelers, villages, and just as in the journey to the train trestle, Ralph was known. Cassius glanced at Ralph to view him from a white's point of view. A fat, grizzled old uncle, salty haired with silver stubble defending his chin and cheeks who would bring next to nothing at slave auction. They would not know he only pretended to rejoice when seeing this or that fool, and that he mumbled insults through his smile. Cassius was initially unaware of his words, but after he'd heard the quiet mutterings a half dozen times, he leaned in and caught the nodding grinning remark about "waistcoat can't hide that watermelon abdomen, Alistair y'old peahen," and Cassius laughed out loud. Alistair glanced back over his shoulder and Ralph looked at Cassius as if he'd gone brain simple on the spot, and he urged Carolina forward and did not mutter again.

Cassius gauged the sun and estimated they had reached the noon hour. That meant the halfway mark, assuming Ralph was correct. They approached a small town nestled among a dense cluster of trees, a white church spire jutting from the middle of all that green, and as they rounded an elbow in the road they came upon a black man swinging by his neck from the stout branch of a white oak. He had been hanging a few days, his corpse bloated and gray, a sad swaying message to someone somewhere. Then Cassius started because the man's eyes moved. He leaned forward as the buckboard crawled closer and saw it was just the flies vying for position inside the man's eye cavities. He stared at the man, his whole head turning as they passed by, but neither he nor the swinging man uttered a word.

"Martin, of Orchard Bloom Plantation," said Ralph. "Good worker."

You knew him?

"Well enough."

Cassius twisted around in his seat to watch the man grow smaller behind them.

"Ran one too many times."

Had to be worth something if he was a good worker, said Cassius.

"Ran so many times they ended up payin the catchers and

paddyrollers more'n he was worth. Nothin more than a business decision."

They rode through town. A hand-painted sign with black letters dripping into the grass leaned against the side of the church: "God Loves You." Cassius looked at the men and women engaged in their daily affairs and thought the sign was intended for them. He wondered which of the dapper gentlemen owned the swinging man, which one of them insisted Martin remain squeezed at the neck dangling. He wished to punish them for their casual capricious greed. He surprised himself, knowing that just a few months before he would not have imagined such a thing—as a slave he had endured in silence the horrors perpetuated by white men, and yet here he contemplated retribution. He was different and he did not know if that change was for the good.

Ralph stopped at the railroad tracks on the far side of town, out of the shade of trees and beside a water tower.

"This is it."

Thought you said it would take all day, said Cassius.

"All day for me. I got to get back," said Ralph. "You wait. Train'll be along soon enough."

Wait here?

"'Less you care to walk. Long way to Gordonsville. Train'll make it a good deal easier."

Why would it stop for me?

"Wouldn't. Stop for water." Ralph pointed at the water tower. "Talk to the boys in the freight cars, they likely help you."

What boys, who are they?

"Slaves, Cassius, like you."

On a train?

"Work for the Confederate Army."

Cassius was surprised to learn such men existed. A body servant going to war with his master, yes, but slaves working for the army?

"Godspeed," said Ralph, as he turned Carolina and was off the way he came. The dust from the buckboard gradually settled against the road and Cassius was alone. Cassius listened to the afternoon insect song, a unanimous chorus from the meadow that built in tone and volume until the entire meadow trembled with sound. Then it ended in a great inhale of silence, only to begin all over again starting on a low note that gradually began to swell. He watched cows in a distant field, and for a time watched a dog sleeping on his back in the shade of a thatch of fountain grass alongside a fence, pink-spotted belly visible, rear legs bent up in the air, front legs and head rolled to the side. He envied the dog's leisure.

Cassius stood in the sharp sun for a time. Within his unknowable journey, his situation had taken yet another unanticipated turn. He had thought it would be easy to track an army, a creature so massive as to leave a conspicuous trail in its wake, but no such army had even glanced off this town. He stood enmeshed in uncertainty, seeing his grand plan evaporate before his eyes. He was not even clear from which direction the train would come.

Someone emerged from the shade and walked along the tracks toward him. At first he thought it was a boy, but the pitch of his amble betrayed mileage and age. As he got closer, Cassius saw he was indeed old and tiny, hands tucked into the top of his trousers. Cassius fingered the pass hidden in his pouch, but did not bring it out. When the old man reached hailing distance, Cassius called out: I'm a friend of Ralph.

"Whyn't you get out the sun, y'damn fool."

Cassius nodded and moved to sit in shade provided by the water tower.

The man set about working the pump. Cassius heard water rush into the tower above his head, and understood the man was there in anticipation of the train. Coming out of the southeast, he saw the familiar billow of smoke, as he had seen it on the trestle the day he met Morningside the telegraph man. He was again thrilled by the sight of such a commanding beast. He felt its reverberation and heard its bell clang out a warning. He hoped to get close enough to touch it. He was on his feet and as the train came closer he instinctively took a step back, not knowing what it would be like to have it pass close to him.

The train decelerated and the horizontal connecting rods that drove the large wheels slowed, their long oval motion hypnotic. Sand dropped out of a small pipe onto the tracks directly in front of the wheels, and the wheels ground to a halt. The locomotive stood massive and majestic before him and he admired each part of it, the pleasing triangular shape of the cowcatcher carried his eye from the tracks up to the long thick cylindrical gray body. Rising over the front of this drum was an enormous smokestack, expanding from a narrow waist up to a proud full chest, shaping the emergent smoke as it entered the air. A noise over his head spooked him and he looked to see the tiny old man lower the end of a long pipe from the water tower. The engineer came out of his cab to open the steam dome and help guide the pipe into position. Cassius was enthralled, with the train, with the operation, with every part of this moment. He wanted the men to yank on the rope and ring the bell again. He walked closer to the looming engine and reached to feel the metal with his palm, but the searing heat forced his hand away. Water poured through the chute to the steam dome and splashed over the boiler, exploding into a cloud of vapor, ripping the air with its harsh sound.

Cassius walked toward the rear of the train, trailing along the line of boxcars until he came to one with open doors. A group of five blacks sat in the car with their legs dangling. None wore shoes and their clothes were filthy and tattered. He had heard whites call poorly dressed slaves "tatterdemalion negroes" and these men certainly qualified.

I'm going north, to meet my master, said Cassius.

'Course y'are, said a high yellow man with prominent freckles across his nose and cheeks.

He's with the army, said Cassius.

Freckles and his friends laughed, all but one who scowled at him with half-lidded sour eyes.

Not enough food for you since out of the five of us, we got six hangin on, said Freckles, and the others laughed at his joke.

You got the wrong railroad, boy, we don't cater to no runaways, said Sour Eyes.

Already got your quota? said Cassius, and immediately regretted his smart mouth. He tried to recover by saying: You don't got to feed me.

You got that right, said Sour Eyes.

Look, I'm just trying to get north, Ralph left me here and went off—

You come with Ralph? Whyn't you say so, brother, climb aboard, said Freckles.

Owlcrap, said Sour Eyes, shaking his head. 'S all we need, one more broke darkie.

Cassius climbed in and looked around the boxcar. He tried to disguise the pleasure he felt in anticipation of riding on the train. Sun slanted in through the vertical slats, falling on the stacks of some unidentifiable wooden objects that resembled boats.

What are those? said Cassius, pointing them out.

Pontoons, boy. Goin to the front, ain't that where you say you goin? said Freckles.

Where's the front?

Darkie gets on board, don't even know where he goin, said Sour Eyes. And he say he ain't no runaway.

Never been this far north.

Owlcrap.

Don't matter if you believe me, but I'm going after Lee's army, said Cassius, resigned to the hazing.

Well, you on the right train. This here the Virginie Central and we goin stop in Gordonsville. Army been through there couple weeks back, kicked up some shit with the bluebellies, said Freckles.

What're you boys doing here? said Cassius.

We the loaders, said Freckles.

The tall meager one cleared his throat.

All right, three of us loaders, them two is unloaders. We just ridin along, back and forth, army feed us sometimes, and this here better'n most roofs, said Freckles.

Noisier, too, said the tall meager one.

Now you a loader, too, said Freckles. Till you ain't. 'Less you want to be a unloader. But I'm warnin you, that job be crap.

The train lurched and Cassius was thrown against a pontoon. The loaders laughed, and the tall meager one offered him a hand up.

You git your train legs soon enough, he said.

The journey was a jerky stop-start ride that, around sharp curves, threw him against the boxcar's walls and would at one point have thrown him out the open door if one of the men hadn't caught him. Smoke blew into the boxcar, his eyes and throat burned and he struggled to breathe, but even that did not diminish Cassius's pleasure in the ride. They approached a bridge that spanned a deep ravine and he leaned far out the door, holding on with one hand to look straight down, and it was a very long way to the distant ground. He had never before been at such a height, and the experience frightened and exhilarated him. The river below appeared small, the trees minuscule, and, impossibly, a flock of birds flew beneath his feet between the girders. Something inside his chest urged him to leap into the air and join them in their flight. He shouted aloud with pleasure, not at all aware that he was making the noise. In time, as his initial enthusiasm waned, he watched the now flat landscape roll by with great curiosity. The land passed swiftly. He saw straight rows of crops stretch out and, by a trick of the eye, seem to repeat in a pattern so consistent it was as if the rows moved along with them. He sat there for hours, watching the world change, mile by mile. He had had no conception that the world was this large. They traveled so far that he expected to run directly into the army at any moment. In the evening, they approached Gordonsville, and he watched the setting sun drop behind mountains running south. Freckles sat down beside him.

You ain't lyin, never been up this way before.

First time. Those mountains got a name?

Them's just some itty bitty hills, couldn't name 'em if I tried. Blue Mountains are beyond, they bigger. But if you goin north, you miss 'em if you follow the army.

So you're working for the Grays, said Cassius.

Not so bad workin 'round the army. They call these the rear jobs so's the whites can fight.

Why? If they're fighting to keep you slave, why do it?

Why d'you?

Cassius was trapped by his own story about traveling to be with his master.

You ever been close to the Yankees? said Cassius.

Close enough. They overran the cook wagons once, shootin and hollerin.

Why not go along with them? Be a contraband.

Freckles was offended: You lookin at a patriot, boy. I know the truth of things, South be our real friends. End of the war, whites'll be grateful we supported 'em and give us better rights and priv'liges. I am loyal, and all the ones I know think the same.

Cassius thought about the man's words. He had met few blacks who thought like Freckles, and while Cassius did not believe the South was his friend or that his rights would improve after the war, he did wonder about his own loyalty in the face of his being a piece of property. Could a man be loyal when he was coerced into his situation? He thought it was a possibility, although he wondered about the idea of coercion for someone born into that situation. Maybe that meant he had coerced himself. He knew he had been unable to coerce himself out of it.

Jackson's regiments took this train to Gordonsville, said Freckles. See them lights over there? Cassius looked, saw the lights, then looked above them at the stars. A cool breeze whipped into the freight car.

Gonna be a cold one tonight, said Sour Eyes.

The train stopped in Gordonsville, and Cassius was sorry to say good-bye to it. He slipped away in the darkness, after helping unload most of the pontoons. He heard Freckles call out after him, but he kept going.

Cassius knew to spend no time in town. He found a road that skirted the main streets, but even from that vantage point he saw the effects of the army's bivouac. The town looked as if it had been scraped and shaken. He traveled beyond the outskirts of Gordonsville and kept track of the Drinking Gourd pointing out the North Star. Once he was far enough outside the town, he abandoned the road and crossed a field. Evidence of bivouac surrounded him, soldiers had cooked their meals here and trampled down grass. Cassius reached the far border of the field and entered a wooded area and set himself on the ground. The night was cold and clear and he slept well.

He woke to a light frost that covered the ground as well as his shirt and trousers, and the fabric was stiff when he stood. He separated out a small portion of his provisions from the haversack and ate, then began to walk quickly through the field back to the road.

Sometime in the afternoon he caught up to the tail of the supply train and walked alongside, moving forward among the wagons. He had removed his shoes and hidden them in his haversack so that others would not requisition them, as he was surrounded by barefoot men, both white and black, all dressed like beggars. He was mistaken for a member of the company, and as such no one paid him any mind. Someone offered to let him ride in one of the covered wagons; he did so, and his feet thanked him.

He spoke to a white teamster in the covered wagon who told him they were following in the footsteps of Old Pete, who had taken his corps due north to White Plains. The teamster admired General Longstreet, and went into close detail about a battle that had just been fought at a place called Manassas Junction; a battle he could not have witnessed, yet spoke of as if he had been there killing the dirty Yanks himself.

Cassius asked if he knew Captain Whitacre. The teamster spat into the dust alongside the wagon. Cassius took his response as an affirmation. Cassius asked if Whitacre was with the wagon train.

"What do you think of his hat?" said the teamster, ignoring the question.

You don't like his hat? said Cassius.

"Ain't the hat I argue with so much as the man looks like he run into a tree, the way his brim got stuck up in front."

Maybe got tired of scorching the underside lighting his cigars, said Cassius.

The teamster laughed and said, "Whitacre gone on ahead of the wagons a week ago, maybe more."

The supply wagons crawled forward. Cassius knew he could travel more quickly on foot, but these wagons were certain to find Lee's army, and he was not. Progress was pitiful. Wagons often became stuck or would throw a wheel, holding up whatever portion of the train was behind them until they could be repaired or dragged out of the line. Cassius pitched in to help free the immobile wagons, but never did the speed improve. After interminable days they reached Salem and the Manassas Gap Railroad, made a hard right turn to White Plains, and followed the tracks in the direction of Manassas Junction. The closer they moved to Manassas, the more the men bragged about the victory, which had caught their imagination because it was the second victory in the same location and it felt like a perfect bookend. The war should end on such a poetic note. The overall mood of the men in the supply train was high, as they assumed the Bluebellies to be demoralized. To a man, they sensed that the war would soon be over. With the South victorious, they would return to life as it had been, the way God intended. That Lee was about to take it to the Yankees in their own country became a certainty on a journey that rode on gossip, where a rumor could travel in one direction, wagon to wagon, for miles, and then come back again as something different. Men repeated the phrase "Carry the war into Africa," which Cassius understood to mean Pennsylvania. What excitement, what joy, what anticipation followed when it was decided, independent of actual proof or knowledge, that Lee's target was Harrisburg, a center of Northern commerce where supplies for the Union Armies were manufactured. Once the idea was confirmed by repetition, the men projected themselves in brand-new uniforms and shoes, carrying the good Yankee rifles and plentiful ammunition.

Cassius had mixed feelings about the news. The Confederates fought for their way of life, which included slavery, but he had learned from newspapers that the Federals were no better. They fought to keep the South as part of the Union. If they won, Cassius did not see how things would change for blacks. Their President Lincoln had said he was *against* equal rights for negroes. Lincoln was known to dislike slavery, but his ambition was to keep it out of the territories, as the country expanded west, not eradicate it altogether.

The supply wagons turned north around Manassas Junction, then ground to a halt yet again, and this time they were stopped for a full day. Cassius saw that the army had been in the area recently and thought that he could now follow it on his own, so he climbed down from the wagon in which he was riding and set out alone. He walked past wagons for what seemed like miles, until he was in front of them. Once out of sight, he returned his shoes to his feet, and his speed of travel increased.

He came to the outskirts of a town that he learned from a local black was close to Leesburg. The army had camped at Leesburg, and had crossed the Potomac into Maryland only a few days before. Lee was in the North. The optimism that had infected the wagon train haunted Cassius, and he saw the inevitable: Lee would now win the war for his country. This thought depressed him more than he had thought possible. The overcast day brought rain, and he traveled more slowly.

Foraging for food was difficult and time-consuming, although he was less likely to be challenged in the rain. The Army of Northern

Virginia had blanketed the area around Leesburg and consumed what there was to consume. In an orchard near a farmhouse, Cassius found a crock of peaches that looked as if they had been rejected, growing soft gray fuzz. The rotting slick flesh slid out from under thick peach skin and turned to dripping mush in his hands. He dug down in the crock until he found portions of peach flesh that were almost firm and not overly infested with insects, and those bits he ate ravenously, finding the fruit both overly sweet and bitingly sour. The juice ran off his chin and he stood in the rain and wondered why he was there, cold and wet and miserable, until he remembered his vow.

The rain stopped and night fell. He again deserted the road to cross a field, again choosing a clump of trees for sleep. Patches of ground under the trees were dry, and he was nodding off when he heard someone or something in the field coming directly to where he lay. He raised his head to see only one man approaching, but the man carried a rifle. Cassius watched him inspect the area in the dark. Cassius was not afraid of one man, unless he proved to be a scout at the head of a unit. The man kicked the ground in the dark, and in a moment would have located Cassius's ribs. Cassius came to his feet, his hand grabbing for the man's rifle, but he caught only night air, as the man hurled himself to the ground with a squeal. The rifle went out of his hand.

What the hell you doing? said Cassius.

"Jesus, I was just looking for a place to sleep, you didn't have to scare me like that," said the man in a high-pitched voice.

You almost kicked me.

"I didn't see you there, can't see nothing in this place."

The man patted the ground around him for his rifle. Cassius stepped to where the rifle had fallen and put his foot on it. He bent to pick it up.

"Okay, all right, listen, I don't know you and I can just get out of here, you found this place, it's yours."

Cassius set down the rifle where he intended to sleep. When the man said nothing, Cassius lay down beside it, watching the man's silhouette.

Do what you want, said Cassius.

"Well, then, if you don't mind, I think I'll just rest here for the night. I am mighty tired, and this ground is mercifully dry and I don't much wish to drag my sorry self through the wet grass again. These sad trousers are heavy enough."

Up to you, said Cassius.

"Name's Purcell. James Purcell. With the Nineteenth Georgia."

Cassius merely grunted.

"Little behind my unit. Wasn't feeling well. Fell behind. You know how it is."

Cassius said nothing.

"Not that they miss me. I ain't much for fighting. You'd probably like to go back to sleep. I'll just shut my mouth, I been known to talk too much. Still feel my hands tingling after you stood up like that, whoo-ee, never been so scared in my life, 'cept maybe facing those goddamn Yanks."

Cassius rolled over to face the other way; anyone who talked so much was probably harmless.

He woke in the morning with the man looming over his legs, admiring his shoes. Cassius sat up quickly, coming face-to-face with him.

"Now now, friend, you only get to do that to me once," said James Purcell.

Cassius felt the rifle, which the man had not taken back, then looked to see that they were alone.

"I did not know last night that you were a negro. That was a secret you kept, wasn't it? Handsome shoes."

Cassius saw that James Purcell was barefoot, in threadbare gray trousers and a shirt that had once been green. He was emaciated, and appeared to be in worse overall condition than the loaders on the train. They were alone, and Cassius was glad to see, in the light of a day that promised to warm up, that the road was far away. Cassius thought he could easily snap this man in half like a toothpick. He did not feel threatened, but remained on his guard.

"Not that I'm interested in your shoes, my feet are too small for those, no sir, those would hurt my feet something terrible, worse than walking barefoot, and by now, my feet have calluses thicker than your soles. You look hungry. Are you hungry? I was just going to look for something, you want I should find something for you?"

Cassius handled the man's rifle. It was poorly kept, and unlikely to fire. He tossed it aside.

"Not much of a weapon, is it? I only carry it to scare away pests."

Where you say you were going? said Cassius.

"Back to my unit, but not on an empty stomach, I can tell you that." James Purcell looked over his shoulder at the field behind him. "You see any hint of food around here?"

Army been through, picked it clean like a plague of locusts.

"We got hit bad by the cicadas couple years back. Right now I'd gladly roast up a pan of cicadas and eat for a week. Been living on a steady diet of pickled doorknobs and candied tenpenny nails."

Cassius did not mention that he was hungry as well.

"Tell you what, you seem like a decent fellow, we'll go into town together, see if we can't find ourselves a meal," said James Purcell.

Cassius looked at him suspiciously.

"You wonder why I'd make such an offer."

Cassius waited.

"If you saw the officers in the Army of Northern Virginia, you'd know most of them look a whole lot like me in their uniforms. Sure, there's fancy ones still got decent clothes, but they are few and far between. No sir, we done walked right out of our shoes and our uniforms ain't far behind. So let's say I walk into some kitchen with my 'body servant,' maybe people think I am somebody and show me a little respect. You play along, and we'll both get to eat."

Cassius considered the man. He did not trust him, but his proposal was not unreasonable and Cassius might well benefit from it. His thoughts must have played out on his face.

"Listen, I got no weapon, I'm a long way from my unit, you think I care what you're doing out here?"

James Purcell assumed he was a runaway. A reasonable assumption.

They followed the road back to the town near Leesburg, an easy walk, and Cassius noticed that James Purcell's feet were split on the bottom, and he walked with pain.

See much action? said Cassius.

"Feel like I've been fighting my whole life. Been in it since the beginning, Manassas last year."

My people lost one of theirs at Manassas.

"A lot of fine men gone," said James Purcell.

They walked a little farther, and James Purcell began to laugh.

"Who am I fooling? I not only don't have my musket, it wasn't working anyway. I ain't no soldier. I'm nothing but what they call a parlor soldier. I mustered in at the start, but I've been ducking the fight ever since. Found myself staring at Yankee guns and the minute the first bullet buzzed my cheek, I was up and running like a rabbit with a bayonet poking its tail. Found myself a spot back in the rear, and put my head in the ground. Surprised they didn't shoot my cheeks off."

You don't say, said Cassius.

"The God's truth, every word."

Hard to disbelieve a story like that, said Cassius. He relaxed somewhat. If the man was being truthful, and confession to cowardice made him appear veracious, he was on the road to earning Cassius's trust.

"I have turned being yellow into an art. Once I smell a battle, I get the sublime urge to wander off to forage, or maybe find a private place to evacuate. Sergeant, got the dysentery bad this morning, you mind if I go over there and set a spell? All right, Purcell, but get back here 'fore the shootin starts. And I skedaddle, always finding my way back once things are clear again. And I ain't alone. Others doing it too. Boys up front, they tough sons a bitches, they good at fightin, they *know* how to kill. Found themselves a comfortable place with it, inside." He tapped his chest. "*How* they do it, I couldn't say. I'm what you might call one of those nervous types."

What you do for a living?

"Ain't you listening? I run yellow for a living."

I mean before, your profession?

"Hard to remember anymore, but I guess I was a teacher. College in Tennessee."

Cassius nodded.

"Was up in Maryland not two days ago. Said we'd be welcomed like liberators, Maryland being a slave state and all, forced to stay with the Union by that bastard Lincoln. And here comes the Army of Northern Virginia to set you free and you can join up with us because once we come into the North, those Yanks are going to throw their hands up in the air and ask us to kindly go home and the war will be over. Well, if there was a welcome, I missed it. And the order come down, No looting, boys, because we want all them Marylanders out there to *like* us. Pay for everything, boys, show them respect. Well hell, what if you got no money? There we are surrounded by crops, none of it harvested, a whole damned state full of food and we can't touch it. You imagine that? Sure, some of the officers bought up whole fields of corn, or apple orchards, out of their own pockets, and the Marylanders even took Confederate money, but how much corn can you eat without your insides turning to rusty water? Speaking of which," he said and scampered off the road, pulling a newspaper out of his haversack, going out of sight. Cassius sat down on a rock and waited for him to finish, and when James Purcell came out of the woods, he was carrying what was left of the newspaper he had used to clean himself. The front page was still intact, and Cassius saw it was the *Baltimore Sun*, dated September 4.

Mind if I look at that? said Cassius.

"You read?"

No, just never did see a newspaper before.

James Purcell handed him the newspaper. He pointed to the top and said, "That says *Baltimore Sun*, that there's a newspaper from the North."

Cassius looked at it as if he were amazed to see something so fantastic. But he read quickly, learning that all of Baltimore was in an uproar, people fleeing into Pennsylvania with their belongings because Lee was rumored to be coming. James Purcell took the newspaper back and folded it into his haversack.

"Maybe I'll read some of it to you later. You doing all right? Feet feel good? Not too hot?"

I'm fine, said Cassius. He could not remember a moment in his life when a white man had asked about his condition. It was an odd feeling.

So you were a teacher.

"War started and I wanted to do my part before they came after me, I mean, I don't own no twenty niggers, and I didn't have no six hundred dollars to buy a substitute to fight in my place like some of the planters, so I thought I'd just go. Joined the Nineteenth Tennessee."

A bell rang in Cassius's head. The night before, James Purcell had said he'd joined the 19th Georgia. When he'd said he taught school in Tennessee, Cassius had let that pass, imagining Purcell had gone to Georgia to enlist when that state seceded. Now he knew the man was telling tales. While an innocent explanation might be forthcoming, Cassius kept this knowledge to himself. Purcell wouldn't have known, in the dark, the color of his companion. Cassius might have been military, might have ordered him to his unit, so a lie might have been in order. It was also possible that James Purcell was a harmless storyteller. He might have suffered a head wound, leading to legitimate confusion, although Cassius saw no scars. By tomorrow he might wholeheartedly believe he had deserted from the 19th Alabama.

They kept to the main road that ran into the center of town, leaving behind farmland. Cassius lowered his head, but furtively scrutinized everyone who passed him, on foot or by buggy. No one seemed interested in him, until he noticed, half a block ahead, a young man wearing a small bowler hat. The young man had a great red mustache that covered his mouth and part of his chin, making him resemble a goat. The red goat stopped dead and looked directly at him. Cassius turned his head away, but a shiver ran down the backs of his legs.

He walked with Purcell past the occasional home until buildings began to cluster creating a business district. As they passed an alley, Cassius thought that he saw the red goat again, and he had an overwhelming sensation that the man was following him. Cassius became so obsessed with his presence that he almost missed seeing a brick slave auction house on a perpendicular street to his left. They continued on for half a block when, without warning, James Purcell stopped.

"I don't know that I can go another step. I need to eat soon."

Cassius nodded.

"Thought I saw a place on that last block. Why don't you have a sit down and rest your feet, I'll go back and have a look. Maybe they'll serve us both instead of you having to be out back."

Cassius entered a patch of shade in an alley where he wouldn't be conspicuous and he scanned the street up and down for the red goat. No sign of him. He looked back in time to see James Purcell turn right onto the perpendicular street they had just passed. Cassius began to move. Purcell had turned in the direction of the slave auction house.

Cassius walked in the opposite direction as rapidly as he thought

could be interpreted as casual, but he was not quick enough, because
a moment later James Purcell and a slave trader came on the run,
rounding the corner behind him.

"Fugitive slave! Fugitive slave!" James Purcell yelled, and the fat
slave trader joined him in the chorus, "Stop him, fugitive slave, by
law it's your *duty* to stop him!"

Cassius ran full-out. He turned at the next corner and his eyes
darted, for places to hide or alleys to utilize. He needed to get out of
sight, but he had to be careful not to trap himself. He felt the lack of
food as his weak legs struggled to reach top speed. His arms pumped
but felt soft, as if the bones had turned to rope. He glanced over his
shoulder and saw the slave trader round the corner, a man whose
profession gave him the wherewithal to eat and drink in prodigious
quantities, and yet for all his girth he ran easily. James Purcell was
not with him. Cassius pushed harder. He ran by people who didn't
understand or hadn't heard the man yell "fugitive slave," and were
therefore slow to react. He glanced back again and James Purcell
was finally around the corner, too weak to keep pace with a slave
trader who made his living in chases. Cassius wished he knew the
town so he might make smart choices. He could only run and turn
randomly, hoping to get far enough ahead of the slave trader to duck
out of sight.

People in front of him were beginning to understand the situation, and two burly men squared up to intercept him. He saw them
crouch, shoulders close together, and knew that he faced real trouble. He had seconds to decide. They waited, he was close now and he
faked left and went right. The man on the left bought it, and shifted,
opening a small space between them. The man on the right was not
fooled, keeping focused, staying in front of Cassius, reaching for
him. Cassius made one last move, going between them instead of
around, and the men, off-guard, grasped for him and caught each
other and he was past. Women scurried out of his way. In one case,
in her hurry, a woman blocked another man from getting to him,
and both man and woman tumbled in the street.

Just ahead, he saw the red goat. His heart sank. The man had
been on to him from the moment Cassius walked into town, and
now he would grab him. Cassius began to slow, looking for some
way around him, knowing he could not retreat, as that would lead

him back into the arms of the slave trader. The red goat, however, did not crouch or set his feet, or do anything to intercept him. Instead, he brought his hand deliberately to his earlobe and tugged on it. Then he turned and walked quickly around the corner out of sight.

What had he seen? Cassius had mere seconds to make a decision as he ran toward the spot, wondering if the red goat would grab him at the corner or if something else was in the offing. Shedd's words returned to him. Had he witnessed a signal? Was the man part of the Underground Railroad? Or was he scratching an itch, indulging a nervous habit? Cassius reached the corner, decision upon him. He could keep running from determined townspeople compelled to capture him by the Fugitive Slave Act, or he could trust Shedd and hope this man represented an escape. He turned the corner. The red goat hovered in a doorway. The street was momentarily empty. The red goat tugged his earlobe again, an obvious and deliberate gesture, and Cassius hoped he wasn't a slave chaser imitating Underground Railroad tactics. Cassius hurled himself at dumb luck and followed him through the doorway. The red goat closed the door behind him and raised a finger for silence.

Cassius struggled to be silent as he fought to catch his breath. The red goat cracked the door and watched the street. Cassius heard the slave trader. "Fugitive slave, where is he?!" He had stopped in the middle of the street, turning in a full circle.

The red goat closed the door and gestured that Cassius follow him, then led him up a flight of stairs to a dining room. At the far end, using his fingernails, he struggled to pry something loose from the wall. After a moment, a waist-high panel of wainscoting came free and revealed a hidden space. Cassius went inside. The red goat left, then returned with a lit lantern, which he passed in to Cassius. He replaced the wainscoting and Cassius could only see the square edges of light. He heard the red goat's footsteps walk away.

He inspected the hidden space. Blankets were piled on a bench and smelled of fresh soap. A pitcher of water sat near the opening, while at the back was a clean chamber pot. Cassius thought none of it had been used before.

Cassius heard a pounding at the door downstairs. He heard the red goat's footsteps as he descended the stairs, heard him speak to someone, then heavier footsteps came up the stairs and tramped through the rooms. Cassius waited to be taken. They came to the dining room and he heard a man say, "You see, no one is here but me."

Gruff words were exchanged, but the heavy footsteps retreated. The front door closed. It was a while before he heard fingernails clawing at the wainscoting.

"You are safe for now," said the red goat. "My name is Bill Bryant and I help the Underground Railroad."

Cassius decided to offer little information. Bryant would make assumptions. That was fine.

"We will get you to Canada. We've had great success with our route, and our conductors have yet to lose a passenger. Now I just want to tell you, so you won't be concerned, that my wife will be coming back shortly. When she arrives, the door will open. I promise you, it will only be her, nothing to worry about; it won't be the slave catchers coming back. Nothing to worry about, she's an abolitionist as well. In fact, she once spoke with Harriet Beecher Stowe. May I offer you tea?"

Bryant took down two cups and two saucers from a cabinet and set them at the table.

Cassius thought that Bill Bryant was likely a nice man, despite his frightening visage—the heavy mustache, the grim eyebrows—but he detected no humor in this young man whatsoever. Bryant spoke as if to make certain that Cassius understood that he considered him an equal. In a cruel assessment, Cassius thought Bryant would be more upset to commit a social faux pas with a passenger than to lose him to the slave traders. Cassius had preferred the company of the devious rat James Purcell. For all his disingenuousness, he was at least entertaining and considerably more comfortable in his own skin, able to tell tall tales with sincerity.

The front door opened, and despite Bryant's warning, Cassius did start, dropping his tea cup, which clattered against the saucer loudly. Bryant quickly had a towel in hand and wiped up spilled tea as he spoke soothingly, nothing to be concerned about. Bryant's young wife came up the stairs and bustled in, petticoats rustling, her tiny round face consumed by unmistakable joy at his presence. "Praise the Lord!" she said.

Ma'am, said Cassius.

"The entire town is positively abuzz with the news of the commotion. I only prayed we would get you in time," she said. "I ran all the way here!"

"I was lucky to be there when he was running," said Bryant.

I was lucky to be running where he was being, said Cassius, attempting levity.

But she was as completely earnest as Bryant. "Oh, you were lucky indeed," she said, and reached out to take his hand and look into his eyes.

Cassius smiled and sighed inside. Two of them.

Bryant and his wife excused themselves elaborately to step into another room. They returned together to face him.

"We want you to know that you are welcome, most welcome, to remain here as long as you like," she said. "As long as you *need*."

I appreciate your help, ma'am, but I best be going soon as possible, said Cassius.

She smiled widely, and turned to look at Bryant, as if this was the most perfect answer imaginable.

"Perhaps in a few days," said Bryant.

Better tonight.

"They know you are still in town, they'll be waiting for you," said Bryant.

"That dreadful man Griggs is across the street. He watches us," said his wife.

Yes, I see, said Cassius, and the news that the house was under surveillance made him more determined to leave.

They closed every curtain in the house. He sat with them, all three at the same table, for a meal, and he was grateful to eat well for the first time since his journey began. But their style of food preparation was unusual, and he found the meal bland, as they used little salt; the provisions in the quarters were packed in salt to prevent spoilage. They served him wine in a glass with a stem. The Howard family owned such glasses, but Cassius had never used one, and it felt delicate and awkward in his hand. He had to concentrate to be sure to keep it upright so that the liquid did not spill. He had also never tasted wine, and it paled in comparison to the whiskey he bought from the patrollers, albeit much less abrasive. He watched them eat and attempted to imitate their actions as well as their manners. He found Bryant's excessive use of a cloth napkin confusing. He was grateful when the meal came to an end.

He learned that they had been married for less than a year; that they had each come from families with money; that they alone, in each of their families, were abolitionists and that they had moved near the border intentionally to help the Underground Railroad. He finally stopped paying attention as they told him the rather standard stories of their young, brief lives.

They led him to a bedchamber where he was to sleep and shut the door behind them, speaking quietly to each other as they moved down the hall to their own room. Cassius could not have been more uneasy. Never in life had he slept in what the planters thought of as a bed. It was high off the ground, with wooden legs and an open space underneath, and he feared if he didn't fall through the middle of it, then he still might slip off the side while sleeping and land on the floor. He found he could not fall asleep, and spent much of the night at the window observing the street. He identified two men watching the Bryant residence. By morning he had been forced to use the chamber pot, which was set inside a wooden commode that had pillows set on top to cushion the seat. As he was unable to step outside for any purpose, much less to use the privy, he could not dispose of the contents. The idea of a white man or woman emptying his slops made him deeply uncomfortable.

The following day, there was no end to their politeness, no moment where their hospitality was anything less than ideal. No sign of tension had flared up between them. Nothing suggested that this awkward situation in any way reflected on their temporary guest. He was grateful for their kindness, but he found it easier to be in the company of hostile planters. In that situation he understood the rules and was able to act accordingly.

Bill Bryant went out and brought back a newspaper that was a few days old. They read aloud a story about the Confederate invasion of the North, and how, in the town of Urbana, Maryland, J.E.B. Stuart had invited charming young women from a Female Academy and thrown a dance for his officers. During the dance, word came that the Yankees had attacked a Confederate position a few miles away at Hyattstown. Stuart's cavalry had left the ladies, leaping upon their horses to ride into the night, putting down the attack, only to return fresh from battle to the Female Academy, where they continued the dance.

"That is unimaginable, unthinkable," said Bryant's wife.

"Unthinkable," said Bryant.

Cassius was secretly amused by the tale, a perfect example of Southern gallantry. He thought again that the South would not lose the war, exhibiting such dash in the enemy's homeland. He wondered if Jacob had been among the cavalry, as in his previous letters he had mentioned that the 7th Virginia Cavalry on occasion rode with Stuart.

Cassius asked Bryant's wife: Will others come to this stop, to be conducted north?

"Yes, if we're lucky," she said.

"Yes," said Bryant, "if we're very lucky."

I see, said Cassius.

"Although perhaps not soon, as we do have spying eyes upon us," she said.

I'll go tonight, said Cassius.

"Tonight?! But that would be out of the question. What about the men, what about them?"

They want me here, thought Cassius. I could live out the rest of my days right here in comfort. I am the abolitionist prize to be awarded to the most virtuous.

Smart to go sooner than later, said Cassius. They know I'm hiding, they think I'm here. If I didn't go immediately, then they'll know you won't move me. They don't expect anything now. In a day or two, maybe.

"You make an interesting point," said Bryant's wife. "Let me speak to my husband."

Bryant and his wife huddled again out of earshot. Bryant returned alone.

"Of course, we hope to eventually guide you to Canada and freedom. But we recognize that you make an excellent point," said Bryant. "I will conduct you out after dark."

Bryant laid out a plan that included back windows and fast horses. His wife joined them and Cassius listened and nodded.

A fine plan, said Cassius. You have thought it through and it is admirable. But there are times when it is best to be simple. If Madam might complain of a malady.

"But I am perfectly well," said Bryant's wife.

"My wife is never ill," said Bryant.

A summer cold, said Cassius. And if Madam would wrap herself in a shawl and cover her head with a bonnet while keeping a handkerchief at her nose, she might depart the front door for a visit to a doctor.

The Bryants exchanged confused looks.

Madam returns home, then departs once more so the men across the street will be well acquainted with her attire, said Cassius.

"I believe I understand," said Bryant to his wife.

Would you say the sun sets behind your home?

"Why yes I would."

Would you say it then would be directly in the eyes of someone on the far side of the street?

"Why, yes. At this time of year, that would be the case," said Bryant.

Cassius had seen that very circumstance the previous afternoon, and knew it to be so.

At sunset, I would ask to borrow your shawl and bonnet, ma'am, and Mr. Bryant, perhaps you might bring the carriage around front. The men will be blind in the sun and I will wear the bonnet and the shawl and hold the handkerchief to my face. You might wish to instruct your horse to walk, respecting the Missus's malady.

Bryant and his wife looked at each other.

"That is a fine plan," she said.

Once we're gone, ma'am, you need to stay indoors, said Cassius.

"Of course."

Sunset came, and Bryant did as Cassius suggested. Cassius wore the shawl with his own hat and haversack hidden beneath. The sun blared into the faces of any curious onlooker across the way. Cassius had to admonish the nervous Bryant to drive slowly, very slowly.

⤙ Chapter Seventeen ⤚

BILL Bryant intended to transport Cassius to Edward's Ferry and cross with Cassius playing the role of his body servant. He informed Cassius that from there, they would report directly to an Underground Railroad station in Maryland at Poolesville. He had been informed that it was the house with the Jocko, a small painted statue of a black groomsman. If a green ribbon was tied to it, or if it held a flag, it was safe to enter. A red ribbon would warn them off. From there someone would guide him through the intolerant North up to Canada.

Cassius expressed his heartfelt appreciation for all that Bryant had done, and then suggested they cross where Lee's army had crossed. The red goat was appalled at the suggestion, but Cassius pressed on, as it would be more difficult to find the army once he was embraced by the Underground Railroad. He appreciated them for all they had done and all they planned to do, and wished they had been the ones to help Joseph, but Cassius had other plans; any strategy that would guide him to his freedom was in abeyance. Cassius looked in the decent eyes of the good man and said that if there was trouble, he would pretend to be a Confederate officer's body servant working his way to the front lines. Bryant nodded.

The ferry means more whites, more danger. Safer to cross at a ford, said Cassius.

"White's Ford is not so far from Poolesville. But it will be difficult to cross with the horse and carriage."

I go alone.

"Out of the question, I cannot allow you to do such a thing," said Bryant.

You and your wife already risked your lives for a stranger, a negro, said Cassius. You have my true gratitude.

Bryant drove him to White's Ford.

Cassius sent Bryant back to his home, and was much relieved to be on his own.

He moved through the undergrowth and eventually came out on the southern bank of the Potomac River. He was rendered breathless, and his hope abandoned him. Never before had he set eyes on such a river. The far bank was five hundred yards away, but to Cassius, it might have been five hundred miles. He could not imagine how anyone could ford such a vast expanse of swiftly moving water. As if to answer his query, a man emerged from brush a hundred yards downriver, removed his shoes and trousers, and walked into the river up to his waist and did not sink. Cassius watched him walk the entire distance, the water only occasionally rising as high as his chest, emerging to claim the far bank in safety.

Cassius re-concealed himself in the undergrowth and remained hidden until after midnight. He had a clear view of the night traffic as many more men made the crossing. As he waited, he counted out the days on his fingers and determined it was the 13th of September; no, it was after midnight, so the 14th. He watched closely each individual that crossed and imagined them stragglers attempting to rejoin their units, but he did not know if they were Yankee or Rebel. Each successful crossing rebuilt his hope. When there had been no travelers in close to an hour, he decided to venture out, following the bank downstream in the open to where he had seen the others embark.

He removed his shoes and trousers, as he'd seen them do. He waded into the Potomac. The water moved quickly, washing up against his shins, then his knees, thighs, and waist. He hesitated. The bottom was sandy and unstable beneath his bare feet. He looked back, then forced himself to face forward. He tried to maintain a steady stride, and hummed to himself to take his mind off of his situation. As he walked, his eyes were drawn to the water flowing around his torso and he stepped into a hole, water splashing to his chin. He looked up and saw that while concentrating on the water, he'd gotten turned and had walked parallel to the bank along with the current. He quickly returned to the shallow ford, and in a panicked moment did not know which direction to go. He caught his breath and located the moon and then the Drinking Gourd, which told him where he was.

He had watched so many men cross that he had imagined he knew how long it would take, but time moved at a different pace out here and he was only halfway across. He looked back. He shivered. He was alone and surrounded by fast water that delighted in luring and tugging him downstream, and he had a superstitious moment wherein he expected the river to carry away the footing and swallow him whole. He now wholly doubted the success of his crossing, and his breathing grew ever more shallow. His head felt light and his desperate mind took control of his reason; he had to return to Virginia as Virginia's ground was firm and the path ahead was chancy. He stopped then, turned his eyes on the constant moon, then considered the current, which also remained constant. He began to trust that the bottom would remain underfoot. He forced himself into a place of calm and pictured the dozen or so men he had witnessed complete the crossing successfully. His sane mind took hold again and reminded him that it would take no longer to reach the far side than it would to go back. He pressed on to Maryland and while he concentrated on the distant bank, he pictured what it would be like to get his hands on Whitacre, and before he knew it, the shore was close, very close, then he was knee deep, ankle deep, and he was on dry land.

The ground beneath his feet was Maryland. He stood on Federal soil. Maryland may have remained slave, but the dirt of this ground, which he bent to collect in his palm, was the North. He was not free, but he was closer to being free than at any time in his life. As he let the dirt sift between his fingers, he was surprised to find himself in giddy spirits.

He relocated the Drinking Gourd in the sky and walked toward the North Star. When daylight arrived, he moved to the road's shoulder to watch the emerging foot and wagon traffic. The road began to suffer supply wagons and the occasional Union soldier on foot. He saw a surprising number of blacks manning the wagons, and he imagined them to be contrabands working in support of Federal troops. How easy it would be for him to throw in with them. He stepped out of his place of hiding and entered the meager parade. He had grasped the tail of the army, and now he and the other fleas gradually made their way to the body. The Union soldiers were ragged, but not as ragged as James Purcell. He was aware that the men around him stayed clear of him, leaving him a wide path, and he had that old sensation of forced invisibility. He passed a limping soldier in baggy red pantaloons with a red sash around his waist, an extensively embroidered short blue jacket, and a red fez on his head. He might have thought the man a mental defective or perhaps an actor, but he used his rifle as a crutch and his outfit was filthy and worn in the way of the soldiers dressed in regular uniforms. Cassius was careful not to laugh.

The day was hot, the road dusty, and travel was slow. He walked for quite some time before he felt comfortable enough to enter a dazed private reverie, keeping up with his shadow, watching it shift to his left, his right, then back to his front as the road ambled and twisted. Someone fell in step with him. He initially thought nothing of it until the presence did not stray. He looked to see a well-muscled Union soldier keeping his pace. He looked at the man's shadow and saw something long growing out of his head that was too thick to be a feather. With a glance he saw it was a bucktail rakishly attached to his dark blue kepi, sweeping back off the front band, waving on the bounce with every step he took. He carried a different kind of rifle, not a traditional musket. The soldier made a soft grunting sound that Cassius took to be a greeting, and Cassius nodded, wishing the man away. They walked along like that for a half mile.

"Seem like you got all the parts," said the man with the bucktail on his hat.

What parts? said Cassius.

"Got a head, two arms, two legs, same number of fingers."

Got a tail rolled up, hidden in my trousers, said Cassius.

The man with the bucktail on his hat suddenly laughed loudly enough that other men on the road looked at him.

"Got a working brain, too," said the man with the bucktail on his hat.

I'm thinking you never met a black man before, said Cassius.

"A few contrabands, but they ain't much for conversation. Curious about 'em, you hear a lot of things."

Extra heads, three arms, like that? said Cassius.

"You hear a lot of things," said the man again, emphatically.

Cassius remembered Purcell and his friendly ways, and the cautious geniality forthcoming from this man put him on his guard. He looked at the man's feet and was relieved to see he wore shoes.

They walked together a little farther.

Cassius wondered if he might get away from the man. He walked faster, but the man matched his pace. He walked slower, and the man stayed with him but showed no indication that he was aware of Cassius's intent.

Finally Cassius gave in, and said: Where you from that you don't see negroes?

"Mountains of Pennsylvania. Wildcat district, McKean County. We don't bring in outsiders to do our work, we do it ourselves."

What sort of work?

"Lumberjack."

Something growing out your hat, said Cassius.

"Bucktail. Regimental badge of honor. You don't know it?"

I don't.

"Never heard of us?"

Never did.

The man did not seem insulted, but he did appear surprised. "We're the first rifles. Sharpshooters. Still nothing?"

I believe you.

The man looked at him with a tilt of the head, but this time his laughter was softer and he continued walking alongside Cassius.

"Might I inquire from where you hail?"

Virginia.

"Virginia's a large piece of property. Any particular place?"

Tobacco country.

"Bring any with you?"

Did not.

"Field hand?"

No.

"Something else?"

Yes.

"That's all I get, ain't it?"

So far.

"Contraband?"

Could be.

"You remind me of my pappy. He don't much like questions, neither. Mind if I walk with you a spell? I enjoy meeting new people."

Not like I got much choice.

"Wife says I can be a bore, so you tell me if I go on."

You think that a likely occurrence, that I'd tell you something like that? said Cassius.

"I'll try to be mindful of it myself," said the man.

The man introduced himself as Hugh McLaren, and Cassius told him his name. A limping soldier saw McLaren from a distance and hurried to catch him, putting his weight on a walking stick he had fashioned from the trunk of a young tree. When he reached McLaren, he saw Cassius and his face fell. He backed off a step.

"That you, McLaren?" said the limping soldier, but his glowering eyes never left Cassius's face.

"Happy to see you, Seymour," said McLaren.

"Sure that's you? 'Cause the McLaren I know wouldn't be walkin with the likes of him," said the limping soldier, indicating Cassius with his thumb.

"Well, now, Seymour," said McLaren, but the limping soldier did not wait for McLaren to finish his reply. He turned aside and shuffled in the other direction.

McLaren glanced at Cassius but said nothing, while Cassius stared straight ahead. What may have been a curiosity for McLaren, making idle conversation with a black man, was something else for other Union soldiers. But Cassius was impressed that McLaren continued to walk alongside him, all the way to the foot of Sugar Loaf Mountain, and on up toward Buckeystown.

Hugh McLaren had been shot at a place called Second Bull Run. A bullet had hit his thigh but missed the bone. In what he referred to as a miracle, the doctor had not amputated his leg. He related a lengthy narrative concerning his wait in the line for the sawbones, but the doctor had passed him by as a fresh group of mangled and screaming soldiers were littered in. As his wait grew, McLaren found his pain tolerable, so he dressed his wound, noting that the bullet had made an exit hole; it had passed clean through. He didn't need to be bled, as the wound itself had done that to his satisfaction. He dragged himself over to the Bull Run Creek, not far from the doctor's tent, and bathed his wound and then himself. The water no longer ran red by then. He camped there and washed the wound twice a day and washed his bandages as well.

After a day or two he thought he saw improvement. He now took pains to avoid the doctor, as the doctor had a wicked look in his eye and was a fair hand with a hacksaw. When the doctor did see McLaren, he indicated that he intended to have the leg. McLaren began to think it unnecessary to experience such a sudden drop in weight, and since he was *attached* to his leg, he would go to great pains to keep it joined to his hip at least until the next bullet. Weren't a large crop of one-legged lumberjacks in the mountains of Pennsylvania.

One morning, he awoke with less pain so he tested the leg, standing without a crutch. He took one step, then another. They weren't what you would call pretty steps, he said, but he found he could walk without dragging his leg. The extraordinary number of wounded had been housed in local homes and churches to recuperate, and he used this time to help the nurses. It was pleasant to spend time with the female gender. One afternoon he saw the sawbones heading his way and he held his ground. The doctor told him that it had been his plan all along to force him to hang on to his leg, and it was time for him to rejoin his unit. That put him here, walking through Maryland, aiming to plant as many Johnny Rebs as possible in the ground of his homeland and send the rest home.

At some point in McLaren's story, Cassius understood that Second Bull Run was the same battle as the one called Second Manassas by Confederates.

I saw a man on the road, said Cassius. Unusual looking, wore red pantaloons and a strange red hat, but he carried a musket.

"One of the Zouaves," said McLaren.

Fighting man? said Cassius.

"Oh, he's a fighting man, all right. Zouaves brought their uniforms when they volunteered. Started with the French. Met one who'd been a firefighter in New York, I think he said his whole unit was firefighters."

So he means to dress like that.

"Yes, that's intentional," said McLaren with a laugh.

Never saw a rifle like yours, said Cassius, indicating McLaren's weapon.

"Barrel's got grooves inside, makes the minié bullet go three, four times farther. More accurate, too. Breech loader, so it loads faster, too."

Sounds like a benefit.

"That it is, lad, that it is."

They took time to scrounge for food. It was close to harvest time, and the state of Maryland had much to offer, even after the main army had passed through. They had little trouble finding fruit and vegetables. McLaren spoke to a farmer and came back with bacon and flour.

McLaren led him off the road for the night, and when Cassius made to wander off to find his own place, McLaren called him back and invited him to bed down near him. He made a fire and they cooked the food they had scrounged, and one or two others came off the road and joined them, casting an uncertain eye toward Cassius.

One fellow not much over the age of sixteen landed heavily on the ground near the fire, his shiny extra gear clanging, his new boots kicking dust into the flames.

"Go easy there, lad. May need that fire for your supper."

"Say," said the sixteen-year-old, his eyes wide, "I seen hats like that before!"

McLaren smiled.

"You a Bucktail is what you is. I ain't never seed a Bucktail before."

"A Bucktail is what I am."

The sixteen-year-old turned to the others around the fire, as if they hadn't noticed McLaren's hat before that moment. "This here's a Bucktail. Wildcat sharpshooters, they send these boys up to the front line when we're meetin the Rebs. Say, Bucktail, do the Rebs really run when they see you comin?"

"Been known to happen," said McLaren.

"Hell, they's excellent marksmen, the Bucktails, best marksmen in the country, hell, best in the damned world," the boy said to the others. One of them hid his eyes behind his hand, cringing at the awe of this green recruit.

"Looks like a new uniform," said the man behind his hand.

"Just joined up," said the sixteen-year-old. He turned his attention back to McLaren. "With you boys around, I'm thinkin the Rebs ain't got no chance a'tall."

"Well, the Rebs may look like they fit every scarecrow in the South with a uniform, but who knew scarecrows could fight so hard?"

The youth gulped. Cassius imagined that he hoped things would go easy on him, that the worst fighting was over and the war would end and he wouldn't die.

"Say, I heard you boys killed Turner Ashby, that true?"

Cassius sat up. Jacob had ridden with Ashby, and had revered the man.

You killed Colonel Ashby? Cassius said to McLaren.

"Sure enough," said the sixteen-year-old. "Ashby of the Confederate Black Horse Cavalry. Bucktails got him. Maybe it were you?"

"Naw, warn't me," said McLaren. "They say it was Bucktails, but some New Jersey Cavalry picket been talkin like he did it. Since New Jersey said he didn't know who it was he shot that day and didn't find out Ashby was dead till the next day, and only then decided it was him, I guess I'll stick with the Thirteenth. We were there, all right, outside Harrisonburg. Reckon it was early June."

"June sixth," said the sixteen-year-old.

"And I reckon you know a little something about Ashby," said McLaren.

The boy looked sheepish. "I used to read about his exploits."

"Well, then, you probably know he was General Ashby that day. Made General couple days before."

The men were silent, as if that ironic observation was the way of the war. Time and again when something good happened for a man, it was but prelude to his death.

"My favorite part of that day was old Sir Percy," said McLaren.

"Sir Percy?" said the sixteen-year-old.

"Sir Percy Wyndham. Soldier of fortune, Britisher. Boasted that morning that he was going to 'bag' Ashby. Word got back to Ashby on that. I met Old Percy once, he was a braggart and an adventurer, but not a bad soldier. Sir Percy charged Ashby's rear guard, but he neglected to notice he was charging all by himself. His men hadn't followed, and then Ashby bagged him. I did love to hear that. Comes the end of the day, Ashby had Virginia and Maryland infantry sent over to him, gave an order to charge, they all get up and they're running and we shot his horse down, but Ashby, he's right back on his feet to lead the charge on foot, waving that shiny sword, and a bullet went right through his heart just a few feet from his horse."

Again they were silent, staring at the fire between them.

"Same day that Colonel Kane was captured. That was some hard day. We got him back in August, I fought with him at Second Bull Run. Hear they might make him a general for that skirmish at the bridge. What day is it?"

"Sunday."

"Sunday. Maybe I'll sleep now."

On the morning of the 15th of September, they caught up to the rear echelon of the Union Army of the Potomac at Turner's Gap in South Mountain. A fierce battle had been fought the day before and the Union had broken through for the first notable Northern victory that summer. Cassius saw the detritus of the battle spread across the rock-strewn ground, and it was a bad sight. Men were burying bodies under the hot sun, digging on the spot and dropping their friends into holes. He looked forward to where they were headed and saw both armies in the distance, no more than fifteen miles away.

McLaren came upon the body of a friend and stopped to bury him. The sixteen-year-old went on, anxious to catch up to the battle that he thought was sure to start at any moment. Cassius found a shovel and worked alongside McLaren.

They spent the night at Turner's Gap and in the morning set off to cover the distance to Sharpsburg. It was hot and dry, but Cassius read the sky and thought the weather was about to turn.

By late afternoon they had come upon the two enormous armies camped up against one another on a rolling, confusing ground that hid whole regiments from his view, exposing them only after he had walked past them. He and McLaren walked by rows of tents that stretched out and vanished beyond a rise, only to reappear continuing on but smaller in the distance. They passed wagons and food and horses, they smelled food and burning campfires. There were cannons and more cannons, and shells piled up alongside the cannons, dropped off by supply wagons. Cassius saw things that he would not have imagined in his most extravagant dreams. How could this Federal army be so large, how was it managed, how did it move? How could the Confederates put up a fight against so many men? The ocean of blue jerseys stretched on and on, in all directions around him. He would not have been surprised to find them under his feet or flying overhead. To see this many men in one place was more than impressive, it was positively daunting. He had been hearing a distant tink and crack throughout the afternoon, and now he knew it was the incidental burst of musket fire. But was this the sound of war? It was so puny compared to the manpower arrayed around him. No, he decided, the majority of the two armies were not engaged at this time. The clashing occurred in snarling pockets of rage that began and ended suddenly. This was but prelude.

The ground was confusing; they walked on land that had appeared continuous from a distance, but suddenly dropped away to reveal a creek and an arched stone bridge.

The afternoon light was almost gone with low clouds moving in, and he and McLaren crossed the bridge, dodging wagons and troops. He stopped for a moment to look down at the small creek that flowed below him, some fifty or sixty feet across. They asked after the 13th Pennsylvania, but usually before they could speak their question, men were pointing, having seen McLaren's hat, sending them off the road along the river up a modest hill. They reached another road and were told to make a hard left.

"Just stay on Smoketown Road," someone advised.

They heard rumors of a skirmish that had just ended, that the Bucktails now had partial control of a patch of woods just ahead. The news put McLaren in high spirits until he saw bodies of men with whom he was acquainted being littered back to the creek, one with his bucktail hat resting on his chest. McLaren's mood darkened.

They reached the woods and located his unit, and it was then McLaren discovered the price that had been paid to take that ground. Twenty-eight Bucktails killed, including Colonel McNeil. Sixty-five wounded. McLaren was angry, and he spoke of McNeil as a fine and noble officer. He was not alone, as the Bucktails to a man were in great despair over the death of an officer they admired. McLaren was ready to enter the fight then, but his friends spoke words to cool his passion and said that tomorrow would be soon enough. Cassius recognized recklessness in the man's rage and moved away from him.

He picked his way to the far side of the woods, found what seemed to be a good spot, and settled down to sleep. The night was filled with pickets firing, small pockets of distant cracks that would come in a burst, then stop, followed by the occasional explosive sound of a nearby musket or rifle firing in retort. He lay on his back, and through the heavy tree foliage above he saw, through the open patches, artillery shells flying, as sparks of their burning fuses glimmered against the low clouds. Cassius heard the men around him restless in their attempts at sleep. He planned to cross to the other side once he understood the lay of the land in daylight, so that he could be behind Confederate lines in the morning before the battle began. Then he would look for Whitacre. If it still mattered after that, he would look for Jacob.

◆ Chapter Eighteen ◆

CASSIUS woke just as the sky was growing light. He had slept poorly, between the late night drizzle that had turned to rain before dawn and the sounds of the occasional musket shot, which gave the night an unending offbeat rhythm. Throughout the night he had sensed that the men around him were awake. He rose and was hungry. The sky was brighter and he saw he was on the edge of an area of woods by a cornfield. He still intended to cross the line to the Confederate side, but first his belly wanted to know if the corn was ripe. He heard a closer shot this time, then another closer still. Fog hugged the ground, the rain had stopped and the trees dripped.

He entered the cornfield at the same time as two Union soldiers. The stalks reached over his head, and he was comforted by the familiar crop. He waded in deeper and found the corn ripe. Faced with this bounty, he became choosy and moved from one stalk to the next. He was dimly aware of a handful of others wandering nearby. He glanced at them in their dark blue coats and saw eyes glazed with fatigue, rifles carried in the crooks of their elbows. The morning fog kept him from seeing little more than a few feet in any direction, as if swathed in a cloud. He moved slowly under the not unpleasant burden of sleeplessness. His fingers tested the sheathed, unpicked corn until he hit upon a substantial ear and twisted it free. It was satisfyingly plump in his palm. The drowsy corn stalks rustled. The fog would burn off, the day would be hot, and the predawn rain would bring humidity, but for now he was content. He took hold of the corn silk at the top of the ear and pulled down to reveal white nubs perfectly aligned. He smiled, looked at his neighbor to share the perfection, and saw the closest man wore a gray jacket. Cassius hesitated, knowing something was out of place, and it was a moment before he identified what it was. He looked back at a blue coat a few feet away, and the blue had not seen the gray, just as gray was unaware of blue. The light was diffused and the colors were gorgeous in the fog shroud, the leaves and stalks near him vivid green and true, while a few feet away, the haze softened the color to a subtle greenish gray. The soft light toned down the deep blue Federal coats and made creamy the butternut gray of the Confederate coats. Cassius held his perfect ear of corn and turned in a circle, losing his sense of direction as he saw another gray coat just visible there, then watched vanish two blue coats in the murk and stalks behind him.

A series of overlapping extraordinary booms sucked the air, the sky shrieked, and from above a huge sudden stunning concussive burst squeezed his skull and slapped his body flat against the ground, knocking his breath completely away. Deaf, dirt-mouthed, desperately fighting for air, ears filling with a gush of rushing white river noise that quickly narrowed into a high-pitched whine. His alarm urged him to flee but his body was unable to move. Slowly, precious breath came and filled him, his sluggish ears cleared and he made out tinny crackling gunfire. After a moment he knew that the whine in his ears was real and not the ringing aftermath of artillery. His head was stupid, aching, his hands explored his body to know if he was still of a piece. Artillery boomed close and splattered him with dirt and corn, his chest and legs and bowels quaked and he dug his fingers into the soil and knew the ground shuddered beneath him. On hands and knees he scrabbled back to the woods, throwing himself down. Bucktails were cramped behind logs and stones, aiming

Sharp's rifles and firing, dense clouds of smoke blinding, then consuming them after each shot, the smoke hovering, thickening the local fog. Return fire came from within the woods, too close. An inconsistent shiver gripped the leaves around him as minié balls chopped through them. Bucktails cracked their smoking weapons open in the middle, grabbed from a small box a whitish linen cartridge, shoved it into the bore, raised the breechblock which sheared off the back end of the cartridge, brought the rifle back up, and fired, all in a matter of seconds. Cassius had never seen a breechloader in action. Astonishing the speed, the accuracy; indeed they were dangerous marksmen who well deserved their reputation. He heard and felt the whiz and zing, then the sickening thumps that he hoped were projectiles drilling trees but knew to be the impact of bullets smacking men's bodies.

Artillery was constant, a gross thunder that raged from both sides and encircled him no matter which direction he turned. The plan to find Whitacre blew out of his brain, as how could anything survive the very air being shredded to bits? He thought of birds and squirrels and insects, and wondered where they would hide.

A piercing cry rose up around him, a violent wildcat yell, and the Bucktails were up and flowing past, firing as they moved. He saw Confederate skirmishers rise from their positions right there, not twenty yards away, to turn and run out of the woods and across the road. The Bucktails drove forward to the snake-rail fence bordering Smoketown Road and settled in and continued their terrible accurate firing.

Artillery shells blundered overhead, some crashing high up into the trees, and giant chunks of shagbark hickory and black walnut and green ash came thundering down, killing a man not ten feet from him. Splinters sprayed and a four-inch sliver stung his shoulder and stuck deep. He eased it out, felt it bleed, and knew it was time to move. He rushed forward in a crouch, dodging bodies and branches, to where a line of Bucktails shielded themselves behind the low fence along the road. Cloaked by woods' edge, he took in the landscape. He was south of the line of corn with an open clover field to his right. The clover field bordered the road on its north side; below the road were a farm and a plowed field. The entire vista revealed an undulating land of tricky rises and swales. The Bucktails sent their accurate fire into Confederates hunkered down in the plowed field, who also endured artillery shelling from the far side of the creek to the east. His eyes followed Smoketown Road southwest up a grassy rolling swell to a small white building turned bright orange by the rising sun, heavy woods beyond it. Confederate artillery sat upon the rise and great blooms of smoke burst from the snouts of their big guns, the sound coming after, the clouds spreading and merging with the smoke of the other guns, all of it rolling down the hill toward and past him to the creek. The natural fog dissipated and this new fog replaced it, borne of muskets and cannon.

His eye was drawn back to the plowed field as a long line of Confederates rose up and opened fire into the Bucktails' position, the space around him coming fantastically alive as bullets cleaved the air, searing perforations that demolished everything in their path. So many projectiles, so many that it seemed the air itself was enraged, spewing vengeful hornets riding hurricane winds. The Confederates knelt to reload, biting off the ends of paper charges, emptying powder into the far end of their musket barrels, dropping in the ball, tamping it down as the patient Bucktails waited, and within a minute the Confederates stood to fire and the Bucktails timed it just so and gave them a crippling volley. Cassius watched the gray men catch the singing fusillade and fall. He noted the harsh sun in their faces and the long shadows thrown out behind them, and knew it was barely past six in the morning with the dead already piling up.

The Bucktails were running low on ammunition and were ordered to fall back. Cassius looked to say good-bye to McLaren but did not see him. Fresh Blues moved in to take their place, and Cassius stayed where he was, feeling a false security as he had so far survived and any venture into the snarling air seemed insane. Out on the plowed field he saw the Confederates turn their weapons away from him and angle them to his right. He looked over his shoulder across the clover and saw, coming through the cornfield, two glorious flags waving over the stalks, leading an unknown force to the southern rim of the corn.

The Bluecoats emerged from the corn rows in parade formation, glorious in their precise emergence. Then, from the turnpike up near the small white building—and Cassius had not noticed them before—coming from behind a wooden fence a vicious fire erupted against the Blue troops—God what smoke!—and the Grays in the plowed field rose as well, perfectly coordinated, as if one man, reflected a hundred times, abruptly stood, and they opened fire catching the Blues in a murderous crossfire. A stunning number of Federals dropped instantaneously in the perfect rows of their formation, as if a giant scythe glinted across their ankles. Survivors dove back into standing corn to escape. Artillery canister from the bald area near the small white building screamed into the cornfield and split men apart as if the human body were little more than a rag doll with poor stitching.

This was killing on an impossible scale, and Cassius could not wrap his brain around the images in front of his eyes. He tried to remember that each one of these men had a life, a family, mother, father, children, fears and hopes and ideas; each one worked and dreamed and had once been a child, and now screamed in astonished agony. He lost his sense of reality, as if his intelligence shut down to preserve him from madness. Unable to comprehend the meaning of such an immense horror, he began to see falling men as unreal, no different than the soldiers he carved. These were white men being killed by white men who were the same but for the color of their uniforms; mindfully, purposely slaughtering one another by the dozens, by the score, by the hundreds, by the thousands. Cassius saw how easy it was to devastate a man's body and rob him of his valuable life. And yet those who survived remained on the battlefield and fought on.

He watched because it was impossible not to watch. He stayed in one place until he moved, and his reasons for moving were no greater than his reasons for staying, unmotivated by fear or superstition. Heat and humidity tormented him, but it was worse for the combatants who held smoldering weapons and did their work on the water in their canteens. Time lagged, and the order in which events occurred began to slam together until it was a confused nightmare of attack and retreat on both sides. More Blues came through the cornfield, but in smaller groups, and not in formation. More Grays reinforced the plowed field and died; others fired; still others ran. A handful of Gray skirmishers slipped into the cornfield between two Blue brigades and sat between them picking off men in both directions, so that when the Blues fired back, they killed their own.

Still more Blue troops came through the cornfield from the north to reinforce their decimated brethren, and the thinned and exhausted Grays fell back to the far woods. The Blues chased them firing, but they too were losing men and running short of ammunition, and then they gave up the field and fell back to the corn. The Grays regrouped and rushed back to their original positions, and all the dead to date were for nothing. He remembered a moment when Grays from the plowed field rose to charge his position, but the gunfire around him caught them climbing a fence and they fell back. He began to doubt that he had actually seen it, even though it had been clear and purposeful and had set his heart racing. Confederates set fire to the farmhouse next to the plowed field, and he knew that was true because the smoke occasionally blew in his direction and choked him, more intense than the passing smoke of artillery.

The cornfield was thinning, acres of stalks flattened by bodies and artillery, and it was patchy and smoking and smelled of sulfur, but the fighting over it did not stop, as if this patch of ground was the key to the war. He saw men go mad. He saw men hurl their weapons at the enemy. He saw men forget to remove the ramrod from their muzzle and fire so that it flew like a spear. He saw men weep. He saw men scream, he saw men throw their weapons aside and crawl among the dead for a fresh weapon. He saw dead men piled atop one another where they had fallen, and others using those bodies as shields to fire on their enemy. He saw a man of rank open his mouth to shout an order, only to have a bullet drive through it and out the back of his head. He saw fresh Gray troops charge the cornfield—someone saw their flag and said Texans—and drive the Blues back, the stalks thinning badly now, and he heard artillery from just north of the cornfield, canister fired at close range, that chewed the Texans apart and only a handful came back. He heard sudden whoops and yells from somewhere to the northwest and knew another battle raged there, and he wondered how many men could be fighting at once. He wondered when they would run out of men, and if they did, would that stop it or would the wind and the trees take up arms and carry on?

It had to be after nine o'clock in the morning, Cassius guessed, looking at the sun that was somehow safely up over South Mountain. The cornfield, what was left of it, belonged to the Blue. The fight was now in the clover field and the plowed field just south.

Cassius got to his feet. He struggled to stand, his leg muscles knotted and strained. He walked into the cornfield, out into the open where here and there a stalk still stood, frayed and uncertain. He stepped cautiously around the dead, an intricate chore as they carpeted the area. Artillery had rent bodies into fetid fetal lumps sprayed across the earth. In some areas, severed body parts were so thoroughly shredded by canister they were hard to identify. Blue bodies covered Gray bodies on top of Blue that rested on green stalks and smashed bits of white corn. He was barely aware of the sounds of battle surrounding him. He heard the zip of the occasional bullet and ignored the one that went clean through his shirt without touching his skin. He cringed at the stench, the ammonia smell of unbathed men, the odors of sulfur and sour vomit, slick oily feces and the first breath of decay. Delirious frenzied flies massed and dove and spewed their cream into open wounds. Flattened cornstalks were splattered with gore, and blood collected like dew in the curled fallen cups of the leaves. The charnel smell chafed his nostrils and burrowed into his sinuses and brain, seeping under his armpits and up his ass, marinating his skin down to his bones until his teeth tasted of rot from within.

Gunfire and artillery stopped at the same moment on both sides. There came over the field a sudden and shocking shroud of silence, and Cassius looked up with alarm and wonder. It lasted only a few breaths, but in that time he was more afraid than he had been all morning.

When the gunfire and artillery resumed, he was able to move again. He stepped over something that shifted like a snake but was in fact greasy uncoiling intestines roasting in the sun.

He grieved, he grieved as he looked at the men piled dead alongside the actively dying; he grieved that they would so willingly give up so much just to keep him in subjugation. He looked at them littering this giant field and he knew that he would never be free. He saw the fate of his people in their twisted faces and dead open eyes, and he knew that he would be a slave forever.

He heard a sound and saw movement, and knelt down to roll a body aside. A Union soldier looked up at him, shot in multiple places but alive, a survivor in the cornfield. Cassius knelt to give the man water from the canteen still stretched across his chest. The man was so parched that he could not find sound to accompany his mouth forming the words "thank you." Cassius decided that this one man would not die, not here, and he lifted him onto his shoulders. The man grunted in pain but did not cry out. Cassius was surprised to find him frail and weightless. He toted the man back through rows of cornstalks that no longer stood, through the woods east of the cornfield to the road just around the bend from the action, where men who had yet to see the elephant sat waiting. They took the man from him and placed him on a litter, and Cassius followed, walking, as they ran him down the road.

As the battle raged in multiple places over there, he stayed out of the way, in the shade of an old maple on the east side of Antietam Creek, unable to understand why he had so much difficulty convincing himself to stand up.

But he did stand. He looked around. He was again thinking about crossing to the Confederate side. He headed back from where he had come, but a soldier bumped into him, an older man who looked hard into Cassius's eyes.

"What's with you, boy, you lost? Where you think you're goin?"

Over there, said Cassius, indicating the small, nondescript, white building in the distance.

"So you got a tongue in your head," said the older soldier unpleasantly.

Cassius gave him the smallest of nods and turned to move away.

"That there building's a church," said the older soldier. "You ain't goin there."

Don't look like a church, said Cassius.

"German church, Dunkers. Pacifists. You go there, them Rebs send you right back where you belong. Say, you think them Pacifists is mad, watchin all this? You think maybe them Pacifists is fightin mad?" He laughed at his own joke.

Could be, said Cassius, without conviction.

"Gettin mighty hot over there," said the man. A battle was taking place in the distance, up and down the turnpike near the Dunker church, a push-pull attack and counterattack. Cassius watched it dispassionately.

"You be a smart boy, wait till it dies down 'fore you give yerself back to them Rebs."

Cassius found the ford point north of the middle bridge and crossed the creek, sludge and sand filling his shoes. He followed the smoke from the burning farmhouse, then cut directly south, staying clear of another farmhouse where beehives had been hit by artillery, which meant another sort of trouble. The battle had moved and a great concentration of Federal troops was massed in a field and moving south toward a rise. He continued on below the farmhouse, walking parallel to the Yankees, and he had this area of the field to himself. Beyond the Federal troops, over near the turnpike, he saw where the big Confederate guns had repositioned themselves. He walked a little farther, so that from his vantage point he could see the far side of the rise that the Federal troops were approaching. What he saw within sixty feet of the rise caused him to drop down on one knee.

Before him was a farmer's road that had been carved out of a swale, worn lower over the years by carts. On the north brow of this sunken road, fence rails were piled and he could see where the rails that had earlier lined the south side of the road—the land rose up a few feet on that side to meet a cornfield—had been carried to the north side to fortify the position. Confederate soldiers had taken cover in this low place, a natural defensive position, hundreds of them spread prone along the bank, aiming their rifles and using the fence rails as protection and foundation. Looking down the stretch of sunken road, halfway toward the turnpike, the road came to a soft arrow point and angled off to the left, traveling southwest, and while more men defended that position, Cassius could not see around the corner to know how many more. They expected an attack, and Cassius saw what they could not see, the Federals coming up the rise on the far side. The crest of the rise was so close to the lane that Blue and Gray could not yet see one another, but when the Yanks hit that crest, they would be very nearly on top of them.

Cassius watched them march, young men in fresh blue uniforms with clean, cream-colored boot guards. Cassius knew from their demeanor that they were not so much Blue as green, climbing the rise in splendor; what a magnificent way to walk into a massacre. Once over the crest they would be so close to the Gray position that the protected Confederates could not miss those young men in their new uniforms with their cream-colored boot guards who were so obligingly lined up shoulder to shoulder. And so they came and so they crested and so they died. They died in rows, and a second group crested behind them and stepped over them and they died. The few left standing turned and ran down the rise on the far side. They tried to warn a third contingent of soldiers just approaching, but these soldiers were veterans. They did not have clean uniforms or fresh faces, they were war-hardened, and they stopped on the far side of the crest, using it as cover, and they stood to fire, then ducked back down, giving it back to the Confederates crouching in the lane. The Confederates were three deep, the men in back loading and passing muskets to the better shots in front, but it wasn't like picking off those first green troops. Artillery hit the lane, and more Blues came from new angles, and they charged and were repelled, then others charged and were repelled, and the sameness of the killing left Cassius numb. Almost an hour passed, and the killing was constant and many of the attacks were pointless and wasteful, but Federals kept coming and made progress, and after a while fewer Confederate muskets fired back.

Cassius had watched the hat in the sunken road for some time before he became fully conscious that it was familiar. He emerged from his daze to try to identify the face of the small man on which rested the tan slouch hat with the brim turned up in front. Now and then the man lifted his head or turned to call to someone behind him, and Cassius thought he wore a beard with no mustache. If it was indeed him, how had he come to this place? He later thought that the man might have been delivering ammunition from the supply wagons and had found himself in the middle of it when the attack began. Cassius imagined him thrilled to be forced into action; an opportunity, as glory would speed his promotion.

Something happened then. Federals charged and broke through at the arrow point, firing down the road in enfilading fire. An order was given and Confederates retreated, trying to go up the south bank, Federals shooting them down as well as slaughtering the men still lined up on their bellies, filling the road with corpses and blood. Cassius watched the tan slouch hat escape into the cornfield, and now Cassius moved with purpose, sideways to see if he could keep track of the hat in the corn, and here and there through the rows he saw it. He ran at an angle, finally entering the corn himself, anticipating its destination from the last place he had seen the hat. His hands and arms separated stalks making a path, head swiveling to see every runner, catching the occasional hatless retreater to search his face in case the man had lost his, throwing him aside when it wasn't the man he sought, hearing sounds of others crashing through the corn over the sounds of distant gunfire and artillery. Then, without warning, the short man in the tan slouch hat with the upturned brim was there, and Cassius grabbed him by the upper arms, his full rage gathering. Whitacre's face was stretched long, mouth shaped into an oval soundless scream, eyes aghast, warped to unrecognizable by terror. His eyes met Cassius's eyes and where Whitacre recognized nothing, Cassius saw the enormity of the man's hell, where his broken spirit unhinged his sanity.

He had him in his hands. Whitacre struggled to escape, but Cassius held him, examining his uncomprehending eyes. His fingers dug into Whitacre's shoulders, one hand moving to his throat. But Whitacre did not understand what was happening. Artillery exploded and fragments cut horizontally across the corn, shearing down stalks a row away. Whitacre flinched, ducking, shrieking, shitting his trousers, but Cassius did not let go. He further studied the man's eyes, and they were the eyes of a feral animal, not of a sentient human being.

Emoline, said Cassius. Emoline Justice.

He raised his voice to be heard over gunfire and artillery, but received no response. A cornered fox would have understood more. Cassius was about to repeat her name again; even in Whitacre's mental absence he was willing to try him for his crime, right here, right now, in the corn, but he saw he would be trying and killing a man out of his mind, a man who did not know what he had done, a man who would not know his own name.

He let go and Whitacre bounded away, as if he had never been stopped.

Without giving chase Cassius watched Whitacre vanish in the corn, running alone with no weapon in his hands to slow him down.

The afternoon aged. Battles continued around him, one concerning a bridge that spanned Antietam Creek somewhere to the south. But Cassius had chosen his position wisely and was not obliged to move. As night came on, the fighting diminished. The sun set before him on his expansive view of the battlefield, the ground shockingly littered with objects that had once been men and horses, until they vanished into the complete blackness of night. He listened to their gruesome screaming and weeping as they slowly died in the dark. He watched pinpoints of light creep across the battlefield, moving, stopping, then moving again, the lanterns of looters, as bodies were stripped of their possessions. He slept finally, and when he awoke the following morning, the bodies remained but the moaning and weeping had grown feeble, and Cassius was glad he did not have to listen to it. He instead heard a peculiar silence, even as the two armies remained interlocked like oddly shaped puzzle pieces. Cassius waited for the artillery to begin. It did not.

He wandered the battlefield. The Federals controlled most of the territory over which they had so desperately fought, and they carted their dead and wounded from the field while Confederate dead were left behind. Over every rise, gathered in every swale, Cassius discovered more of the same.

He found his way back to the sunken road and looked around what was left of the nearby cornfield, the last place he had seen Whitacre. He walked in the direction where he had watched Whitacre run. He passed a civilian who was meticulously picking through the belongings of dead men. The civilian reared up in surprise when one of the dead men moved and looked at him, and the civilian grunted as he backed away, "I'll come back later."

Cassius stopped at the edge of the open space behind the corn field, bordered on its south end by an east-west turnpike, and surveyed the area. He watched for a time a group of Federals as they piled Confederate bodies, one on top of another, preparing to inter them in a mass grave. He looked away, and saw that he was not the only one watching this activity. Standing off to the side of the Federals was another interested party, a woman. Women were not an unusual sight, now that the battle was done, but this was a black woman and she was strikingly familiar. He continued to look at her with skeptical eyes, finding it odd and unlikely to have come across her, although it was not in the least bit impossible, as he had earlier seen her master. She did not dissipate like fog, so he walked toward her.

Maryanne sensed someone coming directly for her and she

turned to see Cassius approach. She looked at him as if he were someone she knew but could not remember if he had lived in her dream or was simply a shade come to life.

Maryanne, said Cassius. Her entire body shuddered in surprise, thinking the shade had spoken. You remember me?

She leaned forward and looked him hard in the face and her expression changed. A new wonder came over her, and she laughed, as if she found this moment to be ridiculous and hilarious.

What're you doing here? said Cassius.

I go where my master go. That always the way it be, I follow ol' Cap'n Solomon, said Maryanne.

Well I've been looking for him.

You done found him, said Maryanne.

That was yesterday, but I've spent all morning—

She nodded her head to the pile of Confederate bodies. He turned and saw, among the corpses and the gray uniforms, among the kepis and the haversacks and the canteens, a tan slouch hat with an upturned brim.

An odd sensation flowed through him, as if his muscles had become liquid. He walked directly to the bodies, took hold of a dead man's arm, and pulled on it to drag him off another, thus revealing Whitacre's calm face. A Federal corporal came on the double.

"Son of a bitch, what the hell you think you're doing there? Just because they're Rebs don't mean you can desecrate their bodies, these were *men!*"

Looking for a family member, said Cassius.

"Family member? But these are *white* men."

So it seems.

The corporal looked at Cassius, trying to understand if he was being made the object of derision, but Cassius did not smile. Cassius looked back eye to eye with the corporal, and something there made the corporal pause. He had more than enough work ahead of him on this day, so he retreated.

Cassius now turned his gaze to Whitacre and viewed the man's empty face with a deep and penetrating sadness. Here was her murderer, slain himself in a senseless battle. And yet the pit of rage, one he had kept close concerning the murder of one woman, one woman in the face of the excessive slaughter of multiple battlefields, still burned fiercely and would not be quenched. His journey was at an end, and still he ached.

H e approached the provisional line that separated Federal from Confederate. Pockets of opposing soldiers swapped food, swapped stories, and he found it curious that one day they were butchering one another and the next exchanging pleasantries. He looked back at one point and noticed that Maryanne had followed him onto Confederate-held ground. She had also found no difficulty traveling from one army to the other. He did not know why she shadowed him, but he was frankly unconcerned, as he walked with purpose.

Soldiers in butternut treated him no differently than had the soldiers in blue. He stayed away from men in groups, approaching individuals to ask after Major Jacob Howard. Some of the soldiers looked at him as if at a wooden door or a porch swing. Others seemed not to hear him. One soldier had never heard of Major Howard, but knew a Corporal Holland.

Cassius reconsidered his approach. The next man he came to, he asked after the 7th Virginia Cavalry.

"Seventh Virginia? Think they's somewheres round the West Woods."

Which is the West Woods? said Cassius.

The man pointed toward the Dunker church. "Back side of the church."

Cassius went in that direction. Once near the church, he asked again. After a few rude responses, he came upon a captain inspecting the fetlock on the right rear leg of his horse. The horse would not put weight on that leg, and the captain's hand came away cupped with blood.

Cassius asked for the 7th Virginia Cavalry. The captain did not look at him, just pointed beyond the West Woods, and said, "Nicodemus Heights." The captain brought out his sidearm, put it to the horse's head, and pulled the trigger. The sound shocked Cassius, as it was the only battle sound he had heard that day. The horse went down in an instant and briefly twitched. The captain turned away with tears flowing freely down his cheeks.

Cassius walked along Hagerstown Turnpike, and passed the Dunker church. He glanced back and Maryanne continued to trail behind him. He did not care. He cut through the woods and walked up a hill to high ground that had more than a dozen guns, many of them still operational. They had been hit hard by Union artillery on the previous day. Behind the guns were cavalry units, and Cassius walked unchallenged between the batteries. He picked his way around tents and campfires, but this time he did not ask for Major Howard. If Jacob was alive, he did not want him to be warned of Cassius's approach.

He saw a horse that had the distinctive markings of Jacob's mount. He was unsure, as this horse was appreciably thinner, but then Cassius recognized Jacob's saddle. He went to the horse, which shied nervously away. He laid his hand easily on its neck and the horse calmed as if it recognized him.

"Ho there, boy, what you doing to my horse?" said a voice behind him.

Cassius turned. He thought that if this stranger was the horse's owner, then Jacob was dead. He took his hand from the horse's neck and felt an unexpected sadness that his old master would not be coming home. Then he started. He cocked his head, looking beyond the heavy beard and mustache and the gaunt face that was ten years older than Jacob had been ten months ago when he had left Sweetsmoke.

Jacob Howard, said Cassius. Never before had Cassius called him anything but Master Jacob.

Jacob Howard squinted. "Cassius," he said, with unmistakable surprise. "How have you come here? Did my father send you? You have come a great long way."

I'm sent by your mother, said Cassius.

"Cassius. Of all people. And my mother, she is well?"

Well enough. Your father not.

"My father will outlive us all." Jacob looked around at the sad scarecrow men, at the bodies being buried, at the weapons and horses. "That will by no means be difficult."

She calls you home. Says you won't see him alive again if you don't come along.

"I may never see anyone alive again. I may not survive this day."

I got her letter for you, said Cassius. He pulled the letter out of

Jacob's old haversack. It was crumpled and stained with grease. Jacob took it and put it into his pocket without opening it.

"There is a good place to sit over there," he said pointing. "We are close to the river."

They walked until they came to a spot that gave Cassius a view of the wide Potomac and sat side by side, a few feet from each other. Cassius had time to observe Jacob's actions, and was taken by surprise. Jacob had developed a nervous twitch in his right hand, and he blinked often. His shoulders slumped and he grimaced as if he had chronic pain, but Cassius could not guess where the pain would be.

"William is dead," said Jacob, speaking of his personal servant.

Thought he might've become contraband.

"That thought did not cross his mind."

You know that? said Cassius.

"Oh, I knew William."

Cassius simply smiled.

"Killed at South Mountain a few days ago. Seems longer. If you wanted to, you—"

No. I won't be your body servant, Jacob, said Cassius.

"No. Will you join the contrabands?"

Cassius said nothing.

Jacob looked at the river through sleepy eyes.

"So my mother wants me home," said Jacob. "What an effortless solution."

Ought to read her letter, said Cassius. She runs the plantation. Other planters don't like a woman master.

"No, I reckon not," said Jacob, but he did not remove the letter from his pocket. "I should read it and show it to my commanding officer and return home at once, ride away from all this." Jacob smiled but his right hand twitched with greater force.

For your father, said Cassius.

"You are the one who should be there for him, Cassius."

Cassius frowned.

"He had a great affection for you."

Never knew my own father. I do know it wasn't Hoke Howard, said Cassius plainly, a simple declaration.

"I did not say you were his son, only that he looked on you with affection. Do you remember Ahab?"

No.

"That great bay? No memory of him?"

No.

"That horse was to be given to me, and he let you ride him first."

I don't remember, said Cassius.

Jacob shook his head, an important piece of his history that was not important to others. He thought for a while before he spoke again.

"It can be difficult to love your son at times," said Jacob. "You want him to be some version of you, the best of you, but also something better, and then he grows up to have his own mind, his own thoughts, his own opinions. Tragic, really." Jacob smiled. "In his actions, his choice of words, he continually reminds you of the parts of yourself that you wish to suppress, the parts you deliberately avoid in the looking glass."

Wouldn't know. Didn't get to raise my son, said Cassius coldly.

Jacob looked at him with mild surprise. "No, you did not, did you? I have a son, of course. He is a rank little turd, the very worst parts of his mother and father and grandparents. I do not miss him."

Jacob stared at the river, and Cassius thought that he had lost his train of thought.

"A pet is something to love, a dog particularly. He loves you without opinion or judgment, he does not speak to you indignantly, he does not confuse your affections with foolish ideas and odd perspectives; he merely loves. I sometimes think of how easy it was for my father to favor you, Cassius."

Cassius fumed at the idea that he had been Hoke's pet, and then he thought that this was Jacob's justification, arrived at after years of resentment. Or maybe just a way to get back at Cassius for Ahab.

If only he'd protected me from you, said Cassius, swinging back.

"From me? Was I also injurious to you, Cassius?" Jacob looked to be humoring him. "How intriguing, that I might be as injurious to you as I felt you were to me."

You only did what I expected. He could've stopped you.

"What you expected of me. Whatever it was must have been dastardly indeed, and yet you don't blame me because it was in my nature," Jacob said, in wonder.

Cassius held his tongue, and fought to keep his temper in check.

"Look at you, Cassius. You would kill me if you could. Is that why you came here?" Jacob did not sound concerned about the prospect.

No. Not to kill you, Jacob.

"What was it that I did that so angers you?"

Young Master Jacob fathered my son, who was sold to protect you.

Jacob laughed.

Cassius felt every expulsive bray of his laughter. He listened to it roll down the bank and saw it embraced by the wide Potomac, carried downriver to coat the Commonwealth of Virginia with a layer of mocking mirth.

"That is what you think? That I lay with Marriah? Poor Cassius. Marriah did not share with you the truth. Your Old Master Hoke was the baby's father. I did not touch her."

Hoke? said Cassius.

"My mother sold that boy so she did not have to confront daily her husband's moment of weakness."

Cassius's thoughts reeled back. Hoke, in his moment of delusion, had said, "I killed her," and Cassius had thought at first he referred to Emoline, then to Tempie. But it had not been delusion. His torment was Marriah. His indiscretion had led to his acquiescence in the sale of his infant son, and that in turn had led to Marriah's self-slaughter, and Hoke bore that in self-loathing.

Why? said Cassius.

"Have you no looking glass, Cassius?"

Cassius was confused by the question and answered with a simple: No.

"My father admired you. You think not? You were strong and virile, things he doubted in himself. He protected you in the way he wished he had been protected by his father, and you repaid him with admiration. How I hated you. How little he had left for me. Marriah was his way of experiencing your strength as his manhood faded. You were strong and loyal, you made him feel loved, and he craved more; he wanted more control."

He owns me, said Cassius with astonishment. He controls me.

"That is merely the law. This was deeper. He wanted your soul."

I'm a black man, a slave, said Cassius, a surge of rage overwhelming him. He wanted more?

"Yes," said Jacob. "The perfect compliment to you, as a black man and a slave."

They were quiet together for some time after that. Cassius was about to stand up and leave, but Jacob spoke again.

"You made a serious gamble with your life, coming here," he said.

I never bet more than I can afford to lose, said Cassius.

Jacob nodded, recognizing Hoke's words. "Spoken as a true Howard."

M aryanne waited until Cassius left Jacob behind at the river. She carried a haversack in her hands and approached him.

Why do you follow me, what do you want from me? said Cassius unkindly.

She offered the haversack to him.

Want you should take this, said Maryanne.

What is it?

Cap'n Solomon's bag. Got his personals in there. Figured you know some way to get it back to his widow.

You're staying.

Stay and be contraband with them Yanks, cook for 'em.

Better than Edensong.

Maybe one day get free.

Cassius opened the haversack, and among Whitacre's personal items he found a kerchief with something wrapped inside. He brought it out and unwrapped it. A small amount of jalap bindweed, old and withered, was revealed.

That what I think it is? said Cassius.

Jalap is what that be, said Maryanne. Cap'n use it regular. Ain't no more left after that, didn't know where I was goin be findin more. Seem like I don't need to, now.

Don't need to give it to his widow, said Cassius, returning the jalap to her, but keeping the haversack. He had seen the quarter-master's wagons preparing to return south, most of them empty, but some would carry the badly wounded and limbless soldiers, those who would never fight again, to return them to their homes across the Confederacy. Among those wagons he would find one that would pass near Edensong, and with it, send Whitacre's belongings.

Maybe use it for someone else, said Maryanne, as she rewrapped the jalap and put it in a pocket in her apron. Then she stared off with something on her mind. Cassius waited for her thought to emerge.

He sure didn't look like much, said Maryanne.

Your captain?

Lyin dead like that, he sure didn't look like much.

No.

'Cause of him is how I connect up with Emoline, said Maryanne, patting her apron.

For the jalap, said Cassius.

That first time I be lookin for some for Cap'n Solomon and heard 'bout Emoline in town. She tryin to grow it in her garden, got someone else who use it, but she done share a little with me. Not so easy to find, partic'lar this far north. Hers be real scrawny and sad.

Hard to grow in this climate, said Cassius, nodding.

Went lookin for it in her garden that night, but it be tore out.

What night? said Cassius.

That night I seen you in the window. Looked there 'cause Cap'n Solomon be runnin low.

You knew where she grew it in her garden?

Sure I did. Every bit of it pulled out, roots and all.

Cassius remembered the hole there, and he began to understand something that he did not want to understand.

It was possible someone else had come along after she was dead and pulled out the jalap plants. But why not other plants, why not harvest the whole garden? Why just the jalap?

Emoline would not have pulled up all of her jalap at once. Her son Richard had not done it; he was digging for her money. Gabriel Logue had not done it.

At that moment, Cassius believed that the one who had done it was her killer. He had no proof, but pieces fit together for him, like a perfectly planed tongue and groove. Whitacre might have done it, but then he would have had more than enough bindweed and

Maryanne would not have needed to look for more in Emoline's garden that night. In a sudden jolt, Cassius knew what he had to do.

N ight fell and the Confederate army made rapid, discreet preparations to leave Maryland. Cassius met with Jacob by lamplight to collect the letter Jacob had written to his mother that afternoon. Cassius asked why the Confederates were leaving, and Jacob said that they were obliged to leave, that Lee had lost one-quarter of his army in that single day of fighting. Jacob then told Cassius what Cassius already knew, that he would stay with the 7th Virginia Cavalry. He would not return to see his father. He would not return to take control of the plantation.

Cassius walked away from Jacob Howard and his men, but once he was out of their sight, he stopped. He took an unattended lantern, and under its light opened Jacob's letter, which, as was his usual, was not sealed. He scanned it, but Jacob's cautious words to his mother did not interest him. With a pencil, Cassius added something to the bottom of the letter underneath Jacob's signed name. He then re-folded it and returned it to the envelope.

Cassius walked down Hagerstown Turnpike toward Sharpsburg and found the quartermaster wagons that were preparing to return to Virginia. There was great confusion as the army also prepared to depart, and Cassius used the confusion to his advantage. He came upon wagons where soldiers loaded crippled and damaged men while teamsters coupled horses into their harnesses. Cassius was directed to a wagon that would travel near the vicinity of Edensong and Sweetsmoke. From a short distance, he examined the faces of the men going in the wagon and was grateful to discover that none of them would recognize him. He approached the teamster, a corporal, and gave him both the haversack and Jacob's letter. The corporal accepted them without comment and placed them with the other mail, barely acknowledging Cassius in the process.

Cassius stepped away in the dark.

-⊛ Chapter Nineteen ⊛-

E LLEN Howard was distracted from her calculations in the
plantation's ledgers by movement out the window of the study.
She saw her husband wandering in the yard and she watched him as
he shuffled along. He walked with his head pressed forward, as if his
curious mind wished to hurry his slow, stiff legs. She saw that he
again carried, in the pocket of his coat, the September newspaper
that reported Lincoln's address, delivered at Sharpsburg a week after
the battle. Lincoln had made a proclamation in that speech, calling
for the emancipation of the slaves. Ellen was convinced that Hoke
did not comprehend the contents of the newspaper, as he now saw
the world around him more simply, but he had discovered it was
quite pleasurable to carry it on his person. When he was around the
servants, he would draw forth the newspaper from his pocket and
hold it up. The house people all responded with smiles and nods. He
took pleasure in their reactions and repeated the exercise time and
again until the house people made excuses to escape. She had initially

believed that they humored him, but grew to understand that they knew precisely what was in that newspaper, despite the fact they could not read it for themselves. Ellen wondered how they knew. She shook her head, the gesture reflecting her inner thoughts. It seemed there were many small mysteries concerning her people that she would never understand. Hoke now moved out of her sight and she returned her attention to the ledger, noting that she still held her pen in midair. The air was drying the nib, and she set it back into its well.

Her patterns had altered since Hoke's illness and the majority of her time was spent in his ground-floor study. She scanned the room, thinking again about adding something of her own personality to the furnishings, now that Hoke no longer haunted his former sanctuary. She missed the leisure time spent painting in the afternoons, and considered telling Pet to bring down a few of her finished watercolors to decorate the walls. The one change she had made was to put away, in a drawer, his fancy wooden boxes. She had never shared his affection for trinkets and collectibles.

She opened and closed her writing hand to release a cramp, then rapidly shook it out sideways. Her fingers collided with the inkwell, and blue ink escaped to form a puddle on Hoke's desk. She leapt to her feet, grabbing the ledgers and stepping back to save her dress, calling loudly for her servant. She kicked Hoke's chair out of the way with frustration, and the chair struck the side of the desk loudly.

Pet came quickly, and Ellen reflected that she had been alarmed by her missus's abrupt call and the subsequent thump. Pet saw the spill and pulled off her apron, dropping it over the ink to sop it up before it rolled to the edge and then to the floor. Ellen saw, as Pet mopped, that the ink soaked into the wood and would leave a stain. She noted the blue that discolored her fingers, something with which she had lived for months now, and imagined it to be permanent.

She thought ahead to the spring, hoping that by then things would have calmed down. After Lincoln's speech, other plantations had suffered runaways, but the patrollers and planters had responded surely and assertively, tracking down those bold few, bringing them back in chains and inflicting extreme—in one case fatal—punishment as a warning to all. No one from Sweetsmoke had run, not yet. But rude anticipation was in the air of the quarters. Something in the world had turned on that day, or maybe it was the week before, when

Lee had given up his invasion of the North and come back to Virginia. Any talk of England and France recognizing the Confederacy vanished in that instant, as if Lincoln had wrapped the conflict in a moral imperative. But Ellen believed in Lee, and was ashamed by her shortsighted countrymen. Lee would regroup, Lee would reinvade the North. In due time, he would end the war, as he should have done in September. But what a shock it had been, she reflected, to learn that Lee was driven back at Sharpsburg, beaten for the first time. Her gaze was again drawn to the outdoors, through the window. November. The light was harsh, the dry leaves baked brown against the cold ground, the sun low in the sky, the afternoons rushing to a swift close. If she was to be in the quarters when the hands returned from clear-cutting, she would need to leave while there was still light. After the proclamation, she had increased her presence on the lane, to discourage any foolish notions in her people.

The business of running a plantation was beginning to suit her. Over the previous months, she had paid strict attention to the choices made by the other planters in their dealings, and had grown to appreciate their thought processes, adapting the ideas she found wise. Only occasionally did she view their decisions as inexplicable. Recently she had heard that Orville Sands, master of Philadelphia Plantation, had agreed to sell two female slaves to Gabriel Logue. These were the very two she had forced Hoke to sell to Sands years before, and she detested the idea of the daughters of Emoline Justice going free. She had tried, unsuccessfully, to dissuade Orville from making the sale. Now there was nothing to be done about it. But it had struck her as odd for business reasons as well; Orville was a rational man who valued his slaves, and as far as she understood, Philadelphia was not facing unusual financial difficulties. She also wondered what the Angel Gabriel planned to do with two females. He had impressed her as a man who preferred to be unencumbered by possessions, in order to facilitate his trade.

Ellen had also emulated Hoke's aura of command, particularly in the early days of her tenure, acting decisively to show Mr. Nettle her resolve and establish her power. She had purposely made an unpopular decision and returned Gus to the position of driver. Gus had seemed appropriately chastised after his demotion. In the past, Mr. Nettle had been lax with Gus. It now fell to her to control them both.

She sighed without realizing it, falling more deeply into reflection. Joseph, Savilla and Abram's son, had returned to work and now labored with the others to clear-cut the new parcel, the one to be planted in the spring. Joseph moved gingerly on his hobbled leg, but, in a bit of good luck, his work had suffered little. An image of his walk came into her mind, and it reflected Hoke, head forward, legs struggling to keep pace. The harvest had gone well, better than anticipated after the hornworm blight, and barring any unforeseen catastrophe, Sweetsmoke would roll along for the first half of the following year. She'd had a second tobacco barn built out of sight on the property, and a significant portion of the harvest cured therein so that it could not be requisitioned by Jeff Davis's government. She thought of Joseph functioning as the lead carpenter on that shed, and was reminded of an incident years before, when Shedd had run, and how quickly he had come to nearly full strength after his punishment.

She glanced out the open door, to the greeting room where Sarah swept down the stairs in her blue dress, her servant trailing behind. How well Sarah wore that dress. How thoroughly Sarah had taken charge of the household. She had stepped in to fill the void Ellen had left when Ellen took over Hoke's business. Sarah now managed the servants like the general of an army. It was as if she had stored up a fount of strength while lingering in her bed all those months. Anne simpered with discontent, chafing under her control, while Genevieve was beside herself with indignation. Ellen could not imagine why, as neither Genevieve nor Anne had shown the slightest interest in maintaining the big house. Perhaps it is my fault, thought Ellen. I encouraged Sarah, after all. But what a welcome surprise on that morning, when Sarah had risen, like Lazarus, from her bed, to join the household at the table, fully dressed with her hair carefully pinned. No one had spoken a word about it at the time, as if her presence were the most natural thing in the world. But afterward, out of Sarah's earshot, it was all anyone could speak of for a full week. And how Quashee had blossomed! As Sarah shouldered the household burdens, Quashee emerged as the predominant servant. Pet had tried, God knows, to manage the household when Ellen was in charge, but she was too clumsy, too easily distracted. Despite the graceful way Quashee instructed her, poor Pet now dwelled in a perpetual sulk, at loose ends.

Ellen ran her fingers along the side of the desk and happened upon a gouge. She bent to examine it with a scowl, realizing it was fresh and she had been the cause, at the moment she had thrust aside the chair. She closed her eyes in melancholy irritation. Hoke would no longer care about the degradation of his desk, but she remembered how he had loved it, how proudly he set his hands flat against it to feel the smooth wood, and she mourned the man who no longer existed.

Ellen became aware of a sudden bustle of activity and saw Sarah rush to the front door. Out the window, she saw the carriage returning from town, Beauregard arriving with the post.

She rose from her chair, her heart tinging high in her chest as it always did when there might be news. She feared that she would discover he had been dead for days or weeks while she had blithely continued her petty existence. She joined her family as they poured from the house and closed in from around the yard, Genevieve and Nanny Catherine, Mrs. Nettle and Anne, Pet and Mam Rosie, Quashee following Sarah, and even young Charles and the other children, all hungry for news. Hoke was not there, but he would come eventually, in his good time. Beauregard stayed on the buckboard's bench, holding Sam's reins, waiting for his missus to join them; he had been well trained by John Corey. Sarah nodded to him as Ellen arrived, and he spoke:

Letter come from Master Jacob, Missus, said Beauregard.

"Let me have it, then," said Ellen.

She opened the envelope and removed the folded letter. Her entire family watched, and with so many expectant eyes upon her, she found herself moving more slowly than usual. She read his handwriting, *Dear Mother,* handwriting that was altered by a slight tremor. She imagined him less arrogant since he had gone to fight. *It saddens me greatly to hear of my father's unfortunate accident.* He was not coming home. Cassius had reached him, and he was not coming home. Her eyes flew down the page where she found excuses in a tone that rang hollow. At the bottom of the page, beneath his signature, in a rushed hand, she read the words *Cassius was killed at Sharpsburg.*

She looked up at everyone, saw their anxious eyes.

"He will not be coming home. Jacob will remain with his cavalry and fight on for his country, as is the right and proper thing."

A general sigh filled the air, a deflation of expectations, and already they began to move away, knowing the letter would reach their hands sometime later in the day, when they would have their own opportunity to savor Jacob's every word.

Ellen noted Sarah's reaction, and thought that, in her erect carriage, she expressed relief. It meant for Sarah that she would continue in her current position without the interference of a husband.

"He also writes that Cassius is dead," said Ellen.

She saw Quashee falter, saw Mam Rosie go to her, but then Beauregard stepped in to lend his support, leaving Mam Rosie stranded with her hands reaching. Ellen had not been aware of the connection between Quashee and Cassius, and she wondered when it had happened.

Ellen looked again at the words at the bottom of the page, and spoke aloud, but so that only she could hear: "So. He did not keep his promise."

The buckboard rolled down the road in the twilight, returning to the Chavis farm. He watched Weyman, drowsy on the bench, reins held lightly in his palms, and he thought to step out in front of the horse, but then thought better of it, as he did not want to shock Weyman into accidentally running him down. He stayed where he was among the trees, and as the buckboard moved past, he emerged and leapt up in the back, putting a hand on Weyman's shoulder from behind.

Dear Lord Jesus! said Weyman, shocked beyond reason that someone was behind him, and then shocked again to realize it was Cassius.

Good seeing you, too, Weyman, said Cassius.

What the hell're y'all doin, scarin old Weyman like that, gave me such a fright I ain't likely to recover.

See anyone else on the road? said Cassius.

Quiet out here. Jesus Lord, never thought to see y'all again, said Weyman.

Here I am, said Cassius.

Figured you for Canada.

Made a promise to come back.

Now that is the Cassius I know, y'all belong here, with me.

Picked up some things for you along the way.

Now, that is some good news, business been quiet. You got 'em now?

No, but get away tonight and we'll meet. Come to Emoline's.

Weyman looked over his shoulder at Cassius's face.

Maybe we could meet somewheres else, said Weyman.

Emoline's is best, nobody bother us there. Travel on foot, so you don't let your old Master Thomas know.

I don't know, Cassius, I ain't real comfortable with ghosts.

Never knew you to be superstitious, Weyman. Way I figure, she'll protect us.

Weyman considered, then nodded.

Good, said Cassius. I'll be getting off right up here, before you go around that bend. And Weyman. Don't say you saw me.

Don't say?

Not to Bunty, not to your Thomas, not to your Thomas's wife.

Why don't you want me to say?

You want I should give the goods to someone else?

No, I gotta have 'em, I won't tell nobody if that's what you like.

After tonight, you tell anyone you want, said Cassius with a smile, and he leapt off the back of the buckboard and was gone into the trees. He saw Weyman look around after him, and thought Weyman was questioning if Cassius had really been there.

Cassius settled to wait in the woods until it began to grow dark, then made his way toward town. He stopped at the little bridge and watched the motion of the water as it rushed by under him until the last of the light left the sky. When he could no longer see, he stayed awhile longer just to listen.

C assius held a lantern in one hand and Emoline's pages in the other, with the page that diagrammed her garden on top. He looked at the hole in the ground where plants had been wrenched out, and on her map he confirmed it as the location of the jalap bindweed. He paused then, glancing at the names on the other sheets, and was reminded that Emoline refused to tell the fortunes of blacks; the burden and pretense of influencing the future was left to the whites. He folded the paper and replaced it in his pouch. He looked at the rows of vegetables and remedies, all dead or dying. No one had come to harvest her garden. They were all too superstitious. Her daughters would do it in the spring.

He went inside to wait.

Weyman came some time later, and he looked shaken. He had narrowly avoided the patrollers. They had been drinking and their moods were foul, hoping for trouble. He was concerned that he would encounter difficulty returning to the Chavis farm.

Don't worry about that, said Cassius. I'll fix it.

How you do that? said Weyman.

Write you a pass.

Write me a pass?

Been doing it for years.

Y'all can write?

Cassius nodded.

Read, too?

Read, too.

Don't that beat all, said Weyman. That some little secret you been keepin from Weyman. I could'a used you in my business.

Could be why I didn't say.

Speakin of business, what you bring back for me?

Left it outside, said Cassius.

Cassius led him to the garden and they stopped at the hole in the ground where the jalap had once grown.

Where is it? said Weyman.

This is it, said Cassius.

Ain't nothin here but a hole in the ground.

That's because I brought you a mystery.

This ain't funny, y'all. You got somethin for me or not?

You were getting remedies from Emoline.

What you on about, Cassius?

Something you couldn't remember. Started with one of the letters of the alphabet, what was it you said? "M," I think you said "M." But it wasn't "M," was it, Weyman?

I ain't followin.

It was "J."

Okay, it was "J." So?

Jalap bindweed. Sound familiar?

Maybe so. All right.

One more piece of the puzzle dropped into place, and Cassius knew a sadness expanding inside him.

She was growing it for you. Remember that? said Cassius.

Sure I remember.

You pulled the whole thing out of the ground.

She didn't need it no more.

Because she was dead.

That right. She dead.

You pulled it out the night she died.

How you figure?

Knew you wouldn't get any more from her, so you took all you could.

Think I better get goin, said Weyman.

What if the patrollers are still out there?

Weyman looked over his shoulder. He looked back at Cassius. Then he smiled.

This some kind of joke. I get it, Cassius. You messin with my head, look to see if you can get me in trouble.

Yes, a joke. Let's go inside.

Cassius followed Weyman back inside Emoline's house, looking at the back of Weyman's head. Weyman moved to Emoline's favorite chair, the one she had slept in when Cassius was recuperating. Cassius stayed on his feet.

You had me goin there, Cassius. Didn't know what you were on about.

No.

So you don't got nothin for me from up North, said Weyman.

Not too many people in the world I care about, said Cassius. A girl back at Sweetsmoke. Maybe one or two others. Maybe even you. And Emoline Justice. I did care for her. She did more for me than just about anyone could want. Mended me, but you know that. Taught me to read and write. Even taught me a new way to think. You think we trust too much in hope?

Don't know what you talkin 'bout, said Weyman.

No, you don't. She gave me hope. Taught me to trust my own thoughts. And then you killed her.

Weyman's eyes went strange, he stood up from her chair and Cassius knew he was right. Something closed down inside of him. He crossed the room and stood over the stain.

Happened here, said Cassius. You hit her and she went down and bled.

You don't understand, said Weyman.

Help me understand, said Cassius.

She was wantin me to join her.

To join her?

She was spyin for the Federals. Bet you didn't know that.

I knew that.

Well, then you understand. She done ask me to help her spy, knew I got some freedom to move around, bein with Thomas and all. I said no, and she got mad.

She got mad, said Cassius.

Attacked me, said I know too much 'bout her spyin.

That little woman attacked you.

She done come at me, Cassius. If I hadn't'a killed her, she was gonna kill me.

She run at you backwards?

You fuckin with me?

Emoline was hit on the back of the head. You hit her from behind.

Weyman sat back down in her chair. He stared at Cassius and was smart enough to hold his tongue.

She never asked you to spy for her, said Cassius.

No, said Weyman.

She knew better. You couldn't keep your mouth shut if you were in a room full of bees. But you found out what she was doing.

Came for jalap, came in the door and saw her puttin stuff in a hiding place. She told me what it was.

She was proud of what she was doing, said Cassius, knowing that was consistent with what he knew of Emoline, a proud woman absolutely certain of her mission. Yes, he could imagine her telling Weyman about what he had seen.

Weyman looked off for a moment, then looked back up at Cassius.

I got it good here. You seen it. I live with whites, eat at the same table, sleep in the same house, work with 'em every day and I don't got to work no harder than Thomas. It's the closest I ever be to free. Almost like bein free, only we ain't never goin to be free, don't matter what that Lincoln says. This the only way I get a decent life. She was goin to ruin everything I got. I know what it like otherwise, I done picked cotton till my master died and I got sold to Thomas. I know what it was, and I know what it can be. I had to kill her, had to stop her from helpin the Union.

Cassius was cold inside. His temper did not raise its head.

What you goin do, Cassius?

Not going to do anything, said Cassius.

Nothin? said Weyman hopefully.

Fact that I know, that you got to live with yourself while I know, that's your punishment. I know what it would do to your farm if something happened to you. The Chavises are good people for slave owners. Working people, put all their money into buying two men to help with their farm. Losing a man to them would be like a fire burning down their barn with their entire harvest inside, along with their mule, and all their chickens. Without you, they'd lose their farm. Without you, they'd lose everything. They couldn't afford a new man. Never be able to make up for your work.

Cassius, I ain't sure what to say.

I'm tired, said Cassius. Maybe you best go.

Yeah, said Weyman. But maybe you do that thing you said?

What thing? said Cassius, but he smiled inside, having known that this moment would come.

You said you write me a pass.

That's right. I made the mistake of telling you I could read and write, didn't I? All right. I think Emoline had some paper over here somewhere.

Cassius crossed to a drawer and found a sheet of paper, a pen and an inkwell that still held some ink, so he didn't have to mix it from powder.

He sat and wrote. Weyman watched.

You really doin that, ain't you? said Weyman. Then he laughed happily, the laughter of relief: Y'all was somethin, keepin such a thing a secret.

Cassius finished the note and handed it to Weyman.

This'll get you home, said Cassius.

Weyman held up the pass as thanks, moving to the door.

Got enough jalap to last you?

Enough to last.

Good.

Weyman went out the door and Cassius followed to watch him walk down the road in the direction of the Chavis farm.

Once out of sight, Cassius took the lantern, closed Emoline's front door, and ran in the street to the German part of town.

He stood outside the *bierhaus*. He knew that if he entered, they would know he was alive, and then everything he had planned would be near to impossible. But he had to alert Mueller. He was on the verge of writing a note when he saw the fifteen-year-old, Mueller's brain-simple son. Cassius made certain that no one else was on the street, then stepped out and caught the boy's arm just before the boy went inside.

Can you give your father a message? said Cassius.

"Message? What you mean?" said the boy.

Can you remember what I say, and repeat it back to him?

"Sure, ain't stupid, you know," said the boy. Cassius thought that the boy was not as brain-simple as he had heard, and he began to doubt his decision. But the boy did not recognize Cassius, so he went on.

Then listen close. You know that one of the patrollers, Bornock, been accusing your father of taking his gun? said Cassius.

"I hear 'bout that all the time," said the boy.

I know where that gun is.

"You ain't gettin no reward, boy."

Cassius started, not having anticipated that reaction. He knew he had to play out the moment.

Maybe just a little something? Cold out here.

"Nothin for you. Now you come in, you tell my papa."

Maybe better if you do it. Then he'll be happy with you. Yes?

Cassius watched the boy's eyes light up. He started to nod, and Cassius nodded with him.

You go tell your papa. You tell him the man who has Bornock's gun is on the road, walking back to his farm now.

"Walking back to his farm now," repeated the boy.

Tell him those words. The man who has his gun is named Weyman.

"I know Weyman," said the boy.

Weyman is on the road now and he has the gun. Tell your papa to get his patroller friends, and they'll catch him.

"I will," said the boy, and he ran into the *bierhaus*.

Cassius backed up and hid in the shadows, waiting to see that the message would be delivered. He still had time to write a note if it was needed.

Mueller came out in a hurry, dragging on his coat and pressing his hat on his head. He ran past Cassius's hiding place and headed for the stable, and Cassius heard him when he was down the street, calling aloud for Bornock and Lang.

Cassius set out on the road, traveling in the same direction as Weyman. He was already out of town when he heard the horses coming on behind him. He stepped out of sight and the patrollers thundered past, whipping their mounts and kicking up dust. The cold night air tightened the sky and made the stars hard and he felt winter coming on fast now. He came back out and continued walking along the side of the road, letting the beam of his lantern pick out the way.

He heard them ahead, on the far side of the elbow in the road, and he sat down on the cold hard ground to wait. He could see light from their lanterns poking through the leaves and trees, and he listened to the sounds of what was happening there. Fifteen minutes later they rode fast in the other direction, returning to town. Cassius put out his lantern and sat in the dark by the side of the road and watched them go by. In the quiet that followed, he thought about Emoline and knew that she would not have approved.

He waited a little while longer until the cold earth made his thighs numb. He found a Lucifer match in his pouch, relit the lantern, stood up slowly, and set back out on the road. He rounded the elbow and walked toward something white on the ground.

He picked it up; the same piece of paper that Weyman had thought was a pass. He angled his lantern and read his own hand-writing: *I got that pearl-handle gun to sell. Meet me tonight.*

He angled the lantern's beam to the level of Weyman's feet, swinging gently. One of his feet still wore a shoe.

He folded the note and tucked it in his pouch.

He continued to walk down the road toward Sweetsmoke. The pit of rage inside him slowly, slowly burned out.

Cassius came through the woods, skirting the quarters and Mr. Nettle's place to approach the big house well before dawn. He entered the open area and crossed to the privy, hidden as it was from the big house by a stand of trees. He dragged a stump over to where he could see it from a hiding spot he had chosen in the woods.

He took a cigar from his pouch, knelt to the frayed cuff of one of his trouser legs, and unraveled a small length of thread. He tied it around the cigar, near the lip end, and placed it on the stump, pointing it at the place where he would wait.

She came out in the early morning, as he knew she would, but she was not alone, and she no longer carried the chamber pots herself, as he had expected. She was directing Pet and Anne's girl, Susan, and he knew that things had changed for her in the big house.

He watched her with his heart full. His memory during the time he had been away had done nothing to enhance her; in fact, she was prettier than he had remembered, and she warmed his lonely eyes.

She kept her distance from the privy. His heart, which had soared when he saw her again, now began a rapid drumbeat as he feared she would not notice his marker. He did not know another safe way to let her know where he was. This was the moment; it had to be now. Cassius saw Pet intentionally drop a chamber pot when Quashee looked away. Quashee grimaced at the prospect of having to help clean up the mess, and then she stopped. Cassius held his breath. He saw that she was looking at the stump. He saw her take a step toward it. He experienced an idiot delight at this success, because he knew she had seen the cigar. But he had expected a different reaction from her, and his pleasure fled as he saw her do battle with shock and confusion when she recognized his signature. Pet asked her a question, and she did not respond. Pet asked again, a little louder, but from where Cassius watched, he could not hear what it was.

Quashee looked up at Pet, attempting to cover the astonishment that ruled her face, and she waved Pet back to the big house. Susan, who was more clever than Pet, looked to where Quashee had been looking. Cassius recognized the danger in this moment. Quashee walked quickly to the stump and sat on it, thus hiding the cigar, bringing her foot to her knee as if to examine a sliver. Quashee indicated that Susan should follow Pet and take the empty pots, and after a moment, she was alone.

Cassius watched as Quashee took the cigar in her hands, finger and thumb running along its length, stopping at the thread, and then, as if suddenly picturing something that she dared not believe to be true, she lifted her head. She turned in the direction that the cigar had pointed and looked directly at Cassius. It was a jolt to meet her eyes, but he knew she could not see him, hidden as he was. She knew that if he had come back, then he was right there.

Quashee stood, a hand at her breast, running suddenly, directly, toward him. After a few steps, she forced herself to slow, throwing a glance over her shoulder toward the big house, but she kept on coming, the longest walk Cassius had ever experienced. She entered the trees with their naked limbs, leaves crunching beneath her feet, and she looked this way and that for him. When he knew she could no longer be seen from the big house, he stood up. She stopped dead in her tracks.

Still twenty feet away, she lifted her hand toward him, but came no closer. She was in the presence of the dead come back to life. She opened her other hand and revealed the cigar in her palm.

You, said Quashee in complete amazement.

I've come for you. To take you with me. To the North.

You're dead. Jacob's letter.

I wrote that in his letter. To keep them from looking for me.

What that did to me. To hear you were— And now you're here, you're alive, she said.

I had to, I'm sorry. I came as fast as I could.

She moved to him then, stepped up very close, close enough to breathe his breath, but she did not touch him until she put her hand on his chest to be certain that he stood there. Slowly her hand moved and he felt it graze his neck and cheek, running over his eyelids, his forehead, stopping to rest on his lips. He pressed his head forward against her fingers, kissing them, then kissing her lips. He said quietly and deliberately: I've come for you. I'm here.

Yes, you're here, yes, said Quashee, her face against his chest, and he heard a small, joyful laugh well up from deep inside her. Her narrow arms wrapped tightly around him, and then, of a sudden, she let go and stepped back. As she stepped, she shook her head.

I was done, I understood, it's what we have in this life, it's what we are. I was prepared to be lonely, prepared to mourn you. I'd already started.

Cassius spoke warmly, explaining: We'll go tonight. The nights are long now, so there's more time to travel. Patrollers say they're on alert, but it's winter. With the cold, the whites rather stay inside. Even the patrollers like to be warm, in their homes. We stay alert, stay away from towns and keep moving, we can make it.

You went off, like you said you would. Never thought to see you again. A man on the road, those were your words. It was different than the man I had at John-Corey's. Worse, so much worse than when he got sold. Didn't even know I was still waiting for you until Jacob's letter. I was relieved, Cassius, do you understand? I was relieved to know for certain you were dead.

He did not move toward her. He thought that was too risky, as any sudden movement might startle her, like spooking a cautious deer who had already stepped too close.

You said if you don't take the good too, then you got nothing, said Cassius. Just pain.

But you were right. Don't love nothing in this life. You only give them power over your mind as well as your body.

I'm here to take you away. To a place where it's safe to love something again.

I can't go with you, she said.

You can.

No. My father.

Bring him.

They think you're dead. They won't look for you, not now, not ever. If you go alone, you'll be safe. What will they do if two house servants run?

They'll come after you, but I can get us through, I know the way.

You know the way of a ghost. But they'll catch flesh and blood

and make it pay. You won't make it with me. I won't let you give up
your freedom.

He had no answer for that. There was no point to argue. Everything he had seen in their future rushed away from him.

Don't stay here, said Quashee. Go now. Go tonight. Get away
from this place, I can be happy if I know you're away and safe.

He wanted to say that he would find a way for them to be together. He wanted to tell her how it was to see her again. But he said
none of it.

Maybe the war will end, said Cassius.

He reached out, but she backed away, shaking her head no, her
palms out to keep him from touching her. He knew her resolve was
shaky, but he also knew that it would return if he touched her, so he
dropped his hands to his side.

She turned and walked out of the trees into the open, back to the
big house and her day's work. He moved to the edge of the trees to
watch her go.

He saw the bantam rooster flit across the yard, come to a sudden
halt at Quashee's approach, lift up on his toes, and flee in the other
direction. He saw Pet pass by a second-story window carrying pillows. He saw Old Hoke come outside with a blanket, walking un-
certainly, stopping to look in both directions, then deciding to
approach a chair near what had been the vegetable garden during
the spring and summer. He watched Hoke sit, then fidget in the
chair, finally drawing his legs up under him and covering himself
with the blanket, curled up like a child.

She left the backyard, entering the big house without looking
back, and he saw her no more.

He wanted to stay there for the rest of the day, to watch for
glimpses of her, anything to fill the well of emptiness inside him. He
vowed that he would come back, somehow, someday, for her.

He watched Hoke for a time, saw his body relax and knew that
he had fallen asleep under the blanket. Cassius thought of all that
had happened between them, and the small flame of his anger
started. But then something came over him, quickly and in a surprise: He smelled that sweet smell of the curing tobacco, and it was
good and rich, warm with captured sunlight, and the aroma was in-
toxicating for him again. The younger Hoke Howard returned to

him, the man who had taught him, who had even cared for him. Now he looked across the open ground at the big house and Cassius saw only an old man fallen asleep. Finally, for a moment, he let go of his disgust and acknowledged the fact that Hoke was the only father he had ever known. He wished him a silent good-bye, turned away, and walked deeper into the woods, to wait for dark, when he would begin his journey to the North.

He was glad to know the rooster was not yet made into a meal.

◈ Acknowledgments ◈

To acknowledge every source would require an extensive bibliography, and would need to include documentaries, films, and Internet sources. Particular thanks must go to Eugene D. Genovese, Harriet Jacobs, Frederick Douglass, Zora Neale Hurston, John Hope Franklin, Loren Schweninger, Peter Kolchin, Kenneth M. Stampp, Ira Berlin, Charles Johnson, Patricia Smith, James D. Russell, Ervin L. Jordan, Jr., The Virginia WPA, Paul Erickson, Anne Kamma, Ellen Levine, Kay Moore, Jason Goodwin, Iain Gately, Webb Garrison, Edwin C. Fishel, Joseph L. Harsh, John Michael Priest, Stephen W. Sears, Douglas S. Freeman, Shelby Foote, James McPherson, and Bruce Catton. These were my primary sources. Finally, to Patrick O'Brian, from whom I borrowed the occasional word that helped keep me in the nineteenth century.

Grateful acknowledgment is made to my family at Hyperion, especially Ellen Archer for her contagious enthusiasm; and Leslie Wells, who made both novel and writer better.

To Deborah Schneider, fierce and wonderful.

To the long line of Fuller writers, including my father, John G. Fuller; and to my mother, Joyce V. Fuller.

Liz Sayre is my patient supporter, co-conspirator, and true companion. This book would not exist without her. Our sons, Tom and Mark, were born shortly before the idea for this novel was hatched. As they have lived with it their entire lives, it truly belongs to them.